...iful tales for her ...n. Amid the gorgeous ...majestic Rocky Mountains, ...gination with the natural beauty surrounding her. Karen now lives in north Texas, writes full-time and volunteers for a boxer dog rescue. She shares her life with her hero of a husband and four to five dogs, depending on if she is fostering. You can email Karen at kwhiddon1@aol.com. Fans can also check out her website, karenwhiddon.com

Also by Amanda Stevens

Criminal Behaviour
Incriminating Evidence
Killer Investigation
Pine Lake
Whispering Springs
Bishop's Rock (ebook novella)
The Restorer
The Kingdom
The Prophet
The Visitor

Also by Karen Whiddon

The CEO's Secret Baby
The Cop's Missing Child
The Millionaire Cowboy's Secret
Texas Secrets, Lovers' Lies
The Rancher's Return
The Texan's Return
Wyoming Undercover
The Texas Soldier's Son
Texas Ranch Justice
Colton's Christmas Cop

WITHOUT A TRACE

AMANDA STEVENS

COLTON'S LAST STAND

KAREN WHIDDON

MILLS & BOON

First Published in Great Britain 2020
by Mills & Boon, an imprint of HarperCollins*Publishers*
1 London Bridge Street, London, SE1 9GF

Special thanks and acknowledgement are given to Karen Whiddon for her contribution to *The Coltons of Mustang Valley* series.

ISBN: 978-0-263-28036-4

0620

This book is produced from independently certified FSC™ paper to ensure responsible forest management.

For more information visit: www.harpercollins.co.uk/green

Printed and bound in Spain
by CPI, Barcelona

WITHOUT A TRACE

AMANDA STEVENS

Chapter One

On the night of the disappearances, a blood moon had hovered over the piney woods in East Texas. The old-timers called it an omen. Tom Brannon had considered it just plain bad luck. He'd forgotten his flashlight when he rushed out of the house and the lunar eclipse provided weak illumination as he'd traipsed along the banks of the lake, hoping against hope that by the time he got back home, he'd find the girls safe and sound in his sister's bedroom.

Fifteen years had passed since that fateful night, but Tom still got a chill when the moon turned ruddy and a pine-scented breeze blew in from the lake. He stood outside the sheriff's station gazing up at the sky, telling himself to get back to work and forget about that moon. He had more important things to worry about at the moment, like budget cuts and rising crime rates, not to mention the mountain of complaints that seemed to grow exponentially higher with each passing day. On and on it went. The job of a rural county sheriff never ended.

He thought about his sister, Ellie, out there alone on Echo Lake. Miles from town. Miles from anyone. He'd asked her once if she ever got lonely, but she'd scoffed at the notion, insisting that the isolation kept her sane. Besides, it was only a twenty-minute drive into town, where she could find all the company she wanted. She seemed content these days, but Tom had to wonder if the nightmares ever came back. If she hid under the bed or at the back of her closet until the monsters went away. He didn't ask. He and his sister were close, but there were things they didn't talk about. Of the three girls who had entered the old hospital ruins on the night of the blood moon, Ellie was the only one who had come out whole. Survivor's guilt could be a powerful thing. Tom understood only too well.

Maybe it was the moon or maybe he was being overly protective, but he felt the need to check in with her tonight, hear her voice to calm his disquiet. He should have called earlier. She'd already be on the air by this time. She produced and hosted a syndicated radio program called *Midnight on Echo Lake*, which she broadcast from a small studio behind her house. She wouldn't answer her cell right now, but he could call in to the program. Talk about space aliens or the Bigfoot creature that some of the locals claimed to have seen in the woods near the lake. She'd get a kick out of that, though she'd later scold him for mocking her callers.

Things happen that can't be explained, she would tell him. People need someone they can talk to about their experiences without fear of ridicule.

Yeah, and some people are just plain nuts, Tom would retort.

Maybe he was one of them. He couldn't seem to shake the uneasiness that had gripped him all evening. He didn't believe in premonitions, but he knew enough to pay attention to his instincts. Something was brewing. He could feel it in the wind. He hoped it was nothing more than a summer storm.

"Evening, Sheriff."

He turned to find his newest recruit striding across the parking lot toward him. He checked his watch out of habit. The department ran on a six, two and ten schedule. Tom had been there since six that morning. He'd worked straight through two watches.

"You're early," he noted. "That's a good habit to get into."

"Yes, sir," the young officer replied with a solemn nod. A recent graduate of the East Texas Police Academy, Billy Navarro was a young, eager rookie who reminded Tom a bit of himself ten years ago. His father had been winding down his nearly thirty-year career as the Nance County sheriff when Tom had come on board. He'd served under his dad for only a year before a heart attack had claimed Porter Brannon in his sleep. Tom had then served under his father's replacement for another nine years, going from patrolman to criminal investigator to the deputy sheriff in less than a decade before running for office two years ago.

The campaign had gotten nasty and personal, fueled by a hostile opponent and an onslaught of negative commentary from the editorial pages of the *Echo Lake Star*. Everything from Tom's age to his integrity had been called into question, and there had been times when he wondered why he had ever thought it a good idea to try to follow in his father's footsteps. In the end, he'd won in a near landslide, no doubt a bitter pill to swallow for the Cavanaugh clan, who had spearheaded the campaign against him. He suspected the animosity between the two families would only worsen as the next election approached.

"Beware the blood moon," Billy muttered beside him.

Tom slanted him a frowning glance. "What did you say?"

"That's what my grandmother told me before I left the

house tonight." He shifted uneasily. "What kind of goodbye is that for a guy going out on patrol?"

"It's just an old wives' tale. Keep your eyes open and your mind on the job. You'll be fine."

Tom would never point out to a rookie that patrolling the town of Belle Pointe and the outlying country roads was hardly the same as taking on the mean streets of a crime-ridden city. He wanted Billy aware and on guard. Nance County was rural, but their home turf had more than its fair share of drug-related crime. Meth dealers had taken to scoping out abandoned houses in the country where they could cook their product in mass quantities. Then they used the nearby interstate to transport the drugs to points north and south. Big business. Big money. Synthetic weed was becoming a problem, too, along with fentanyl and the old standbys of crack cocaine and heroin.

Beside him, Billy searched the sky. "I know it's just a superstition, but there's something in the air tonight. Can you feel it?"

Yes, he felt it, but Tom didn't want to spook the rookie any more than he already seemed to be. He shrugged off his foreboding as he turned to go back inside. "Static electricity," he said. "Storm front moving in."

"There's not a cloud in the sky," Billy said.

"Not yet," Tom allowed. "Who's riding with you tonight?"

"Naomi Clutter."

"Tough as nails. Nobody better in three counties. You run into trouble, she'll have your back. You just make sure you have hers."

"Yes, sir."

Tom went back inside and crossed the nearly empty squad room to his glassed-in office at the front of the building. Long windows looked out on the street. He kept the blinds open so that he could see all around him, both within and without. The space hadn't changed much since his dad's time. The desk was the same. The vinyl chairs that faced him had been there for decades. Even the pictures and citations on the walls brought back memories. Tom had been meaning to change things up, bring in a few personal touches, but he never seemed to have the time. Never enough time for anything these days. He couldn't remember when he'd last asked a woman to dinner or a movie. He lived in town with neighbors all around him and yet in recent months he'd become as isolated as his sister.

He rubbed the bridge of his nose and then his temples. A headache nagged and exhaustion had set in, but paperwork kept him chained to his desk. Settling in with a fresh cup of coffee, he opened the latest budget report. The hours passed by quietly. He didn't take a break until right around midnight when he got up to stretch his legs.

When the call came in about the missing girl, he was standing at the window staring up at the moon.

RAE CAVANAUGH FINISHED loading the dishwasher and then wiped down the counters and set the timer on the coffee maker. She hated doing kitchen chores so late, but she'd fallen asleep after dinner in front of the TV. The house was so quiet and peaceful tonight. A welcome respite. She'd been burning the candle at both ends for as long as she could remember. A little downtime was just what she'd needed.

Her niece, Sophie, had roused her when she came in a few minutes ago. The girl had muttered a good-night and then gone straight upstairs to her room. Normally, music would be blasting through her closed door, but

Sophie had seemed a bit subdued. Maybe she was coming down with something. Or maybe she'd had a fight with her boyfriend. Hard to tell with a sullen teenager.

Rae wondered if she should go up and try to talk to her, but she discarded the notion almost immediately. One, she was too tired to cope with the girl's moods, and two, she wanted to give Sophie her space. Wasn't that the whole point of this prolonged visit? To allow Sophie and her parents a much-needed breather?

Rae knew things must have gotten bad at her brother's house if he'd come to her for help. At his wit's end, he'd said. She'd never known Jackson to admit defeat, let alone to her. They'd been in bitter competition with one another since childhood. It didn't help that she'd always been their dad's favorite, but West Cavanaugh's partiality toward his daughter hadn't kept him from handing over the reins of Cavanaugh Industries to his only son. Rae was the chief financial officer—a glorified bookkeeper, she sometimes thought. Between the job and looking after their father, she had her hands full. And now Sophie. Poor kid. None of this was her fault. Rae blamed her brother and sister-in-law for letting things get so out of control. They'd lavished everything but attention on the girl without bothering to set boundaries. Now they were at loggerheads, with Sophie pushing for more independence and Jackson realizing a little too late that his princess might be headed for trouble.

Rae poured herself a glass of wine and took it out to the backyard, but she left the drink untouched as she gazed up at the moon. *What a strange night.* She felt unaccountably uneasy, and it wasn't just the argument she'd had earlier with Jackson or the troubling discrepancies she'd found in the financials. Or even the lawsuit that had been brought against Cavanaugh Industries by a neighboring rancher. That would all be sorted out soon enough.

Nothing Rae could do about any of it tonight. Her father would handle the lawsuit. He had a way of coming out of these things smelling like a rose. He and Jackson had spent untold hours sequestered with their corporate attorneys, discussing possible witnesses and devising strategy. Rae, of course, had been kept out of the loop, which suited her fine. Plausible deniability in case things went south.

She glanced up at her niece's window. The lights were out but she could see a muted glow from the laptop screen. Time for her to turn in as well, Rae decided. She carried the glass back into the kitchen and poured the wine down the drain before taking one last look at the eclipse through the window. Then, turning off the lights, she went upstairs, pausing on the landing to listen for any sign of life from Sophie's room. She could hear music playing, softly this time, and the murmur of Sophie's voice as she talked to someone on her cell. Rae didn't bother knocking or calling out. *Let the girl have her privacy.*

In her own room, Rae collapsed on top of the bed fully dressed and threw an arm over her eyes. She'd get up in a minute, wash her face and brush her teeth, but right now she just wanted to drift. Forget about Sophie down the hallway and her brother off on a deep-sea fishing trip with his buddies. His wife, Lauren, had gone down to New Orleans to visit friends. Now that they didn't have to worry about their daughter, they were footloose and fancy-free. Rae tried not to begrudge them a carefree weekend. She tried not to condemn their selfishness and poor parenting skills. *God knows after Mother died, I certainly failed Riley.*

Beautiful, smart, tenderhearted Riley. Rae's younger sister by two years. The girl who had entered the old hospital ruins on that fateful night fifteen years ago and had never been seen or heard from again.

Riley and her best friend, Jenna Malloy, had spent the night at Ellie Brannon's house. The parents had been called away on an emergency and Tom had been left in charge. He'd been sixteen when it happened. Same age as Rae. Old enough to know that you didn't go out partying when you were supposed to be minding the store. Never mind that the girls had been fourteen, also old enough to know better. Tom had been the one left in charge. He should have kept them safe.

Over the years, Rae had come to accept that her feelings toward Tom Brannon were at best irrational and at worst malicious, but old grudges never really died. They just crawled off into some back corner of the mind and waited.

She rolled over in bed, hugging her pillow as she stared out the window. She could see the moon through the pine trees. A blood moon, just as it had been on that night fifteen years ago. Rae wouldn't think about that now. She wouldn't think about her sister, Riley, and how much she still missed her. How much she would always miss her.

But it was Riley's smiling face she saw when she closed her eyes. It was Riley's anguished cry for help that echoed in her dreams when she finally fell asleep.

SOPHIE WAS TEMPTED to use the flashlight app on her phone, but there were houses on the lake and she didn't want to attract attention. The moon was up, dulled by a lunar eclipse, according to her science teacher. Sophie didn't much care about the reason. She just wished she could see where she was going as she made her way along the bank toward the Ruins, a hollowed-out shell of a building that had once housed a psychiatric hospital. Or so rumor had it. That was long before Sophie's time.

The place had always been spooky, but more so after those girls had gone missing. Sophie hadn't been born yet when her aunt had vanished from the Ruins. Ellie Brannon had come back. Jenna Malloy had eventually come back—at least physically—but Riley Cavanaugh had disappeared without a trace that night. And now here Sophie was, fifteen years later, headed for the same destination.

She wasn't frightened. Not really. The lake looked eerie in the muted moonlight, with cypress stumps rising from the shallow water and the banks curtained with Spanish moss. But as far as Sophie was concerned, there were scarier things back in town. Still, she couldn't help glancing over her shoulder now and then.

Her aunt Rae had been sound asleep when she'd slipped down the stairs and out of the house. Sophie couldn't get her license for another few months, so she'd ridden her bike out to the lake bridge and abandoned it beneath the supports. She had to go the rest of the way on foot. She was almost there now. She could see the smokestack from the old boiler room rising above the treetops. That gave her pause. So creepy. She was starting to get a little nervous now. She always did when her turn came, but she would never admit her unease to the others.

A twig snapped behind her and she whirled, peering all along the edge of the lake and into the woods. Nothing stirred except for the sway of the moss in the breeze and the gentle lap of water against the bank. A mosquito buzzed her face and she waved a hand to shoo it away. She should have brought insect repellent, but too late now.

She remained motionless for another long moment

before turning back to the path. Up the steep bank she climbed, clutching vines and roots to help propel her to the top. When she reached the summit, she stood with the lake at her back and the Ruins silhouetted before her. Three stories of crumbling brick and mortar and broken-out windows.

Drawing a resolved breath, she picked her way through the weeds and brambles and entered through one of the arched doorways. Taking out her phone, she used the flashlight to illuminate the interior. She'd been here many times before, always in daylight until lately. She knew about the gurneys and wheelchairs that had been abandoned at the back of the building. She knew about the open elevator shaft upstairs and the caged area on the third floor. She angled the light beam over the biblical graffiti on the walls and the mural with the demonic face that had been painted on the ceiling.

Preacher. That was the name given to the former psychiatric patient who had continued to sermonize from his makeshift pulpit long after the hospital had closed down and the patients without families or financial means had been left to their own devices. Some had assimilated into nearby towns, or so the story went, but Sophie thought that might be another urban legend.

Whatever. She was here now. *Let the game begin.*

She crept from room to room, playing the light over the walls as she searched for a symbol that would guide her to the next level. The roof was missing in places and she had an image of the whole structure toppling down upon her, burying her in an avalanche of dark secrets and old misery. Would her aunt Rae blame herself? Would her parents? Would they even care?

The softest of steps sounded behind her. Phantom footfalls that sent a shiver down her spine. She turned slowly, the light beam capturing a silhouette for one split second before the shadow darted away.

Rae tried to swallow away her fear as she drew a quick breath. "Preacher," she said in a small voice. "Is that you?"

RAE AWAKENED WITH a start. She wasn't sure what had roused her this time. In her dream, someone had been pounding on the front door. She lay still for a moment, listening to the dark house, but the only noise she heard was the scratch of a tree limb against her window.

She crawled out of bed and headed for the bathroom, then paused in midstride as her gaze went to the bedroom door. She was certain she'd closed it earlier, but now it hung open, as if someone had stood in the hallway peering in at her.

Which was crazy. If Sophie had needed something, she would have barged right on in, turned on the light and called Rae's name until she woke up. The girl could be as subtle as a sledgehammer at times. Still, Rae thought about her niece's wan expression when she'd come home earlier. Something had obviously been bothering her, and now Rae regretted that she hadn't been a little more curious.

She went down the hallway and listened at Sophie's door. She could hear music inside. Maybe the girl was still up, still in need of a sympathetic ear. Rae knocked softly. When she didn't get a response, she knocked a little harder and then tried the door. She expected to find it locked from the inside, but to her surprise, the door swung inward, revealing the usual mayhem and clutter. Music played from the laptop on Sophie's bed. The window was open, allowing the night breeze to blow in. The lights were off except for a night-light that burned from the adjoining bathroom. Rae crossed the room and peeked inside, wincing at the mess. Damp towels had been tossed into a corner and the vanity was littered with cosmetics. But no Sophie.

Apprehension tickled at the back of Rae's neck, but she told herself there was no cause for alarm. Sophie had probably gone down to the kitchen for a snack. Rae checked the hallway bathroom before heading downstairs, turning on lights as she went. Sophie wasn't in the living room, den or kitchen. Not in the downstairs bathroom or out on the screened back porch. She wasn't on the front porch, either, or in the detached garage. She wasn't anywhere.

Don't panic. She'd probably sneaked out of the house to meet her boyfriend.

Disregarding the late hour, Rae called the kid's house, rousing his dad, who gruffly assured her that Dylan was in his room and had been since he'd come home around ten. Rae insisted he go check to make sure, which he'd begrudgingly agreed to do. Then he'd put Dylan on the phone and the kid had sworn he hadn't seen Sophie since he'd dropped her off at home at 10:00 p.m.

Rae sat out on the front porch and called everyone else she could think of. None of Sophie's friends had seen her. No one knew anything. How could she have slipped out of the house without Rae knowing? She was usually such a light sleeper.

Okay, just stay calm. It's not that late. A few minutes after midnight. Well past curfew for a school night but Sophie wasn't one for following the rules. Rae tried the girl's cell phone for the umpteenth time and then sent her a barrage of text messages.

Where are you?

I'm starting to freak out a little. Call me as soon as you get this message. Just let me know you're okay.

Sophie, call me! Call me right this minute! I'm serious!

You're not in trouble, I promise. Just call me. I need to know you're okay.

Sophie, please call me.

I'm worried.

After a bit, Rae got up and went back inside. She climbed the stairs to Sophie's room and checked the laptop, then searched through the dresser drawers and closet looking for a clue as to where the girl might have gone. Then she got in her car and drove through town, up one street and down the other.

By the time she got back home, she could no longer keep panic at bay. It didn't matter that Sophie had been missing for only a couple of hours. It didn't matter that her niece had once pulled a similar stunt on her parents. Rae was responsible for the child now. She was the one in charge.

Plopping down on Sophie's bed, she sent off another volley of texts before reaching for the laptop once again. Then she called the last person on earth she had expected to talk to that night.

RAE CAVANAUGH WAS the last person Tom had expected to hear from that night…or ever. He automatically checked his watch when the call came in. He should have left for home an hour ago, but he supposed it was just as well that he hadn't. No matter the time, a call from a Cavanaugh would have been forwarded to his cell phone or landline. They were important folks, the Cavanaughs, and they weren't shy about letting you know it.

He figured the call had something to do with the kid he had in lockup, one of their young roughnecks who'd gotten himself into a little trouble earlier in the evening. Tom wasn't in the mood to be raked over the coals, but he could face Rae's wrath now or in the morning. Didn't much matter to him. He'd developed a thick skin when it came to the Cavanaughs.

"Sheriff Brannon." He answered the phone in his usual manner, fully expecting a surly comeback.

"This is Rae Cavanaugh."

She sounded out of breath. Distressed. Tom frowned. "What can I do for you, Rae?"

"Sophie's gone missing."

The unease that had niggled all evening deepened. "Sophie?"

"My niece. Jackson's daughter. She's been staying with me for a while. I went to check on her earlier and she's not in her room. I called everyone I could think of. All her friends, her boyfriend. No one has seen her. Tom..." He could imagine her clutching the phone as everything she'd done to find her niece came pouring out in her panic. When she finished, she took another moment to gather her poise. "You and I have had our differences in the past, but I didn't know who else to call. I don't know what else to do. I've looked everywhere. She's not answering her phone or my texts. I just keep thinking about that night—"

"Hold on," he said. "You say she came home at ten and went up to her room. It's just after midnight now. At most she's only been gone a couple of hours. Teenagers sneak out of the house all the time."

"I know that. I keep telling myself she's just gone off with a friend, but I checked with the girls I know she's close to. No one has seen her."

"Maybe she has a friend you don't know about."

"It's possible. She hasn't been living with me that long. Tom." Dread crept into her voice. "I found something on her laptop just now. She has dozens of pictures of the Ruins. I think she took them herself. They look recent. You don't think—"

"I was just leaving the office. I'll make a run out there before I head home."

"I'm coming, too. It'll be faster if I meet you there."

"Maybe you should stay home in case she comes back," he said.

"I'll leave a note and I'll take my cell phone. I can't sit in this house and do nothing. I'll go crazy with worry."

He sighed under his breath. "Okay, but if you get there first, wait for me by the bridge. Don't go any farther without me. Understand?"

"Tom…"

"What is it?"

She hesitated. "Aren't you going to say it?"

"Say what, Rae?"

"This is my fault. She's my responsibility."

"Let's just find her and bring her home."

Tom ended the call and then went out to the squad room to speak with the dispatcher. A patrol car would meet them at the bridge. They could all traipse through the woods together. Most likely, the girl was out partying somewhere, but Tom didn't take chances with missing kids.

As he went out to his own vehicle, he couldn't help glancing skyward once more. The moon had disappeared behind a storm cloud.

Chapter Two

Rae's car was pulled to the side of the road by the time Tom got out to the lake. He half expected she'd already taken off for the Ruins alone, but he called out to her anyway. To his surprise, she answered back immediately.

"Down here!"

He used his flashlight to pick his way down the embankment, half running, half sliding in the loose dirt and pebbles. His light flicked across Rae. She stood at the edge of the lake peering up under the bridge. His heart skidded but he kept his voice calm as he greeted her.

"Glad you waited for me."

"I found her bike," she said over her shoulder. She used her flashlight beam to guide his attention. "See it up there under the braces?"

"You sure it's hers?"

"I'm certain. She brought it with her when she came to stay with me."

"How long has that been?"

"Nearly three weeks. There was trouble at home," she admitted reluctantly.

"What kind of trouble?"

"The usual stuff. Jackson doesn't approve of her friends or the way she dresses or the music she listens to, and you know how well criticism goes over with a teenager. Even under the best of circumstances, Sophie's a handful and my brother has never been the most tactful or patient person in the world. They all needed a break."

"So you came to the rescue." Tom hadn't meant anything by the comment, but he regretted how it might sound to her.

"I offered to help. That's what families do."

"The good ones." As he turned to scan their surroundings, his light caught her again. She seemed unaware of his quick scrutiny. The bike had her full attention. She looked uncharacteristically unkempt, her light brown hair tangled down her back, freckles exposed across her nose, clothing rumpled. Understandable under the circumstances. She'd undoubtedly left the house in a hurry, but what Tom couldn't help noticing was that her frayed demeanor did little to disguise her appeal. He'd always admired Rae Cavanaugh's good looks if not her disposition. As far back as high school, she'd been a real piece of work. Prickly, suspicious and obnoxiously competitive. Riley had been the sweet one. It pained Tom even now to think about her.

He kept his voice neutral as he asked the necessary questions. "You two didn't have an argument, did you? Maybe she left the house to cool off. Or to teach you a lesson. Kids are like that."

"We didn't fight. We've been getting along reasonably well, considering."

"Considering?"

"Like you said, she's a kid. I don't have a lot of experience dealing with teenagers except for..." She trailed off.

Except for Riley.

Tom finished her sentence in his head. Their mother had died when the Cavanaugh kids were still young. West Cavanaugh had remarried a few years later and there'd been a string of nannies and housekeepers in between. But Rae was the one who had looked after Riley. She'd been fiercely protective of her sister, so much so that Riley had taken to spending all her free time at their house just so she could have a little breathing room.

Tom wondered if Rae ever thought about that in those late hours when she couldn't sleep. He wondered if she remained so hard on him because it was easier to attack than to reflect.

A car engine sounded on the road. Doors slammed and voices carried down to the lake. He called out to the patrol officers and both Billy Navarro and Naomi Clutter responded. A moment later, their flashlight beams bobbed in the dark as they hustled down the embankment.

Tom made short work of the introductions and explanations. Then they left the bridge and the abandoned bike and headed toward the Ruins, dread dogging their every step. Tom told himself it was much too early to worry. Two hours, going on three was nothing in the life of a teenager, especially one who might be acting out because of a difficult home life. He didn't know Jackson and Lauren Cavanaugh well, but he'd had enough run-ins with the former to know that he could be a real jerk. The wife appeared to be the high-maintenance type, and Tom could well imagine how a spirited teenage stepdaughter might get in the way of spa treatments and country-club luncheons. Not a fair assessment, he readily admitted, but he wasn't inclined to be all that generous when it came to the Cavanaughs.

None of that mattered at the moment anyway. *Just find the girl and we'll sort the rest out later.*

The eclipse had entered its final stage. The moon drifted from behind a cloud, glimmering like quicksilver on the surface of the lake. Somehow the illumination made the woods all around them seem darker, thicker. No one said much. Billy and Naomi had taken the lead, Rae trailed behind them and Tom brought up the rear. He couldn't stop thinking about that night fifteen years ago when he'd raced along the water's edge alone. He couldn't help brooding about the outcome.

Rae slowed and fell into step beside him. "Your sister lives out here somewhere, doesn't she?"

"Her house is on the other side of the bridge." Tom glanced over his shoulder. "If you look close enough, you can see the lights on her antenna flickering through the pine boughs."

"I've listened to her show a few times. She has a soothing voice, but her callers are pretty strange," Rae said. "Where do those people come from anyway? Are they for real?"

"She gets the occasional prank call, but most of them are real and they call in from all over the place. They just need somebody to listen to their story. At least, that's what Ellie tells me."

"I don't see her in town much anymore. How is she?"

"She's fine. Busy. Likes her solitude."

Rae shivered as she glanced over the water and then turned her head and gazed up at what could be seen of the Ruins. "I would go crazy out here."

"The Cavanaugh ranch is pretty isolated," Tom pointed out.

"That's different. People are always around. My dad, the housekeeper and all the ranch hands coming and going. It's like a small town out there. One of the last big cattle ranches in the area," she said proudly.

And quintessentially East Texas, Tom thought as he conjured an image of an Angus herd grazing peacefully in lush green pastures dotted with pumper jacks. The peaceful scenery in his head was a far cry from the disturbing reality of their current surroundings. Echo Lake held too many bleak memories, too many deep, dark secrets.

As if reading his thoughts, Rae glanced out over the water with a shiver. "I've heard people say that when the air is still and the hour is late, you can hear the screams of the patients echoing across the water. I never put much stock in all those old legends, but being out here like this… One can imagine almost anything."

"Most likely what they hear are the peacocks from the old Thayer place," Tom said. "They've roamed the countryside ever since Mrs. Thayer passed. My sister walks over a few times a week to feed them."

Up ahead, Billy and Naomi had already begun the ascent to the top of the embankment. Tom knew better than to offer Rae assistance. She was too proud to accept his hand. Instead, she propelled herself up to the summit like a seasoned climber and stood waiting for him to scramble up behind her. Then they all took a moment to gaze at the Ruins.

Moonlight glinted off the windows, giving the place a strange sense of animation. Of being alive. Tom scoffed at himself. Maybe Rae's trepidation had rubbed off on him. Maybe he was letting his own imagination get the better of him because if he listened closely enough, he could hear the creak of a door somewhere inside. Or was that the squeal of a rusted gurney? With very little effort, he could conjure ghostly images behind the broken windowpanes and phantom whispers rippling down through the trees. He shook off those visions, reminding himself that a place couldn't be evil or haunted. The only real monsters were human.

"We'll check around back," Naomi said.

Tom nodded. "We'll take the front. Call out if you find anything."

"Roger that."

She and Billy headed off into the darkness and Tom turned to Rae. "Are you sure you don't want to wait for me outside?"

"No, I need to go in with you. If Sophie's inside and she sees you come in alone, she might get scared and think she's in trouble. I don't want to take the chance that she could run off again."

She had a point. "Okay, but we need to stick together. And watch your step. I don't trust the integrity of this place. One wrong move and the whole structure could come down on top of us."

"It's been standing for decades," Rae said. "Even been through a few tornadoes. I think we're safe enough, but your point is taken. I'll be careful."

They entered through one of the archways, pausing to rake their flashlight beams over the graffiti.

"I always wondered what this place was like on the inside. It's even creepier than I imagined," Rae said in a hushed voice. Her light lingered on the ceiling mural. "What's that?"

"Preacher." Tom swept his light over the demonic fresco. The eyes seemed to glow, but he knew that was only an illusion of paint and moonlight. "So you've never been inside before? That's surprising. Spending time at the Ruins has been a rite of passage in these parts ever since the place closed down."

"I was never much of a follower, and then after Riley disappeared..." She trailed away. "I've been outside plenty of times, but I could never make myself enter. After it happened, I'd drive out after school and walk around the area calling my sister's name even though

I knew she was long gone. I tried to picture where she might be. Tried to put myself in her place, imagine her fear, her screams…"

Tom heard a tremor in her voice. He was having flashbacks of that night, too. He'd been so panicked by the time he entered the building, he hadn't stopped to assess the risk. On some level, he'd been aware of the structural danger and the possibility of rattlers or copperheads, but the human menace had eluded him until he heard the softest of footfalls behind him. By then it was too late. He was struck across the back of his head, so hard he fell to his knees. Another blow knocked him out cold.

He came to the next morning at the bottom of the rise, his hair and clothing stained with blood. He'd been rolled down the embankment and left for dead, no doubt bleeding so profusely that the assailant hadn't bothered to finish him off. Tom had found Ellie lying facedown at the water's edge. How she'd gotten away from her attacker or why she hadn't drowned was anyone's guess. Tom had administered CPR and then carried her all the way to the bridge, up the embankment and out to the road where he'd left his vehicle the night before.

Eighteen stitches and a week in the hospital later, he'd still blamed himself for not being able to save the others, even though he knew in his gut that Riley and Jenna had already been taken by the time he regained consciousness.

Beside him, Rae froze as she angled her beam along the cracked floor tiles. "Tom, look at this."

He came over to stand beside her. Then he squatted, focusing his light on the red droplets.

"Is that blood?" she asked fearfully.

He touched his finger to a drop. "It's fresh, but there isn't much of it. Let's not jump to conclusions." Too late for that. He heard the sharp intake of Rae's breath as she swung the flashlight wildly around the crumbling interior, tracking up the stairs and searching in all the dark corners.

"Sophie! Are you in here? Sophie, it's Rae. Answer me!" He heard another gasp. "I saw something!"

He rose. "Where?"

She positioned the light at the top of the stairs. "Someone was up there watching us. A man, I think."

"Stay here." Tom unholstered his weapon as he moved toward the stairs. Running the flashlight beam along the landing, he started up, testing each step with his weight before moving on to the next. When he got to the top, he angled the beam down the long corridor, taking note of open doorways and piles of debris, places from which he could be ambushed.

"Sophie!" he called out. "Are you up here? This is Sheriff Brannon. You're not in any trouble. Your aunt is with me. We just want to make sure you're okay." Gun in his right hand, flashlight in his left, he eased down the corridor, shining the beam inside the empty rooms. He heard footsteps on the stairs. "Rae, is that you?"

"I'm coming up," she said.

He didn't bother to argue. "Watch your step. The floor is rotting through up here."

He heard her behind him, but he didn't turn. Up ahead, in one of the gloomy recesses, he'd caught the glimmer of human eyes. "Whoever you are, put your hands behind your head and come out where I can see you." Rae was at the top of the stairs now. He said over his shoulder, "Stay where you are, Rae."

"Who's up here?" she asked on a breath.

"I don't know yet. Stay by the stairs."

In front of him, a shadow darted across the corridor. Startled, Tom called out, "Freeze!"

A face peered back at him for a split second before disappearing. Just vanished before Tom's very eyes.

He moved forward cautiously until one foot found nothing but air. He found himself teetering on the brink of the old elevator shaft. A rope swung wildly from a rafter as if someone had rappelled down into the chute. He leaned over the opening, allowing the flashlight beam to peel away the inky layers. Something was down there, crumpled on the floor.

"Tom?"

He threw out an arm to halt Rae's progress. "Careful. Long drop. Looks like it may go all the way down to the basement."

"What is it?"

"The old elevator shaft. Someone's rigged up a rope. I think whoever was up here used it to lower himself down."

Tom holstered his weapon and reached for the rope, rocking precariously for a moment before Rae grabbed his arm and pulled him back. "Are you crazy? You don't know how old that thing is. Who knows how much weight it'll hold."

She was right. A broken leg wouldn't help them find Sophie. "Let's see if we can figure out another way into the basement."

They backtracked along the corridor, down the stairs and through a maze of hallways to the back of the building. Outside, Tom glanced once again at the sky. The eclipse was nearly over. He wanted to take that as a good sign, but the blood drops inside, coupled with the crumpled form he'd seen in the elevator shaft, didn't bode well for a happy outcome. Beside him, Rae remained tense and silent.

He could see the deputies' flashlight beams bobbling in the dark. He called out to them. "Stay alert. We saw someone inside."

"Any sign of the girl?" Naomi called back.

"Not yet. We're looking for a way down into the basement. One of you stand guard out here, the other go around to the front. Make sure no one leaves this place without our knowing."

They split up, Billy taking the rear while Naomi went around to the front. Tom and Rae searched along the house until they located the outside basement entrance. A set of concrete steps led down to a metal door that hung open on one rusty hinge. He pulled back the door and then angled his flashlight beam into the cavernous space.

An odor of sour mud and dead fish emanated from the cellar, reminding Tom of a bog. He imagined there were plenty of rats and snakes in there, too. He didn't relish an exploration, but he wasn't about to delegate that job to a rookie.

He said over his shoulder, "You two wait out here. Keep your eyes peeled."

"I'm coming with you," Rae insisted. "Sophie is my niece. She's my responsibility. I need to help you find her." She touched his sleeve. "Please, Tom."

He stepped back. "Can you smell that? You still want to go in there?"

"I don't want to, no. I want to be back home asleep in my bed with Sophie safe and sound down the hallway. But I'm not leaving here until we've searched every square inch of this place."

"All right, then," he said. "Let's get it done."

Rae put the back of her hand to her nose as she followed Tom into the basement. That smell! As if she hadn't been apprehensive enough. The stench of sour mud and rotting vegetation permeated her nostrils and clogged her throat. She swallowed past her gag reflex and braced herself. She had to do this. Now was not the time to go wimpy and squeamish. She had to find Sophie. Nothing else could be allowed to matter.

She cleared her throat, dropped her hand from her nose and took a few tentative breaths until she felt clear-headed and steady. The building was on high ground, but enough rainwater had seeped in over the decades to allow mold, mildew and all manner of creeping things to take up residence. Even now Rae could have sworn she heard dripping water, but they hadn't had rain in weeks. Maybe it was condensation. The air was damp, and the stone floor felt slippery beneath her sneakers.

She resisted the urge to cling to Tom's shirt as they made their way through small mountains of discarded equipment and debris. She didn't want to think about the original purpose of all those old contraptions, but already she had visions of restraints and drain tables dancing through her head. Once upon a time, the hospital had had its own morgue. She wondered if that was where they were now.

The elevator was just ahead. She tried to get a better view, but Tom's broad back kept blocking her, as if he wanted to shield her.

"What are you doing?"

He glanced over his shoulder. "What do you mean?"

"You keep moving in front of me. Why? What are you afraid I'll see?"

"I've got a weapon and you don't," he said. "We don't

know who or what we'll find down here. It's best that you stay behind me."

"You saw something from above, didn't you?"

"I don't know what I saw," he admitted. "Will you just stay behind me?"

"You think Sophie's—"

"Alive," he said. "We've no reason to think otherwise."

"Except for the blood we found."

"A very small amount and could be animal blood, for all we know. Just stay focused. Let's finish this job."

They approached the elevator shaft and Rae moved around Tom despite his protests. Her heart thudded when her flashlight beam connected with something on the floor. Tom moved quickly to investigate.

"It's just a bunch of old clothing," he said.

Was that relief she heard in his voice? "Are you sure?"

He picked up a metal rod from the floor and prodded the pile. "See?"

No sooner had Rae let out her own relieved breath than a sound brought her up short. She couldn't identify the direction of the noise. The basement had an echo effect that disoriented her. Why had she insisted on coming down here with Tom? She could have remained outside with the officer and no one would have thought less of her. She hated close places. Hated the dampness even more. Hated the sensation that something or someone lurked in the shadows, just beyond the reach of her flashlight. Rae wasn't one for allowing her imagination to get the better of her, but this place held too many trapped memories.

Tom called to his deputy. "Billy?"

"Right here, sir." His voice came from the top of the outside steps.

"You see anything out there?"

"No, sir. Everything's quiet. What about down there?"

"We're about to find out," Tom said.

Rae moved her flashlight beam around the room. Near the entrance, something glinted.

"Tom?" Her voice was barely a whisper. "Someone's down here."

Icy fingers slid down her back as she gripped the flashlight. She used her other hand to steady her wrist as she vectored in on a silhouette. Human. Tall, lanky with longish hair and a scraggly beard. She thought for a moment her fear had conjured the man, but then she caught the glimmer of his beady eyes before he dropped to the floor and scurried crab-like back into a yawning black hole beside the entrance.

"Did you see—"

Tom swore under his breath as he sprinted across the room, Rae at his heels. She wasn't about to be left behind.

A metal gate hung open, revealing the dark void into which the man had scuttled.

"What is that place?" she asked on a quavering breath.

Tom knelt to shine his light back into the opening. "Looks to be a crawl space or a tunnel of some sort. I can see some old pipes. Lots of cobwebs, too."

"You're not going in there," Rae said.

"Get Billy down here."

"Tom, you can't—"

"Make sure he knows where I'm going."

She didn't argue further, but spun on her heel and ran up the steps. She called to the deputy, told him about the tunnel, and by the time he'd followed her back into the basement, Tom had disappeared.

THE CRAWL SPACE went on and on. Tom walked hunched over, occasionally dropping to his hands and knees when the floor and ceiling tightened. He'd never been bothered by close places, but the tunnel unnerved him. It was damp and moldy and he could smell something fetid up ahead. Something that churned his stomach and stiffened his backbone.

Dead rodents, he told himself, but the dark passenger of dread climbed upon his shoulder and whispered bad things in his ear. He shook off the presentiment, reminding himself that Sophie had been missing only a few hours. For all they knew, she was out partying with a friend or lying low someplace to teach her parents a lesson. No reason to believe the worst. They still had plenty of time.

But the clock was ticking and the crawl space seemed endless. After a bit, Tom felt a slight ascension, as if he were heading back up to ground level.

Rae called out to him. His muffled name reverberated through the narrow passage, sending a shiver down his spine even as he took comfort in the sound of her voice. "Just stay put," he called back to her.

He didn't know if she'd heard him or not. Surely she wouldn't try to follow him through the crawl space. He couldn't worry about that right now, though. He had to follow this thing to the end, had to discover the source of that smell.

He plunged on, eventually arriving at another gated opening. Instead of getting closer to the source of the smell, the odor had faded. He could feel fresh air on his face. The crawl space had led him from the main building back to the old boiler room. Tall windows allowed in enough moonlight so that he could make out the metal grates that would have restricted the flames.

Perching at the edge of the opening, he shone his flashlight into the room before he dropped down to the floor and stood gazing around. The space was littered with discarded food cans, an old mattress and what looked to be a camping stove. Someone had been living there.

He caught a movement out of the corner of his eye and turned just as an emaciated man with a heavy beard leaped out of the crawl space and flung himself at Tom, knocking him off balance. He swore as he scrambled to his feet. Once he regained his equilibrium, he had no trouble fending off the scrawny attacker.

"That's enough," Tom said, holding the flailing assailant at bay. Then he pushed him away and the man dropped to the floor, cowering and whimpering.

"I didn't do nothing. You got no call to hurt me like that."

"You're the one who jumped me," Tom pointed out. "I was just defending myself."

The man cringed and hid his face.

"Look at me." Tom trained the flashlight beam on the badge he wore clipped to his belt. "My name's Tom Brannon. I'm the Nance County sheriff. What are you doing in here? Have you been living in this place?"

The man sat up and scratched a bony arm. "I stay here sometimes when I'm passing through. No law against that, is there?"

"Depends on what you've been up to." Tom flicked the beam around the room. "What's your name?"

"Marty."

"You got a last name?"

"Booker."

"Have you seen anyone else at the Ruins tonight, Marty?"

"Like who?"

"A girl." Tom had been moving the flashlight around the room, but now he froze the beam on the floor. He used one of the disposable gloves he kept in his pocket to pick up a cell phone in a pink silicone case, gingerly holding it by the edges. "Where did you get this?"

"Found it."

"Where?"

Marty gave a vague nod toward the door. "Over yonder. Somebody dropped it, I reckon. Finders, keepers."

The phone wasn't locked. Tom kept an eye on the man while he scrolled through the contact numbers. Before he had time to get through the list, Rae burst through the door with Billy Navarro behind her.

"We saw a light out here and then we heard voices." She halted when she saw the stranger shrinking in the shadows. "Who's he?"

"Says his name's Marty Booker." Tom held up the phone. "Do you recognize this?"

Her eyes went wide with shock. "It's Sophie's. Where did you find it?"

"It was lying on the floor in plain sight." He handed the phone to Navarro. The deputy produced a plastic evidence bag, dropped the phone inside and sealed it.

"Lying on the floor in *here*?" Horror crept into Rae's tone. "Where did it come from?"

He nodded toward the man in the shadows. "That's what I'm trying to determine. He says he found it in the main building."

Rae took a step toward the stranger. "You saw Sophie tonight?" When he didn't respond, she advanced closer. "You took her phone, so you must have seen her. Where is she? *Where is she!?*"

The outburst startled even Tom. He had no doubt Rae would have gone for the man's throat if he hadn't caught her arm and held her back. She tried to shrug out of his grasp. "Let go of me!"

He held her tighter. "Settle down."

"But he knows something!"

In all the commotion, Marty Booker shrieked and buried his head in his arms.

Rae was unmoved. "If you've hurt my niece in any way, I swear to God I'll—"

"Just cool it," Tom warned. "We're not going to get anything out of him if you keep threatening him like that."

She jerked away. "Why aren't you doing anything?"

"I'm trying to do my job if you'd let me."

"That would be a first!" she shot back.

Okay, truce over, Tom thought. He wouldn't hold it against her under the circumstances.

Marty Booker took a peek from between folded arms, his gaze darting from Tom to Rae. "I didn't do anything, I swear it. I would never hurt anyone."

"But you saw a girl out here tonight," Tom said.

He hemmed and hawed before he shrugged. "Maybe I saw her."

"Where?" Rae demanded.

He gave the same vague nod toward the entrance. "I see them over there sometimes, but they don't see me."

Tom held up a hand to silence Rae. "Who?"

"Those kids. *Him.*"

"Him?"

Booker's eyes lifted to the ceiling as if he were searching for the mural. *"Him."*

Tom said to Rae, "Do you have a picture of Sophie?"

She fumbled for her phone and then scrolled through the camera roll.

Tom took the phone and held up the screen so that Booker could see the shot of Sophie. "Did you see this girl tonight?"

He hesitated. “Maybe it was her. I don’t see so well at night.”

“Do you know where she is now?”

“He took her.”

“Who?” Tom pressed.

“Preacher,” he whispered. “Preacher took that girl.”

Chapter Three

By morning, word had gotten out about Sophie Cavanaugh's disappearance and a small crowd had gathered outside the station waiting for news. Tom's deputies had returned to the Ruins at first light and were now scouring the building and surrounding area for evidence. The blood sample collected hours earlier at the scene had been sent to the lab for analysis, and Tom's IT specialist, a young deputy named Noah Goodnight, was going through Sophie's cell phone and laptop.

A call to the sheriff in the next county verified Marty Booker's claim that he had family living nearby. The sheriff was well aware of the man. "It's a sad story," he told Tom. "Suffered a severe head trauma when he was just a kid. Hasn't been right since, but as far as I know, he's never been violent. Just wanders around the countryside until he gets ready to come home."

Tom was inclined to agree. He didn't think Marty Booker was responsible for Sophie's disappearance, but he suspected the man had seen more than he was willing to admit. Scared, maybe. Or unable to process what he'd witnessed. Either way, spending the night in a holding cell hadn't done him any harm. If nothing else, he'd gotten a shower, clean clothes and a hot meal.

As for his claim that Preacher had taken Sophie, Tom

wasn't sure what to make of that. Silas Creed hadn't been seen or heard around Nance County since Riley Cavanaugh and Jenna Malloy had gone missing. It was a widely held belief that Creed had taken the girls and held them captive in an abandoned house. Law enforcement personnel and untold volunteers had scoured the countryside for days. When Jenna Malloy had been found wandering down a rural road weeks after she'd been taken, she'd been in a near catatonic state, too emotionally fragile and confused to identify her abductor, let alone lead the police to where the girls had last been held. Jenna had spent the next fifteen years of her life in and out of psychiatric facilities. Tom had lost track of her a long time ago, but he sometimes wondered if Ellie still kept in touch.

He seriously doubted that Silas Creed had returned to Nance County after all this time. He'd be almost sixty by now. Most likely the man was long dead. However, Tom couldn't afford to discount any possibility. He pulled every file he could find on the previous abductions, noting with a pang his father's handwritten notes in some of the margins.

He had everything spread out in his office ready to dig in when he decided to take a ride over to Rae Cavanaugh's place. Things had gotten a little heated the night before and Tom knew he hadn't been as tactful as he should have been. He understood only too well that feeling of utter helplessness, and a part of him wanted to hang back and give her some space. But they were well into the critical twenty-four-hour window and Tom needed her cooperation and he needed her trust. Sophie's life could depend on it.

She lived in one of the town's older neighborhoods. Quaint and private. Unlike the newer subdivisions out by the interstate, all the houses here were different—tidy ranches, stately colonials, a few scattered Victorians. Rae's house was a white prewar bungalow with black shutters and flagstone walkways. Oak trees shaded the front yard, the gnarled branches hidden by whiskers of Spanish moss. The air was thick with the scent of roses. Belle Pointe was situated on the Texas-Louisiana border, and Tom had always thought his hometown more Southern than Texan, though there was no shortage of Lone Star spirit and pride in the area. Life was a little slower here, a little quieter until you probed beneath the surface. Until you remembered that young girls had gone missing.

He didn't recognize the car in her driveway when he pulled up. Rae drove a brand-new midsize SUV and he doubted the aging coupe belonged to Jackson or Lauren Cavanaugh. Not their style. He took note of the license plate number and glanced inside the car as he walked up the driveway.

Rae answered the bell immediately, pulling back the door in anticipation before her expression fell when she saw him. She glanced past him to the street. "Have you found her?" The question was blunt, her tone filled with a heart-tugging mixture of hope and dread. Little wonder, given her previous experience.

"No. That's not why I'm here," Tom said. "I wanted to touch base. But I guess your reaction means you haven't heard from her, either."

She shook her head, looking bleak.

"I thought we could go back over everything that happened last night," he said. "Memories have a way of returning once the dust settles."

She stepped back and motioned him inside. "I don't know what more I can tell you, but it's certainly worth a try." She wore jeans, sneakers and a plain gray T-shirt. Her hair was pulled back into a careless ponytail and she hadn't bothered with makeup. "I was thinking about heading back out to the Ruins," she said. "I can't sit here all day and do nothing."

"I've got deputies combing the area. But organizing a search party isn't a bad idea." It might be a little early for that, but the abandoned bicycle and those drops of blood worried Tom. Not to mention Sophie's cell phone. At the very least, recruiting volunteers would give the family something to do.

"We're already on that." A girl Sophie's age appeared from another room. She walked up to Rae. "Sorry. I wasn't trying to eavesdrop, but I couldn't help overhearing."

"It's okay," Rae said. "Sheriff Brannon, this is Hannah Tucker, one of Sophie's friends."

"Her *best* friend," Hannah clarified as she extended her hand.

"Hannah came by first thing this morning," Rae explained. "She's been helping me compile a list of Sophie's friends, acquaintances, favorite hangouts. That sort of thing."

"Good idea." Tom shook the girl's hand and then followed Rae back to the kitchen, where she'd turned the breakfast table into a workspace. A teenage boy with dark hair and a brooding expression sat at the island with his laptop. He glanced up when they walked in and then did a double take when he recognized Tom. He ducked his head and averted his gaze just a little too quickly by Tom's measure.

"This is Dylan Moody, Sophie's boyfriend."

"Glad you're here," Tom said. "I'd like to ask you and Hannah a few questions if you don't mind."

"Is that legal?" Hannah asked. "We're both minors.

Not that it matters. I'm glad to do anything I can to help bring our Sophie back home, and I'm sure Dylan is, too."

"It's legal," Tom said. "But as a general rule, you don't have to talk to the police without a parent or guardian present."

"What is it you want to know?" Dylan turned to face Tom. "We've already told Detective Jarvis everything we know," he said, referring to Tom's chief investigator.

"I understand, but I have a couple of follow-up questions. Just trying to get the timeline straight in my head. I know this is difficult." He offered a sympathetic smile. "You dropped Sophie off around ten last night. Is that right?"

"Yes. She has a weekday curfew since she's been staying here." He flashed an enigmatic glance in Rae's direction.

"Where did you go during the evening?"

"Just drove around. Grabbed some burgers. Listened to music. Usual stuff." He shrugged.

"You didn't notice anything unusual when you dropped her off? No strange cars parked on the street? Anything at all out of the ordinary?"

"Everything was normal."

"What about her behavior?"

He took a moment too long to answer. "She seemed fine."

"What about you, Hannah? When was the last time you talked to Sophie?"

"She texted last night after she got home. Nothing important. She had some questions about our chemistry assignment and I asked about her date."

"She didn't say anything to either one of you about going out to the Ruins?"

"Not to me. What about you, Dylan?"

He gave Hannah a frowning glance before he said, "No. But she's always had a thing about that place. She likes to take pictures out there. She once said the Ruins spoke to her. I didn't pay much attention. She's always been a little weird."

"That's why we love her," Hannah added.

"Kids don't still dare each other to go out there at night?" Tom asked.

"We can't speak for everyone in school," Hannah said. "But our group is a little more mature than that."

"What about you, Dylan? Were you ever dared to go out there?"

He looked uncomfortable. "Like Hannah said. We don't really do that sort of thing anymore."

"I've never thought Sophie the type to bend to peer pressure anyway," Rae said. "If anything, she's more of a ringleader. Or am I wrong about that?" She glanced from Dylan to Hannah and back to Tom. He had a hard time reading her expression at that moment. Did she suspect, as he did, that these two were holding out on them? Or did she take their earnest expressions at face value?

"Definitely a ringleader," Hannah agreed.

Tom caught an odd look on Dylan's face before he turned his attention back to the laptop.

"You mentioned a search party," Hannah said. "We have enough kids lined up to comb the whole area as soon as you give us the go-ahead. We'll take shifts and search all weekend if we have to." She turned to Rae. "If there is anything we can do for you, just name it. Sophie was like a sister to me. We've been best friends since first grade."

Tom's gaze sharpened at the girl's use of the past tense. An innocent mistake or something more sinister?

"Thank you both for your help," Rae said. "You've

been wonderful. But if you'll excuse us, I need to have a word with Sheriff Brannon."

"Of course." Hannah smiled sweetly as she tucked back her straight brown hair. "We need to get to school anyway, but if it's okay, I'd like to check in with you later."

"Yes, I'm sure we'll talk again," Rae said with a brief nod.

She walked them to the door. When she came back into the kitchen, Tom stood at the window looking out over her backyard. He turned when he heard her footsteps, his gaze taking in her weary expression and the tired slump of her shoulders. She didn't look as if she'd slept a wink the night before. Tom could relate. He hadn't gotten any rest, either. Every time he closed his eyes, he saw too many bad things. He'd finally given up and gone back to the station.

"Coffee?" she asked.

"If it's not too much trouble."

She crossed the room and got down fresh mugs. "Cream and sugar?"

"Black is fine." She carried the cups over to the table and sat down. Tom came over and joined her. "Thanks," he said as he took a tentative sip. "This hits the spot. The coffee we have at the station tastes like feet."

She cradled her cup in both hands as if trying to absorb the warmth. "What did you make of those two?"

"What do you mean?"

She frowned. "They're hiding something. I may not have kids of my own, but it hasn't been that long since I was a teenager. The averted eyes. The cagey glances. Maybe I'm letting my imagination get the better of me, but I think they came over here to find out what I know."

"I don't think you're imagining things," Tom said slowly. "I think they're hiding something, too."

Her blue eyes deepened. "You don't suspect they had anything to do with Sophie's disappearance, do you? They're good kids, from what I know of them."

"Even good kids do bad things," Tom said. "At the very least, I think they knew Sophie was going to the Ruins and now they're too afraid to say so. I'll have them come down to the station separately to give statements. One of them is bound to crack. My guess is it'll be Dylan. Hannah is one cool cookie."

"Tracy Flick," Rae murmured.

Tom gave her a puzzled look. "Who?"

The barest hint of a smile flashed. "A movie reference. Never mind. What did you want to talk to me about?"

"I'd like to take a look at Sophie's room if that's okay."

"I've been through all the drawers and every square inch of her closet. And one of your deputies came and got her computer, so I doubt you'll find anything useful."

"You never know. Another pair of eyes," he said.

She drew a weary breath and stood. "I'll show you up."

The dark circles under her eyes against her pale complexion gave her a vulnerable air, a descriptor Tom would never have thought he'd apply to Rae Cavanaugh. She'd always seemed tough as nails. He hadn't realized how tiny she was, either. When he rose, she barely came to his shoulders. He supposed her commanding personality had always made her seem larger than life, but in the homey confines of her kitchen, she just looked small and scared and lost.

"Tom—"

"We're not even twenty-four hours in," he said. "We've still got time."

"Promise me you'll find her."

"I can't make that promise, but I swear to you I'll do everything in my power to bring her home safely."

Rae sighed. "I guess that will have to do."

TOM BRANNON DIDN'T wear a uniform. Rae wondered if that was because he wanted to set himself apart from the rest of the sheriff's department or if he desired to avoid the inevitable comparisons to his father. Porter Brannon had worn his khaki uniform with a great deal of flair. He'd been a tall man, like his son, and heavyset in his later years. A formidable figure in his Stetson and cowboy boots. Tom wore boots, too, but his were far less pretentious than the full-quill ostrich his father had favored. Nevertheless, his whole rustic, urban chic vibe—low-slung jeans, dark shirt and tie—worked for him. Worked for a lot of the women in town, too, Rae suspected.

Odd that she would be focusing on something as mundane as Tom Brannon's wardrobe when her niece was still missing. Maybe she was just trying to distract herself. Concentrate on something besides the phone call she'd made to Jackson in the wee hours of the morning. That call had been the second hardest thing she'd ever had to do. The first had been letting go of the notion that Riley would someday come home.

She paused outside Sophie's room, picturing her niece sprawled on the bed texting away on her cell phone. *Please, please, please let her be safe.*

"This is it," she said as she pushed open the door. She stood back for Tom to enter. The once sophisticated guest room had been made over into a girlie retreat. Band posters on the wall, photos taped to the dresser mirror, pink-and-white chenille spread on the bed. None of it was to Rae's taste and the clutter drove her crazy, but then, she wasn't fifteen anymore. Sometimes she wondered if she'd ever been that young. "Sophie has a fondness for pink," she said unnecessarily.

Tom glanced around. "I can see that. Reminds me a little of my sister's bedroom when we were kids."

The room was large and airy with a row of windows that let in plenty of natural light, but somehow Tom Brannon seemed to dominate the space, as only a tall, confident man could do. Rae wanted to resent him for the easy way he commanded his surroundings, but right now she just wanted him to find Sophie. If she had to pay tribute to the Brannons for the rest of her life, so be it.

"I talked to Jackson a few hours ago," she said. "He's on his way home. Fair warning—he'll be loaded for bear."

"A man's daughter goes missing, he has a right to be angry and scared."

"That's generous of you."

He gave her an inscrutable glance before he went back to his search. "You think I don't have compassion for what he's going through? You think my dad didn't have compassion for what your dad went through? It was a bad time for all of us," he said. "But your family suffered the most. No one in my family was unaware of that."

His words hit her like a physical punch. "I promised myself I wouldn't talk about that night. I wouldn't even think about it. This is a different time. Different girl, different situation. But what that man said last night." She paused with a shudder. "Do you think it's possible Preacher has come back?"

"I'm not even sure there ever was a Preacher," Tom said. "Silas Creed was a troubled man. Preacher was a fairy tale. A made-up bogeyman to keep kids away from the Ruins."

"For all the good that did. If he didn't take Riley and

Jenna Malloy, then why did he leave town after they went missing? No one ever saw him after that night."

"My dad always figured Creed had someone in the area who helped him disappear. A relative, maybe. They probably knew he'd get blamed and felt sorry for him. Or maybe he really did take those girls. All I know is that whoever split open my skull that night had enough strength to drag me out of the Ruins and roll my body down the embankment."

"You were lucky you weren't killed," Rae said.

"You don't have to tell me how lucky I am. My sister, too. If I could go back and change the outcome—"

Rae turned away abruptly. She didn't want to hear Tom Brannon's regrets. She had enough of her own at the moment. "Why would Marty Booker say Preacher took Sophie if he didn't?"

"Marty Booker is also a troubled man," Tom said. "The description he gave of the abductor matched the face on the ceiling in the Ruins. He's confused at best. I'm not sure he even knows what he saw. His sister is coming in later to pick him up. Maybe she can get more out of him."

"You're just going to let him go?"

"For now. But don't worry. We'll keep an eye on him."

Rae dropped to the edge of the bed. "I wish there was more that I could do to find her. I feel like I should be out there beating the bushes with your deputies."

"Let them do their job right now. You're doing everything you can. Just try to relax."

"Easier said than done."

"I know that." He leaned in to examine the photos taped to the mirror. "Does Sophie keep a diary or journal?"

Rae traced a pattern on the bedspread. "I have no

idea. But kids keep all that stuff online these days. Their whole lives are spread out all over social media. I can't even keep up with all the platforms."

"Do you know if she has accounts under different names?"

"No. But it wouldn't be unusual if she did. I have different accounts for business and personal use." Rae tracked him for a moment as he glanced behind the mirror and then tested the floorboards. "What are you doing?"

"Teenagers create hiding places for things they don't want others to find," he said.

"Sophie's been living under my roof for less than three weeks. You think she already ripped up the floorboards?"

"She had time to redecorate, didn't she? Kids her age are resourceful. I've seen it all."

Restless, Rae stood and walked over to the window to stare down at the garden. Despite the heat of late summer, the roses were still in bloom. She could almost smell the lush scent through the double-pane glass. She'd gotten her start from her mother's prized bushes, everything from American Beauties to Winter Sunsets. Rae didn't have her mother's green thumb. She was lucky to get a few decent blooms per season, but she was too stubborn to give up on the garden.

She said without turning, "Tell me about that night."

He didn't bother pretending to misunderstand. "You said you didn't want to talk about it or even think about it."

"I changed my mind."

"Wouldn't it be better if we focused on Sophie instead?" He sounded tired. And wary. Rae could hardly blame him, given their past.

She turned and leaned a shoulder against the window frame. "We are focusing on Sophie. I know it's a long shot to think the disappearances could be connected, but what if they are? What if Preacher really has come back to town? Anyway, I'd like to hear your version of that night."

He lifted a brow. "My version?"

She rested her head against the frame. "Your story. Your account. Call it whatever you like. I know you've told it before. Dozens of times, I'm sure, but I don't think I ever really listened. Why did you go out that night? Why did you leave the girls alone when you promised your folks you'd look after them?" She tried to keep her tone neutral, but a hint of accusation crept in. *Just tell me why.*

She wouldn't have been surprised if he had refused to answer, but he said in a resolved voice, "I drove out to that party to see a girl."

"Who?"

"Ashley Reardon. Do you remember her?"

Rae straightened from the window, conjuring the image of a pretty blonde cheerleader. "Ashley? Yes, I remember her. I never knew the two of you went out."

"We didn't. We were just starting to notice each other. After everything that happened that night…" He trailed away. "Whatever we had or could have had fizzled."

A lot of things had fizzled after that night. The world as Rae knew it had never been the same. She didn't know if Tom's candor made her feel better or worse. For as long as she could remember, she'd wanted to punish Tom Brannon and his family for failing to protect her sister. *His* sister had come home, after all. But how could she keep blaming Tom when she was the one who had really failed Riley? She was the one who was supposed to look out for her little sister. And now her niece had gone missing on Rae's watch. Payback had never tasted so bitter.

Guilt had never felt darker or heavier than the curtain of regret that descended upon her shoulders.

"Ashley called that night and wanted to see me," Tom said. "I didn't want to say no, so I drove out to the party. We only talked for a few minutes. I was away from the house less than an hour, but when I got back, the girls were gone."

"How did you know where to look for them?"

"I called around and badgered my sister's friends until one of them told me about the dare. I drove straight to the bridge and ran all the way to the Ruins. By the time I got there, I was in a cold sweat. I knew that I would be in trouble if my parents found out, but I didn't care about the punishment. I had a bad feeling something was wrong the moment I set foot in that place."

Rae shivered. "And then you were ambushed."

"Another stupid mistake. I let down my guard."

"You were sixteen."

Their gazes connected for a moment before he glanced away. "Nearly seventeen. And I was old enough to know better."

"Then what does that say about me? I was asleep when Sophie left the house. I didn't hear anything. I knew she had something on her mind when she came home earlier, but instead of trying to talk to her, I took the easy way out."

"You couldn't have known she'd leave the house."

"Neither could you."

Tom looked taken aback, but he couldn't have been any more stunned by her defense of him than she was. He'd been her enemy for fifteen years. A target for all her anguish and guilt. So why did she now feel the need to understand him? Why the desire to reach out to him, to draw comfort from his strength and resolve? Why did she wonder, all of a sudden, what it would be like to have his arms around her, holding her close as he murmured in her ear that all would be well?

She was just tired and worried and scared. She wasn't thinking straight. Hugging her arms around her middle, she looked anywhere but into Tom Brannon's troubled gray eyes.

He stirred restlessly. "I'm done in here."

Yes, so was Rae. She needed to be alone to regroup. Everything seemed strangely tilted in Sophie's room, as if the lingering emotions and confusion of a teenager had somehow infected Rae's common sense.

She led Tom back into the hallway and then turned to close the door. He was already at the top of the stairs when her phone rang. She fished her cell out of her jeans pocket and lifted it anxiously to her ear.

"Hello?"

"Rae, it's Dad. Don't say a word. Just listen. Something's happened. I need you to drop everything and get out to the ranch as quick as you can."

Chapter Four

Rae clutched the phone. “Dad? What’s going on?”

He paused for so long she thought he might have hung up. “Are you alone?”

She glanced at Tom, who waited on the landing.

“Sheriff Brannon is here,” she tried to say without inflection.

Her father muttered an oath. “Get rid of him.”

“He was just leaving. He came to search Sophie’s room. No, we didn’t find anything. Not yet.” She shot Tom another look. “Try not to worry. I’ll drive out as soon as I can.”

“Get out here *now*.” West Cavanaugh hung up without another word.

Tom watched her carefully. “Everything okay?”

She slipped the phone back into her pocket. “My father is having a difficult time, as you can imagine. Sophie’s disappearance is bringing back a lot of painful memories. I need to go out to the ranch and be with him.”

“I’d like to talk to him,” Tom said. “To Jackson and his wife, too, as soon as they get back in town. Maybe I should drive out to the ranch with you.”

Rae bit her lip. “Would you mind waiting until I have a chance to calm him down? I can usually get through to him if there aren’t any distractions. He hasn’t been in the best of health lately. He had a mild heart attack last winter."

"I didn't know that." Tom turned back to the stairs. "Are you sure everything is okay? Nothing else you want to talk to me about?"

"I've told you everything I know," Rae said. "I'm well aware that our best chance of getting Sophie back unharmed is to cooperate fully with your office."

"I'm glad to hear you say that."

They were in the foyer now, standing face-to-face. Tom stared down at her for the longest moment. He probably sensed something was up. Rae had never been that great of a poker player, but she couldn't exactly fill him in when she had no idea why her father had called. She resisted the urge to check the time on her phone. She needed to get out to the ranch. She needed to be there for her family. But Tom lingered.

"If you think of anything or hear of anything—"

"I'll call," she said as she reached around him to open the door and then ushered him onto the porch. "You have my word."

Trailing him down the steps, she stood on the sidewalk and gave him a brief wave as he backed out of her driveway. She waited until his vehicle had disappeared around a corner before rushing back inside to grab her purse and car keys. Then she backed out of the garage, glanced both ways and laid down rubber as she wheeled into the street.

Fifteen minutes later, she pulled through the gateway arch that led to the Cavanaugh ranch. Speeding along the curving lane, she was oblivious to the pine trees and honeysuckle thickets that crowded the shoulder. Even with the sun shining down through the bowers, a perpetual gloom hovered, but she was used to all those shadows.

She made the last corner and the trees thinned, allowing an expansive view of the rolling countryside. Light glinted off the pond where a mother duck and her babies skimmed across the surface and a heron fished in the shallows. In the distance, black cattle grazed peacefully against a backdrop of robin's egg blue.

The pastoral scene seemed obscenely incongruent with Sophie's disappearance, but the sight of the sprawling limestone-and-cedar house never failed to comfort Rae. Her happiest moments had been spent on the ranch. She and Jackson and Riley riding horses on a frosty evening. Coming home to a crackling fire and the smell of baking bread and their mother's soft laughter as she bustled about the kitchen. Their father sipping whiskey in his recliner, a dog at his feet and a cat curled up on the hearth. Summers were even better. Waterskiing on the lake. Tubing on the river. Lounging on the back porch as thunderheads rolled in from the east.

After Rae's mother died, everything had gone to hell. Her father had eventually remarried and then divorced, Riley had disappeared and Rae and Jackson had grown so far apart she sometimes wondered if her brother actually hated her. If he didn't before, he certainly would now, she thought with dreaded certainty.

She pulled around to the back of the house and started to go in the kitchen entrance as she always did when she heard raised voices coming from the direction of her mother's rose garden. Stepping off the porch, she slipped unnoticed along the flagstone pathway. The French doors to her father's study were open, allowing in the morning breeze, and Rae paused to savor the garden before facing whatever terrible news waited for her inside.

As she stood there wrapped in the luscious scent of

her mother's roses, she heard Jackson's voice lift in anger. So her brother was already back.

"How can you blame me for any of this? I wasn't even here!"

"Which is precisely why I hold you responsible," her father countered. "You're the girl's father, yet you had no qualms about pawning your only child off on your sister even though you know she has no experience in dealing with someone like Sophie."

"Someone like Sophie? What's that supposed to mean?"

"Do I have to spell it out for you?"

"She's a spirited girl," Jackson defended.

"She's a spoiled brat and you know it. That child has always needed a firm hand and a watchful eye. You've given her neither. And that wife of yours is no help. Although she does know how to spend money. I'll give her that."

"It's not enough to disparage my daughter, but now you have to set in on my wife?" Jackson grumbled bitterly. "Under the circumstances, I would have hoped for a little more understanding and compassion. The last thing I need is another lecture from you."

Her brother's sullen tone grated on Rae even as she berated herself for eavesdropping. She knew she should make her presence known, but she stood motionless in the garden, rooted by an indefinable worry. Why were they arguing about Jackson's second wife when his daughter had vanished from the Ruins just as Riley had? Didn't they understand that none of their petty grievances mattered anymore?

"I'm only telling you these things for your own good," West insisted. "When this is all over and Sophie is back home safe and sound, you need to take a long, hard look at yourself. You're nearly forty years old, Jackson. It's high time you grow up and take control of your life. You've made plenty of bad decisions in the past few months and the business has suffered as a result. You're away from the office at all hours. You drink too much, and you've allowed your wife to spend you to the verge of bankruptcy. I'm beginning to think I should have put Rae in charge."

"I'm surprised you didn't. She's always been your favorite." That sullen tone again. Rae winced.

"Your sister is a hard worker. She's earned my respect and devotion, and if I play favorites now and then, maybe it's because she's the spitting image of your mother. But you're my only son. I've always had high hopes for you. Maybe those expectations have been too much of a burden. I don't know. What I do know is that none of this matters a whit if we lose Sophie. Instead of worrying about Rae, you need to figure out how you're going to get your daughter back."

"How *I'm* going to get her back? Do you have any idea how cold you sound right now? She isn't just my daughter. She's your only grandchild. Or doesn't that mean anything to you?"

"Of course it means something to me. We're all in this together. Why do you think I asked Rae to come out here?"

"Where is she anyway? Shouldn't she be here by now?"

"She'll be here when she gets here," West said. "Stop that infernal pacing and try to relax."

"I need a drink," Jackson muttered.

"It's barely ten o'clock in the morning," West said reprovingly.

"Yes, and my daughter isn't home yet. If I want a whiskey, I'll damn well have one."

"Suit yourself."

Rae drew a breath and started to enter through the garden doors when a car sounded in the driveway. She retraced her steps around the house just as Lauren Cavanaugh exited her luxury sedan and strode up the walkway to the front entrance, using her key to let herself in. Rae went back around to the rear door and came in through the mudroom and kitchen, allowing her sister-in-law time to disappear down the hallway. The last thing she wanted was a confrontation with Jackson's wife. She'd never warmed up to the woman. Never really trusted her. But if Jackson was happy in his second marriage, then Rae's opinion didn't matter. As far as she could determine, no one in that household had been happy for a very long time, least of all Sophie.

Rae spoke to the housekeeper for a moment before heading down the long hallway to her father's study. Lauren was already seated on the leather sofa with her long legs crossed, revealing the red soles of her expensive heels. She wore a white dress belted at the waist and a gold-and-diamond bracelet around her wrist.

A former model, Lauren Cavanaugh was a tall, pale blonde with expensive tastes and a distant nature. She gave Rae's jeans and T-shirt a dismissive once-over as she accepted a mineral water from her husband. He sprawled on the sofa beside her, weary and anxious and yet somehow still defensive. Even under such distressing circumstances, the two made a striking couple. Rae's light brown hair and freckles came from her mother's side of the family while Jackson had inherited their father's height and dark good looks.

Rae went over and kissed her dad's cheek. As always, he smelled of fresh-cut grass with a hint of witch hazel. She drew in the scent, taking comfort in the familiar.

The leather furniture, the paintings on the wall, all those well-loved books…

How she wished she could go back in time, to a point where Sophie was safe and sound and everything else was mundane. Maybe even further back so that she could see Riley one last time.

"I'm glad you're here, Rae." Her father patted her shoulder.

She straightened, her gaze moving from her father to her brother. The tension was as thick and choking as smoke. "I came as soon as I could. What's going on? Has there been news of Sophie?"

"Yes, we have news." West took her hand. "Brace yourself, honey. We've received a ransom demand."

AFTER LEAVING RAE'S HOUSE, Tom drove straight back to the station. The morning remained hot and sunny, and yet an eerie pall had settled over the town. Sophie Cavanaugh's disappearance had stirred a lot of bad memories in Belle Pointe. A lot of old fears and suspicions had been resurrected.

Tom wasn't immune. He'd been fighting a sense of déjà vu ever since Rae had reported her niece missing. He didn't want to believe Sophie's disappearance had anything to do with the incident fifteen years ago, but someone had picked the night of a blood moon to lure her to the Ruins. Surely not Preacher after all these years, but someone with knowledge of the past. Someone who knew the significance of the eclipse.

He itched to be out combing the countryside with his deputies. He felt powerless behind a desk, but if Sophie Cavanaugh didn't turn up soon, a million details would have to be coordinated. The investigation had to be done right. He couldn't afford to get careless.

Taking a momentary break, he leaned back in his chair and glanced outside. He could see the street from his desk. Traffic was light for a weekday morning. Little wonder. People who had heard the news would be staying close to home. Parents would want to keep an eye on their kids. Imagining themselves in a similar situation would strike cold terror in their hearts.

Tom's gaze lit on a solitary figure in the park across the street. Dylan Moody had been sitting on a bench in the shade of a pecan tree for the past ten minutes. He'd obviously ditched school. Maybe he just needed some time to himself, but the proximity of the park to the station led Tom to wonder if Sophie Cavanaugh's boyfriend was trying to work up the courage to come in. Tom thought about walking over and confronting him, but then he decided it might be better to let the boy stew for a while.

"Sheriff?"

He glanced up to find his civilian assistant hovering in the doorway. "What is it, Angie?"

She angled her head toward the squad room. "You've got a visitor. Says his name is Blaine Fenton."

Tom glanced through the glass partition to the front of the building, where a dark-haired man paced nervously. He looked vaguely familiar, but Tom couldn't place him.

"Did he say what he wanted?"

Angie looked worried. "Says he needs to talk to you about the Cavanaugh girl."

"You'd better send him in, then." Tom turned back to the window. Dylan Moody was still out there, sitting hunched over as if he had a bad stomachache. *What are you hiding, kid?* What had him all torn up inside?

As if drawn by Tom's scrutiny, Dylan glanced across the street at the station. His gaze moved over the brick facade before coming to rest—Tom could have sworn—on his office window. The boy sat transfixed for the longest moment before he finally got up and hurried away, casting a worried look over his shoulder before he disappeared into the trees.

A shadow appeared in the doorway and Tom tore his gaze from the park.

The man hovered on the threshold, shuffling his feet as he ran a finger around the brim of his Stetson.

He's nervous, Tom thought. "Blaine Fenton?"

The man cleared his throat. "Thank you for agreeing to see me, Sheriff."

Tom swiveled his chair around and leaned an elbow on his desk. "How can I help you?"

"I'm hoping I can help you."

Tom sized him up. "You know something about Sophie Cavanaugh's disappearance?"

"Not directly. But I know something."

"That's plenty vague. Everybody knows something." Tom straightened and motioned to the chair across from his desk. "Maybe you'd better sit down and tell me what's on your mind."

The man took a seat and placed his hat on the floor beside his chair. He looked to be in his late thirties, tall and fit with the air of a man accustomed to hard work. He wore jeans, boots and a plaid shirt with pearl snaps up the front. Ordinary attire for Nance County.

"You may not know this, but our dads used to be friends," he said. "Pop always spoke highly of the sheriff. He said Porter Brannon was one of the finest men he ever knew."

"That's always nice to hear," Tom said. "What's your dad's name?"

"Bill Fenton. He owns a small ranch north of here.

Part of his property borders the Cavanaugh spread. We're small potatoes by comparison, but we always got on well with the family. Jackson and I played baseball together when we were kids and I used to ride horses with Rae. Sometimes Riley would tag along. Real sweet kid. Shame what happened to her."

"Yes, it is."

The man's thoughts seemed to drift for a moment before he reined in his focus. "After I left the military, I worked for the Cavanaughs for a time."

"I get it," Tom said. "You go back a long way with the family."

Blaine Fenton nodded. "About two years ago, Pop got bad sick. Lung cancer. No insurance. The medical bills piled up quick. He went to West Cavanaugh and offered to sell him the water rights to a parcel of land the family had been trying to buy for years. Cavanaugh had the papers drawn up and my dad signed them. It wasn't until they started moving heavy drilling equipment onto the land that Pop realized he'd also signed away the oil and gas rights. This happened just months before the discovery became public of the new natural gas deposits in the Haynesville-Bossier Shale."

Tom gave him a long scrutiny. "You think West Cavanaugh knew about the discovery before he signed those papers?"

"Of course he knew." Bitterness crept into Blaine Fenton's voice. "Why else would he have slipped that clause into the contracts?"

"Didn't your dad have an attorney look over the paperwork before he signed?"

Fenton's lips thinned as his tone sharpened. "Yes. An attorney recommended by West Cavanaugh. You have to consider how sick Pop was back then. Between the chemo and radiation, he wasn't thinking clearly, and the Cavanaughs took advantage of his frailty."

"Where were you during this time?"

A look flashed across the man's face that Tom couldn't name. Could have been guilt. Could have been annoyance at a perceived implication. "I'd been living out west for a few years. I came home as soon as I found out about Pop's illness."

Tom fiddled with a pen on his desk. "Sounds like your family has had a rough go of it and I'm sorry about that. But what does any of this have to do with Sophie Cavanaugh's disappearance?"

"I'm getting to that." Outwardly, Fenton's nerves appeared to be under control, but beneath his calm surface, he was still a man on edge. "After I found out what happened, I hired an attorney willing to take our case on contingency. She's believed all along that we have a good chance in court. Folks around here don't appreciate anyone taking advantage of the elderly. Or anyone swindling a sick man out of hundreds of thousands of dollars by one of their neighbors. Having public opinion on our side means a sympathetic jury pool."

"Still waiting for your point," Tom said.

Fenton leaned in. "After more than a year of delays and mediation, the case is set to go to trial next month. Just weeks away from the court date and Sophie Cavanaugh disappears, reminding people of what happened to West Cavanaugh's youngest daughter. All of a sudden, sympathy shifts to his side."

"Let me see if I follow," Tom said slowly. "You think West Cavanaugh had his own granddaughter abducted in order to sway public opinion?"

"Yes. That's exactly what I think. Don't get me wrong. I'm not suggesting he'd have the girl harmed. She's probably stashed away in some fancy spa or maybe out on the ranch somewhere. She'll turn up in a few days none the worse for the wear. The family will keep her out of the public eye until after the trial so that imaginations can run wild. In the meantime, they'll use all their resources, including their kin at the *Echo Lake Star*, to smear my dad and challenge his mental state. People forget that the Cavanaughs have a stake in the local paper, so they don't always see the bias."

"Maybe you're not giving people around here enough credit. And maybe you're placing too much importance on a small-town weekly," Tom said. "No one relies on local newspapers anymore."

"People who serve on juries do."

Tom allowed that he might have a point.

Blaine Fenton scowled across the desk. "Think about how they used to go after your dad. Sheriff Brannon could never catch a break. Nothing he did was ever good enough. That paper hammered him for years and you know damn well West Cavanaugh was behind those attacks. I always tried to give the old man a break for his bitterness. Losing a child like that…" He shook his head. "But now I think he went after your dad because Porter Brannon couldn't be bought. And the Cavanaughs will do the same thing to you if you don't watch your back."

Tom thought about all the nasty rumors and innuendos that had been launched by his political opponent and the heated rhetoric that had been sanctioned on the editorial pages of the *Echo Lake Star*. All through that campaign, Tom had had to remind himself that politics was a dirty business and he couldn't allow himself to take any of it personally. But he was only human. The attack on his character had stung. He knew firsthand how brutal the Cavanaughs could be when they viewed you as the enemy. Even so, he didn't want to attach too much credence to Blaine Fenton's theory. The man obviously harbored a grudge and everything he said had to be filtered through that lens. Yet a seed of doubt had been planted.

"It's an interesting theory," Tom said. "But that's all it is. Not much I can do without hard evidence."

"You can keep an open mind," Fenton said. "That's all I'm asking."

Tom sat back in his chair. "Are you sure you aren't trying to stir up trouble because of an old grudge?"

"I'm not stirring up anything. I haven't said a word to anyone else about my concerns. But it's been on my mind ever since I heard about the girl's disappearance. I figured I needed to come in and say my piece. Whatever happens now is out of my hands." He picked up his hat and stood. "Thank you for your time, Sheriff."

Tom rose, too. "Leave your contact information with my assistant in case I need to get in touch with you."

Fenton hesitated. "I don't know why you would. I've told you everything I know. I'd as soon my name is kept out of it. People might assume as you did that I have an ax to grind." He paused as another frown flashed. "Just don't make the mistake of underestimating West Cavanaugh. He's done a lot of good in Nance County, fooled a lot of people, but my father learned the hard way that he's as ruthless as they come. And from what I can tell, the apple doesn't fall far from the tree."

Tom leaned a hip against the corner of his desk. "Are you now suggesting Jackson Cavanaugh had something to do with his daughter's disappearance?"

"I wasn't talking about Jackson."

The insinuation blindsided Tom, though he wasn't sure why. "You think Rae Cavanaugh is somehow involved?"

Fenton said grimly, "Put it this way, Sheriff. Jackson

doesn't have the smarts or the stomach to pull off something like this. I grew up with those kids, and in my experience, people don't change that much. Riley was the sweet one, Jackson was the hothead and Rae was always one step ahead of everyone else."

Rae was smart, no question, but Tom couldn't imagine her having anything to do with her niece's disappearance. She'd been genuinely distressed when she called last night and even more so this morning. Or was she that good of an actress?

Fenton gave him a knowing look. "Don't let that pretty smile fool you, Sheriff. Way down deep, Rae Cavanaugh's every bit as cunning as her old man."

Chapter Five

Rae stared at her father in stunned disbelief. A ransom demand had never entered her mind. She supposed she'd subconsciously melded Sophie's disappearance with Riley's. In her sister's case, there had never been any communication with the abductor, much less a final resolution. The day Riley went missing had started out as any other and then she was just…gone.

But a ransom demand implied that Sophie could still be alive.

Tears flooded Rae's eyes, but she blinked them away and tried to remain resolute. Kidnappings for ransom didn't always turn out well, either. So many things could go wrong. But Sophie had been gone for less than a day. Tom Brannon said they still had time. Rae clung to that.

"When? *How?* What are the demands?"

"The call came in on the landline just before Jackson arrived," West said. "I was here alone. The caller used one of those electronic gizmos to disguise his voice. I couldn't tell if I was speaking to a man or a woman. Whoever called demanded a cool million in twenty-four hours for Sophie's safe return."

Rae's stomach knotted with dread. "How do we know it isn't a hoax? Maybe someone heard about Sophie's disappearance and is trying to cash in."

"We don't know," West said. "Not yet. We've only had the one call."

Rae took a moment to calm her thudding heart. "Twenty-four hours isn't much time to raise that kind of cash."

"But you can do it, right?" Lauren had been silent since Rae arrived. Now she rose and went over to West's desk, placing her palms on the surface as she leaned in anxiously. "You can get the money. It isn't that much, really. Not by Cavanaugh standards."

"A million dollars is a great deal of money by anyone's standards," West snapped. "Contrary to what you seem to think, money doesn't grow on trees around here."

"Dad, please," Jackson pleaded.

"Please what?" West demanded.

Lauren whirled to face Rae, her eyes clouded with anguish. Rae had never seen her sister-in-law's facade slip, but something that might have been fear clawed its way up to that cool, placid surface. "There must be something you can do. Holdings that you can liquidate. Lines of credit that you can tap into. Don't tell me there isn't a way!"

"Let's just try to stay calm." Rae was scared, too, but she deliberately kept her tone even. "I'll talk to the bank if that's how we want to play it. We should also call Sheriff Brannon. He needs to know about this."

"No cops." West was blunt and adamant. "The son of a bitch said he'd kill Sophie if we involve the authorities."

Lauren gasped. Jackson swore. A cold chill shot through Rae.

West pressed home his point. "We've got to be smart about this. Porter Brannon never did a damn thing to bring Riley home. I'm not about to put Sophie's life in the hands of his son."

"I don't think that's fair," Rae said. "Tom isn't his father."

Three pairs of eyes stared her down. No one said anything for a long, tense moment and then her father's gaze narrowed. "What did you say?"

Rae wavered in the face of her father's hostility, but she didn't back down. "Just because Porter Brannon couldn't find Riley doesn't mean Tom won't find Sophie."

Jackson stepped forward, fists clenched at his sides. "I can't believe what I'm hearing. What is wrong with you? Don't you remember anything about the night our little sister went missing? Tom was supposed to be watching those girls, but instead he left them alone while he went out partying. What happened to Riley was his fault."

Rae took a breath. "Then what happened to Sophie is my fault."

She hadn't really expected Jackson to leap to her defense, but the white-hot fury in his eyes shook her to the core. "Damn right it's your fault. If anything happens to my daughter, I will never forgive you."

"That's enough," West said. "It doesn't help Sophie if we turn on each other. We need to keep our heads on straight, so we don't make any stupid mistakes."

"I'm sorry," Rae said.

Jackson turned away with a shrug.

Rae dropped down onto an armchair. She'd been bracing for the confrontation with her brother ever since she'd discovered Sophie missing from her room, but nothing could have truly prepared her for Jackson's scorn. She told herself he was just scared. Even without the history of a missing sister, any parent would be terrified in his place. But Riley had to be on his mind. She was on everyone's mind. If he needed to take his fears out on Rae, then so be it.

But there was something about his behavior that struck

a wrong note. Yes, he was scared, but he also seemed jittery, as if he'd mainlined a gallon of black coffee. He couldn't be still. He sat down on the sofa only to pop back up a moment later to pace to the window. Lauren watched with hooded eyes, her gaze keen and calculating. For whatever reason, Rae's mind went back over the accounting discrepancies she'd found recently. Invoices from companies she couldn't track down. Cattle bought and sold without proper documentation. She didn't like where her thoughts were headed, so she forced her attention back to her father. He sat back down at his desk and stared at the phone as if he could somehow will it to ring.

"Dad?"

He glanced up with a frown. "What?"

"If you don't trust the county sheriff's office, what about calling the FBI? They know how to handle kidnappings."

He glared at her. "Did the feds find Riley?"

"They were called in late—"

"Yes, and I remember the guy they finally sent down here." He gave a derisive snort. "Fresh out of Quantico. Green behind the ears. About as useful as any of Porter Brannon's idiot deputies."

"I just think—"

Jackson had been pacing in front of the window, but now he stormed over to her chair and got in her face. "Enough, Rae! No cops means *no cops*. Local, federal or otherwise. You heard what Dad said. This time we take care of things our way."

Rae put up a hand warning her brother to back off. "Our way? What does that even mean?"

"It means we get on the same page right this very minute." West's gaze swept the study with steely resolve. "Nothing we say leaves this room. Are we clear on that?"

"I understand how you feel," Rae said. "But even if we come up with the ransom, there's no guarantee they'll let Sophie go. We need backup. We're taking an awfully big risk not bringing in the authorities."

Jackson gave her another contemptuous glance. He'd retreated a few steps, but he still hovered. "Don't cross us on this, Rae. You always think you know better than anyone else, but this is not your decision to make. You've already done enough without going behind our backs to the cops."

"I'm not going behind your back. Since when am I not entitled to an opinion?"

West leaned forward. "Do you trust me? Forget this ridiculous feud with your brother. Do you trust *me*?"

She sighed. "Of course I trust you, Dad."

"Then believe me when I tell you we'd be taking a far bigger risk by calling in the authorities. For all we know, someone could be watching the ranch at this very moment. They may even have planted surveillance inside the house. If we call the cops, they'll know it."

"They?"

"I got the impression more than one person is involved in this thing. It's likely we're dealing with professionals."

Her father was starting to sound paranoid, but Rae couldn't help glancing around the room with another shudder. Jackson was back at the window staring out at the garden. He'd distanced himself from the conversation, but Lauren clung to every word. She seemed fascinated by the back-and-forth.

"Something you want to add?" Rae couldn't help asking.

"What's there to add? West is absolutely right. It would be a mistake to bring in the police."

He spared her a withering glance. There had never

been any love lost between West Cavanaugh and his daughter-in-law, so he wasn't likely to be swayed by her truckle. After a moment, he dropped his gaze back to the phone in dismissal. "If we want Sophie back alive, we have to do exactly as the kidnappers say. We have to trust that all they want is money. But I won't give them one red cent until they provide proof of life."

"When should we expect another call?" Rae asked nervously.

"I don't know. I was told to stay close to the phone."

She nodded. "Then I'll handle the financial arrangements. Jackson can stay here with you."

"I've already phoned Glen Stafford," West said, referring to their longtime banker. "I didn't give him specifics and he didn't ask for any. We've done business long enough that my word is good enough for him. All you need to do is go down to the bank in a few hours, sign the papers and bring the money straight back here."

"A few hours? How is that possible? First National is a small bank," Rae said. "They don't have that kind of cash on hand, do they?"

"Leave the details to Glen. He said he'd have the money. He'll have the money."

Jackson turned from the window. "If you already had it worked out with the bank, then why didn't you say so? Why put me through hell with all that talk about getting my house in order? You couldn't have waited until we have Sophie back to tear into me?"

"I told you some hard truths," West said. "When this is all over, we're going to make some changes around here, starting with you two." He pointed a finger at first Jackson and then Lauren. She stiffened, but didn't turn away. "No more expensive trips, no more shopping sprees, no more anything until you work yourselves out of debt. As for you." He turned to Rae. "I've always had complete faith in your judgment, but if you're going soft on Tom Brannon, I may have to rethink my position."

She frowned. "I'm not going soft. I'm just trying to be fair."

"Was it fair that Porter Brannon's daughter came home and mine didn't? Was it fair that his son left those young girls alone in the house that night? Nothing about this situation is fair, Rae. Keep your head on straight and let's just get through this. We'll deal with Tom Brannon later."

"SHERIFF?"

Tom turned to find Angie back at his door, this time with her purse hooked over her shoulder.

"Going somewhere?" he asked.

"It's Friday noon. I'm out of here until Monday morning."

"Is it that late already?" He glanced at his watch. The hours had flown by.

"Boy Wonder's in the back," she said, referring to Noah Goodnight. "He says he's found something on Sophie's phone that you should take a look at."

Tom nodded. "I'm headed that way now. You have a good weekend."

"You sure you don't want me to stay?"

"I'll call you back in if I need you. Otherwise, go home and relax."

"Thanks. I intend to. You try to get some rest, too. You've been up all night and half the day. You look like hell," she said in her usual direct manner.

"I feel that way, too." Tom followed her out into the squad room and they parted ways as he headed down the hallway to the back of the building to find his deputy.

A graduate of Sam Houston University with dual

degrees in criminal justice and forensic studies, Noah Goodnight was one of Tom's most successful recruits. Tom was under no illusion that a deputy of Noah's caliber would remain in a place like Belle Pointe forever. He'd eventually get bored and move on to greener pastures, most likely to a midsize city like Tyler at first and then to Dallas or Fort Worth. Tom would never be able to match the incentives or salary of a big-city police department, but for as long as Noah remained in Nance County, Tom intended to take full advantage of the man's skills.

He pushed open the door and nodded to both Noah and Craig Jarvis, the senior detective in Criminal Investigations. Craig was a twenty-year veteran on the force. He wasn't flashy or cocky like some of the younger officers. He preferred the background to the limelight, and his hunched shoulders and easygoing demeanor could sometimes be mistaken for a man cruising toward retirement. He and Tom had been partners early in Tom's career, and he'd quickly learned that beneath Craig's low-key exterior lurked a clever and determined investigator. He had been the first to encourage Tom to run for his dad's old office, the first to congratulate him when he won and the first to stand shoulder to shoulder with him when resentment had reared its ugly head in the department.

Tom pulled up a stool and sat down at a counter across from Noah. "You've got something for me?"

The young deputy gave him a brief nod. "Two things. The blood analysis came back from the sample that was collected last night at the Ruins. It's not a match for Sophie Cavanaugh or Marty Booker."

"So we have conclusive proof a third person was in that building last night," Tom said.

"It's not a match for Silas Creed, either, for whatever that's worth," Craig added.

"No big surprise there," Tom said. "But it's always good to eliminate every possibility, no matter how slight. What else?"

The younger officer held up the pink encased cell phone Tom had found in the boiler room. "I've been going through Sophie's text messages. It's mostly just high school stuff, but I came across a series of group texts that could be important."

"I'm all ears," Tom said.

"There are four people texting back and forth in this particular group, including Sophie, Dylan Moody and Hannah Tucker. I haven't been able to trace the fourth number to anyone in Sophie's contacts. They've all replaced the letters in their names with symbols. See?" He turned the screen so they could take a look. "Those kids have been going out to the Ruins for weeks. I think they're involved in some sort of game."

"I saw Hannah and Dylan at Rae Cavanaugh's house this morning," Tom said. "They told me flat out they didn't go out to the Ruins anymore and had no idea why Sophie would have gone there alone."

"They told me the same thing," Craig said.

Noah shrugged. "Kids lie all the time. Question is, why are these two lying?"

"What do you think these symbols mean?" Tom asked.

"Think of them as Monopoly pieces. Each player has a unique token. Remember the photos of the Ruins that Rae Cavanaugh found on Sophie's laptop? When I blew up the images, I found these same symbols on some of the walls inside the building." He turned the laptop around so that Tom and Craig could scrutinize the images.

Tom leaned in to get a better look.

"From what I can piece together from the texts, the rules of the game are pretty simple," Noah said. "The first player enters the Ruins, probably at night, to hide his or her symbol somewhere inside the building. On a wall, on the floor, the ceiling, wherever. The second player arrives on a different night with the objective of finding the first player's symbol. Player Number Two then hides his or her symbol elsewhere so that the third player has to find both. They go deeper into the building with each trip and the game becomes riskier. The more symbols a player finds, the more points he or she is awarded. It's kind of like a scavenger hunt."

"A creepy scavenger hunt, if you ask me," Craig muttered.

"That's not even the creepiest part," Noah said. "The symbols seem to represent people who were connected to the disappearances of those girls fifteen years ago."

"You're right. That is creepier."

"Connected how?" Tom asked.

"Sophie's symbol is a gemstone—a Riley. Dylan Moody uses a six-point star." Noah pointed to the badge clipped to Tom's belt. "Your father was sheriff back then. The star probably represents your sister or you or maybe even your whole family. Hannah Tucker uses a lightning bolt. That one took me a while to figure out. Then I remembered that the girl who was found wandering on the side of the road—Jenna Malloy—was in and out of psychiatric hospitals for years. The lightning bolt is probably meant to represent electroshock therapy. The fourth player uses a cross."

Tom felt a chill along his spine. "Preacher?"

Craig gave a low whistle. "Now Booker's account is starting to make sense. When he told you that Preacher had taken Sophie, we assumed in his confusion he meant Silas Creed. But what if he saw *this* Preacher?"

Tom nodded. "He also said, 'I see them, but they don't see me.' I assume he meant the players." He turned back to Noah. "So the fourth player—Preacher—is the number you haven't been able to track down."

"I tried calling and texting. Nothing. No voice mail or anything. I figure it's a burner that got tossed after the prepaid minutes were used up. We can trace the number back to the point of purchase, but that takes time and it still may not tell us who bought the phone."

Tom glanced at Craig. "Is Marty Booker still in lockup?"

"His sister picked him up a little while ago."

"We'll need to bring him in again. Or better yet, see if you can talk to him at his sister's house. He may feel less threatened in a friendly environment. We'll need to bring in Hannah Tucker and Dylan Moody, too. Call their parents and get them to agree to a time. Let's do this by the book."

"I'm on it."

"Any objection to me running out to the Ruins and taking a look at these symbols in person?" Noah asked. "I don't think there's much else to be found on Sophie's phone."

"Go ahead." Tom pushed the stool up under the counter. "Both of you keep me posted. I'm on my way out to the Cavanaugh ranch. Sophie's parents should be back in town by now. I'll see if they know anything about this game. At the very least, maybe they can tell me if Sophie has made any new friends recently."

Craig stuffed his notebook into his pocket. "Does it seem strange to anyone but me that none of the Cavanaughs have been by the station this morning? They're not exactly shrinking violets. You'd think they'd want an update on the investigation. If it were my daughter or granddaughter, I'd be camping out on your doorstep."

"A lot of things about this case are strange," Tom said.

Chapter Six

Rae picked up the money at the bank after lunch and then left through Glen Stafford's private entrance to avoid curious stares. She didn't ask how he'd managed to come up with the cash so quickly. She was just grateful *he* didn't ask questions.

Storing the bag in the back seat of her SUV, she eased around the building and pulled onto the street. She tried to remain calm and alert, but she felt as if a big target had been painted on her back. All the way home she kept an eye on the rearview mirror. Even though she didn't see any suspicious vehicles behind her, she didn't rule out the possibility of a tail. For all she knew, she could have been followed from the moment she left the ranch.

Gripping the steering wheel, she shifted her focus to the road ahead of her. The county highway had plenty of cutoffs and wooded areas where someone could lie in wait. She was starting to feel a little paranoid, but if her dad's hunch was right, the whole family could be under surveillance.

Turning off the main road, she breathed a sigh of relief as she drove through the metal archway. She felt safer now that she was on her home turf, but she didn't let down her guard until the house was in sight. Even then, her reprieve was short-lived. A full-size SUV sped up the driveway toward her. Panic welled until she spotted the lights across the top of the cab. She couldn't see the driver or the emblem on the door, but she knew the visitor was Tom Brannon.

Rae bit her lip, wondering if she should pretend she didn't see him and take the money inside or if she should wait for him beside her vehicle. Might be a good idea to speak to him first before he talked to the others. She could at least find out what he wanted. If he had news of Sophie, then she would be able to prepare her family.

She got out and locked the doors, then lifted a hand to shield her eyes from the sun as she watched the vehicle's approach. The day was hot and humid. She could feel dampness gathering between her shoulder blades, but the perspiration was more from nerves than heat. She pulled the T-shirt away from her skin and tried to assume a poised demeanor as she waited for the big SUV to circle the driveway.

Tom Brannon got out and strode toward her, tall and formidable, a man on a mission. His cuffs were rolled back, and he'd loosened his collar and tie in the heat. He might have been anyone from a businessman to a cowboy save for the glint of his badge and the gun at his hip.

Rae took a step toward him. "Tom? What are you doing here? What's happened? Have you found Sophie?"

"No, it's nothing like that."

"Thank goodness." She drew a sharp breath. "That came out wrong. I don't mean I'm thankful you haven't found her. It's just—"

"I know what you meant." He walked over to where she waited beside her car. Her heart skipped a beat when he glanced through the tinted windows. The bag sat on the back seat, in plain sight if he peered closely enough. "It's a difficult time for your family."

"You've no idea." She shifted her position, drawing his attention away from her vehicle.

He stared across the space between them, peering into her eyes instead of through the car window. The effect did nothing to ease Rae's disquiet. She could see herself mirrored in his sunglasses. She looked pale and anxious and not altogether trustworthy. Abruptly, she turned away.

Tom said, "I told you earlier I need to talk to the rest of the family. I never heard back from you about a time."

"I'm sorry. I meant to let you know. I'm not thinking too clearly right now."

He nodded. "No problem. I saw you in town just now. I tried to flag you down, but I guess you didn't see me."

She turned back to him in distress. "You saw me in town? Where?"

"You were pulling onto the highway. I figured you were on your way to the ranch."

"You followed me?"

"I was headed out here anyway." He took off his sunglasses and tucked them into his shirt pocket. "Is your brother back yet?"

The question *sounded* routine, yet Rae detected a subtle note of annoyance—or was that suspicion?—in his voice. She tried to swallow past her anxiety, but the steadiness of his gaze sent a ripple of awareness along her spine. Tom Brannon was nobody's fool. He could tell from her behavior that something was wrong. He would give her some leeway because of the situation, but that would go only so far before he started picking apart her body language.

With an effort, she looked him in the eyes without flinching, focusing on the attractive crinkles at the corners rather than the depth of his gaze. "He and Lauren both got in a little while ago."

Tom glanced away, turning his attention to the wooded drive and the highway beyond for a moment. His silence seemed ominous.

"What aren't you telling me?" Rae demanded.

His gaze came back to her. "There've been some new developments in the case."

She tried to remain calm, but her heart pummeled her chest. "What new developments? Tell me if I need to prepare myself."

His gaze softened. "We haven't found Sophie, but we do have some new information. For one thing, the blood we found at the Ruins last night isn't a match for Sophie or Marty Booker. We now know for certain a third person was in the building last night."

"But we already knew that." Rae rubbed the back of her arm, hoping he wouldn't notice the chill bumps popping on her skin or the tremor in her fingers. "You and I talked about it this morning. Marty Booker said that Preacher took Sophie."

"The blood isn't a match for Silas Creed, either," he said. "We can eliminate that possibility."

"You never believed he'd come back anyway."

"No."

"But he could still be alive."

"It's possible," Tom said. "My guess is he's long dead."

Rae glanced out over the property, frowning into the sunlight. Was someone out there right now watching them, taking note of her interaction with the sheriff? Would they punish Sophie if anyone in the family made a wrong move? She closed her eyes on a shiver. "So we still don't know who took my niece. With each passing moment she could be slipping farther away from us."

"You can't lose hope," Tom said. "It's early yet, and like I said, we have new information that could turn into a significant lead. Can we go inside? It'll save time if I explain everything to all of you at once."

Rae hesitated, keenly aware of all that money on the back seat. The doors were locked and the vehicle in plain view of the house, but that was a lot of cash to leave lying around. Still, she couldn't very well open the door and remove the bag without arousing Tom's suspicions.

She wasn't overly trusting of law enforcement, particularly after their failure to find her sister. Despite that, her instinct was to come clean with Tom. She wanted desperately to trust him, but he was a Brannon and she was a Cavanaugh. Fifteen years of misgiving and animosity didn't disappear overnight. And anyway, her brother was right. It wasn't her call. She'd already made one bad mistake. Sophie had gone missing on her watch. What if she went behind Jackson's back and told Tom about the ransom demand? What if the kidnappers really were watching? What if they hurt Sophie because Rae hadn't followed their orders? She'd never be able to live with herself.

But what if they hurt Sophie anyway? What if this whole thing blew up in their faces? Could she live with herself then?

Doubts churned as she opened the front door and motioned Tom inside. The living space had been remodeled a few years ago into a wide-open concept. The foyer led into a spacious family room with plank flooring and a beamed ceiling. Rae could see all the way through the dining room into the kitchen. Lauren stood at the island pouring a glass of wine. She glanced up when she heard the front door. She walked around the island and came through the dining room into the family room.

"Rae? What took you so long—" She broke off when

she spotted Tom in the foyer. Then her gaze darted back to Rae. "You didn't—"

"Forget to call Sheriff Brannon? I'm afraid I did." Rae gave her a warning look. "He tried to flag me down in town, but I didn't see him. So he drove all the way out here to speak to the family. There've been some new developments in the case."

Something flickered at the back of Lauren's eyes. "What new developments? Is Sophie—"

"She hasn't been found yet," Rae said. "Let's just go into the study. Is Jackson still in there with Dad?"

"Yes, but I wish you'd tell me what's going on."

"I've told you everything I know. Sheriff Brannon will fill us in on the rest. Oh, and I'd advise you to leave the wine." She nodded to the stemware in Lauren's hand. "You know how Dad disapproves of imbibing before five, much less before lunch." She made a point of glancing at her watch even though she already knew the hour. Why she felt the need to antagonize her sister-in-law at a time like this, Rae couldn't say. Maybe it was because Lauren had never really given Sophie a chance and Rae felt defensive and resentful on her niece's behalf. Maybe it was because both Lauren and Jackson had leaped at the chance to dump their responsibilities so that they could take off for sunnier ports.

Or maybe she just wasn't a very nice person, Rae acknowledged.

Lauren polished off the wine and gave her a defiant glare as she set the glass on a nearby side table instead of returning it to the kitchen. Tom hadn't said a word during the whole confrontation. He hovered in the doorway waiting for his cue.

"This way," Rae said and turned on her heel.

They walked down the hallway together and Rae

knocked sharply before opening the double doors. Her brother and dad looked up expectantly. Their gazes lit on Tom, but before they could utter a protest, Rae said, "Sheriff Brannon needs a word."

Her father was seated behind his desk while Jackson stood silhouetted against the French doors. He stood frozen, his gaze going from Rae to Tom and finally to Lauren. She walked around Rae and took her usual place on the sofa. No one said anything for the longest moment. It was as if the presence of a Brannon in West Cavanaugh's inner sanctum had rendered them all speechless.

Then Jackson's surly nature rallied. He came forward, his expression both puzzled and hostile. "Rae? What's going on?"

"Tom needs to talk to you about Sophie. I'm sure he has a lot of questions for all of us. He is the sheriff, you know."

"That fact hasn't escaped any of us."

"Try to keep a civil tongue." She gave her brother the same warning glance she'd shot Lauren earlier. "We need to hear what he has to say."

West sat forward. "Have you found my granddaughter yet?"

"No, sir, I'm afraid not. But we do have a promising lead." Tom came all the way into the room then, commanding the attention of even his enemies. Rae had to admire his professional aplomb. The simmering aggression in the study was butter-thick and razor-sharp, but Tom's tone was all business. He told them about the blood analysis first and how it disputed Marty Booker's claim that Preacher had taken Sophie. Then he launched into a lengthier explanation about the text messages and symbols found on Sophie's phone and how they seemed to relate to the pictures of the Ruins that were on her computer. When he finished, they all stared at him with a mixture of incredulity and anxiety.

Rae hardly knew what to make of any of it. "Sophie was playing a game?"

Tom nodded. "The best we can tell, she and her friends have been playing for weeks."

Jackson looked beside himself. Every muscle in his body tensed as he balled his hands into fists at his sides. "That's it? That's the promising lead?"

"It's more than we had this morning," Tom said.

Jackson shook his head as if he, too, were trying to make sense of it all. "You found some text messages on my daughter's phone and now you think someone kidnapped her because of a stupid game?"

"We think the game may have been used as a ruse to lure Sophie to the Ruins alone."

"But you said she and her friends have been playing the game for weeks," Rae said. "Why wait until last night to take her?"

Tom shrugged. "Could have been a matter of timing and circumstances. Or the suspect may have had to work up his nerve. We just don't know."

"*His* nerve?" Rae asked.

"If Sophie was abducted, the suspect is most likely male, but we're not ruling out any possibility at this point." Tom turned back to Jackson. "Has Sophie talked about any new acquaintances lately? Have you seen her with anyone outside her ordinary circle of friends?"

Jackson remained brusque and uncooperative. "You'd have to ask my sister. Sophie has been staying with her for the past three weeks."

Rae winced. The accusation in his voice was like the point of a dagger in her heart. Guilt made her a tender target. Maybe that was why she'd felt the need to goad her sister-in-law. Just like after Riley's disappearance, Rae found it easier to blame and deflect than to examine too closely her own culpability.

If she were honest with herself, she'd have to admit that she hadn't exactly been Sophie's champion. Rae had been too caught up in her own life. She'd never taken the time to get to know her niece like she should have. Would it have killed her to take Sophie shopping or to a movie now and then? Was it that much of an inconvenience to sit down and have a heart-to-heart with the girl? What if it was too late to do any of those things now? What if Rae never got the chance to tell Sophie how much she cared about her? What if she never got the chance to say goodbye?

At the back of her mind, Riley materialized, but only for a moment before she melted back into the misty unknown. Tears welled in Rae's eyes, but she blinked them away. She had no right to cry.

Tom said, "We've reason to believe the game originated while Sophie was still living at home."

Jackson's eyes flashed angrily. "Just what the hell are you implying?"

His outburst seemed to surprise Tom even though she'd warned him about Jackson's disposition. "I'm not implying anything. I'm trying to establish whether anyone new had come into Sophie's life before she went to stay with Rae. The fourth player remains a mystery. We'd like to find out who that person is."

Rae thought about Sophie's time with her. "Hannah Tucker and Dylan Moody were the only two who ever came to my house. You saw them there this morning. If Sophie hung out with anyone else, I never saw them."

Jackson pounced. "Have you questioned the Moody kid yet? I wouldn't put anything past that punk. Look at how he was brought up. His old man's never been anything but trouble. I've known Dwight Moody since high school. You try to cut him a break, he's apt to turn around and stab you in the back. But if there's one thing he's good at, it's sniffing out easy money. I wouldn't be surprised if he and the kid are in this together."

Tom said slowly, "Are you saying you think Sophie was taken for money?"

Too late Jackson realized his mistake. He opened his mouth and then shut it again as he searched for a way out.

Whether her intent or not, Lauren came to his rescue. She gave him a contemptuous stare. "You're jumping to conclusions because you don't like Dylan. That boy didn't take Sophie. He'd never do anything to hurt her."

Jackson spun to face his wife, transferring his frustration onto her. "And you know this how?"

"I've seen them together. He's crazy about her." Defiance sparked as Lauren lifted her chin and glared at her husband. Something was definitely going on between them. An undercurrent of hostility that couldn't be feigned. The pair had never been shy about arguing in public. They both had quick tempers and acerbic tongues, but the rancor simmering between them now was something new. Something dark and disturbing.

Lauren's taunt pushed all the wrong buttons, as she had undoubtedly meant for it to. Jackson took a step toward her. "Why are you defending that little creep? If I didn't know better, I'd almost think—"

"What?" Lauren rose slowly to confront him. "What would you think?"

He stared her down for a moment without speaking. Then he jabbed a finger in the air in Rae's direction without looking at her. "You're as much to blame for this as she is. If it wasn't for you, Sophie would still be home, where she belongs."

Lauren's eyes flared knowingly. "I'm not the reason Sophie left home. She couldn't wait to get away from *you*."

The nasty argument dissolved into another stare down. Rae sat watching them in dread and fascination. Why were they doing this in front of Tom Brannon, of all people? Didn't they know he would be taking all of this in? Rae's gaze darted to the sheriff. One thing was certain. The confrontation had taken the focus off Jackson's gaffe. Without another word, her brother whirled and started toward the door.

"Where do you think you're going?" Lauren called after him.

"To find that stupid kid. I'll beat the truth out of him if I have to."

Rae jumped to her feet and grabbed her brother's arm. "Just calm down—"

He shoved her aside. She stumbled and fell back against the chair. Tom was in Jackson's face in a flash. "Touch her again and I'll put you in cuffs."

"Get out of my way or I'll have your badge."

Tom didn't budge. "You can try, but it won't stop me from doing my job. You start trouble with that boy and I'll have no choice but to take you in."

"He's right," Rae said. "Just back off and let the man do his job."

"Do his *job*? You mean the same way his old man found our sister?"

The phone rang just then and Jackson's sneer vanished. Rae could see her brother's profile. In that moment, his rage deflated and he looked as terrified as she felt. Her gaze flashed to her father's desk. Everyone in the room seemed to freeze, including West Cavanaugh. Then he lifted the handset to his ear. After a gruff hello, he listened for a moment and then said, "I can't talk now. You'll have to call back later." He slammed the phone down and stood.

"Dad?" Rae half rose, too.

He put up a hand to stop her. "I'm going outside for some air. Don't anyone try to follow me. I've had my fill of the lot of you." His gaze pierced Jackson. "Get yourself together. If you have to air your dirty laundry in this house, do it behind closed doors. And you." He turned to Rae. "You brought the sheriff in here, you can damn well show him to the door."

Chapter Seven

West stepped out into the garden and slammed the door behind him. Rae wanted to follow. She wanted to know if one of the kidnappers had been on the other end of that call, but she couldn't say anything with Tom still present. Jackson wavered as if debating on whether or not to defy their dad's wishes. Then he turned and stormed out of the room. Lauren followed him out into the hallway, where they continued to bicker until their voices faded behind another slammed door.

Tom turned to Rae. "That went well."

She gave a shaky laugh to relieve tension. "Didn't it? As well as could be expected, knowing my family the way I do. Come on. I'll walk you to your car."

All the way down the hallway, she was conscious of Tom's sidelong gaze. He had to be curious about the scene that had just gone down between Jackson and his wife, about the phone call, Rae's behavior and everything else. He said nothing, but his silence spoke volumes.

Once they were outside, she surreptitiously glanced in the back seat of her car on the way to his vehicle. The bag was still there, thank goodness.

She leaned against his door and turned her face to the sky. A hawk circled overhead. She watched for a moment, but the sky was so brilliant she had to look away. Exhaustion tugged. With very little effort, she could drift off. Just close her eyes and float away from this whole awful mess. How could a day be so beautiful on the surface and so ugly underneath?

"Rae?"

She opened her eyes.

"Are you okay? You're very quiet all of a sudden."

"Just lost in thought. I can only imagine what you must think of us after that embarrassing display."

"I think you're a family in crisis," he said. "You've lost a mother, a sister, and now you're afraid you may be facing another tragedy."

His compassion brought tears to her eyes. She took a moment to gather her composure. "It's true what they say about the waiting. The not knowing. It wears on you. All the terrible things that go through your head. Your mind never shuts down. You can't sleep.You can't eat. You start to dread the sound of the phone. Then comes the time when the phone stops ringing and the silence is even more terrifying."

Tom gave her one of those soft gazes, the kind that tore at her resolve. She thought again how nice it would be to feel those strong arms around her, to have his broad shoulder to lean on. She wasn't a needy person. She'd always been fiercely independent and proud of it. But this wasn't about need. It was about comfort and understanding. The solace of having someone next to you who'd have your back no matter what. Rae loved her father and brother, but she couldn't honestly say that she trusted them to always have her best interest at heart. They were too arrogant and single-minded.

"I know it's hard," Tom said. "But Sophie isn't Riley. She didn't disappear without a trace. She left a trail."

Rae tucked back her hair. "You mean the text messages?"

"Among other things. We won't rest until we follow every bread crumb." He glanced over his shoulder at the house. "Your brother worries me, though. I meant what I said inside. If he goes after the Moody boy, I'll have no choice but to lock him up."

"He won't," Rae said. "He was just letting off steam."

"Does he always get physical when he lets off steam?"

She frowned. "You mean what happened just now? That was nothing. A sibling skirmish. Besides, I'm the one who started it. I grabbed his arm, he pushed me away and I tripped. Please don't make more of it than it was. Don't you and your sister ever fight?"

"We have the occasional disagreement."

"Occasional." Her smiled turned bitter. "Most families aren't perfect."

Tom's gaze was still on her. She didn't want to look up into those rain-colored eyes, but she couldn't help herself. He moved in, not so close as to be threatening, but enough so that the space between them grew intimate. She could almost imagine his hand on her arm, his knuckles scraping softly against her cheek. *Everything will be all right, Rae.*

Instead, he said, "I'm not your enemy. You need to trust me."

She let out a slow breath, releasing the anger she'd been harboring for hours. Not at Tom this time, but at her brother. At her niece's abductors. At her feeling of helplessness. "I'm trying to. I want to trust you. It's just…"

"My sister came home and yours didn't."

"Yes." She folded her arms. "As irrational and petty as that still sounds."

"Then I don't know what more I can say. Do you honestly think my dad didn't do everything in his power to find Riley? Do you think he wouldn't have given his own life to bring her home safely? Do you think I wouldn't? Not a day goes by that I don't think about what happened. I've asked myself a thousand times what I might have done differently to change the outcome. If I'd gotten to the Ruins sooner or if I hadn't let down my guard. If I'd never left the house that night in the first place." He paused, but his gaze never wavered. "I don't know why my sister and I were spared. I don't think it was intentional. I've always believed we were left for dead. What I do know is that Ellie wasn't breathing when I came to. I had to act fast. Make a split-second decision. I could have left her there on the bank to go back and search the Ruins, but letting my sister die wouldn't have saved yours. Deep down, I think you know that."

His blunt assessment took Rae's breath away. Her brother wasn't the only one who could wound her with words. "We all do what we have to do," she murmured.

She wondered if he would be so understanding of her decision to keep quiet when he found out about the ransom demand. If the kidnappers let Sophie go, all would be forgiven eventually. But if her niece never came home, Rae would spend the rest of her life playing the same terrible game of what-if. What if she'd told Tom the truth? What if she'd gone to him with the ransom demand and asked for his help?

His gaze narrowed. "What did you mean by that?"

"Just what I said. Most of us do what we think is right in any given situation. Second-guessing is pointless. I just wish there was something more I could do right now. Some way I could help with the investigation."

He was still eyeing her with what Rae thought might be suspicion. "What can you tell me about Blaine Fenton?"

The name took Rae by surprise. "Blaine? Why do you want to know about him?"

"His family owns an adjoining ranch. I understand his father is suing Cavanaugh Industries. There must be bad blood between the families."

Rae shrugged. "I can't tell you much about that lawsuit. I'm not involved."

He looked skeptical. "You're the money person in the business. How can you not be involved?"

"My brother calls the shots now. He and my father have deliberately kept me out of the loop. I like to think they're trying to protect me, but I suspect the attorneys have advised them I could have a conflict of interest."

"What kind of conflict?"

"Blaine and I were once engaged."

The gray eyes flickered though his voice remained steady. "When was this?"

"About a hundred years ago," Rae said with a grimace. "We dated before he went into the service. When he came home, we tried to pick back up where we left off, but it was too late. I wore his ring on my finger for all of a week before I realized I wasn't ready for that kind of commitment."

"You broke things off? How did he take it?"

Rae sensed a sudden tension. She said carefully, "About as well as you can imagine."

"Did he get violent? Make threats? Anything like that?"

"No. He left town without a word. We didn't keep in touch. I heard that he came back when his dad got sick, but I haven't seen or talked to him." She slanted Tom a puzzled glance. "Why all these questions about Blaine? You don't think he had anything to do with Sophie's disappearance, do you?"

"He's convinced your family swindled his sick father out of a lot of money. That's a powerful motive. So is rejection."

"You think he's carrying a grudge against *me*?" The notion that Sophie had been taken because of Rae's past was another painful blow. "If that's true, why didn't he come after me personally? Why take Sophie?"

"She was living with you when she went missing. He'd know how her disappearance would affect you."

She was silent for a moment. "I don't believe it. It's been too many years. Besides, Blaine wouldn't do something like that. He's always been a good guy."

"You said you hadn't had any contact with him in years. People change. Or sometimes something happens to bring out their true nature."

"That's a scary thought."

"People do scary things," Tom said. "Is there anyone else you can think of who might have it in for you or your family?"

"We've been in business for a long time. My dad and brother aren't the easiest people to deal with. We've had our share of bitter competitors and disgruntled former employees, but I'm not aware of any physical threats. As for me personally, my opinion pieces for the *Star* have ruffled a few feathers. I don't tend to pull punches."

"I'm well aware of that fact."

"Tom." She suppressed a shiver. "Do you really think Sophie could have been taken because of me?"

"Whatever the abductor's motive, this isn't your fault."

He stared deep into her eyes as something shifted between them. Any rancor that might have remained melted in the face of his compassion. Before Rae could stop herself, she placed her hand on his arm, unconsciously reaching for his warmth. "Find her, Tom. I can only imagine how frightened she must be. Please bring her home."

"I'll do everything in my power. You know that."

She nodded and dropped her hand as her gaze traveled down the long drive, probing into the woods and then returning to skim the shadowy windows. Physical contact was inadvisable. Someone could be watching. From outside the house and from within.

RAE DIDN'T LEAVE the ranch again until late that night. After Tom drove away, she'd taken the money inside and locked it away in the safe. The housekeeper had made sandwiches and iced tea for a late lunch, but no one was hungry. The casserole she made for dinner went virtually untouched, as well. They sat huddled in her father's office until the sun set over her mother's rose garden and the bats came out of their houses. Rae stood at the French doors and watched them circle until they vanished against the deepening sky. One by one the stars twinkled out and the moon rose over the treetops. And still no word of Sophie. Still no phone call from the kidnappers.

They were all scared and bone-deep weary. Rae wanted a shower and her own bed, but she was reluctant to leave her father alone on the ranch with all that cash. Not that he would be truly alone. The housekeeper had quarters off the kitchen and the ranch foreman lived on the property. The house was well secured and her father well armed, but if he was right and they were dealing with professional kidnappers, anything could happen.

"Go home," Jackson finally insisted. "You're dead on your feet and no help to anyone. I'll stay with Dad. I want to be here in case we get another call. Just let me run home and change clothes before you leave. Lauren can stay at our house in case anyone decides to call the landline there."

Lauren nodded her acquiescence and the two of them

left. They were barely speaking by this time. Maybe it was a good thing they had another night apart.

Jackson returned a little while later and Rae hugged her father good-night. All the way home, she kept an eye on the rearview mirror. Once, a car came upon her so quickly she became certain someone was trying to overtake her to force her off the road. She gripped the wheel as the car passed and sped off into the night. By the time she drove into town, her neck and shoulders ached from tension.

Fueled by the strain and a pervasive dread, her imagination went to bad places. She'd never noticed before how dark the streets were in her neighborhood. The old-fashioned streetlamps were quaint but not effective in holding the night at bay. Everywhere she looked, she saw lurking shadows.

Pulling into the garage, she lowered the door all the way before getting out of her car. Once inside the house, she turned the dead bolt. She rarely bothered with the security system, but she felt the need to activate the sensors tonight. After checking to make sure the garden doors were secured, she went straight upstairs to the shower and stood under the hot water until phantom sounds drove her dripping from the bathroom. Wrapping herself in a towel, she padded across her bedroom into the hallway, then to the staircase, where she glanced down into the foyer.

No one's there. You're safe. Sophie was the one in danger.

But even as Rae shrugged off the night sounds, uneasiness dogged her back to the bathroom. She couldn't shake the sensation that someone had been inside her house while she was away. Finishing her bedtime routine, she opened the door to the hallway before crawling between the cool sheets. If a sound came from anywhere in the house, she would hear it.

She didn't think she'd be able to sleep a wink, but she grew drowsy the moment her head hit the pillow. She'd just dozed off when one of those sounds catapulted her upright in bed.

No one could get into the house through a door or window without tripping the sensors and setting off the alarm. But what if someone had already been inside when she got home?

Throwing off the covers, she swung her legs over the side of the bed and perched on the edge as she listened to the house. She'd almost convinced herself she'd dreamed the noise when she heard it again, so low and distant she couldn't pinpoint the source or location. She padded to the hallway door and glanced out. She'd left a light burning at the top of the stairs. Keeping her back to the wall, she eased once again to the landing and glanced into the foyer. She started down the stairs when the noise froze her again. She recognized the muffled reverberation this time. It was the sound of a phone that had been set to both ring and vibrate.

Returning to her bedroom, she grabbed her cell from the nightstand charger and checked her screen even though she knew the strange ringtone wasn't hers. Then whose?

Was someone in the house with her at that very moment?

She pocketed the cell and returned to the hallway, tracking the sound past the guest bathroom and bedroom to Sophie's room. Pushing open the door, she hovered on the threshold as she gazed around. Moonlight and a night breeze flooded in through the open window. Her pulse leaped as the curtains billowed. For a moment, she was certain someone stood behind them. Then the wind died away and the gauzy panels flattened. Only then did she remember closing the window the night before. It had been shut that morning when she stood looking down into the rose garden as Tom searched the room behind her.

The ringing had stopped by this time. Rae checked the bathroom and closet and then dropped to the floor to search under the bed. Rising, she crossed the room to the window and peered down into the garden. Was someone down there watching her? A shadow moved and she jumped. A dog barked and she jumped.

Hand to her heart, she turned to scan the room once more. Her gaze fell on the bed and she traced a faint impression in the chenille spread as if someone had been lying there recently. The idea was so frightening and repugnant, Rae wanted to run screaming from the house, but the sudden *vzzzzt* of that vibrating ringtone froze her.

As if in a dream, she walked to the bed and picked up one of the pillows. Sophie's image stared up at her from a cell phone screen. She was bound and gagged, her face bruised and tear-streaked. But she was alive. Or had been when the photo was taken.

Reluctantly, Rae accepted the incoming call. "Hello?"

A metallic voice said in her ear, "Call the police and she dies. Call the FBI and she dies. Come alone to the drop or you die."

Chapter Eight

The next morning, Tom stood at the back of the conference room while Craig Jarvis updated the department's active investigations on the whiteboard and handed out assignments to the assembled officers. He tried to concentrate on the business at hand, but his mind kept straying to the previous day's events, in particular to the scene he'd witnessed at the ranch. The bitterness between Jackson and Lauren Cavanaugh had been palpable. He'd been shocked by the nastiness of Jackson's attack and the underlying viciousness of Lauren's volley. If they fought like that on a regular basis, no wonder their daughter had wanted to run away.

He thought about Rae, too, and her revelation that she'd once been engaged to Blaine Fenton. Tom didn't know how he felt about that. The relationship was ancient history and likely had nothing to do with Sophie's disappearance. On the other hand, the bad blood between Fenton and the Cavanaughs provided a motive and Tom wasn't about to leave any stone unturned. A cursory background check had turned up an interesting detail and Tom thought it might be time to pay Fenton a visit.

After the officers had filed out of the room, he and Craig conferred for a few minutes and then went their separate ways. Back in his office, Tom scoured a county map, familiarizing himself with the terrain surrounding the Fenton ranch. Then he plugged the address into his GPS and headed out. The excursion took him deep into the swampy bottomland of Nance County. As the road narrowed, the pine forest grew denser until only streamers of sunlight filtered down through the bowers. The air was steamy and pungent, the shadows so deep on either side of the road that Tom could understand how the primitive landscape spawned tall tales of swamp creatures and black panthers.

A metal cattle guard across a paved lane marked the entrance to the ranch. The one-story brick house was modest in comparison with the Cavanaugh spread, but the trim looked freshly painted and the roof appeared new. Despite the hardships the family had suffered, someone had recently infused money into the property.

Tom got out of his vehicle and took stock of his surroundings before climbing the porch steps to knock on the door. When no one answered, he followed a footpath back to the barn. One of the double doors hung open and he thought Blaine Fenton might be working inside.

Calling out the man's name, he stepped from bright sunlight into the dim, cavernous interior. A barrage of scents greeted him—leather, hay and diesel mixed with the lingering aroma of horses. The animals were long gone, replaced with a small fleet of four-wheelers. Tom walked down the row of empty stalls, checked the tack room and was on his way back to the front when a furtive sound halted him. His gaze lifted as a few bits of hay floated down through the cracks in the loft.

He went up the steps as quietly as he could, pausing at the top to reconnoiter. The space looked like any other barn loft he'd encountered with a wide-plank floor and overhead rafters. Some of the bales of hay had been broken apart and piled on the floor, creating a cozy mattress where someone had recently slept. An old blanket had been neatly folded and stored on a bench, along with a towel and a bucket of basic toiletries.

The only occupant up there now was a fat yellow tabby that crouched at the top of the haystack, eyeing the intruder with sleepy-eyed suspicion. Tom had a quick look around before the hum of a four-wheeler drove him back down the steps. By the time he got to the front of the barn, the motor had died. A moment later, Blaine Fenton appeared in the doorway with a shotgun.

Tom approached with caution, moving his hand to his side where he could draw his weapon if he needed to.

"It's Tom Brannon," he called out.

Fenton hesitated and then took a step inside, dropping the barrel of the shotgun toward the floor. "Sheriff? What the hell are you doing in here?"

His tone wasn't as cordial or deferential as he'd seemed in Tom's office. Fair enough. He'd been caught by surprise. Tom tried to defuse the situation. "I need to have a word. I knocked at the house first, but no one answered. When I saw the barn door was open, I thought you might be back here working." His gaze flicked to the shotgun. "Mind putting that away while we talk?"

Fenton propped the weapon against the wall. "Sorry about that. I'm in the habit of arming myself before I go out. I don't even think about having it with me anymore."

"You expecting trouble?"

"In this part of the county? Damn right. We're remote and lousy with meth heads. They'll steal anything that isn't nailed down. And they tend to get violent when confronted. I guess I don't have to tell you that."

"Pays to be careful," Tom agreed. "But if you're that worried about thieves, I'd suggest locking up before you leave. Unless you're expecting someone." He chin-nodded toward the loft. "Looks like someone's being staying up there. One of your ranch hands?"

"Pop has a few regulars that come by now and then. He gives them a hot meal and a place to clean up and sleep."

"What do you mean by regulars?"

"Not PC to call them hoboes anymore. Guys that ride the rails. They get on and off at the crossing by the river. Pop's been letting them stay here for years. Harmless for the most part, but I've warned him about keeping the doors up at the house locked."

For the most part. He had Tom's attention. "When was the last time someone came by?"

"I'd say a couple of weeks at least." Fenton appeared more relaxed now. Leaning a shoulder against the wall, he slid his hands in his pockets. "What did you want to talk to me about? I said everything I had to say when I came by the station."

Tom studied the man's expression, his posture. Fenton had reverted back to his polite comportment, but there was a troubling vibe in that barn. "Why didn't you tell me that you and Rae Cavanaugh were once engaged?"

Fenton shrugged but the tension seemed to amp up a notch. "That was a long time ago. What happened between Rae and me has nothing to do with anything."

"I don't know about that," Tom said. "It gives you a motive."

And just like that, the polite veneer vanished, allowing a simmering bitterness to cast a shadow over the man's features. He flexed his fingers as if to remind Tom that the shotgun was still within easy reach. "A motive for what? Maybe you'd better get to the point of this visit, Sheriff."

"You made some pretty bold accusations about Rae

and her family. A broken engagement could explain why you were so keen to paint her in an unflattering light."

"I take it she's the one who told you about our split?"

Tom didn't comment.

"I don't know how she presented things to you, but there's always another side to the story. I won't bother telling you mine. What's past is past." Fenton shrugged again, as if trying to free himself of an unwanted ghost. "Rae Cavanaugh could be an angel these days, for all I care. I came to you because I wanted you to know about the lawsuit. About *their* motives. If I'd known you'd try to turn it all back on me, I would have kept my mouth shut."

Tom waited a beat before he said, "You also didn't tell me about your record. Assault with a deadly weapon is serious business."

He could see the man working to control his temper. "So you pulled my sheet. Before or after you talked to Rae?"

"Does it matter?"

"If you've done your homework, then you know the original charge was downgraded to a misdemeanor. I did nine months in a county lockup, but the arrest was bogus from the get-go. Guy came at me with a knife and I defended myself with a broken bottle. We both ended up in the ER, but he had connections and I didn't. You know how that goes. The sentencing judge was removed from the bench and did time himself for accepting bribes. I was clean before that night and I've been clean ever since. Nothing in my past has a damn thing to do with why I came to your office."

"Where were you on Thursday night?"

Fenton's gaze narrowed. "On the night of the kidnapping, you mean."

"It's a routine question," Tom said.

He could have sworn the man's gaze strayed to the shotgun before he answered. "I was in Dallas. Pop is in the hospital again. I stayed with him for most of the day, took care of some business, and then I had a bite to eat with a friend. I got back to the ranch around midnight."

"Can anyone corroborate your arrival time?"

"Like I said, Pop's in the hospital, so there's no one here but me. You can talk to him, I guess. I can give you my friend's number if you insist, but I'd rather not get her involved."

"I may need her name," Tom said. "But that's all for now. I'll be in touch."

Fenton walked him outside. "Have you talked to the Cavanaughs? Did you question them about *their* whereabouts?"

"I've talked to a lot of people, but I can't get into any of the details of those conversations."

Fenton's tone turned grim. "I hope you find that girl soon, Sheriff. If the family didn't set this up, she could be in real trouble. I keep thinking about Riley."

"We're all thinking about Riley," Tom said as he glanced around the property. He made sure Fenton remained in his periphery as he took note of the other outbuildings. "You're right about one thing. You are isolated out here. Keep a sharp eye as you go about your business. You see or hear anything suspicious, give me a call."

Fenton put up a hand to shade his eyes as he, too, scoured the countryside. "Lots of abandoned houses and barns in these parts. People use them for all sorts of unsavory activities. I try not to snoop in the wrong places. I don't want to get my head blown off. But I will keep an eye out. And next time you want to talk, maybe you should call first. Like I said, I arm myself before I leave the house. You can't be too careful these days."

Tom nodded. "I'll keep that in mind."

Fenton closed and latched the barn doors before trailing Tom back to the house. He climbed the porch steps, but he didn't go inside. Instead, he stood leaning against the railing as he watched Tom get into his vehicle. Tom gave a brief nod, but Fenton didn't bother responding. He'd left his shotgun in the barn, but Tom had no doubt the man had more than one weapon at his disposal.

After a decade in law enforcement, Tom appreciated the need for caution and self-defense. Drugs and human trafficking had created a dangerous situation in rural areas all over the state. Nance County was no exception. Gone were the days when people routinely left doors and windows open at all hours or when kids could roam the countryside without fear of being accosted or nabbed. Tom thought about his sister out there alone on the lake. Her place was secure, and she knew how to use a gun, but Tom still worried about her. Sometimes he thought they might both be living on borrowed time.

He glanced in his rearview mirror as he drove away from the house. Blaine Fenton was still on the porch staring after him. Tom wasn't sure how he felt about their discussion. On the one hand, Fenton had been forthcoming about the nature of his incarceration; on the other, he'd kept that information to himself until confronted. Tom had to wonder what else he might be hiding.

He slowed as he neared the cattle guard. Before he could cross, another car whipped off the road and braked. Tom recognized Rae's SUV. Rather than reversing to let her pass, he put the vehicle in Park and got out. Rae got out, too, and they met on her side of the grid.

She looked shocked to see him and, unless Tom misread her averted gaze, a little guilty. Unease niggled as she approached him. "Tom? What are you doing out here?"

The sun beat down on his shoulders as he gave her a long scrutiny. He could see freckles beneath her suntan and the dark purple half-moons of fatigue and distress beneath her eyes. "I think it's best if you answer that question first."

She hesitated. "I guess you could call it an impulse."

"What kind of impulse?" The question came out harsher than Tom meant, but Rae didn't seem to notice. Her gaze drifted to the narrow road behind him. Even though they were out of sight of the house, he imagined Blaine Fenton up on that porch staring back at her.

A shadow passed across her features as if she'd had the same thought. "I keep going over our conversation yesterday and your implication that Blaine might still hold a grudge against me. I don't think it's true. The breakup was a long time ago. But on the slim chance you could be right, I wanted to see his face when I asked him flat out if he had anything to do with Sophie's disappearance."

"You drove all the way out here to confront him? That's not a good idea, Rae."

"Why not?" A frown flitted as her gaze turned defiant. "I'll be able to tell if he's lying."

"You sure about that?"

"It's worth a shot, isn't it?" She wore her hair down today and the mild breeze that stirred the long brown tresses seemed to annoy her. She tucked the errant strands behind her ears with a jerky movement.

Tom tried to keep his voice neutral without seeming to patronize her. "Just think it through for a minute. Aside from the fact that you haven't seen Fenton in years, what if he really did have something to do with Sophie's disappearance? What do you think will happen if he feels threatened? He'll tie up loose ends and make a run for it."

She looked stricken. "Tie up loose ends? What do you mean?"

"Leave no witnesses behind." Tom hated being so blunt. "We can't take that chance."

"Then why are you here? He's bound to feel more heat from you than me. What makes you think he won't panic and run after you talked to him?"

"Because I'm the law. I'm asking a lot of questions of a lot of people. He'll know that if he has his ear to the ground. Given his history with your family, it would seem strange if I didn't talk to him." Tom tempered his tone as he gazed down at her, resisting the almost physical need to touch her. What was it about Rae Cavanaugh that had him wound up so tight? Why couldn't he just do his damn job and keep emotions out of it? "You have to trust that I know what I'm doing. Just go home and let me handle this."

"I can't go home, Tom. I can't stand the waiting." She turned to gaze off into the trees. "I was out all morning searching the woods around the Ruins and walking up and down the lake. I saw your sister. She said officers have been out there since sunrise. I know that's your doing. Thank you for that. Thank you for not giving up."

"It's way too early to talk about giving up."

She nodded. "I wanted to go inside the Ruins, but the doors are cordoned off."

"That's standard procedure," he said. "Not that tape is much of a barrier in a place like that. People are curious about such things. We don't have enough manpower to keep them out."

"Then it's okay if I go inside?"

"Why would you want to? We've been all through that building, including the basement and boiler room.

If anything besides Sophie's phone had been left behind, we would have found it by now."

"You mentioned symbols yesterday. I want to see them for myself."

"Why?"

She seemed at a loss. "I don't know why. Maybe I'm curious about such things, too. Maybe I'm wondering why Sophie would willingly play a game that trivialized Riley's disappearance."

She looked so distraught standing there gazing up at him. So earnest and desperate, and Tom felt dangerously protective even though Rae Cavanaugh could take care of herself. She was worried, yes. Scared, yes. But there was a dauntless quality to the way she held herself, a steely resolve to the set of her jaw and chin when she didn't want to be told no. Her intrepid nature made him want to protect her all the more, which made no sense. His feelings for Rae Cavanaugh made no sense. He'd known her for most of his life. Had admired her good looks from afar since they were kids, but never once had he thought about her in *that* way. She'd been off-limits. A prickly nemesis who had kept him and most every other man in Nance County at arm's length. But not Blaine Fenton.

A vision crept around Tom's subconscious, unnerving him in the morning heat. He wasn't jealous. That would really be pushing boundaries. But he didn't like thinking about Rae and Blaine Fenton as a couple. He didn't like imagining them together or wondering if she'd told him the real reason she'd shown up at the Fenton ranch so early in the morning.

He especially didn't like all those gnawing doubts.

She looked distressed as her gaze moved back to the road behind him. "Do you think he can see us from the house?"

"No. Those trees block the view." Tom glanced over his shoulder anyway. They couldn't be spotted from the house, but her question prodded him. "Let's get moving. We're standing on Fenton property and your ex-fiancé could head this way at any minute with his shotgun. I'd rather not find out how willing he is to use it."

"Tom?" Her eyes held him enthralled. "I was never in love with Blaine Fenton. I'm not sure why, but I want you to know that."

TOM FOLLOWED HER as far as the arched entrance to the Cavanaugh ranch, and then with a honk and a wave, he headed back toward town. Rae drove only a short way before she pulled to the side of the road and cut the engine. Her hands shook. She lifted them from the wheel and observed the tremor in her fingers. Tom Brannon had done that to her. Unsettled her. Intimidated her. Made her want to wrap her arms around his neck and kiss him until all her dark thoughts fled.

Lowering the window, Rae drew in the pungent air. She'd parked in deep shade, and the breeze blowing through the pine forest felt cool against her overheated face. She told herself to buck up. She couldn't let the family see her so rattled. They needed her. She'd always been the steady one, a rock in times of crises, but at that moment, she'd never felt less in control. Sophie's disappearance had leveled all her defenses, and her unwelcome attraction to Tom Brannon had only intensified an already desperate situation.

She chided herself for the weakness. How could she feel anything at that moment except frightened? The kidnapping had her all knotted up inside and yet somehow Tom Brannon had managed to pierce through her fear. Maybe it really was as simple as needing a friend, a strong shoulder, and if anyone could understand her angst, it was Tom.

Still, she had to be careful. He was a lawman trained to look for nuances and tells. The more time she spent in his company, the greater the chance she'd let something slip. She hated keeping secrets, especially with Sophie's life on the line, but the kidnappers had left her no choice. *Call the police and she dies.*

After receiving that message loud and clear the night before, Rae had raced back to the ranch, calling on the way so that her father and brother wouldn't be alarmed when she turned up at the door. They'd huddled around the kitchen table, downing shots of whiskey as they discussed the next step. Jackson had wanted to take charge of the kidnappers' phone, but Rae refused. The burner had been left in her house. The threat had been made directly to her. For whatever reason, she'd been designated the point person.

Keeping that phone close, Rae had gone out at the crack of dawn to search for Sophie. Maybe that was the wrong thing to do. Rationally, she knew the best way to help her niece was to sit tight. They had the money and they had proof of life. The rest was a waiting game. But Rae had never been strong on patience. The futile search had been more for her benefit than Sophie's. She couldn't sit around drowning in despair. Taking action, no matter how pointless, kept her focused and grounded, which was why she'd gone out to the Fenton ranch.

She didn't really believe Blaine could be involved, but what if he was? She needed to see his face, stare deeply into his eyes to know if there was anything left of the old Blaine. Even as kids, she'd always been able to tell when he lied. He'd been an open book. Or so she'd thought. But how well had she ever really known him? They'd drifted together because of the proximity of their family ranches and a common upbringing. He used to say that East Texans were a different breed, a mixture of Southern gentility and backwoods cliquishness, so they had to stick together. He was one of the few people who understood her, one of the few people who had never tried to change her. Undemanding and uncomplicated, Blaine Fenton had been an easy man to like, and for a time, Rae had tried to convince herself that she could love him. That hadn't worked out. Maybe she wasn't the marrying kind. Or maybe she'd sensed something even then, hunkering down deep inside him.

Taking out the burner, Rae studied the photograph of Sophie. She looked so young and helpless and scared. Tenderly, Rae traced the girl's battered features with her fingertip. The gag was hard enough to witness, but the scratches and bruises that marred the smooth cheeks tore at Rae's heart.

She's alive. That's all that matters. Just do as the kidnappers instruct and this will all be over soon.

Rae desperately wanted to believe in a positive outcome. Sophie wasn't Riley. This could still work out if they all kept their cool—

A cloud of blackbirds lifted from the woods in a flurry of flapping wings. Rae's head snapped up as she scoured the countryside. Something had startled them from the treetops, but everything else had gone silent. On any given day, at any given time, the forest teemed with life, but the rabbits and squirrels had scurried to the safety of their hidey-holes.

Into that deathly hush came the sound of the kidnappers' ringtone. The burner phone vibrated in Rae's hand. Several clicks went by before she pressed the accept call button. She put the phone on speaker and the grating sound of that mechanical voice filled her vehicle.

"You talked to the cops."

She suppressed a gasp at the accusation. "No, I didn't. I didn't talk to anyone."

"You talked to the cops."

"I didn't! I saw Sheriff Brannon this morning, but I didn't say a word and I won't." She gulped back her panic. "He's investigating Sophie's disappearance. He has questions. If we don't appear to cooperate, he'll get suspicious—"

The call dropped.

A moment later, the phone dinged an incoming text. Rae clicked the message icon and a video appeared. Her thumb hovered over the arrow before she pressed Play. Sophie came into view. She was tied to a chair with a high window behind her, but not much light filtered in. Either the video had been shot in the dark or the grounds outside were in deep shadow.

Rae tried to take note of the surroundings, but her gaze remained riveted on her niece. She looked terrified but determined as she struggled and strained against the bindings. Then she went suddenly still. Her head pivoted as if someone had entered the room. The sound of a gunshot startled Rae so badly she screamed, and then the video ended.

Numb with shock, she stared at the screen in helpless fear. Then she shook the phone as if she could somehow bring Sophie back.

"No. Please, no..." *Please, please, please, please...*

A split second of mindless panic crawled by before Rae realized the gunfire had come from the woods and not the video. Another flock of birds had taken to the sky in alarm. Someone was out there.

Leaning forward to peer out the windshield, she reached for the ignition and then her hand froze. Was Sophie nearby? The gunshot had been a warning, but if the weapon had been fired from the location where Sophie was being held—

Rae was out of her vehicle in a flash, standing in the middle of the road with her ears trained on the woods. Conjuring a map, she tried to recall any nearby buildings, old barns and farmhouses where the kidnappers might hold Sophie. *Where are you?*

Jumping the ditch, she moved to the edge of the trees. "I know you're out there!" she yelled. "I know you can hear me! We have the money! All we want is Sophie! Please, please don't hurt her!"

No sound came to Rae, nothing so much as the snapping of a twig, but she could sense a presence. *Who are you?*

"Just tell me where to leave the money. We can end this today. No one has to get hurt."

Her voice echoed back to her as she stood there searching the trees. She thought about Tom's theory that the game had been used to lure Sophie to the Ruins alone, which meant at least one of the kidnappers knew her. A friend or an acquaintance. Someone familiar with Riley's abduction and Sophie's fascination with the past.

For one terrible moment, rage clouded Rae's vision, a white-hot fury that someone could be so cruel as to terrorize a child in order to extort money from an already devastated family. Rae's impulse now was to tear through the woods until she found the offenders. She wanted nothing so much at that moment as to feel her hands around a throat. To hear that voice on the phone plead with *her.*

Tamping down such a reckless inclination, she called

out again. "Tell me where to leave the money! *Please*. We just want her home."

The blackbirds circled as a chill invaded. She could stand there all day begging and bargaining, but the kidnappers wouldn't make contact again until they were ready. They knew what they were doing, how to instill fear and cooperation. Sophie's abduction had taken long-term planning and skill. A trap had been patiently laid. Nothing had been left to chance. And no loose end would be left untied when it was over.

"Please," Rae whispered. "Just take the money."

She jumped when the phone vibrated in her hand. Accepting the call, she scanned the woods. Off to her right, a shadow moved, or was that her imagination?

The robotic voice said into the quiet, "Be smart. We're watching you."

Chapter Nine

Later that morning, Dylan Moody and Hannah Tucker appeared at the station at the agreed-upon time. One of Tom's detectives had already conducted an informal interview with both kids, but Tom wanted to get them on the record. Plus, it was easier to evade and outright lie in the safety of their homes than it was in an institutional environment. They had no idea what the police already knew or who might be observing—and contradicting—their statements through a two-way glass.

Unlike Hannah, who waited in another area of the station with her mother, Dylan had come in alone. He said his old man had been too busy to accompany him. Too hungover, more than likely. Jackson Cavanaugh wasn't the only one who'd had unpleasant dealings with Dwight Moody. Back when Tom was still on patrol, he'd been sent out to the Moody place on any number of 10-16s—domestic disturbances—before Dwight's girlfriend had finally left him for good. Dylan hadn't been so lucky.

He sat with his shoulders hunched and his eyes downcast, his posture and demeanor a far cry from the punk whom Jackson Cavanaugh had described the day before. Craig Jarvis conducted the interview while Tom observed from a dimmed area on the other side of the glass. Dylan's answers had been mostly monosyllabic at first, but once

Craig mentioned the group text messages, the kid's head came up and the floodgates opened. To Tom's surprise, Dylan readily copped to his participation in the game.

"I don't understand," Craig said. "You saw Sheriff Brannon at Rae Cavanaugh's house yesterday morning. Why didn't you tell him about the game then? You made it sound as if you never went out to the Ruins."

Dylan pushed back a lock of dark hair from his forehead. He seemed willing to talk, but he was nervous as hell about something. "Sophie made us promise not to tell anyone. She said her stepmother already wanted to get rid of her. If she found out that Sophie was sneaking out of the house at night, she'd make sure her dad sent her away to boarding school."

"You didn't think her safety trumped that promise?"

Dylan winced. "I didn't think she was in any danger. Not at first." His legs were jittery beneath the table. He wiped his hands along the tops of his thighs. "I thought she was just hiding out. Or maybe she ran away. She's done it before. I kept thinking she'd call or text, but she hasn't. Now I don't know what to think."

"When was the last time you saw Sophie?"

"Around ten on Thursday night when I dropped her off at her aunt's house."

"You didn't talk to her after that? No calls or texts?"

"No, sir."

"How were things when you left her? You two have a fight?"

Tom's gaze narrowed as he studied the boy's facial expressions through the glass. Dylan hesitated only infinitesimally before he answered the detective's question. "Everything was fine. We didn't have a fight."

"Let's talk about that game. Do you know the identity of the fourth player? The one who uses a cross for a symbol?"

Dylan shook his head. "We all got texts one day explaining the rules of the game and inviting us to play. I wasn't interested at first. I thought the whole thing sounded pretty stupid. But Sophie wanted to play, so I went along. I didn't see the harm. I figured she was the one who had sent those texts anyway. Seemed like something she'd dream up."

"Did you ever ask her if she was the fourth player?"

"Yeah, but she would never admit it even if she was. She likes keeping secrets."

"What kind of secrets?"

"I don't know. All kinds, I guess."

"You said you thought she might have run away. Do you know of any place or anyone she'd go to? A friend or family member, maybe?"

"No, not really. Sophie's popular at school, but she doesn't have a lot of close friends. And I know she wouldn't go to any of the Cavanaughs. She'd be afraid they'd tell her dad. Her mom's family—her real mom? They're pretty much all dead or live out of the state." He paused as if something had just occurred to him. "I don't know if this is important—"

"Everything is important at this point," Craig assured him.

The boy looked uneasy. "Her grandparents on her mom's side left her some money. She always said she was going to use the cash to leave town. Go someplace where no one could find her."

"She had access to the funds?"

"No, that's the thing. All that money from her grandparents is gone."

"What do you mean?"

"There's only a couple hundred dollars left in the account."

"What happened to the rest?"

Dylan shrugged. "Her dad told her he invested it, but Sophie didn't believe him. She thinks he used the money to pay off her stepmother's gambling debts."

Craig cast a glance toward the window. "Lauren Cavanaugh gambles?"

Dylan shifted in his chair, still fidgety. "She's hardcore, from what Sophie says. There was an incident a while back that really spooked her. Two men showed up at their house while she and her stepmother were home alone. Big, tough dudes with hand cannons. Sophie stayed inside while Lauren went out to the driveway to talk to them. Things got dicey, she said. Lauren was white as a sheet when she came back inside. Wouldn't say much about it. But a few days later, Sophie found out her money had gone missing and she put it all together. That's when she decided to go live with her aunt. There was a big bust-up over it. Sophie threatened to tell her grandfather about the missing money if her dad tried to stop her from moving out."

"Did Sophie ever see those two guys again?"

"Not that she told me."

"Can you think of anyone who may have it in for Sophie? Someone at school, maybe? A jilted boyfriend?"

"I don't think so."

"What about one of your old girlfriends?"

Dylan had been fairly animated while talking about Sophie's problems at home, but now he shifted nervously and averted his gaze.

Craig leaned in. "Is there someone like that? Come on, kid. The best way you can help Sophie is to be honest with me."

"It's not like she'd ever do anything to hurt Sophie," Dylan mumbled as he studied the cracks in the tabletop.

"Who are we talking about? Give me a name."

Dylan glanced up, wary and defensive. "Okay, but you have to understand we only went out for a little while before Sophie and I got together."

"A name, Dylan."

"Hannah."

Craig sat back in his chair. "Hannah Tucker?"

"It wasn't serious. At least…not for me," he added reluctantly.

"What about her?"

The kid looked miserable. "I guess she was pretty upset when we broke up."

"Define *upset*."

"She wouldn't speak to me for a long time afterward. Some of my buddies said she started rumors about Sophie."

"What kind of rumors?"

"Just dumb stuff. She was mad, okay? But she got over it. We're all friends again. Like I said, she would never do anything to hurt Sophie. They're like sisters."

"Like sisters, huh?"

"Yeah."

Craig glanced down at his notes. "Anything else I should know about your relationship with Sophie?"

"What do you mean?"

"Like I said, any and everything is important at this point."

Dylan's expression grew earnest, but Tom didn't trust his sincerity. Teenagers these days were pretty sophisticated. They knew how to deceive and deflect when the pressure was on.

"Sophie is a good person," Dylan said. "People have

the wrong idea about her. They think because her family has money, she's all stuck-up and stuff, but she's not. She wouldn't go out with someone like me if that were true." He placed his hands flat on the table as he leaned in. "You have to find her. I don't know if she ran away or if someone took her, but she must be in trouble. She would have called me before now if she could."

"You're sure about that?"

The kid jutted his chin. "She would have called."

"Okay, son. That's all for now. You're free to go." When Dylan started to rise, Craig added, "Don't leave town."

Tom watched as Dylan exited the room. He'd been polite and cooperative, but something about his manner still niggled. His concern for Sophie seemed genuine, and after his initial reticence, he'd answered every question. So why was Tom's gut warning him to dig deeper? Had the kid been a little *too* obliging? A little too willing to throw Hannah Tucker under the bus?

The door opened and Craig poked his head in. "What did you think?"

"Deliberate or not, he sure painted Hannah as a person of interest."

Craig nodded. "Maybe I should call him back in and lean on him a little harder."

"Give him some time to simmer. Let's hear what Hannah has to say."

Tom returned his attention to the window as Hannah and her mother were ushered into the interrogation room. Hannah sat down at the wooden table while her mother hovered in the background. Craig introduced himself and gave Hannah a word of encouragement before he took the seat across from her.

Unlike Dylan, the girl appeared cool and collected.

She sat ramrod straight in the chair with her hands folded on the table. She wore a simple sleeveless dress with a sweater tied around her shoulders. Her hair was pulled back in a ponytail and her face scrubbed clean of makeup. She looked younger than sixteen and much more subdued than she had at Rae's house the day before. Restrained but not the least bit intimidated. Like Dylan, she readily admitted to her participation in the game.

"It was just a way to pass the time," she explained. "Something different. We never thought anyone would get hurt or…" She trailed off on a tremulous note.

Craig projected a hint of frustration at her response. "Why didn't you mention any of this to Sheriff Brannon when you saw him at Rae Cavanaugh's house yesterday? Why did you lie and tell him that none of your friends went out to the Ruins anymore?"

She gazed across the table with wide, guileless eyes. "Because we all made a pact that we wouldn't tell anyone. Sophie was afraid of what her dad would do if he found out and I didn't want to worry my mom." She glanced back at her mother. "I'm sorry, Mommy. We didn't mean any harm. It just gets so boring around here."

"We'll talk about it when we get home," her mother said. "Just answer the detective's questions."

Hannah turned back to Craig. "There really isn't much to do in this town, you know. That's why we kept playing."

"Do you know who the fourth player is?" Craig asked. "The one who uses a cross for his or her symbol?"

She shrugged. "Dylan and I both thought it was Sophie. She likes mysteries and games, and the Ruins have always fascinated her. She used to go out there after school sometimes and take pictures. I think it's because of what happened. Sophie kind of romanticized Riley's disappearance. She became a little obsessed. She used to say it was strange that she could be so invisible to her family while a girl who vanished fifteen years ago was still all any of them ever thought about."

"Did Sophie talk to you about any other problems she had at home?"

Hannah considered the question with a pensive frown. "She and her stepmother don't get along. Sophie hates Lauren. She calls her a gold-digging slut."

"Hannah," her mother reproached.

"I'm sorry, but I'm just repeating what Sophie said. She called her a lot of other things, too. If you want, I can make you a list."

"Maybe later," Craig said. "Did she ever talk about running away from home?"

"All the time. I used to think she just wanted to get her family's attention, but maybe it was something more. I don't know. Dylan wasn't much help. He egged her on."

"How do you mean?"

"Sophie inherited some money from her mom's side of the family, but she couldn't touch it until she turned eighteen. She didn't want to wait that long to leave home, so she and Dylan used to sit around dreaming up ways to get their hands on that money."

"What did they come up with?"

"Just crazy stuff. I really didn't pay much attention."

Craig's tone dropped imperceptibly. "It must have been awkward for you, listening to Sophie and Dylan make all those plans together."

Hannah's expression remained passive, but her gaze turned shrewd. "Why would you think that?"

"You and Dylan used to go out, didn't you? Wasn't there a part of you that resented Sophie? He broke up with you to be with her."

Hannah's mother moved in closer as if to warn him to tread carefully.

Hannah didn't seem to notice. Her eyes widened in surprise as she shot a glance at the two-way window. "Did he tell you that?"

"He said you were pretty upset when he called things off."

Her voice rose for the first time. "Who wouldn't be? Do you know how embarrassing it was, the way they sneaked around behind my back? Everyone in school knew but me."

Her mother placed a hand on her shoulder. "I think that's enough for now. Hannah wants to help, but it's been a traumatic two days. I'd like to take her home *now* so she can get some rest."

Hannah swatted her mother's hand away in annoyance. "Stop it, Mommy. I'm not tired. And anyway, I've got plenty more to say about Sophie and Dylan."

Craig nodded. "I'm listening."

She sat back in her chair and folded her arms. "It's true I was angry when Dylan first broke up with me, but it wasn't long before I realized that he was much better suited to Sophie than to me."

"How so?"

She gave him a cool smile. "I plan to go to college in a couple of years and someday I'll have a fabulous career. Dylan doesn't want any of those things. He's only interested in the moment. So is Sophie, but it's totally okay for her. She doesn't have to worry about her future because she comes from money."

Was that a trace of resentment in her voice? Tom wondered.

"You told Sheriff Brannon that you talked to Sophie after Dylan dropped her off on Thursday night."

She visibly relaxed. "She texted me about our chemistry assignment and I called her back to explain something."

"How did she seem? Was she upset about anything? What was her mood like?"

Hannah paused. "She seemed distracted."

"Do you know why?"

She cast another glance toward the window, as if wondering who might be listening behind the two-way glass. "I'd rather not say. You'll think I'm just trying to get back at Dylan for what he said."

"Stick to the truth and you'll be fine," Craig assured her.

She nodded as she tightened her sweater sleeves around her shoulders. Readjusting her armor, Tom thought.

"Sophie was worried about Dylan. She said he was getting too clingy. He kept pressuring her to run away with him. Sophie's a big talker, but she's still really immature. She won't even turn sixteen until next month. Leaving town with Dylan scared her. Where would they go? How would they live without any money? She told me she wanted to break up with him, but she was afraid of how he would take it."

"Why was she afraid? Did he ever get physical with her? Threaten her?"

"No… I don't think so. But he…" She trailed away worriedly.

"What?"

"Don't get me wrong—he's a good guy," she hedged. "But he has a dark side. He used to scare me sometimes when he'd get in one of his moods."

"Did he ever threaten you?"

"No, of course not. He'd just get all mopey and quiet.

I think his dad used to knock him around until he got old enough to defend himself. It's no wonder he wants to leave town so badly. I would, too, if I had a father like that."

"Are you sure Sophie didn't say anything about going out to the Ruins on Thursday night?"

"No. I knew it was her turn, but I didn't know when she would go."

"She never said anything about making a new acquaintance? You haven't seen any strangers lurking around town or school?"

She shook her head.

"And you're sure you have no idea who the fourth player is?"

"I told you, I thought it was Sophie."

Craig nodded. "Okay. Thanks for coming in." To her mother, he said, "Keep an eye on her. Make sure she doesn't leave the house without you knowing. Everyone needs to take precautions until we get to the bottom of what happened." He pulled out his card and handed it to her. "If either of you think of anything else, give me a call. In the meantime, stick around town in case we have more questions."

"Detective?" Hannah stood. "Can I ask you a question?"

"Shoot."

"Is Dylan a suspect?"

Craig gave her a direct look. "Everyone in Sophie's life is a suspect at this point. The two of you probably know her better than her own family knows her. Dylan was with her on the night she went missing and you may be the last person who spoke with her. That makes you both material witnesses. You may not think you know anything that can help us find her, but small details and seemingly irrelevant pieces of information are often how we figure out what happened. You need to think back to that last conversation. Try to remember the nuances. It's possible Sophie said something to you that could help us break this case."

She gave him a solemn nod. "I'll do my best, Detective Jarvis. Whatever it takes to find Sophie."

After she and her mother left the interrogation room, Craig lifted a quizzical brow at the window. Tom also had doubts about some of Hannah's responses. Like Dylan, she'd projected an accommodating demeanor, but it had taken her even less time to turn on him. Tom didn't trust either of those kids or their innuendos about the other.

What better way to hide a conspiracy than by casting aspersions on one's partner in crime?

Chapter Ten

Shaken by that second phone call, Rae spent the rest of the morning at the ranch with her father and brother, determined to sit tight until they received further instructions from the kidnappers. That was assuming another call would be forthcoming. Doubts plagued her. What if the ransom demand was a ruse intended to keep the family from looking for Sophie until it was too late?

On and on Rae's mind spun until she became so agitated that the slightest sound caused her to jump. Her father's disposition was no better. He watched the phone on his desk with an almost unblinking focus while Jackson's mood alternated between rage and despair. Rae wasn't unsympathetic to her brother's anguish, but her patience could stretch only so far. He seemed determined to take his fury out on her, and the incessant carping wore on her nerves until she found herself sniping back at him.

He wasn't wrong. Sophie should never have been able to sneak out of the house so easily. Rae should have kept a closer watch. But her brother wasn't without fault, either. He'd literally dropped Sophie on Rae's doorstep on his way out of town. He'd not only expected her to keep an eye on his teenage daughter, but also to take up the slack at work. Rae accepted her part of the blame, but she would allow herself to be a punching bag for only so long before she fought back.

"Rae?"

She started. Jackson had left the room for a bit and the silence had lulled her. Despite her chaotic thoughts, she'd almost drifted off to sleep. "Yes, Dad?"

"Go into town and get us something to eat."

The request surprised her. "Dad, there's a ton of food in the kitchen. If you don't want leftovers, Jetta can whip up something else."

"I gave her the day off. I couldn't stand all that hovering."

"She's just trying to help."

He scowled at Rae. "I know that. But I don't like to be fussed over. I'm not senile or at death's door like some folks like to make out."

Point taken. "Then I guess you don't want me to fix you anything, either."

He sighed heavily. "Can you just humor me for once? I want real food. Go get me the blue-plate special at the Corner Café."

Comfort food, Rae thought. Her father and his cronies often met for lunch at the café to savor Winona Landry's fried chicken, mashed potatoes and buttermilk biscuits while they argued over local politics. Under normal circumstances, Rae might have tried to steer her father toward a more heart-friendly choice, but the circumstances were far from normal and she wasn't about to intervene at a time like this. If he wanted fried chicken, so be it.

Jackson came back into the room then and Rae attempted a truce. "I'm making a run into town. Dad wants fried chicken for lunch. What about you? Can I bring you back something?"

He went straight over to the window to stare out. "I'm not hungry."

"What about for later?"

"I said I wasn't hungry, but do whatever you want. You always do anyway." He gave her a surly glance.

Rae bit her tongue. "I won't be long. I'll take the kidnappers' phone with me just in case we get another call."

Jackson returned his focus to the garden. "Let's hope you do a better job keeping up with that phone than you did with my daughter."

Rae wanted so badly to retort, but then she caught her father's eye. He shook his head slightly as if warning her to back off. She felt instantly ashamed. She was thirty-two years old, educated and accomplished by most standards, yet still in need of an admonishment from her father to do the right thing by her brother.

"Jackson?"

He turned with a scowl.

"I'm sorry I snapped at you earlier. We're all on edge. But we'll get through this. We'll pay the ransom and get Sophie back. Everything will be fine. I really believe that."

Rather than soothe, her words seemed to grate. His eyes darkened with contempt, but before he could attack, he apparently picked up on the same silent cue from their father. He flexed his hands at his sides and swallowed his anger. "I hope you're right," he finally managed.

"We can talk more when I get back if you like." Okay, that was probably overkill, Rae decided. When had she and Jackson ever had a heart-to-heart? Their fierce competition as children had devolved into a bitter rivalry as adults, one that had driven a wedge so deeply between them that Rae had no idea how to comfort her brother. The birth of his child, the death of his first wife, his promotion to CEO of Cavanaugh Industries—all milestones that Rae had let go by with little more than cursory acknowledgment because Jackson kept pushing her away.

How had things gone so wrong in their family when they'd once been so close?

Rae pondered that painful question as she pulled onto the highway. If she had to pinpoint the beginning of the rift, she would guess it to be a moment shortly before her mother's death. They all knew the end was near and had gathered around her hospital bed to say their goodbyes. Jackson couldn't take it. He'd fled the room, but they could hear his sobs from the hallway. Their father had gone after him and Rae had pretended not to overhear the ensuing conversation. Yet every now and then West's harsh words came back to her. *Stop it! You hear me? Wipe your nose and stand up straight. This is no time to lose control. You're a man now. That's not how we act.* Their mother had squeezed Rae's hand as if to say, *Take care of him, Rae. Your brother will need you when I'm gone. Riley, too. We all know you're the strong one.*

Jackson had never been the same after that day. It was almost as if he had to prove his strength to himself and to everyone around him, especially to Rae.

Tears stung her eyes at the memory and at the lost relationship with her brother. She wiped her cheeks with the back of her hand. *This is no time to lose control.*

Just get the food and head straight home. Be there for your family whether they want you around or not.

It was almost noon on Saturday and Belle Pointe would be bustling with weekend shoppers. Rae didn't relish running into anyone she knew, but the café would be packed this time of day. No avoiding all those sympathetic well-wishers and pitying stares, but she would get through the ordeal as she'd always done with a bit of bravado and sheer force of will.

Calling ahead, she was told there would be a half-hour wait for her take-out order. She could have easily jumped the line by giving her name and playing the sympathy card, but instead she left her phone number and murmured her thanks. Killing time, she drove all around town looking for the location where the video had been shot even though she suspected the kidnappers were holding Sophie somewhere remote. But she kept searching anyway, up one street and down another.

Rae must have watched that footage of her niece at least a dozen times trying to spot clues. The high window behind Sophie suggested that she could be locked in a room belowground. That brought to mind the chilling basement at the Ruins. The kidnappers wouldn't keep her there, of course. The cops had been all over that place. But what if she'd been locked away in a place equally terrifying, equally dangerous?

Think of other abandoned places in the area. Other buildings with basements.

Someplace close enough to the ranch that the gunshot had startled the birds from the treetops as Rae had sat shivering on the side of the road. What if she could find that place? Rescue Sophie—

Be smart. We're watching you.

Giving up, Rae drove back to the square and searched for a parking place. As she eased along the street, she felt curious eyes turn in her direction, but the scrutiny was mostly her imagination. Or was it? Maybe the kidnappers had followed her into town and were even now keeping a close watch on her every move.

Rae had just spotted an empty meter when she saw Dylan Moody hurrying along the street. She started to lower her window and call out to him, but he looked upset. Understandable. They were all worried sick about Sophie. However, the way he walked with such purpose—casting a glance over his shoulder before ducking into an alleyway—triggered Rae's suspicions. She told herself there was nothing unusual or nefarious about his movements. People cut through the alley all the time.

But doubts nudged her as she pulled into the parking space and got out to feed the meter. Those kids had been hiding something the morning after Sophie's disappearance. Rae hadn't known then about the game, but she'd picked up on their sheepish behavior. They'd both lied to her face about going out to the Ruins, so she had to wonder what other secrets they might be harboring.

Dylan seemed more approachable and far more malleable than Hannah. Maybe if Rae asked a few questions, she could manipulate him into giving something away. After all, she was Sophie's aunt. It was only natural she'd want to talk to the person with whom Sophie had last been seen. *I'll study his face, his eyes. I'll know if he's lying.*

Right. Just the way she'd known Sophie had been lying to her for weeks.

By this time, Dylan had vanished down the alley. Crossing the street, Rae pretended to window-shop for a moment before heading down the cobblestone lane behind him.

Belle Pointe was an old town, founded on the banks of the Red River before the Civil War on land ceded from the Caddo Indians. The area was steeped in folklore. Rae had never bought into any of the spooky tales. Even as a child, she'd been too pragmatic to indulge in fantasies. But as she crept along in the shadow of the buildings, she suddenly remembered why the backstreet was sometimes called Ghost Alley. As the town grew, the prominent location of the old cemetery had become an inconvenience. Rather than moving the interred to a new resting place in the countryside, the powers that be had built over the graves. The alley between the courthouse and city hall led back to a handful of untouched graves from the original cemetery. People had sworn for years they'd seen strange lights moving up and down the alley after dark. Of course, many of them also swore they'd spotted black panthers stalking the woods and heard phantom screams echoing across the lake.

A latticework gate opened into the cemetery. The creak of the rusted hinges prickled the back of Rae's neck despite her common sense. She tried to shake off the disquiet. The local historical society tended the graves these days, but when Rae was younger, the cemetery had been a popular hangout for the three or four Goth kids in her high school. It had been more convenient than trekking out to the Ruins, and they would gather at midnight in the cemetery with candles and cheap wine. Rae had never paid them much mind. Harmless fringe dwellers, though there had been whispers of rituals and sacrifices after Riley disappeared.

Rae had never paid those rumors much mind, either. She had never been one to judge on appearances. Going by the way she looked, most would consider her a conformist, but she was a fringe dweller in her own way. Her competitive nature had always driven people away. She had no close friends and told herself she was fine on her own. Who had time for a social life anyway? But Rae suspected if she delved deeply enough, she would discover that her drive to be the best was prodded by a fear of never measuring up.

Shaking off that morose thought, she took a quick peek

through the gate. No one was about. Dylan had probably used the back entrance to slip through to the other side of the alley. Rae told herself to stop this nonsense and go home. Let the police do their job. Now was the time to be with her family. What if the kidnappers called on the landline with the next set of instructions while she was out playing sleuth? She would have to drive all the way back to the ranch, and time could be of the essence.

All those things went through her mind as she entered the cemetery. It was shady inside and so quiet she could hear nothing beyond the tinkle of a wind chime and the gurgle of a small fountain. The graves, once badly neglected, were well tended now and covered in seashells. A wooden bench had been installed beneath a tree so that one could pause in the shade to rest or reflect. Rae did neither. She crossed the tiny cemetery to the rear gate and peered through the slats.

Dylan stood several yards down the alley with his back against the brick wall. His head was turned away as a silhouette approached from the street.

Rae recognized the tall, slender figure at once. The regal bearing, the catlike walk. After two years of living in Belle Pointe, Lauren Cavanaugh still stood out, even in a shadowy alley. She was like the proverbial hothouse rose in a field of daisies and dandelions. The comparison would please her, which was why Rae had always kept that observation to herself. Petty of her, but she had never pretended to be a saint.

Why was her sister-in-law rendezvousing with Sophie's boyfriend in Ghost Alley, of all places? Wasn't she supposed to be manning the phone at her and Jackson's house?

Rae wanted to believe it was simply a chance encounter, but why had Dylan paused to wait? Why did Lauren turn to glance over her shoulder? The meeting had obviously been arranged and they were taking precautions not to be noticed.

As Lauren drew even with Dylan, she placed her hand on his arm. The gesture seemed both clandestine and intimate. Rae strained to pick up their conversation. She thought at first Lauren might be comforting Dylan, but when she touched his cheek, he knocked her hand away.

Rae must have made an involuntary movement or sound because Lauren's head snapped around and her eyes narrowed as she peered through the latticework. Quickly, Rae retreated into the cemetery, dropping down on the bench in the deepest part of the shade. A moment later, Lauren came through the gate. She didn't bother glancing around but walked straight across the cemetery to the front entrance. Maybe she'd concluded the sound had been her imagination or maybe she'd heard nothing at all. Maybe a guilty conscience had made her jumpy.

Rae wasn't sure why she didn't call out to her. Why not confront her brother's wife and demand answers? *Why are you meeting Sophie's boyfriend in an alley two days after she disappeared? Why did he lie about going out to the Ruins? Who's minding the phone in case the kidnappers call your house?*

Instead, Rae lay low, holding her breath until the gate swung closed behind her sister-in-law. Then she rose and returned to the back gate to search for Dylan. The alley was deserted. He'd already hustled out to the street, and by the time Rae returned to her vehicle, Lauren had vanished, as well.

Rae stood at the meter glancing around. Surely her sister-in-law hadn't had time to get into her car and drive off. She must have ducked into a nearby shop or restaurant. Rae could walk up and down the street searching for her through plate glass windows or she could circle the block and try to find Dylan, but what would either effort accomplish? What had she actually seen? Nothing untoward. Nothing overtly suspicious, and yet something Jackson had said to Lauren in anger came back to Rae. *Why are you defending that little creep? If I didn't know better...*

"Rae?"

Tom's deep voice jolted her out of her reverie. She glanced up. He stood in the dappled shade of an oak tree, gazing at her curiously. He wore his usual uniform of dark plaid shirt, dark tie and jeans, and her heart thudded despite her resolve. She needed to stay steady, needed to keep her distance. Needed to be mindful that someone could be watching.

When he had her attention, he approached slowly, as if worried he might frighten her away. "Sorry. I didn't mean to startle you. Whatever you were thinking about just now, you seemed a million miles away."

Rae didn't know how to respond. She felt uncomfortably lost. She couldn't bring up the kidnappers' warnings or the ransom demand. Didn't dare tell him about the burner phone or the video. But should she mention Dylan and Lauren? And tell him what, exactly? *I think they're up to something.*

He cocked his head slightly. "You okay?"

"Yes. I was just thinking about Dylan Moody. I saw him a moment ago. I wanted to talk to him, but I lost him down Ghost Alley."

"What did you want to talk to him about?" His tone sounded mildly curious, but there was a deeper emotion swirling beneath the placid surface.

Careful, Rae.

She shrugged, trying to arrange her features in an

appropriate mask. "I just wanted to ask him some questions. That's not so strange, is it? He was the last person to see Sophie before she disappeared."

"Besides you, you mean."

"Yes, besides me. And I suppose Marty Booker saw her, too. He may also have seen Sophie's abductor, so I'm not sure why you let him go."

Tom propped an arm on the meter as he studied the street. "We don't hold witnesses in jail indefinitely unless their lives are in danger. I told you yesterday, we'll keep an eye on Marty."

"Do you know where he is now?"

"I have an officer out looking for him."

Rae said in shock, "He's disappeared?"

"His sister says he never stays in one place for too long. He'll turn up."

"I hope so."

Tom's gaze found hers. He looked cool and calm in the heat while Rae was sweating bullets beneath her shirt. It was hard to pretend not to know things with him. Hard not to blurt out the truth and plead for his help, but she'd been warned. She took herself back to that split second of terror when she thought Sophie had been shot. *Remember that. Use that. Next time could be the real thing.*

Tom took her arm unexpectedly. "I think we need to get you out of the sun. You look ready to pass out."

She jerked away. "I'm fine." His touch sent a shock wave through her battered system and she overreacted.

He dropped his hand with an apologetic gesture. "Just trying to help."

"I know." She regretted her aggressive behavior, but it was all such an impossible balancing act. *Don't get too close, but don't push him away. Don't tell him anything, but try to appear cooperative.* The strain was getting to her. Even now Tom's gray eyes seemed to probe a little too deeply and she worried about how to keep his suspicions at bay. She hadn't eaten or slept in two days. She felt too susceptible, too in need of his strong shoulder, and that knowledge distressed her even more.

For as long as Rae could remember, she'd relied on no one but herself. Even after Riley went missing, she hadn't allowed herself the luxury of a breakdown. Someone had to keep the family together. Someone had to be the rock. But what if she was no longer up to that task?

I'm just tired, she thought. So bone-deep weary she could hardly think straight. She wanted to sink right down to the sidewalk and bury her face in her hands. *Let someone else be in charge for a change.*

"I'm a little on edge these days," she murmured.

"If anyone has that right, it's you, Rae."

She gave him a rueful smile. "My mother would say there's never a good enough excuse for being rude. I'm sorry."

"Don't worry about it." But those stormy eyes were still watching her, still measuring her by some unknown yardstick.

Rae glanced away. "I should be getting back to the ranch. Dad will be expecting his lunch."

"Doesn't he have a housekeeper?"

"Yes, but he gave her the day off. He says her hovering makes him nervous. I drove into town to pick up some food. It should be ready by now, so if you'll excuse me..." She wiped damp palms on her jeans and told herself to stop talking.

"Before you go I need to ask about your brother."

Despite her fatigue, Rae's guard shot back up. "What about him?"

"Let's step over here out of the way." Tom took her

arm to steer her into the shade, and this time she didn't object. It was hot on the street and she needed to keep a cool head.

But even as she tried to remain poised, her gaze strayed to the alleyway. What if Lauren and Dylan were somehow involved in the kidnapping? Shouldn't she say something? What if they could lead Tom and his deputies to Sophie?

A few hours ago she would never have entertained such a notion, but was it really that far-fetched? Lauren liked money. That was no secret. Her spending habits were so out of control that West had felt the need to call her out in front of her husband. *And look how she reacted to the ransom demand.* Rae had thought at the time that her sister-in-law seemed uncharacteristically emotional, not to mention desperate, in her response. *You can get the money, right? A million dollars isn't all that much by Cavanaugh standards.*

As for Dylan's part, it wouldn't be the first time a teenage boy had fallen under the spell of a conniving older woman.

Rae tried to rein in her racing thoughts. Maybe she was being a little overzealous in spinning her theory because she'd never liked Lauren in the first place.

"There you go, drifting away again," Tom said. "Where did you go this time?"

She tore her gaze from the alley. "Nowhere. What were you saying?"

He gave her a dubious look. "Are you sure you're okay?"

"I'm just worried about my dad. I need to get back home. You wanted to ask about Jackson. Can we make this quick?"

He nodded. “I want to talk to you about that argument he had with his wife yesterday. Things got pretty heated.”

“Couples fight,” Rae said. “They both have tempers, so petty grievances tend to escalate, even under the best of circumstances.” She felt obligated to downplay the significance of the conflict even though she’d thought at the time that something more was going on between Jackson and Lauren. Everyone had secrets, it seemed—including Rae.

“Do they fight like that often?”

“I’m not with them on a regular basis, so I wouldn’t know. Jackson has always been able to cut to the quick, but I doubt he gets anything over on Lauren. She keeps her claws sharp, from what I can tell.” Rae paused to scan the street. They’d been standing out there for a long time. If the kidnappers were watching, they might get the wrong idea. She said impatiently, “Why do you care about that argument?”

“I care about everything going on as it relates to Sophie. You said she came to live with you because of problems at home. Lauren and Jackson certainly seem to be at odds. It must have made for a stressful home life. I’m wondering if some of their problems are financial.”

He’d managed to surprise Rae again. “Why would you think that?”

“I’ve been asking a lot of questions for the past two days. I hear a lot of rumors.”

Her voice sharpened. “About my brother?” *About me?*

“Everyone has a theory,” Tom said. “There’s been some talk around town about business difficulties. How are things at Cavanaugh Industries?”

Now Rae’s defenses really came up. He was poking in places he had no business. Or did he? Everything was fair play when a child went missing. He would expect her full cooperation. She thought about those odd discrepancies she'd uncovered at work. Nothing truly substantial so far, but small bits of cash here and there could add up over time.

"What is it?" Tom asked.

Sunlight flickering down through the trees blinded Rae. She used the opportunity to step back, putting a little distance between them. "I'm wondering where you're going with all this."

"Just answer the question. Has there been any trouble at Cavanaugh Industries since Jackson took over?"

"A few hiccups. Nothing major. The company is fine."

"Does either of them gamble?"

Rae's brows shot up. "What? Who told you that?"

"Do they?" Tom moved out of the sun, too, closing the gap between them. His tone remained gently persistent but there was a hard gleam in his eyes that Rae had never seen before.

"I take it you don't mean the occasional scratch-off."

He shook his head slowly. "I'm talking high stakes, the kind where a bad streak can put you under for a few hundred thousand."

She gasped. "Jackson doesn't have that kind of money to lose."

"Then a debt like that could make a person desperate."

Rae stared at him for a moment. She could almost feel the color drain from her face. "You can't possibly think Jackson had anything to do with Sophie's disappearance."

"Maybe not directly. But the gambling industry attracts a dark element. The kind of lowlifes who wouldn't think twice about nabbing someone's daughter to use as leverage."

His line of questioning and the implication of his probe worried Rae, but she took a breath and answered candidly. "I've never known Jackson to gamble. Not even on his beloved Dallas Cowboys. That's just not his thing. As for Lauren, I can tell you that she spends money like crazy. You only have to look at the way she dresses and the car she drives to know she enjoys the finer things in life. But gambling…" Rae trailed off. "I don't know."

"You don't like her much, do you?"

"Is it that obvious?"

Tom gazed into her eyes, causing her pulse to flutter. "Put it this way. *You* should never play poker."

Was she that much of an open book? Rae swallowed. "Luckily, I've never been a gambler, either."

"Have you and Lauren had any trouble?"

What was behind *that* question? "We've had words on occasion. I don't like the way she treats Sophie and I think she brings out the worst in Jackson. But mostly I try to stay out of their business."

"Except when they asked you to take Sophie in. They made her your business."

"Yes. I think we all regret that move."

His voice softened. "None of this is your fault, Rae."

"So you've said."

"She and her friends were sneaking out to the Ruins before she came to stay with you."

"Somehow that doesn't make me feel any less responsible."

"I know about guilt," he said. "I know that it can eat you up inside if you let it."

She avoided his gaze. She didn't want to see the compassion in his gray eyes. Didn't want to think about those strong arms and how good they might feel around her now. "I'll be okay. We just need to find Sophie."

"That's why I'm here. That's why I'm asking all these questions. I know they're unpleasant. I know you think my time would be better spent out beating the bushes, but anything you can tell me is important. Even something seemingly insignificant has the potential to lead us to Sophie."

Rae nodded, gulping down a sudden lump in her throat. If only he knew what she was holding back. "What else do you want to know?"

He hesitated. "Were you aware that Sophie's trust fund has been emptied?"

"I'm only vaguely aware that she has a trust fund. What do you mean it's been emptied? By whom?"

"According to Dylan, Sophie believed the money was used to pay off her stepmother's gambling debts."

So that was the reason for all the gambling questions. Rae pushed back her damp hair as she tried to square the revelation with the encounter she'd witnessed in the alley. Had Lauren tried to persuade Dylan to keep his mouth shut about the trust fund?

She gave Tom a hard stare. "I don't think I like where you're going with this. You said you didn't think Jackson was directly involved in Sophie's disappearance, but you seem to be trying awfully hard to implicate him."

"No. I'm just trying to gather as much information as possible. Like I said, we need to know everything there is to know about the people around Sophie."

"I don't know what more I can tell you."

"Let's start at the beginning with Jackson and Lauren," Tom said. "Tell me how they met."

"How can that possibly matter?"

"Maybe it does, maybe it doesn't. Think of the investigation as putting together a puzzle. You can't always know where a piece fits until you start to see the bigger picture."

She nodded with a weary sigh. "Okay. They met on

vacation in the Cayman Islands. They hooked up in a bar and came back home engaged." How well Rae remembered the day Jackson had brought Lauren home to meet the family. The shock of his impetuous behavior. The uncomfortable and slightly nauseating displays of their infatuation. The mumbled congratulations that had rung hollow even to her ears. "Jackson was head over heels at first. A real goner. His first wife was lovely and sweet. The girl-next-door type. Lauren was something different, a gorgeous and exotic model, of all things. Jackson bought her a huge ring, a new house. Gave her a stack of credit cards. They seemed happy enough for a while, but things started to go south in the second year. For one thing, Sophie never warmed to Lauren. For another, Jackson led her to believe that he had money. I guess he does by Belle Pointe standards, but not ten-carat-diamond-ring money. Not three-weeks-in-an-exclusive-resort money."

"So they do have financial problems."

They were back to his original question. "I guess they do," Rae said.

He looked pensive. "Okay. That's all I wanted to know."

"Tom?" She touched his arm. It would have served her right if he'd pulled away, but instead a half smile tugged as he gazed down at her. She dropped her hand at once. "Why are you smiling?"

"I like the way you say my name."

She frowned. "What does that have to do with anything?"

"Nothing. I just like the way you say my name."

Her tone chilled. "You realize this isn't the time or place for frivolous banter."

"I do realize that. I wasn't trying to be frivolous, Rae. I meant what I said."

She shook her head, trying not to read too much into that smile, his stare. The way he said *her* name. "My niece is still missing."

"I know that."

"Is my brother a suspect?"

"Yes."

"Am I?"

"Technically."

That gave her another long pause. Then she nodded. "I understand. The family is always looked at the hardest. I remember what we went through when Riley went missing. My poor dad…all those questions he had to endure… Please don't do that to Jackson."

"I have to do my job, Rae. You know that."

"Yes, of course." She glanced out over the street. "Let me know if you need anything else. I'll help in any way I can. Right now, though, I have to get going. Dad's fried chicken is getting cold. You'll let me know if you hear anything?"

"The very minute. But you already know that."

She started back to her vehicle and then turned. He was still standing in the shade, head slightly canted, staring after her. He had the oddest look on his face, an unnerving mixture of desire, compassion and suspicion.

Why suspicion? What had she done to give herself away? Rae wondered. Was she really that easy to read or was Tom Brannon getting to know her a little too intimately?

As if intuiting her distress, he dipped his head and then turned to walk away, leaving Rae to stare after him.

Chapter Eleven

Tom didn't get home that night until almost midnight. He was so tired he wanted nothing more than to fall into bed, pull the covers over his head and sleep right through his alarm the next morning. But he hadn't eaten all day, so he fixed a quick bite and then took a long shower, propping his hands against the tile wall and bowing his head so the hot water could pummel his neck and shoulders. Then he stretched out on top of the covers and stared at the ceiling while time ticked away and the quiet of the house deepened.

It had now been forty-eight hours since Rae had first called in to the station about Sophie's disappearance. The hope that she had taken off on her own volition dwindled by the minute. Still, the possibility couldn't be discounted. She had a history of running away and, according to her closest friends, had talked about it incessantly. She fit the profile. Problems at home. Craved attention from her dad and hated her stepmother. Wouldn't be the first time a teenager had hidden out for a few days to teach her parents a lesson. But Tom didn't buy it. He couldn't imagine that Sophie would have intentionally left her cell phone behind at the Ruins. And what about those drops of blood that had yet to be identified? Too many people had motives. Too many people had secrets.

Tom had his problems with the Cavanaughs, but his heart went out to that family, especially to Rae. He knew what she was going through right now. How the guilt and worry would eat at her. The torment of her own thoughts would keep her tossing and turning all night. What was it she'd told him yesterday? *The waiting wears on you. All the terrible things that go through your head. Your mind never shuts down. You can't sleep. You can't eat.*

He pictured her pacing the floor and staring out the window. Pictured the shimmer of fear in her eyes and the soft tremor of her lips. The image made him wince. Rae Cavanaugh was the last person he should be obsessing about tonight. Nothing good could come from that distraction. Too much history and bad blood stood between them.

But he had to admit she was different from what he remembered. She could still be touchy and standoffish at times and he had no doubt she could still carry a grudge. He only had to bring up her sister-in-law's name to glimpse Rae's belligerent side. But she could also be compassionate and understanding. She'd done a lot of growing up since their high school years. Tom liked to think that he had, too. They were not unalike in a lot of respects. She worried about her family just like he did.

His sister would be thirty in another few months and Tom still felt the need to boss her around. Not that she would let him. He'd given up persuading her to move back into town. He figured she had something to prove to herself and to the monsters that chased her by living out there on the lake. He admired her courage and determination, but that didn't stop him from fretting, especially now when another girl had gone missing. What if Silas Creed really had come back? Or worse, what if a predator had roamed the streets of Belle Pointe for the past fifteen years, hiding his true nature as he mingled with his neighbors?

Tom told himself to quit borrowing trouble and get some sleep. Silas Creed was dead and gone. He wasn't coming back to Belle Pointe now or ever. Better to focus on the here and now. Every day brought new challenges to the investigation and he needed to stay sharp. But his mind wouldn't be quiet.

Rolling over, he punched his pillow as he ran through the clues they'd uncovered thus far—the game, the texts, the symbols. All those clandestine visits to the Ruins. The revelations about Lauren Cavanaugh's gambling and Sophie's drained trust fund. Hannah Tucker's sour breakup with Dylan Moody and Rae's broken engagement to Blaine Fenton. The rumors about Jackson Cavanaugh's financial troubles.

Tom didn't have much regard for Rae's brother, but he couldn't bring himself to believe that anyone in the family had masterminded Sophie's kidnapping. On the other hand, Blaine Fenton had a motive. Hannah Tucker and Dylan Moody both had motives.

And who was the elusive fourth player?

On and on Tom's mind churned until he finally got up, dressed and left the house. A few minutes later, he found himself pulling to the curb in front of Rae's place. The whole house was lit up as if she'd aimlessly flipped switches as she wandered from room to room.

He leaned his head against the back of the seat as he watched the windows. This was a terrible idea. What the hell was the matter with him anyway? Even the greenest of rookies would know better than to get personally involved with someone connected to an active investigation. Emotions only muddied the waters. He should head back home before he was spotted, get some sleep and start with a fresh perspective in the morning.

Tom stayed put, though, because his attraction to Rae Cavanaugh wasn't the only thing driving him tonight. Maybe he was trying to justify his surveillance, but he thought she might be holding out on him, too. Keeping secrets just like everyone else. Something had changed in her demeanor and attitude from the time he'd seen her at the edge of the Fenton ranch early that morning to when he'd spoken to her in town later in the day. Something so subtle it might be nothing more than Tom's imagination, but his instincts hadn't failed him in a long time. She'd been nervous and fidgety and had a hard time meeting his gaze. He'd noticed some of that uneasiness yesterday. *What are you hiding, Rae? What aren't you telling me?*

The scent from her rose garden drifted in through his open window. The white flowers lining her walkway shimmered in the moonlight as a warm breeze whispered through the oak trees. It was one of those mild summer nights that stirred memories and aroused a dangerous longing. Tom could imagine Rae up there on her porch, toeing the swing back and forth as she watched lightning bugs flit through the dark. If he wasn't careful, he might picture himself right up there beside her.

She appeared so suddenly at one of the front windows that Tom thought for a moment he'd somehow conjured her. But no. She was all too real as she parted the curtains and peered out into the darkness. Had she seen him? He didn't want to alarm her by his presence, so he got out his phone and sent her a quick text:

It's Tom. Just checking in to make sure everything is okay before I head home.

A few seconds went by before she answered. His text had undoubtedly caught her by surprise.

Tom? Do you have news?

No news. Sorry.

A few more beats went by before she again responded.

Are you at the station? Can't sleep. Thinking about driving over there to talk to you.

Not at the station. His thumbs hovered while he decided what else he wanted to say. I'm parked outside your house.

She reappeared at the window, cupping her hands around her face as she searched the street. A moment later, the front door opened and the porch light came on. Tom got out of his vehicle and strode up the walkway, telling himself he wouldn't linger. He'd make sure she was okay while subtly observing her behavior. Then he'd go home and get some sleep. Tomorrow would be another long day. A search party would need to be coordinated and neighborhoods would need to be canvassed. Sophie's picture would again be shown at the local bus station and it might even be time to consider bringing in some bloodhounds. But he would mention none of that to Rae unless she asked.

A neighbor's dog barked and he glanced over his shoulder, scanning the street warily before turning back to Rae. She stood silhouetted in the doorway, dressed in pajamas that would normally cover as much skin as her regular clothing, but the light from the foyer turned the cotton to gossamer. He tried not to notice the outline of her curves beneath the thin fabric, concentrating instead on her worried expression.

She folded her arms around her middle. “It’s late, Tom. I’m surprised to see you tonight.”

“I know and I’m sorry for coming by like this.” He propped his foot on the bottom step as he gazed up at her. “I had a feeling you’d still be up.”

“I lay down for a while, but I just kept staring at the ceiling and thinking about Sophie. Wondering where she is. If she’s okay or if she’s out there somewhere hurt and frightened. Or if she’s already…gone.” Her voice trailed off to a whisper. She drew a sharp breath as she glanced at the sky. “The moon is so bright tonight. I can’t help but feel I should be out looking for her.”

“Too risky even with a full moon,” Tom said. “People tend to get trigger-happy in the dark. It’s better if we wait and hit it hard in the morning.”

She tucked her hair behind her ears and nodded. “It just seems like we’re wasting time. It’s after midnight. Sunday morning. We’ve entered the third day already. You know what that means.”

He heard a quaver in her voice as he climbed the rest of the steps. He didn’t say as much to her, but he was all too aware of that closing window. Only too cognizant of that ticking clock. “We’ll find her, Rae.”

“You don’t know that. You said you’d do everything in your power to bring her home and I believe you. But even if you look until you’ve exhausted yourself and every possibility, it may not be enough. Forty-eight hours has come and gone, and you said the first twenty-four—”

“I know what I said, but Sophie isn’t a little kid. From everything I’ve learned about her, she’s smart and resourceful. A real fighter.”

“Riley was a fighter, too, in her own way.”

"Sophie isn't Riley."

"Everyone keeps saying that." Rae was silent for a moment. "You know the real reason I can't sleep? When I close my eyes, I see Riley reaching out to me. When I drift off, I hear her calling my name, begging me to come and find her. And then her voice fades and she's gone again. But Sophie is still out there. Maybe she's calling out to me, too. Or maybe she's already losing hope that anyone will ever come and find her."

"Rae." He didn't know what to say to her in that moment, how to comfort her without breaching ethical barriers.

She didn't give him a choice. She moved toward him and Tom just waited while she walked straight into his arms. He was so startled he hardly knew what to do. He hadn't expected this. Not in a million years. He stood stiffly as she clutched his shirt and buried her face in his shoulder. Even then, he tried to remain stoic, but he wasn't so hard-hearted or such a stickler for protocol that he could refuse her a moment of comfort. He tightened his arms around her and held her awkwardly.

"I'm sorry," she said.

"Don't be." He rested his chin on her head and held her. "It's been a rough time for all of us."

But that didn't make it okay. Not by a long shot. He was starting to feel things for Rae Cavanaugh he had no business feeling. What was he thinking, holding her like this? What was she thinking? He told himself to pull back and walk away. *Walk away.* But he couldn't bring himself to disengage. She needed a shoulder and his was right there.

A million thoughts ran through his head, none of them helpful or appropriate. She smelled really nice. Like expensive soap and shampoo. He wondered if she'd just stepped from the shower because her skin felt warm beneath her pajamas. With very little effort, he could imagine how she would look out of those pajamas, but he didn't dare let himself go there even when she slid her arms around his neck and pulled his mouth down to hers.

Tom resisted. He did. For a half second at least. But damn. She tasted like mint and hot chocolate.

He ran his tongue lightly over her lips and felt a shiver go through her. She pulled him closer, deepening the kiss with a needy little moan that set Tom's heart to pounding. He told himself, *Don't be a jerk. You have to stop this.* She was scared and vulnerable and reacting on impulse. *You can't let this happen.*

But, man, did she ever feel good pressing up against him the way she was. Lighting him up. Making him remember and forget all at the same time the last time he'd had sex.

It was that damn dog across the street that finally drew them apart. Tom lifted his head at the incessant barking and turned to search the shadows. Even then, Rae tried to pull him back in. He drew away, casting another look over his shoulder.

"This isn't a good idea."

She glanced past him to the street. "You're afraid someone will see us?"

"I've never cared too much about the gossips."

Even the ones who had speculated behind closed doors as to why Porter Brannon's children were the only ones to make it out of the Ruins that night. When Jenna Malloy had been found on the side of the road weeks later, conjecture about Tom and Ellie had eventually diminished, but by that time, the wounds ran deep. The Brannon family had learned the hard way how quickly friends and neighbors could turn, how thoroughly a small town could be divided.

"I've got a job to do," he said. "This doesn't make it any easier."

She backed away then, running a hand up and down her arm as if she were suddenly chilled. "I'm the last person who'd want to hinder the investigation."

Was she? Or was she deliberately trying to distract him?

She leaned her head against the door frame. "I can't believe we're even having this conversation. I can't believe I kissed you."

He tried not to take her regret personally. "No harm done."

"No, I was out of line and I apologize." Her chin came up then and she met his gaze defiantly. "I don't want you to get the wrong idea. It was just a moment of weakness. My version of letting off steam."

"You don't have to apologize for being human."

She glanced away. "What happens now?"

About the investigation or the kiss?

"We keep looking," Tom said. "We keep asking questions. Someone out there saw something. They may not even know it yet. Sooner or later, that person will come forward."

Her expression was enigmatic in the shadows. "You really believe that?"

Before he could answer, the chime of an incoming text message caught her attention. He heard her gasp in the dark. Then she fumbled in her pajama pocket for her phone and glanced at the screen. A shadow passed over her features before she remembered that he was still staring down at her.

She seemed flustered. "Sorry. It's… Dad. I need to

answer him…" She thumbed a quick message, taking care to position herself so that Tom couldn't glimpse the screen.

"Everything okay?" he asked.

"What? Yes. I mean, no. He can't sleep. None of us can. We're all so worried. And the memories are killing us."

Tom had his memories, too. He wanted to reassure her that everything would be okay, but missing persons cases were unpredictable, and all too often ended in tragedy. No one knew that better than Rae.

He didn't touch her again. He was careful to keep his distance. "Is there anything I can do?"

"Besides find Sophie?" She slid the phone back into her pocket and straightened, all business now that she'd had a moment to clear her head. "I didn't mean that the way it sounded. I appreciate everything you've done so far to find her. And I appreciate you coming over here to check on me. You caught me at a vulnerable time, but I'm fine now and I'd really like it if we could just forget tonight ever happened."

That might be easier said than done, Tom thought, but he nodded and said good-night. By the time he reached the bottom step, he heard the front door close. He climbed in his vehicle and circled the block, pulling to the curb a few houses down from Rae's. Another SUV was parked between his car and her house. He hoped if she looked out the window, she wouldn't be able to spy him.

A few moments later, her garage door opened and she backed her car down the driveway. Gunning the engine, she straightened the wheel and sped away. Tom waited until she made the first corner before he started his vehicle and cut his lights. He followed her all the way out to the highway, running dark and keeping a safe enough distance so that she wouldn't be able to detect him in her rearview. She took the turnoff to the ranch and he cruised on by, telling himself that she'd driven out there to be with her distressed and ailing father. Nothing suspicious about her actions. Nothing dubious about her motives. But those niggling doubts wouldn't be silenced.

He found a place to pull off the road and sat in the shadows as he contemplated his next move. He'd wait ten minutes, and if nothing happened, he'd drive back to town. He needed some rest. Tomorrow would be a day of decisions. If they couldn't pick up a trail soon, he'd have to request assistance from the Rangers and widen the search. The family would start to lose faith. Jackson Cavanaugh might even decide to take matters into his own hands and then Tom would have a real mess to clean up.

Reaching across the console, he removed a .38 from the glove box and placed it on the seat beside him. His 9 mm service weapon was locked up at home where he always kept it when he came off his watch. Maybe he was being too cautious, but it was dark and isolated where he sat. Anything could happen.

He'd started to get drowsy when the sound of a car engine brought him up sharply. He scrubbed his face as he tried to pinpoint the sound. Rae's vehicle emerged from the trees. She drove through the archway and turned left onto the highway, toward town. Tom fell in behind her, once again keeping his distance. But instead of heading to Belle Pointe, she turned right onto Lake Road.

Tom allowed more distance to creep between them. No need to keep her in sight. He knew where she was going.

RAE THOUGHT SHE'D glimpsed a vehicle behind her before making the turn onto Lake Road. Her hands gripped the wheel and she flashed another glance in her rearview.

Nothing. Maybe the vehicle had been heading into town, but why would anyone be out driving this time of night without lights?

You're seeing things, she told herself firmly as she returned her attention to the road ahead of her. Carrying around a million dollars in cash would stoke anyone's paranoia, but she couldn't afford to get sidetracked. She couldn't afford to get careless, either. She had her instructions. She knew where and when to make the drop. The text message had laid everything out. She'd been given only thirty minutes to drive to the ranch, collect the money and then get to the Ruins.

Why there, of all places, Rae couldn't imagine. Seemed risky. Curiosity seekers might be out there even this time of night, though she thought that doubtful. She didn't relish going into the building alone—that haunted, crumbling structure where both Riley and Sophie had disappeared—but what choice did she have? Her niece's life depended on her making the drop at the appointed time and place. She'd let Riley down. She wasn't about to do the same to Sophie. But if someone had followed her from the ranch, she might have to take evasive maneuvers and that could throw off the tight timing.

Something shot across the road in front of the car. Rae had allowed herself to become too distracted by the instructions. Now she overreacted and hit the brakes while simultaneously cutting the wheel. Swerving too sharply, she lost control of the vehicle. The tires skidded off the shoulder into the ditch. The car bounced, scraped bottom and stalled.

No! No, no, no!

What had she done? Why, why, why hadn't she paid closer attention to the road?

Every tick of the cooling engine seemed like the beat

of a countdown clock. The night seemed to swoop down upon Rae as she sat in stunned silence. She tried the ignition, but the engine wouldn't crank. Fear and frustration overwhelmed her. She wanted to stomp the accelerator, grind the ignition and put her fist right through the windshield. How could she have been so stupid? What was she supposed to do now?

She could head out on foot to the Ruins. She'd taken the time to dress and put on sneakers, but even if she ran all the way, she'd never make it in time. The message had warned against any deviation or delay. Everything hinged on Rae getting to the Ruins in exactly—she glanced at the dash clock—thirteen minutes, and she was still at least two miles from the bridge. Then she had to climb down the embankment and follow the lake to the Ruins. The hospital had once had direct access to the highway, but that road had washed out years ago. Nowadays, there was only one way in and one way out. Aside from the history, maybe that was why the kidnappers had chosen that spot. If someone was positioned at a third-story window, he or she would be able to see Rae coming. They'd know if she was alone.

Her only choice was to call for help, but she could hardly expect her dad to come to the rescue. His heart might not be able to handle the stress, and as for Jackson…

She shuddered to think what her brother would say about her incompetence. He'd wanted to make the drop himself, but the text message had been explicit. And anyway, it was better that Rae be the one. Jackson was too close to the situation and couldn't be trusted to keep a cool head. If he came face-to-face with one of his daughter's abductors, there was no telling what he might do. Rae, on the other hand, knew when to keep her head down and follow orders. She'd make the drop and then hightail it back to the ranch to await further communication. Hopefully, in a matter of hours, Sophie would be home safe and sound and they could all put this terrifying episode behind them.

That had been the plan, but instead, Rae sat stuck in a ditch.

Despite the full moon, the thick canopy overhead blocked the light. She grew uneasy, imagining someone easing along the side of the car to ambush her. Checking the locks, she glanced in the rearview mirror. No one was there. No one had followed her. Still, she removed her dad's pistol from the backpack of money and gripped the handle. He had insisted she arm herself before leaving the house. Rae didn't own a weapon, but she knew how to shoot. Rattlers and copperheads were prevalent on the ranch. She'd never been one to go out looking for trouble, but she hadn't shied away from protecting herself and her animals.

Clutching the weapon, she scoured her surroundings. The woods seemed to close in on her. She could imagine all sorts of creatures slinking through the trees, but the only predator that worried her at the moment was the human kind.

Just sit for a moment and let the motor cool off.

She forced herself to count slowly to ten before retrying the ignition. Thankfully, the engine caught, and with a bit of skill and patience, she maneuvered the vehicle out of the ditch and back onto the road.

Now take a breath and calm down.

She could still get to the Ruins in time if she didn't make any more stupid mistakes. If she could reel in her imagination and stay focused. One step at a time. One mile at a time. She wouldn't allow herself to think about

Sophie or that video. She wouldn't entertain for even a second what might have happened to her niece after the footage had been shot. For now she had to believe that Sophie was still alive. She had to get to the Ruins and make the drop. *One step at a time. One mile at a time.*

Up ahead, the trees thinned and she caught a glimpse of the bridge. Fear rippled across her nerve endings as sweat beaded between her shoulder blades. She had no idea whom or what she might encounter inside that creepy building, but she couldn't allow herself to think about that, either. Wiping clammy palms on her jeans, she told herself everything would be fine. The kidnappers were only after the money. No reason to hurt her or Sophie or anyone else so long as they got what they wanted.

Pulling to the shoulder of the road, she eased into the trees until she was certain any chance passersby couldn't spot her vehicle. Moonlight shimmered brilliantly off the lake. She wouldn't need to use a flashlight. She grabbed one anyway and tucked the pistol into the waistband of her jeans. Hitching the straps of the heavy backpack over her shoulders, she tried to keep the weight balanced as she skidded down the embankment. Twice she lost her footing and went all the way to the ground, but she made it to the bank without a broken bone or turned ankle. That was something at least.

Trudging along the treacherous path, she kept a sharp eye. Even the sound of a faint splash chilled her to the bone. She turned to search the woods. Every shadow, every movement set her heart to pounding. She wanted to use the flashlight to chase away those shadows, but she couldn't take a chance on being seen from one of the houses. So she drew another breath and plunged ahead.

The smokestack rising through the treetops guided her toward her destination. Scrambling up the ridge, she paused momentarily to search the gaping windows. Nothing stirred. The night was very quiet, but she knew danger was only an arm's length away. She was being watched. She had no doubt that someone stood at one of those windows tracking her every move.

Adjusting the backpack, Rae headed for the same arched entry she and Tom had used on that first night. How she wished he were here with her now. How she wished she had confided in him about the ransom demand, but too late now. For all she knew, Sophie might be waiting for her inside, and that thought buoyed Rae's courage.

She waited until she was inside to turn on the flashlight, running the beam over the walls and floor and finally up to the ceiling, where Preacher stared down at her.

Moving as quietly as she could, she started up the stairs, testing each step before she applied her full weight. Then she paused at the top, once again using her flashlight to reconnoiter before she eased down the corridor. Somewhere behind her a floorboard creaked, and she whirled, her hand going to the gun hidden beneath her T-shirt. She didn't draw the weapon. Instead, she held her breath and waited. Nothing moved. Even the rats had gone silent.

She turned and continued down the corridor to the elevator shaft. Shrugging off the backpack, she dropped it to the floor and then hovered at the edge to shine her light down into the abyss.

Glassy eyes gleamed up at her.

Chapter Twelve

Rae teetered at the edge. If Tom hadn't grabbed her arm, he was certain she would have pitched headfirst into the shaft. She turned with a gasp, her eyes wide with terror. She tried to fight him off, and for a moment, he worried they might both lose their footing.

He clasped her wrists. "It's me, damn it. Hold still."

She froze at the sound of his voice. "Tom? What are you doing here?"

"I was wondering the same thing about you. Seems like we've been asking each other that question a lot lately."

Moonlight flooded in through the windows and the gaping roof. She looked pale and distressed as she wrested her hands from his grip. "You can't be here!"

"Why not?" He studied her in the pale light. Her fear had turned to flat-out terror. "What's going on, Rae?"

"Do you have any idea what you've done?"

"What *I've* done?" He wanted to give her a little shake, wake her up to the dangers of coming out here alone in the middle of the night where three people had gone missing. Where his own sister had been left for dead. Instead, he kept his distance and forced a neutral tone. "Seems you and I need to have a talk."

A bit of the old Rae surfaced and she looked as if she

wanted to lash out at him, but then she whirled back to the shaft as a shudder ripped through. "There's a body at the bottom of the shaft."

He glanced past her to the opening. "You mean in the basement? It's not a body. We checked it out the other night, remember? It's just a pile of rags and debris."

"This is different. I saw the eyes." She swayed and he caught her elbow. "It can't be Sophie. I did everything I was supposed to."

Tom had a feeling she was talking to herself now. Pulling her gently back from the edge, he took out his flashlight and angled the powerful beam through drifting shadows until he could see all the way to the bottom of the shaft. Someone was down there all right. He spotted twisted arms and legs. A contorted face.

"Is it Sophie?" Rae asked in a fearful voice.

"No," Tom said grimly. "It's Marty Booker."

"Oh, thank God." Her hand shot to her heart. "I didn't mean… I know how that sounds. It's just…" She closed her eyes. "Thank God," she whispered.

"I know," Tom said.

She stepped back up to the rim, steadier now, but her voice was still taut with tension. "Do you think he fell?"

Tom remembered the way Marty had leaped into the shaft and agilely swung down from the rope to avoid him on that first night. The man had known what he was doing. He'd timed his jump perfectly. Why would he suddenly get careless now and miss his mark?

Putting away his flashlight, Tom reached for the rope.

"You're going down there?" Rae asked on a sharp breath. "What if *you* fall?"

"I'm not going to fall. I need to get a closer look and I need you to call 911."

His request seemed to take her aback. Her eyes widened. "But… People will come. The EMTs, cops…"

"That's the idea. We need to get that man some help. He could still be alive, for all we know." Doubtful given the twisted position of the body, but Tom had to be certain. He gave her a hard scrutiny. "What's going on, Rae? Why don't you want to make that call?"

It took some effort, but she seemed to shake herself out of that odd lethargy. Her gaze went back into the shaft as her voice softened with remorse. "I wasn't thinking. Of course I'll make the call. There's nothing else I can do right now."

He wanted to ask what she meant by that. Something was definitely going on with her tonight. Her clandestine trip made little sense to Tom, though suspicion was beginning to niggle. Outwardly, she'd quickly regained control of her nerves, but she still wasn't herself. Tom clung to the rope and wondered. Who texted her earlier when he'd stood on her front porch? What kind of message had driven her headlong out to the ranch and then to the Ruins in the middle of the night? And what the hell was in that backpack?

But those questions and all the others buzzing around in his head would have to wait until he checked the body and secured the area. "Keep your light trained downward so that I can at least see where I'm going."

He could hear her on the phone as he rappelled down the shaft. When he got low enough, he dropped to the ground with a thud and hunkered beside the body. Marty Booker's head lolled at a sickening angle. The eyes were open and staring, his hair matted with blood. Tom searched for a pulse. The skin was already cooling, but rigor mortis had yet to set in. He hadn't been dead long.

Tom gazed up into Rae's flashlight beam, shaking his head to let her know the man was gone.

Her hushed voice echoed down to him. "He's dead?"

"Looks like a broken neck."

"Then he must have fallen."

Tom wasn't so sure about that. Maybe someone had figured out that Marty Booker saw something he shouldn't have on the night Sophie Cavanaugh went missing.

Just as Tom turned back to the body, he caught a movement out of the corner of his eye. He whipped around, pinpointing a crouching shadow for one split second before the silhouette dashed for the outside steps. Tom lunged after him, dodging debris and rusty equipment before sprinting up the stairs behind him.

Arms and legs pumping frantically, the man headed in a full run toward the woods. Tom dived, hitting him square in the back, and he crashed to the ground with a pained grunt. Tom was on him in a flash, pinning his arms to his sides while he pressed his face in the dirt. All the fight seemed to go out of him then and he lay gasping for breath until Tom eased the pressure and rolled him over.

Dylan Moody threw his arms in front of him as if to ward off Tom's phantom blows. "I didn't do anything. I swear. I didn't do it." He tried to scramble away, but Tom yanked him back down.

"Just stay right where you are. Got it?"

"I didn't kill him. You have to believe me. He was dead when I found him."

Tom glared down at him in the moonlight. "Then why did you run?"

The kid looked frantic. "Because I didn't know who you were! I thought you might try to kill me, too!"

Tom grabbed his arm and hauled him to his feet. "What are you doing out here this time of night?"

"Nothing!" Dylan turned and spit blood from a cut lip, then wiped his mouth with the back of his hand. "I just came out here to look for Sophie, that's all."

Tom handed him a handkerchief. "Why did you think she'd be here?"

Dylan blotted his lip with a trembling hand. The action provoked an unexpected response in Tom. He'd been young and scared once, too, and his first inclination was to give the boy the benefit of the doubt, but there was a dead body in the basement and a girl was still missing.

"You're all right," Tom said. He doubted it was the kid's first split lip with Dwight Moody for an old man. "I need you to start talking."

Dylan spread his hands in supplication. "I was desperate, okay? I've been out searching for her all day and I didn't know where else to look. I'd already walked the woods all the way to the river and then I went up and down the lake on both sides. I didn't find her," he added unnecessarily. "It's like she vanished into thin air."

Tom nodded toward the basement entrance. "How long were you down there?"

"Not long. Five or ten minutes, I guess. I heard voices and then I saw the body in the elevator shaft. I got scared and hid."

"You didn't see anyone else here tonight?"

"Just you."

"How'd you get here? I didn't see a vehicle out on the road."

"I left my car on the other side of the bridge. There's a place where you can pull off into the woods."

"Why take the time to hide your car if you were searching for Sophie?"

Dylan seemed stumped for a moment. "I didn't even think about that. It's where I always park when I come out here."

"To play the game, you mean."

"Yeah."

Tom's voice hardened. "That's not the real reason you came out here tonight, is it? You kids aren't still playing some kind of game."

"No. I told you. I came looking for Sophie."

Tom nodded but he was far from convinced. Something wasn't adding up. The kid seemed even more nervous than Rae. Strange how they'd both ended up at the Ruins on the same night at the same time. "You weren't afraid that whoever took Sophie might still be lurking about in those woods? Or that a property owner might see you trespassing and decide to shoot first and ask questions later?"

He met Tom's gaze straight on, squaring his shoulders as if trying to put them on equal footing. "I thought about all those things, but I didn't care. I had to look for her anyway. It's my fault she's gone."

Tom rested a hand on his belt where normally his holster would hang. Inclining his head, he stared back at Dylan through narrowed eyes. It was a stance he'd seen his dad assume many times and it had never failed to intimidate Tom. "How is Sophie's disappearance your fault?"

The kid's gaze dropped. "It's obvious, isn't it? If I hadn't agreed to play that stupid game, none of this would have happened."

"So you decided to come out here and look for Sophie in the middle of the night even though you knew the police had been over every square inch of this place for two solid days."

Dylan's gaze came back up. "The cops don't always get things right."

True enough.

Tom glanced back at the looming structure, wondering again about the timing of the night's events. At some point before Rae had entered the building, Marty Booker had fallen or been pushed into the elevator shaft while Dylan Moody had been conveniently hiding in the basement. Neither Dylan nor Rae had come clean with him yet about their real reasons for being here and he was getting a little tired of their caginess.

Just then, Rae came hurrying around the corner of the building and froze when she saw Tom and Dylan in the moonlight. Then she ran toward them.

"Dylan?" She sounded breathless and upset. "What are you doing here?" She turned to Tom. "What's going on?"

"That's what I'm trying to find out."

She came to a dead stop as if paralyzed by a sudden revelation. Then her gaze went from Tom to Dylan and back to Tom as if she couldn't quite believe what she was thinking. "Where did he come from?"

"Dylan? He was hiding in the basement."

Something flickered across her face that Tom couldn't define. "Is Marty Booker dead?"

"Yes."

She turned on Dylan. "Did you kill him?"

He shook his head violently. "I didn't kill anyone! How many times do I have to say it?"

Tom put up a hand. "Let's stay calm until we figure out what happened here."

"I think it's pretty obvious what happened," Rae said.

"What's she talking about?" Dylan asked. "Why am I being blamed for something I didn't do?"

"Keep quiet, both of you. I need a minute." Tom

stepped back, making sure Rae and Dylan were in his line of sight while he called the station. In the minute or so it took him to explain the situation to the dispatcher, Rae approached Dylan and spoke to him in a low, furious tone. Whatever she said appeared to shake the kid up. He looked pale and scared in the moonlight.

"What's going on?" Tom demanded as he slipped his phone back in his pocket.

Rae's eyes were as cold as a steel moon in January. That shook Tom up. He'd never seen her look quite so much like West Cavanaugh. "I told him if you didn't make him talk, I would."

Her tone worried Tom. "I wouldn't be too hasty with the threats if I were you. He says he came out here looking for Sophie."

"And you *believe* him?"

"Is there some reason why you don't?"

She cut her gaze back to Dylan. Tom almost expected her to lunge for the kid the way she'd gone after Marty Booker in the boiler room. Instead, she said in a deadly quiet voice, "There's only one reason he would have been down in that basement tonight. He's the one who took Sophie."

Dylan jerked back at the accusation. "*What?* No! I would never do anything to hurt Sophie!"

"I didn't say you hurt her. I said you took her."

"That's crazy! I didn't take Sophie and I didn't kill that guy in the elevator shaft. I didn't do anything but play a stupid game! You can blame me for that. I deserve it," he said in a rush. "I should never have let Sophie come out here alone. But I didn't take her. Why would I? I would never hurt her like that. I wouldn't hurt anyone."

"Take it easy." Tom could hear sirens in the distance.

Rae would have none of Dylan's denials. "You were

waiting in the basement when I arrived. That can't be a coincidence."

"What are *you* doing here?" Dylan countered.

Tom turned. "That's a good question, Rae. And I'm still waiting to hear your answer."

"Ask *him*."

"I don't know what she's talking about." Dylan stumbled back, his hands up in front of him defensively. "This is crazy. She's crazy. I'm telling you I didn't do anything."

"Just stay right where you are," Tom advised. "If you try to run, it'll only make things worse for you."

"But I didn't do anything!" Despite the warning, Dylan looked as if he wanted to bolt for the woods. For everyone's sake, Tom decided he'd better restrain the kid. That didn't go over well. "I know what you're doing," he accused sullenly as Tom snapped on the cuffs. "You're going to pin everything on me so you can act like a big shot in town."

"Nobody's going to pin anything on you," Tom said. "This is for your own good so you don't do something stupid while we talk."

Dylan tossed his head back, trying to clear his eyes of an unruly lock of hair. "Are you going to make her tell you why she's here?"

"Stop pretending you don't know," Rae shot back.

"Okay, this is getting us nowhere fast." Tom took Rae's arm and guided her out of earshot. "He's right. I need to know why you're here. The real reason. Stop dancing around and tell me the truth."

He could see the gleam of defiance in her eyes as she lifted her chin. "Why do you keep asking me that question? He's the one you should talk to."

"I'm talking to you right now."

She snatched her arm away. "You can't possibly think

I had anything to do with Marty Booker's death, let alone my own niece's abduction."

Tom kept his voice even. "I never said anything like that. But I would like to know why you decided to take a drive out here in the middle of the night. And why you don't seem to want to give me a straight answer."

As if to prove his point, she narrowed her gaze. "Why are you here, Tom? I assume you followed me, but why?"

"Are you seriously asking me that question right now?" He shook his head. "You're unbelievable, Rae. Am I going to have to take you in to get the truth out of you?"

"Take *me* in? You still have no idea what you've done, do you?"

His voice tightened. "Then tell me. I have a pretty good idea of what's going on now, but I want to hear you say it. You came here with a backpack. I saw you drop it at the edge of the shaft."

"So?"

"What's in it?"

She caved on a shudder. "Ransom money."

"Ransom money," he repeated in a level voice, but a wave of anger washed over him. That was what she'd been up to. This was what she'd been keeping from him. What the whole Cavanaugh family had been hiding from the police. Sophie had been taken for money.

Which meant the investigation had been compromised from the get-go. There was no way of knowing how differently things might have played out if Tom and his men had been given the facts. He thought of all those wasted man-hours and resources. All those futile interviews and searches. But he tamped down his frustration as he studied Rae's features in the moonlight.

"How much?"

"One million dollars in cash."

Tom lifted a brow at the amount. "You came here to make the drop?"

She nodded miserably. "Those were my instructions. I was to come alone and toss the bag into the elevator shaft from the second floor. When I got up there, I shone my light down into the basement and saw the body. I thought… Well, you know what I thought. And then I saw you and I panicked. *I was supposed to come alone, Tom.*"

"How was I to know what you were up to?"

"You could have trusted me."

"Do you really want to open that can of worms right now?"

Her gaze strayed back to Dylan. "You know what happened after that. You went down into the shaft to check the body and you found Dylan hiding in the basement. He must have been waiting for me to toss down the money. Why else would he be there? Maybe Marty saw too much and Dylan killed him."

"Let's not jump to conclusions," he said, but the kid had looked panicked as hell when Tom had tackled him.

Rae's hand crept to her throat. "I never thought of Dylan as being dangerous. He'd seemed troubled to me but was always so quiet and polite. Except his being here *can't* be a coincidence. It just can't be. What are the odds that he and I would both end up here at the same time on the same night?"

Slim, Tom had to admit.

She clutched his arm. "If he's involved in the kidnapping, then he must know where Sophie is. You have to get him to talk, Tom. You have to make him tell us where to find her."

"Oh, he'll talk," Tom said. "Don't worry about that. But I'm not through with you yet."

"What more can I possibly tell you?"

"Everything. I'm playing catch-up and we may not have a lot of time. Start at the beginning and don't leave anything out, no matter how small the detail."

"The beginning," she murmured.

"When did you get the first ransom demand?"

She didn't answer immediately, but Tom didn't get the impression she was stalling. Maybe she was just trying to get everything straight in her head. He liked to think she'd finally seen the light. Her best hope of getting Sophie back alive was to cooperate. She had to trust that he would move heaven and earth to find that girl, but he'd been working all this time with one hand tied behind his back.

"The first call came in on Friday morning on the landline at the ranch," she said. "Dad was the only one there. He said the voice was disguised but he had the feeling we were dealing with professionals. They gave him twenty-four hours to put together a million dollars. They said if any of us went to the police, they'd kill Sophie."

"Of course they'd say that."

"I know." She gazed up at him in the moonlight. "You can believe me or not, but my first instinct was to call you. Dad and Jackson refused. They reminded me that the police hadn't been able to find Riley."

"My dad couldn't find Riley, you mean."

"Please don't make this personal. We did what we thought we had to do to protect Sophie."

Tom nodded. "I get that. You had to make an impossible decision." He'd been in that position before, so he did understand. As frustrating as it was to be kept out of the loop, he couldn't honestly say he blamed Rae and her family for the secrecy. When a loved one's life was on the line, you did what you had to do to protect them. Who was he to say that he would have behaved any differently? "You said your dad was alone when he took the call. When did you find out?"

"Later that morning. He called while you were at my house. He didn't tell me anything over the phone. He just said I should get rid of you and get out to the ranch as quickly as I could. Jackson was already there and Lauren came in a few minutes later. That's when I was told about the ransom demand. Dad was naturally upset. You can imagine what we were all thinking by that time. But still he managed to call the bank and make all the arrangements. All I had to do was drive into town and pick up the money."

Tom gave a soft whistle. "He was able to arrange that much cash that quickly?"

"We've done business with Glen Stafford for years. And we have plenty of collateral." Rae shrugged. "Dad can be very persuasive when he needs to be."

"Still, it's unusual for a small branch bank like First National to have that much cash on hand. It was almost as if the money had been prearranged."

Rae frowned. "What are you getting at? You're not suggesting Glen Stafford had something to do with the kidnapping, are you?"

"I'm not suggesting anything. Just thinking out loud."

Rae wasn't buying it. She gave him a puzzled look before she continued. "I had the money in my back seat when you followed me out to the ranch. I was afraid you'd know something was wrong the moment you saw my face."

"No wonder you were so jittery," Tom said. "You almost jumped out of your skin when the phone rang."

"We thought it might be the kidnappers again."

Despite Tom's empathy, he couldn't help being disappointed in Rae's lack of faith in him. Which was ridiculous because she happened to be right. This shouldn't be personal. Still, he felt the need to press her a little. "You walked me out to my vehicle. We had a long talk about trust and yet you never said a word."

She gazed up at him earnestly, any hint of defiance or anger long gone. "Because Sophie's life was on the line! Try to put yourself in my place. She went missing from my home on my watch. I was in no position to go against Jackson's wishes. She's his only child. It was his decision to make, not mine."

"Even if it put her at greater risk?"

"There was no way we could know that. It was a gamble either way. But even then, even knowing the risk, I suggested that if we didn't trust the local authorities—you—we could go to the FBI. They wouldn't hear of that, either. So it was never about you, Tom."

"I guess that's a relief."

She bit her lip. "Look, when this is over, you can berate me all you want. We can go back to being enemies, for all I care, but right now you need to talk to that boy and find out what he knows about Sophie."

For all I care. "You and I aren't done," he said. Not by a long shot.

Her instinct was to argue. He could tell by the way she stood so rigidly with hands clenched at her sides, but instead of pushing back, she lifted her head as a breeze from the lake ruffled her hair. After a moment, she seemed to relax. "When I got home on Friday night, someone had been in my house. They left a phone in Sophie's room and a call came in. The person on the other end told me that if I talked to the police or the FBI Sophie would die. If I didn't come alone to the drop, I would die."

Tom's voice sharpened. "The voice specifically mentioned the FBI?"

Her gaze flickered. "Yes. Why?"

"Nothing. Go on."

"They sent a picture of Sophie bound and gagged. Her face was all scratched and bruised." Rae faltered. "It was meant as proof of life, I guess. Or a warning."

"You still have the photo?"

"Yes, of course."

"I'll need to see it. The phone, too."

She nodded. "The photograph was hard enough to take, but the next morning after I saw you at the Fenton ranch, I was texted a video. Sophie was tied to a chair struggling to get free. The position of the window behind her made me think she might be in a basement somewhere. The footage was dark and grainy. It ended with the sound of a gunshot."

Tom tensed. "A gunshot?"

She closed her eyes on another shiver. "You can't imagine what went through my mind in that moment."

"I think I have some idea." When he'd found his sister lying facedown in the shallow water near the bank, he'd been certain she was dead. He knew about terror. He knew about panic. Any frustration he still felt at Rae's silence vanished in the face of her anguish.

"I was so terrified of what might have happened that I didn't realize at first the sound had come from somewhere in the woods instead of the video," she said. "That gunshot was a warning to me. They were near and they were watching. Maybe they thought you'd be the one I'd reach out to, so they had to do something drastic to head me off. It worked. I knew then I had to do exactly as they said. They weren't bluffing. They'd kill Sophie if I deviated from their instructions. They told me to come alone to the drop and now you're here. He's here." Her voice rose as she glanced at Dylan. "I thought I could handle myself in any situation. Keep a cool head and all that. I was so worried about what Jackson might do. He tried to come in my place, but I wouldn't let him. The kidnappers wanted me. Now I can only imagine how he'll react when he hears how badly I've messed things up."

"You didn't do anything wrong, Rae."

"Do you really think he'll see it that way?"

Tom kept his tone purposefully measured. "Let's stay calm and think this through."

"Isn't that what we've been doing?" She paused to catch her breath. "I think we can both agree our only hope now is Dylan. If he tells us where Sophie is, he can have the money. We have to get her back."

"You're still assuming he's involved," Tom said. "I'm not so sure that kid knows anything."

"He may know more than you think." She was back to being cagey again.

"Meaning?"

She lowered her voice. "I saw him in town today—yesterday—with Lauren."

Tom refused to react. "I thought you said you lost him in Ghost Alley."

"I did, kind of. But before I lost him, I saw them together. I couldn't hear their conversation. Lauren did most of the talking. She seemed very intense. When she tried to touch him, he slapped her hand away."

"Are you suggesting the two of them are somehow involved?"

"I don't know. But it wouldn't be the first time an attractive woman seduced a younger man into doing her bidding. If she's really that deeply in debt from gambling, I can only imagine how far she'd go to save her own neck. And I keep going back to the timing of all this. That Dylan would come out here looking for Sophie at the exact same time I'm making the drop is just too random. Marty Booker must have gotten in the way. Or maybe he recognized Dylan from the night Sophie went missing."

"You've got it all worked out," Tom said.

"Somebody has to." She looked instantly contrite. "I'm sorry. That just came out. Force of habit, I guess."

"Don't worry about it." But her words cut deeper than Tom wanted to admit. "Jackson seemed to think that Dylan's dad might be involved."

"Dwight?" Rae scoffed at the notion. "He's no mastermind. You think he could have come up with something as clever as that game to lure Sophie out here alone? No, it had to be someone who knew about her interest in this place. Someone who knew about Riley. They even took Sophie on the night of a blood moon. That can't be a coincidence, either."

"It's not a coincidence," Tom agreed.

"What do we do now?"

He scanned the towering facade. So many dark secrets hidden inside that crumbling building. So many ghosts still lurking in all those dark corners. If it were up to Tom, he would burn that place to the ground, but that might serve only to bury the secrets deeper. "As soon as we get some help out here, I'll send someone back inside to get the money. Not a good idea to leave a million dollars in cash lying around in an abandoned building."

"I told you, I don't care about the money. I just want to find Sophie."

"That money is your bargaining chip," Tom said.

She pounced on that. "Then you think Sophie is still alive. You think the kidnappers will call again."

He glanced back at Dylan. The kid had dropped to the ground and buried his face in his cuffed hands. "If he's involved, she's still alive. He seems to have genuine feelings for her. I don't think he'd let anyone hurt her."

"Tom." She touched his sleeve. A soft touch. An innocent touch. Yet Tom felt a brief surge of awareness in the pit of his stomach. Even after everything that had happened, he still hadn't managed to quell his desire for Rae Cavanaugh. If anything, this night had made her even more fatalistically attractive to him. How could he not admire a woman who had so willingly put her life on the line for a child who wasn't her own?

"What is it, Rae?"

"I need to call home. They'll be worried sick if they don't hear from me."

"Just wait a bit. We'll go talk to them together."

"But if they don't hear from me, they'll panic. Jackson may even drive out here to see what happened. Trust me, you don't want him anywhere near Dylan Moody right now."

Tom considered her point and nodded. "Go ahead and call, then. Tell them you're okay and you'll be home soon. But don't say anything about the ransom or Dylan or Marty Booker. Keep things brief. Understand?"

She frowned. "No, I don't understand. Why can't I tell them the truth? They'll know as soon as I walk in the door with the money."

"I'd like to be there when they find out."

A light dawned as his words penetrated. "You think someone in my family is involved."

"You're the one who told me about Dylan's tryst with Lauren," he pointed out.

"But she's not the one you're worried about, is she?"

He didn't answer, just stood there staring down at her in the moonlight. Then they both turned their heads to the sound of sirens out on Lake Road. A few minutes later, the EMTs scrambled up the embankment, followed by a small army of uniformed deputies.

He started toward them, glancing back when Rae said his name.

She looked scared and vulnerable with the Ruins looming behind her, but appearances could be deceiving. Rae Cavanaugh was not, nor ever had been, defenseless. Not for the first time, Tom paused to think about her role in all this. Did she also have suspicions about her own family? About someone closer to her than a sister-in-law? Was that why she'd stayed silent?

Like a taunt, Blaine Fenton's warning suddenly came back to him. *Don't let that pretty smile fool you, Sheriff. Way down deep, Rae Cavanaugh's every bit as cunning as her old man.*

Chapter Thirteen

Nikki Dresden, the Nance County coroner, stood at the top of the basement steps and used the back of her gloved hand to swipe back her dark bangs. She was dressed in jeans and Converse sneakers, a far cry from the all-black outfits she'd worn with combat boots in high school. Tom had known Nikki for most of their lives, but they'd never really been friends. Even as a kid she'd been a loner. Then after both her parents split, leaving her to be raised by an aging grandmother, she seemed to have found her tribe in the small group of Goth kids who had sat at the back of the cafeteria, scribbling poetry in black notebooks as they basked in an air of perpetual gloom.

Nikki had always been smart as a whip, but somehow people were taken by surprise when she'd graduated college with honors and been accepted into the University of Texas Medical School in Galveston. However, no one had been surprised when she'd decided to specialize in forensic pathology. Death seemed right in her wheelhouse. In addition to her duties as the Nance County coroner, she also worked as a pathologist for the Northeast Texas Forensic Science Center, which served most of the rural counties in the Piney Woods area.

Tom admired the woman and all that she'd accomplished at such a young age, but he regretted the circumstances under which their paths always crossed. She hovered at the top of the basement steps, gazing up at the moon as he strode through the weeds toward her.

He greeted her with a nod. "Nikki."

"Tom."

"What's the verdict?"

"Looks like a broken neck, poor guy. He's had it rough for most of his life and now this."

"You knew him?" Tom asked in surprise.

"His family lived down the road from my grandmother for a time." She snapped off her gloves and stuffed them in her back pocket. "He also has blunt force trauma to the back of his head, but I'm not sure either injury killed him. Judging from the amount of blood on the floor and in his hair, he survived the fall. His heart was still pumping when he hit the bottom."

"What did kill him, then?"

"I noticed some faint marks on his throat. Could be thumb impression contusions. If so, the bruising will get darker in a few hours and we'll start to see evidence of asphyxiation."

"So you're saying someone crawled down into that shaft and finished him off after his neck was broken?"

"That's my gut feeling. I think you're dealing with a cold-blooded killer, Tom."

"Or a desperate one," he said. "How soon will you know?"

"I'll pull some strings and get him autopsied first thing in the morning. He deserves that. Have you notified his sister yet?"

"I'm heading over there after I leave here," Tom said. Notifying next of kin was a task he always dreaded.

"She'll take it hard," Nikki warned. "She always looked out for him when they were younger, decking any kid who dared to make fun of him. Marty never made it easy. Always getting into trouble. Always blurting out inappropriate things. Not his fault, of course. Life just plain sucks sometimes."

They both fell silent, taking a moment to remember that behind every case file was a human being.

"Tell you what," Nikki said. "I'll clear my schedule and perform the postmortem myself."

"That would be a big help. I don't want anything to slip through the cracks on this one."

"Consider it done, then."

"What about fingerprints?" Tom asked.

"You know as well as I do that it's nearly impossible to lift latent prints from a corpse. But we may be able to recover some of the assailant's skin cells for DNA testing. First things first, though. Let's get the body bagged and ready for transport. No easy feat getting him out of here."

"Have you worked out time of death?"

"Going by body temp and lack of lividity, I'd put it no more than two hours. Probably closer to an hour. You may have just missed your killer. Unless you already have him in custody." She nodded to where Dylan Moody sat on the ground with his cuffed wrists draped over his knees.

"I have my doubts about him," Tom said. "He doesn't strike me as someone who would climb down into that shaft and strangle a dying man, but I've been fooled before."

Nikki's gaze drifted to Rae. She also sat huddled on the ground, hugging her knees to her chest. As if sensing their scrutiny, she glanced in their direction, zeroing in on Tom for a moment before she turned away.

"Isn't that Rae Cavanaugh?" Nikki asked.

"Yeah, that's her."

"I see her around town now and then. She's mellowed since high school."

"Has she?"

Nikki slanted him a curious glance. "What was that look she just gave you?"

"I didn't see any look."

"Really? She seemed pretty obvious to me. I'm guessing by her presence that this has something to do with her missing niece."

"I'm still trying to put all the pieces together," Tom said. "It's a complicated case."

The coroner's voice softened unexpectedly. "It must be hard for that family going through this again. I remember when Riley disappeared. The whole town turned out to look for her."

"I remember it, too," Tom said.

Nikki lifted her gaze to scan the shadowy building. "I sat up there in one of those broken windows and watched as they dragged the lake. It felt so surreal. Afterward, the search party headed back this way and I hid upstairs until they were gone. I'm not sure why. I guess in the back of my mind I thought they might be coming for me."

"Why would they be coming for you?" Tom asked.

She shrugged. "The way I dressed, the company I kept. You don't remember how my friends and I were treated after those girls went missing?"

"I guess I had too many things on my mind back then."

"For a while the investigation took on shades of the West Memphis Three," she said. "At least it seemed so. My friends and I even talked about leaving town. I decided to stick it out. I'm glad I did, but it was rough for a while."

"Being out here must bring back a lot of bad memories."

"You would think so, but as strange as it sounds, I've

always loved this place. If you strip away all the pain and suffering, the building is really quite beautiful. Back in school, I considered it a haven. My special place. No one bothered me here. Then Riley went missing and it became her place. I guess now it's Sophie's."

"Until we find her."

"I hope that's soon."

"I hope so, too." Tom glanced at Rae. She was staring at him again. He stared right back, letting darkness spin an intimate cocoon around them.

Nikki seemed oblivious to the subtle drama. She tipped her head, gazing all the way up to the eaves. Then she seemed to shake off her dreaminess and turned back to the steps with a purpose. "I'll see you at the autopsy in a few hours. Bring doughnuts."

Tom waited until she'd disappeared through the doorway at the bottom of the stairs before he walked over to Rae. He wondered if she was feeling as anxious and off center as he was tonight. Wondered if anyone else had noticed the looks they'd exchanged and the explosion of sparks every time their gazes connected. Or was the charged air only his imagination?

She rose, clutching the backpack as he approached. "Can we go now?"

"Yes. I'll drive you home."

"I don't need a ride. I left my car on the other side of the bridge." Her tone was even, no hint of anger or censure, and yet Tom felt as if he had been subtly brushed off.

"You can pick it up later or I'll have someone drive it back to your house." He reached for the backpack. "I don't think it's a particularly good idea for you to be out driving alone with this much cash in your possession. If the kidnappers are keeping as close a watch as you seem to think, they could follow you home. Or ambush you on the way. Lots of places to lie in wait between here and the ranch."

"What makes you think they won't try it with you?"

"For one thing, they'll know I'm armed. Taking out a county sheriff is not the attention they want or need right now."

"What about Dylan?"

Tom glanced back. "We'll take him into custody and let him stew in a jail cell for a while."

"Is he under arrest?"

"Not yet, but we can hold him for a few hours on suspicion. Maybe we'll get something out of him before he or his old man lawyers him up."

"I hope so. If we don't find Sophie soon..." She glanced away.

"I know. But nobody's giving up. Right now, the best thing you can do is go home and get some rest."

He slung the backpack over one shoulder as they started down the embankment. Rae was right on his heels. He heard her stumble once and turned to ask if she was okay. She merely shrugged and kept going.

The trek became easier once they reached the lake. She moved up beside him as they walked along the bank. The water looked silky smooth tonight, like spun silver. A light fog had begun to creep in from the other side. Tom wished he were sitting in a boat with a line cast down into those misty depths. He would have liked no more pressing business for the rest of the night than to close his eyes and remember the taste of Rae's lips as he drifted in the shallows.

Her voice brought him back with a jolt. "Do you really think someone in my family had Sophie kidnapped?"

He frowned at the water. "I told you. I'm not discounting anything at this point."

"But what a horrible thing to contemplate."

"We don't know anything yet. You have the money and you have the phone. Let's wait and see if the kidnappers make contact again."

"What if they decide to cut their losses?" Her voice was heavy with dread.

"They want that cash. They went to a great deal of trouble to get it. They'll call."

"What should we do in the meantime?"

"We can put a trace on the landline at the ranch and use triangulation to determine the location of an incoming call on a burner. But neither action is without risk," he warned. "We don't want to scare them off."

"What would you do?"

He paused. "Let's get out to the ranch and lay all the cards on the table. The ultimate decision belongs to your brother."

A scream sounded from some distant point on the lake and Rae jumped. Her hand flew to her heart as she paused to glance over the water. "What was that?"

"A peacock," Tom said. "Something must have roused him from his roost. You've never heard that sound before?"

"Not in the dead of night." She held out her hand. "I'm shaking. I think I could do with a drink."

Tom could as well but he had a long day ahead of him. He hoisted the backpack to his other shoulder as they neared the bridge and prepared for the final ascent. They didn't speak again until they were inside his vehicle.

Rae glanced out the window with a shudder. "I hope this is the last time I ever come out here. Someone should burn that place to the ground."

"I had the same thought earlier." Tom's phone rang just then, and he fished it out of his pocket. His sister's name flashed on the screen. Why would Ellie be calling at this time of night?

He lifted the phone. "You okay?"

"I'm fine. But something's happened that I thought you should know about."

He was mindful of Rae's gaze on him. "What is it?"

"I'm outside the Thayer house. I walked over a few minutes ago when I heard the peacocks. One of them sounded in distress. I thought a fox or coyote might be after them. As soon as I came up the drive, I saw a light through one of the windows. Someone is inside the house."

"Where are you now?"

"I went back out to the road, but I can still see the house."

"Is the light still there?"

"No, it's gone out just now."

"Do you see any cars around? Anything else suspicious besides that light?"

"No. But earlier I heard a boat on the lake. There's a dock out back. Should I go check?"

"No," Tom said quickly. "You just stay put and keep out of sight. I'm two minutes away." Rae's gaze was still on him as he slid the phone back in his pocket. "That was Ellie."

"So I gathered. Is everything okay?"

"She saw a light moving around in the old Thayer house just now. I need to go check it out. Are you okay with that?"

Her gaze widened. "Do you think it could have something to do with Sophie?"

The thought had occurred to Tom as well, given the

proximity of the house to the Ruins. "Let's not jump to conclusions. Probably just a squatter or someone scoping out a place to cook meth. I don't want my sister going inside alone."

"Do you think she would?"

"She might. She's quiet and introverted, but she's also headstrong."

"Then I think we should go check it out," Rae agreed. "I just hope Jackson doesn't show up at the Ruins while we're gone."

A quarter of a mile down the road, Tom killed the lights. When they were within a hundred yards of the overgrown driveway, he pulled to the side of the road and shut off the engine.

"Might be best if you wait here," he said. "Keep the windows up and the doors locked. I'll make this as fast as I can."

She gave a quick scan of their surroundings. "I'm not staying out here alone. Weren't you the one who warned about an ambush earlier? Besides, you may need backup and I have a gun. And, yes, I do know how to use it."

Tom wasn't surprised. She'd grown up on a ranch with a father and brother who liked to hunt. And she had a point. They were miles from the Ruins, miles from help, and they had a million dollars in cash in his back seat. People committed horrible crimes for the change in someone's pocket.

He nodded. "Okay, but keep your head down."

They stayed in the shadows as they hurried down the road. When they neared the drive, Ellie slipped from her hiding place in the bushes to join them.

"I haven't seen the light since I called you," she said. "I think whoever was in there is gone. Or else lying low. No one could have gotten by me on the road. I suppose he or she could have gone through the woods or down to the lake."

"I'll check it out," Tom said. "You two stay here and keep watch. Let me know if you see anything suspicious."

"Tom, be careful," his sister warned.

Rae nodded. "Yes, be careful. And call out if you need me. I'll come running."

He saw Ellie give her a curious look in the moonlight before he turned to ease up the driveway, reconnoitering both sides of the house before he approached the porch steps. The door was locked, but one of the front windows had been broken. He slid up the frame and climbed through.

Betsy Thayer had been dead for only a few months, but already the house smelled musty and his flashlight caught the shimmer of cobwebs hanging from the ceiling. Some of the furniture remained. He traced the outlines with the beam and pinpointed the exits. Once he had the layout in his head, he started to move through the house, clearing one room at a time until he reached the back porch. He could see the lake shimmering through the bushes. If the intruder had left by boat, Ellie would have heard the motor unless paddles were used for a silent getaway.

Tom stood there on the porch listening to the night until the scream of the peacock drove him back inside. He walked through the house again, checking places he may have missed on his first pass. He came across a locked door just off the kitchen. Given the age of the house, well over a hundred years old, he imagined the narrow passage led down into a root cellar that would have also been used as refuge from the killer tornadoes that sometimes swept through the area.

He jiggled the knob and then put his ear to the door.

He heard nothing and yet the hair at the back of his neck rose for some inexplicable reason. Taking a step back, he kicked the door at the weakest point and the wood frame splintered. Another kick and the door flew open. Tom fought his way through more cobwebs as he went down the steps. The basement was larger than he would have imagined for a house that size and crammed full of abandoned furniture and debris.

Against the far wall, a body lay crumpled on the floor.

Tom's heart thudded as he ran the light over the room before coming to rest once more on that motionless figure.

He said her name softly. "Sophie?"

No reaction. No movement. Dread clawed at his throat.

"Sophie Cavanaugh?"

Her head came up then and she scrambled back against the wall, mewling like a wounded kitten as she hugged her knees to her chest. "Don't hurt me. Please. I just want to go home."

Her hair was matted, her face and arms streaked with blood and dirt. Tom didn't know how badly she might be hurt or traumatized, so he approached with caution, keeping distance between them as he knelt.

"I'm not going to hurt you. I'm a police officer. My name is Tom Brannon. I'm the Nance County sheriff. I know your folks. They're worried sick about you."

She buried her face in her arms and whimpered.

"Your aunt is outside. She's come to take you home." He slipped his phone from his pocket. "I'll call her, okay?"

No response.

Before he could use the phone, he heard footsteps above. Rae called out his name. "Tom, are you okay?"

"Down here!"

He sensed her presence at the top of the stairs and then he heard her gasp. She came down the steps so quickly he thought she might trip and break her neck like poor Marty Booker.

"You found her! Oh, my God, you found her!"

Sophie lifted her head at the sound of her aunt's voice. "Aunt Rae?"

"I'm here, Sophie. I'm here, sweet girl." She dropped to her knees and held out her arms.

Chapter Fourteen

Sophie had been taken straight to the hospital, where she was given a comprehensive physical examination and treated for superficial cuts and contusions. Her clothing had been bagged and her fingernails scraped for trace evidence. Physically, she seemed fine and even her spirits had started to lift once her family had descended on her private room, but no one came through an ordeal like that unscathed.

Tom stood in the hallway observing the reunion through the glass panel in the door as everyone gathered around her. She sat propped against a pillow, looking wan and frail, and yet Tom had the uncomfortable notion that she was secretly basking in all that attention.

Like grim guardians, her dad stood on one side of the bed, her grandfather on the other. Rae hovered at the foot, reaching down every now and then to smooth the covers as if reassuring herself the girl was really there. Lauren Cavanaugh took her place at her husband's side, beaming down at Sophie as if she were thrilled beyond measure that her stepdaughter had been found safe and sound. But that smile didn't quite reach her eyes, Tom thought. He couldn't help remembering Rae's insinuation that something might be going on between her sister-in-law and Dylan Moody. The encounter Rae had witnessed might mean something or it might mean nothing at all. Either way, Tom intended to dig a little deeper into the woman's background.

Beside him, Craig Jarvis murmured his own reservations. "Why do I get the feeling she's secretly enjoying this?"

"You mean Sophie? I wouldn't read too much into her behavior. She's been through a lot."

Craig looked doubtful. "Were you able to get a statement?"

"We spoke briefly. She was pretty traumatized when we brought her in. I didn't want to press until she'd been examined. She says she never saw who took her. She went into the Ruins to leave her symbol on the wall and she heard a noise. When she turned toward the sound, someone grabbed her from behind and shoved a cloth to her face."

"Sounds like there were two of them," Craig said. "One distracted her while the other one nabbed her."

"Next thing she knew, she woke up in a dark, damp room bound and gagged and with no idea how she'd gotten there. She says she was moved twice, once in the trunk of a car and once by boat. My guess is they brought her to the old Thayer house because of its proximity to the Ruins. They were keeping her close just in case anything went wrong at the drop."

"That was risky, moving her around like that."

"Probably trying to stay ahead of the search," Tom said. "It's not a lot to go on, but she may remember more once the shock wears off."

Craig gazed through the window. "Remember what Hannah Tucker said about Sophie and Dylan sitting around dreaming up ways to get their hands on her money? A ransom payoff would be a good way to get that missing trust fund back."

Tom would be lying if he said the same thought hadn't already occurred to him. "Did you get anything out of Dylan?"

"His story hasn't changed, and I leaned on him pretty hard once we got him back to the station. We'll see if he's a little more cooperative in the morning."

"Hold him for a few more hours and then cut him loose," Tom said. "But put someone on him. I want to know where he goes and whom he sees. Rae said she saw him in town yesterday with Lauren Cavanaugh."

"Lauren Cavanaugh?" Craig gave a low whistle. "That boy has more mojo than I gave him credit for."

Rae came out of the room just then and Craig conveniently disappeared. Rae took Tom's arm, drawing him away from Sophie's room. "I'm glad you're still here." The way she stared up at him caused his pulse to thump a little too erratically. "You said you would do everything in your power to find Sophie and you did. I don't know how we can ever repay you. What you've done for my family…for Sophie… There are no words."

Tom tried to play it lightly. "Ellie is the one who really found her. If she hadn't called me when she did, we might not have gotten to Sophie in time."

"I'll speak to her again," Rae said. "I want her to know how grateful we are. But you're the one who found her, Tom. You're the one."

"I did my job, Rae."

"If that's how you want to leave it, fine. But we both know you went above and beyond. I won't forget it."

"I'm just glad she's safe."

Rae's eyes gleamed suspiciously. "It's hard not to think of the past at a time like this. Hard not to remember a different outcome. But I don't want to look back. I don't want to keep wondering about what might have been. Sophie is safe. That's all that matters tonight."

Tom wanted to reach for her. To comfort her. To tuck back her hair and kiss away her sadness. Instead, he merely nodded.

"I've carried that around with me for too long," she said. "I blamed you for what happened to Riley because I didn't want to deal with my own guilt. There were times when I wouldn't even let myself see you as a real person. It all seems so petty after everything that's happened. So trivial."

"You had your reasons, Rae."

"I thought so then. Now..." She shrugged. "I'm not under any delusions that everything will just magically blow over. Those scars run deep. But maybe with time... maybe when the dust settles...we could have coffee?"

He allowed a brief smile. "Are you asking me out on a date?"

"God, no." She wrapped her arms around her middle and shuddered. "Dating is too much pressure. Let's just call it coffee."

"Fair enough. I'll give you a call."

"Or I could call you."

"Either way." He gave in to an impulse then. Taking her face in his hands, he leaned in and planted a kiss on her forehead.

The action seemed to take her aback, although he probably hadn't startled her as much as he'd surprised himself. She pulled away, staring up into his eyes before she cupped his face and brought his mouth down to hers.

Not a good idea, Tom thought. Emotions were running a little too high, and anyway, public displays were not his thing. But with her fingers in his hair and her body swaying against his, it was a little too easy to forget they were standing in the corridor of a busy hospital.

"Rae!"

She would have jumped back at the sound of her name, but Tom held her for a moment longer, pressing his fingers into the small of her back before he let her go. West Cavanaugh stood just outside Sophie's room, his narrowed gaze pinning Tom with contempt.

"What the hell is going on out here?" he demanded.

"Nothing." Rae managed to sound perfectly normal. "Tom was just leaving."

West nodded. "Good. This is family time. Whatever questions you have will have to wait until morning."

"That's fine," Tom said. "But eventually we'll need full statements from all of you."

"Then call the house and make an appointment." West turned his attention back to Rae. "Your brother needs to see you."

"What about?"

"Sophie's decided to move back home. You don't have a problem with that, I trust."

"No. It's probably for the best, considering." She glanced at Tom. "We'll talk later?"

"Count on it."

West did not follow Rae back into Sophie's room. Instead, he remained in the corridor, glowering at Tom. "You found my granddaughter and for that I'm grateful, but it doesn't wipe the slate clean. Not by a long shot. I'll never see my youngest daughter again because of you. The hole in my heart will never be mended because of actions you took on the night of her abduction. If you have an ounce of decency left inside you, you'll leave my family alone and let us heal. Rae has a lot on her plate right now. She's likely to have more in the near future. Just step back and let her get on with her life."

Under normal circumstances, Tom would have been goaded to anger, but he kept a tight rein on his temper. "Isn't that Rae's decision to make?"

West Cavanaugh's smile turned sinister. "Don't be flattered by her attention. She's reacting to the situation. When push comes to shove, she'll do the right thing by her family. She's her father's daughter, after all. The sooner you realize that, the better off you'll both be."

AFTER TOM LEFT the hospital, he and Craig Jarvis drove over to Jefferson to inform Marty Booker's sister of his death. As the coroner had predicted, she took the news hard but agreed to meet them at the morgue to make a positive ID. After that, Tom went home to shower and even managed to catch a couple of hours of sleep before he had to be back at the morgue for the autopsy. The preliminary findings bore out Nikki's suspicions, but it would be at least a day or two before she and her colleagues reached a final conclusion. Regardless, Tom had already decided to treat Marty's death as a homicide. He'd wasted no time in getting a forensics team out to the Ruins and another to comb through the old Thayer house.

The ticking clock of a missing persons case had gone silent, but he now felt the pressure of a homicide investigation. He worked straight through two watches, leaving the station only when hunger and exhaustion finally drove him home. He ate a cold sandwich and took a hot shower, but he didn't bother lying down. He was still too keyed up. Pulling on a pair of worn jeans, he took a beer out to the front porch and sat down on the steps to enjoy the evening breeze.

The scent of roses drifting over his neighbor's fence

reminded him of Rae. He wondered where she was at that moment and if she might be thinking about him.

A text message came in and then another. The deputies he had watching Dylan Moody and Lauren Cavanaugh reported in. Everything was quiet. A third ping sounded. It was Rae.

Can't sleep. You still up?

His thumbs hovered before he responded. Yeah. Can't sleep, either.

Come over.

I don't know if that's a good idea.

Come over, Tom.

He rotated his thumbs while he considered the invitation. Then he put away the phone without responding and got up to go inside.

RAE WATCHED FROM the window as Tom pulled to the curb. She waited until he got out of his vehicle and then she turned on the porch light and opened the front door. He was already halfway up the sidewalk by the time she came out to greet him. He paused with one foot on the bottom step, gazing up at her.

Emotions flitted like moths—doubts swarmed. She wondered what Tom saw when he looked at her that way. A lonely, desperate woman? He wasn't wrong. Not tonight. She'd taken care with her appearance. Styled her hair and put on a dress. Maybe she was trying too hard, and wasn't that the very definition of desperate?

He looked just right. Faded jeans, unkempt hair. Shirt only partially buttoned and untucked. So not desperate.

Slowly he climbed the steps. When he got to the top, he reached for her, drawing her into his arms, kissing her back into the house and closing the front door with his foot. Rae leaned against the wall, breathing heavily, as she toyed with his buttons.

"I didn't know if you'd come," she said.

"You knew." He smiled down at her in that way he had.

Rae slid her arms around his neck and drew him to her. "I knew."

THEY WERE IN her bedroom. Tom sat on the edge of the bed as Rae moved around the room, opening windows to the night breeze. She looked ethereal in the moonlight with gossamer curtains billowing all around her. "I smell rain."

"Storm's coming," Tom said. "Not for hours, though."

"Too bad. I like all that thunder and lightning." She lit a candle. The flame danced wildly in the breeze. Music came next and then her dress. She unzipped it slowly, letting it fall from her shoulders and puddle at her feet before she stepped out of it. She wore an old-fashioned slip, lacy and slinky, and Tom thought if he lived to be a hundred he might never again see anything so sexy.

She put out her hand and he took it, letting her draw him to his feet. She melted in his arms and they slow-danced with the shadows. He moved his hands over her back, pressing her into him, and then he tucked aside her hair to kiss her neck.

Her head fell back and she sighed dreamily. She seemed content to savor each moment, but then his hand slid up her thigh, lifting the slip, and she shivered. Drawing away, she crawled between the sheets and lay back against the pillows as she watched him undress.

He slid into bed beside her, pulling her close, kissing and stroking until she was damp and trembling. Then she took him in her hand and her mouth, and Tom thought he might have truly died and gone to heaven.

Pressing her back against the pillows, he pushed up the slip and entered her slowly as the night breeze tangled the curtains. She arched her back on a moan. He moved deeper. Deliberately rhythmic as if they were still dancing. She became frantic, digging her nails into his back as she wrapped her legs around his waist. Lifting her hands above her head, Tom paused to kiss her lips, her mouth, her breasts before he rolled them, so that she rose over him and took the lead.

On and on they moved. Kissing and straining and finally shuddering into a powerful release. Tom wrapped his arms around her quivering body and held her close.

WARM WATER SLOSHED across his naked body as Rae settled back against him in the tub. She'd lit candles again. He would never have thought of her as a romantic. She'd always seemed so pragmatic in her prickliness. But then, he would never have imagined himself as a romantic, either, and yet here he was, enjoying wine and a candlelit bath as music drifted in from the other room.

He slid down deeper in the water. "I think I could get used to this."

"Hmm. Me, too." Rae let her head loll back against his shoulder. "Better than having coffee."

"So much better."

"A week ago, would you ever have pictured us like this?"

"Not in a million years."

"It feels right, though, doesn't it? Comfortable."

Tom fidgeted as her bottom pressed into him. "I don't know about comfortable."

"Tom?"

He closed his eyes and drifted. "Yeah?"

She sat up suddenly. "Did you hear something?"

He pushed himself up and listened. "What did it sound like?"

"I don't know. The windows are still open in the bedroom. Maybe the curtains knocked over something on my dresser."

"Hopefully not a candle."

"I blew them out."

"Shush." Tom turned his head to the bedroom. Then he said against her ear, "Wait here."

He rose and stepped out of the tub, reaching for a towel as he moved toward the door.

"Tom." He glanced back where she sat shivering on the edge of the tub. She spoke softly so that only he could hear her above the music. "The pistol I had earlier is in the nightstand drawer."

"Which side?"

She motioned to his right. He nodded and turned back to the door, letting his gaze roam into all the shadowy corners before he entered the bedroom. Easing open the nightstand drawer, he removed the pistol and then pulled on his jeans. Barefoot and shirtless, he slipped across the room and out into the hallway. The music followed him all the way to the stairs. Before he started down, he glanced over his shoulder to make sure Rae hadn't followed him.

Tom wasn't a kid anymore. He had no excuse. He was

a trained law enforcement officer and had been for the past ten years. Yet he never saw it coming.

The last thing he remembered before the shot rang out was the sound of Rae's scream.

Chapter Fifteen

When Rae awakened, she found herself prone on a cold stone floor. She thought at first she'd collapsed in her bathroom. But the room she found herself in was pitch-black and the air smelled fusty, like the place had been closed up too long. She tried to sit up, but a wave of nausea crashed over her. Groaning, she fell back to the floor and drew her knees up to her chest, lying motionless with her cheek against the stone until the sickness passed and the cobwebs began to clear.

She remembered hearing a gunshot somewhere in the house and then a scream. Her own, she thought. She'd gone into the bedroom to check the nightstand. The pistol was missing. Tom must have taken it. Where was he now? She strained to remember. In her mind's eye, she saw herself picking up her dress from the floor, sliding it over her shoulders as she moved into the hallway, easing on bare feet to the banister to glance downstairs. Tom lay in the foyer in a pool of blood.

Rushing down the steps, Rae had dropped to her knees beside him. Unresponsive. No pulse. Oh, God, where was her phone? She ran back upstairs to the bedroom. Her cell wasn't on the nightstand where she always left it. She turned to scan the dresser and that was when she saw something in the mirror. A silhouette coming up behind her. She screamed and turned to fight him off, but an arm came around her, holding her close while a rag was stuffed against her mouth and nose. Her head spun. Her legs grew weak.

And now here she was in a damp, dark place…

Panic welled and for a moment Rae couldn't breathe from the fear clogging her throat. She pushed herself up, forcing back her terror as she glanced around. She could see nothing, hear nothing. She had no idea where she was.

She scrambled to her feet and shuffled forward until her extended arms made contact with a wall. Then she walked all around the room, running her hands over the stone surface until she was certain she'd explored every inch. No door. No window. No way out.

Pressing her back to the wall, she slid down to the floor and buried her face in her hands. Fear came in choking sobs. Dread tightened her lungs. Was this what Riley had experienced before she died, this paralyzing terror? *My poor little sister. My poor, sweet girl.*

Somehow the thought of Riley spurred Rae and she got to her feet, walking the room again and again searching for a way out. After a while, she started to scream. On and on until she grew hoarse and exhaustion claimed her. She dropped to the floor, throat raw and fingers bloody from scratching at the walls.

Drawing up her knees, she let herself drift into a deep lethargy. It was the only way she knew to preserve her sanity.

TOM HATED BEING so helpless. Even pushing himself up against the pillows brought a jagged pain and a wave of dizziness. He put a hand to his bandaged side and winced.

"Take it easy," Craig Jarvis advised. "You've only been out of surgery a few hours. You're lucky the bullet passed right through, but it'll still take a few days before you're back on your feet."

Tom lay back, breathing hard. He didn't feel so lucky. "Rae may not have a few days. I need to get out of here now."

"I've got every available deputy out there looking for her," Craig said. "We'll find her."

"You don't know that."

"Look, the kidnappers still want that money and we're coordinating with the family. As soon as they call, we'll arrange a swap."

"Assuming that's why she was taken."

"Why else?"

Tom turned his head to the window. "I don't know. This seems like something different."

"Different how?"

"That's what I've been lying here trying to figure out." He reached for the water beside his bed. Raising his head to take a sip exhausted him. "I need to get out of here."

"You need to rest. I'll keep you posted every step of the way. You have my word on that."

After Craig left, Tom managed to sit up, but he couldn't muster the strength to swing his legs over the side of the bed. His clothes must be around here somewhere. If he could just get to his feet—

A phone buzzed. He looked around in confusion until he spotted his cell on the bedside table. Craig must have brought it to him. Or maybe he'd had it in his pocket when they brought him in.

He reached for the phone and lifted it to his ear. "Brannon."

"I know where she is, Sheriff."

His pulse jumped. "Who is this?"

"I saw where they took her. If you want to see her alive, you'll do exactly as I say."

AS IMPOSSIBLE AS it seemed, Rae had almost managed to doze off when a scraping sound awakened her. She lifted her head from her knees and glanced around her darkened surroundings. What was that? Sounded like something heavy being dragged across stone.

She lifted her gaze to the noise. To her amazement, a crack appeared in the ceiling, allowing dim light to filter down into her prison. The opening grew wider and a face appeared.

Rae jumped to her feet, pressing back against the wall. "Who are you? What do you want with me?"

"Move back," a voice ordered.

A wooden ladder dropped down, almost clipping Rae's shoulder before she stumbled out of the way.

The face appeared above her again. "Come on!"

Rae went over to the ladder and stared up into the light. "Dylan?"

"Hurry! He's coming back and I don't know how soon help will arrive."

"Who?" Rae tested the rungs and then started to climb. "Who's coming back?"

Dylan grabbed her wrists and hoisted her through the opening. "You don't know where you are, do you?"

She glanced around. They were in a barn. She could smell hay and motor oil. A welcome aroma to the dank air of her underground prison.

"That Fenton dude brought you here," Dylan said. "This is his barn."

The name shocked Rae, though she didn't know why. Hadn't Tom been suspicious of Blaine all along?

"How did you find me?"

"I've been watching him. After Sophie was taken, I started noticing things. Remembering things. Like how I saw him hanging around outside her house once. Like how he would sometimes come into the Corner Café and just stare at us while we ate."

"Why didn't you tell the police?"

"You think they'd believe someone like me? They tried to pin everything on me. I've had cops on my tail ever since I got out of jail. As soon as I managed to shake them, I came out here to look for proof."

"That was dangerous."

"I guess. But I wasn't going to let him take Sophie again. When I heard you were missing, I figured he'd have you someplace close. That's when I found the trapdoor. I think they must have built the barn over an old storm cellar. No one would ever have thought to look for you down there."

"Except you." She caught his arm. "What about Tom? Sheriff Brannon?"

Before Dylan could answer, the sound of a four-wheeler caught his attention. He swore under his breath. "He's back."

"We should make a run for it," Rae said.

"No time. We'll have to hide and hope that he doesn't check the cellar." He kicked the ladder down into the hole, shoved the cover back into place and spread a little hay over the entrance. He nodded to the loft as he got to his feet. "Up there!"

"What about you?"

"Just go!"

Rae scrambled up into the loft and flattened herself against the floor so that she could peer down through the cracks. Blaine Fenton strode into the barn a few moments later. He put aside his shotgun and then lifted his head to scan the cavernous interior as if sensing something amiss. From her vantage, Rae couldn't see Dylan. She hoped that he was well hidden. Hoped they both managed to make it out of the barn alive. To think that a man she'd once planned to marry had become a cold-blooded killer…

She wouldn't think about that now. *Keep calm. Keep quiet. Please, please let him move on.*

Instead, he moved deeper into the barn, heading straight for the cellar. As soon as he found her missing, he'd search the place from top to bottom. He'd find Dylan's hiding place and then he'd come looking for her in the loft…

A car engine sounded outside and then a door slammed. Fenton reversed course and headed back to the front of the barn, grabbing his shotgun before he opened the door to peer out.

SOMEHOW, TOM HAD managed to get up from bed, dress and make his way down to the lobby of the hospital, where he called Billy Navarro to come and pick him up. The rookie gave him an uneasy look as he climbed into the car.

"Sheriff, you don't look so good."

"I'll be fine. I need to get to my vehicle." He gave the officer directions to Rae's house, where he'd left his SUV. Then he said, "And here's what I need you to do."

A few minutes later, he was headed out of town, deep into the piney forest. Backup was on the way, but none of his officers had had time to study a map of the rural area the way Tom had. They didn't know the back roads. He drove as close to the ranch as he dared and then got out to go the rest of the way on foot.

The effort put too much strain on his stitches. By the

time he had the barn in sight, the wound had begun to bleed. He ignored the pain and kept going. His plan had been to find a side or back entrance into the barn and lie low until help arrived. But his strength ebbed, and his head had begun to swim. He took another step, faltered and then pitched forward to the ground.

BLAINE FENTON BACKED away from the entrance as the newcomer stepped inside. Rae tried to position herself so that she could see them through the cracks. A voice rose, chillingly familiar, and she had to suppress a gasp. A wave of terror washed over and then a sick realization. *No. Please, no.*

Below, her brother said urgently, "I've changed my mind. I want to call it off."

"Don't be stupid," Fenton retorted. "It's too late to call anything off."

Jackson said in a hushed voice, "You mean—"

"I mean we have a deal and I'm holding you to it. Now isn't the time to get cold feet."

Jackson tossed the backpack to the floor at Fenton's feet. "Take the money. You earned it. A million dollars will get you a long way from Belle Pointe. I never want to see you around here again."

"Damn right I earned it. But I'm not leaving town. Not yet. The cops would be all over me."

"Then stay. I don't care. Just let her go."

Blaine moved slowly toward him, his arms extended in supplication. "Let's just talk this through," he said in a placating tone. "Think back to when you first came to see me. You were worried about the business, remember? You said your old man was going to replace you as CEO. He was talking about cutting you out of his will, too, and leaving everything to your sister. Has that changed?"

"No," Jackson admitted.

"If I let her go, you lose everything."

Her brother fell silent. "How will you do it?"

"You leave that to me."

"It needs to be quick. I don't want her to suffer."

"She won't feel a thing. She'll just disappear and no one will ever find a trace. In a few months, the strain will get to your old man. I'd be surprised if he lasts another six months after this. All you need is a little more patience and then everything you ever wanted will be yours."

Rae lay motionless, but inside her heart flailed as her mind raced. Her own brother wanted her dead. He'd hired Blaine Fenton, her ex-fiancé, to kill her. The ransom money was to be his payment. It was never about Sophie. Rae had been the target all along.

A few bits of hay drifted down through the cracks. Jackson held out his hand and caught one between his fingers, then slowly lifted his gaze to the loft.

"Someone's up there."

Fenton glanced up, too, and then, pumping the shotgun, he started up the steps. Rae glanced around, searching for a weapon or a way out.

Then she heard Dylan call out. "Hey, over here!"

The footsteps paused. Rae heard a shuffling sound, and then the sound of a shotgun blast reverberated through the barn. Fenton pumped the weapon and fired again.

Rae leaped to the top of the steps. "Stop it! I'm the one you want!"

Fenton lifted his head with a smile. "Nothing personal, Rae, but a deal is a deal." He lifted the shotgun.

"Freeze!"

Fenton turned. Rae turned. She stared in astonishment

as Tom stumbled forward and took aim, steadying one hand over the other.

"Lower your weapon," he ordered.

Fenton hesitated for a split second before he spun and fired. Tom fired back. For a moment, the barn seemed to explode. When the dust cleared, Rae saw the bloom of blood on Fenton's shirt before he tumbled backward down the steps.

Tom called out to her. "Rae! You okay?"

"I'm okay. Where's Dylan?"

"I'm here. I'm fine. He didn't touch me."

Jackson stood frozen. His gaze went from Fenton to Rae, and for a moment, their gazes clung. Then he picked up the backpack and ran.

Rae wondered why Tom didn't stop him, but then she saw that he had dropped to his knees. The gun fell from his hand. Before she could reach him, he collapsed to the floor without a sound.

"Tom!"

Dylan came out of his hidey-hole. "Is he dead?"

Together they rolled him over. His eyes fluttered open. Rae let out a ragged breath as sirens sounded outside the barn.

Chapter Sixteen

It was Tom's first day back at work. A month was too long for any man to remain idle, but he hadn't exactly been lolling away the hours on vacation. Physical therapy had been a beast. There were days when Tom had wondered if his life would ever return to normal, but Rae had been there to encourage his recovery. *Don't push yourself. For God's sake, take it easy for a change.*

She stopped by every day to check on him and spent most of her nights at his house. She cooked, cleaned and ran errands. Saw to his medicine and doctor's appointments. This on top of her duties as the new CEO of Cavanaugh Industries. Sometimes Tom felt as if they were an old married couple. He didn't mind that feeling.

He sat in a back booth at the Corner Café and watched as she crossed the street. She wore a suit and heels today. Her hair was pulled back in a bun. She looked capable and efficient. A woman ready to take on the world. Tom found himself thinking about that lace slip. He admired the all-business Rae, but he pined for the other Rae.

Reaching into his pocket, he ran a hand over a velvet jewelry box. Tom didn't know what had come over him. He wasn't an impetuous man. It was way too soon to even think about anything permanent, and yet there he sat with a ring in his pocket. He thumbed open the box and admired the sparkle of the diamond beneath the table. Too soon. Way too soon.

She came through the door and he quickly slipped the box beneath his napkin. Sliding into the booth across from him, she gave a weary sigh. "What a day."

"Trouble at work?" Tom motioned for coffee.

"It's always something. I thought I would like being in charge, but I miss the days when I could hide out in my office surrounded by numbers."

"You could always resign," Tom said.

"Maybe I will one of these days." But they both knew she wouldn't. Her family, what was left of it, depended on her. The last Tom had heard, Lauren was divorcing Jackson and selling the house and Sophie had moved in with her grandfather. Rae was the glue holding it all together.

"I have some news," he said.

She looked up from her coffee. "Bad news?"

"I guess that depends on your perspective. Jackson may have been spotted in Costa Rica. It could be just a rumor, but I've asked a buddy down there to check it out."

"What happens if they find him?"

"He'll be arrested and brought back home to face charges."

She stared down into her coffee. "I still find it hard to accept that my own brother tried to have me killed. We've always had a difficult relationship, but what did I do to make him hate me so badly?"

"That's not on you, Rae. Don't take on his guilt."

"I guess." She glanced out the window with a frown. "Jackson's gone. Riley and Mom are gone. Dad's getting frailer by the day. Soon it'll just be Sophie and me. Thank God, she has Dylan. What a hero he's turned out to be."

"People will occasionally surprise you," Tom said.

"You do that all the time."

He scoffed. “I’m no hero. I managed to get myself ambushed and shot.”

“And yet you still saved the day.” Rae reached for his hand. “Funny how things turn out sometimes.”

“Isn’t it?” He toyed with the napkin.

Rae’s gaze sharpened. “What’s that?”

“I need to ask you something. But I think I already know the answer.”

“What is it?”

He slid the box across the table with the tip of his finger. She gazed down and then up in astonishment. “Tom, I don’t—”

“I know. It’s too soon. A month ago, you still hated me.” He squeezed her fingers. “But life’s short, Rae. No one knows that better than we do.”

She opened the box and took a peek inside. Then she snapped the lid closed and put a hand to her heart.

Tom gazed into her flooded eyes. “Don’t say anything. I’ll take the ring back and next time I’ll do it the right way. Flowers, candles, down on my knees. I’m not the most romantic person. I don’t know how to go about these things.”

She rose and leaned over the table to kiss him. “Yes,” she whispered against his lips.

A few people sitting nearby clapped. Someone whistled. Rae laughed at Tom’s discomfit and kissed him again.

* * * * *

COLTON'S LAST STAND

KAREN WHIDDON

Once again, this book is for my husband, Lonnie.
He eagerly awaits each book release and
reads every single one. I'm so happy to have
him in my corner always.

Chapter One

For the first time in her life, undercover FBI agent Fiona Evans truly understood how someone became indoctrinated into a cult. Ever since arriving at the Affirmative Alliance Group center, she'd been bombarded by a relentless onslaught of information, all presented in such a smiling, feel-good, we-only-want-the-best-for-you way that she felt guilty asking for a break. There were seminars and classes, films and audio recordings that were piped into her room at night under the guise of helping her learn while she slept. The other members, so earnestly pleasant and cheerful, were supportive, telling her over and over again that they—and AAG's founder, Micheline Anderson—only wanted to help her become the best person she could possibly be.

Luckily, Fiona considered herself strong and capable, well trained and not the slightest bit susceptible to either criticism or brainwashing. If she weren't, even she might have bought in to the relentless indoctrination of nonsense by AAG.

Teeth aching from all the saccharine, Fiona smiled and nodded and pretended until she thought she would scream, which she did sometimes inside her head while smiling back at them.

Even Micheline, a woman Fiona thought of privately as the cult's supreme ruler, went out of her way to show an interest in her group's newest arrival, sending a personal note of welcome along with fresh flowers. "An honor," whispered Leigh Dennings, one of Micheline's protégées. "So rare. True proof of how special you are."

With difficulty, Fiona kept from snorting at that. Gullible she wasn't, though she definitely wanted Leigh and the others to believe she was. In fact, she'd taken great care to make sure she appeared to be exactly the kind of vulnerable person they sought out as recruits. They'd found her, destitute and alone, on the streets of Mustang Valley, asking where she might find a shelter to get a free meal.

Instead, one of the AAG members had found her and taken her to its lovely and welcoming center, ten miles from downtown Mustang Valley. It had a long, tree-lined dirt drive leading in from the main road, an always open, hunter-green gate, and big potted plants in front. Fiona had stared at the woodsy, yet fancy log cabin exterior, large triangular roof over two sprawling stories, before being led into the large, open lobby. She'd been served complimentary beverages and a light lunch and told someone would be out to speak with her soon.

Affirmative Alliance Group had been founded forty years ago by Micheline Anderson, formerly known as Luella Smith. Ever since the FBI had been given an anonymous tip hinting Micheline's involvement in numerous crimes, including money laundering, they'd researched her. A gifted nurse, Micheline promoted herself as a healer and self-help guru. These days, her followers numbered in the hundreds of thousands, most of those via the internet. Locally, members were only in the hundreds, most of those living in their own homes. Only about twenty people lived in the AAG center full-time, mostly Micheline and her inner circle as well as new recruits who were in the process of being converted.

Like me, Fiona thought grimly. She'd bear it—she had to. As long as she kept her eyes on the big picture, the reason she'd come here, she would survive.

Trying to grab some alone time, Fiona hurried from the crowded room where she'd just attended yet another seminar on becoming your best you—or some variation thereof—and rushed toward the ladies' room. She'd learned early on that around here, the only place they'd leave you alone was either in the shower or the toilet.

Just as she reached the door, someone grabbed her arm.

"I've been looking for you!" Leigh gushed. "You're not going to believe who asked about you."

With difficulty, Fiona kept from rolling her eyes. "Micheline?" she guessed.

Clearly astonished, Leigh giggled. "Wow, you *are* amazing. Smart as well as lovely. Come with me. Micheline asked me to bring you around to talk with her."

Though Fiona actually considered refusing, she reminded herself of her task and nodded. For such a petite and delicate person, Leigh kept an awfully firm grip on Fiona's arm as she steered her down a long hallway, through some double doors marked Private and into a part of the center where Fiona had never been.

Here, plush carpet softened their footsteps to a hush. Elegant mahogany tables displayed expensive-looking vases and statues, matched with clearly valuable artwork hung under muted lighting. Fiona felt as if she'd left the Old West and stepped into the corporate offices of some über-rich CEO.

Giving herself a mental shake, she made a show of gaping around her at everything all at once. Seeing, Leigh laughed, the sound like bells tinkling. "It's something else, isn't it? I remember the first time I saw it. I was overwhelmed, too."

They stopped in front of an intricately carved mahogany double door. Spine straight, like a soldier standing at attention, Leigh knocked three times, the staccato sound sharp.

"Come in." A warm voice, inviting confidences. *Micheline Anderson.* Finally. Playing the role of everyone's friend. Fiona's gut tightened. Funny, in this place, her gut was the only thing she trusted.

Stepping inside, Fiona eyed Leigh, half expecting her to bow. Instead, Leigh murmured something that sounded like, "Here you are," and turned to leave.

"Wait." With a benevolent smile, the leader of the AAG waved Leigh to a chair. "You may have a seat also, Fiona," she offered, making it sound as if Fiona actually had a choice.

"We are to have a special visitor this afternoon." Bright blue eyes sparkling, Micheline pushed back a strand of her well-coiffed blond hair. "My son, Jake. I haven't seen him for twenty-three years. I would appreciate if both of you helped in making sure he feels welcome."

Immediately, Leigh nodded. "Will do," she chirped. "If you could provide me with some sort of list of his likes and dislikes, I'll have staff get to work immediately."

Micheline's broad smile faltered. Just a tad before

she had it firmly back in place. "Honestly, I have no idea. The last time I saw him, he was only seventeen."

Fiona looked from one woman to another. "I'm sorry, but I have no idea why you wanted to talk to me."

Leigh snapped her head around to eye Fiona, her perfect brow creased in a frown. But then, so quickly Fiona wasn't sure if she might have imagined it, Leigh smoothed her expression in a return to the ever-pleasant, eager-to-please beauty queen she was. "Patience, Fiona," she said, folding her hands neatly in her lap.

Micheline watched them interact with the same compassion that had endeared her to her followers. A slight smile curved her red-painted lips as she waited. "You're new here," she told Fiona. "Tell me, what do you think of the AAG?"

Heart skipping a beat, for a split second, Fiona found herself at a loss for words. She recovered quickly, remembering all the hours of intensive research she'd put in. "It's a bit overwhelming at times," she volunteered softly. "I can see so much happiness, so much good. I'm just not sure I could ever be worthy of belonging." There. Textbook. No doubt exactly the sort of thing Micheline had hoped she would say.

"Of course you're worthy," Micheline purred. "I see great potential in you. Which is why I'm going to assign you to my son. Show him around, keep him company while I'm in meetings, and make sure he has a good time."

"She's giving you a great honor," Leigh prodded when Fiona remained silent.

Not sure how she felt about this, Fiona pasted a smile on her face and nodded. Best to play along. "Thank you, ma'am," she stammered, hoping she appeared dazed enough. Her role was to play a grateful and zealous convert while obtaining concrete proof of even one of the crimes Micheline was suspected of being involved in. She already had substantive leads on Micheline's varied schemes, including running a fake marriage counseling center outside town, and scamming people out of money with phony self-help seminars.

Apparently, she did. Micheline leaned back in her chair, her expression satisfied. "You and Leigh will meet him when he gets here. He's driving down from northern Arizona, and I expect him sometime between two and three." With that said, she picked up a stack of papers from her desk and began reading through them, a clear dismissal.

"Come on." Leigh took Fiona's arm. "Let's go up to your room and see if we can find you something suitable to wear."

Allowing herself to be led away, Fiona glanced down at her fashionably torn jeans. "What's wrong with what I have on?" she asked.

Leigh only shook her head.

Once they reached Fiona's room on the second floor, Leigh followed her inside. "Micheline has great plans for you," she announced the moment the door closed.

Every instinct on alert, Fiona turned. "Really? What kind of plans?"

"She's grooming you to become a welcome coordinator like me, to help find people just like yourself who need help and could use the AAG's warm and welcoming family."

"Wow." Pretending to be awestruck, Fiona waited to hear the catch. One thing she'd picked up early on here was that AAG did nothing out of the simple goodness of its hearts. It was all about getting money out of its followers.

"Wow is right," Leigh gushed. "She wants you to focus on Mustang Valley College. Mainly on one particularly lonely, wealthy freshman named Theodore Royce the Third, whose money hasn't brought him happiness."

"But AAG will," Fiona finished, her tone bright, even though her stomach churned.

"Of course. He's already sought us out, attended a few seminars and talking to one of our counselors. You will take over for her." Leigh had begun riffling through Fiona's closet. "You don't have many dresses."

Fiona crossed her arms. "I'm not really a dress-up kind of person."

"Why not? You're so pretty and you have an amazing body," Leigh gushed. "Why not use that to your best advantage and show it off to prospective members? How do you think I became Miss Mustang Valley?"

Weighing her options, Fiona decided to play along. "Such an amazing accomplishment."

"It is, isn't it?" Leigh wrinkled her nose. "Now I'm going to help you. We're going to do a makeover."

"When?"

"Right now, silly." Patting the desk chair, Leigh picked up Fiona's admittedly small makeup bag and looked through it. "This won't do at all," Leigh muttered. "I'll be right back."

And she dashed off, leaving Fiona staring after her. A moment later, Leigh returned, carrying a much larger makeup case. "I want you to pay close attention to what I do," Leigh instructed her. "So that you can replicate the look on your own. I'll let you borrow some of my makeup even, since I have tons more."

As Leigh began rummaging through her stuff, Fiona put her hand on the other woman's arm to stop her. "What's the point?" she asked, honestly bewildered. "Why are you having me change the way I look?"

Batting her long—surely false—eyelashes, Leigh sighed. "To help you attract Jake, Micheline's son. No offense, but Micheline feels you might need just a little help in that department. And I agree with her."

"Attract Micheline's son?" Fiona felt as if they'd entered an alternate universe. "Why would I want to do that?"

"Because he's quite the catch, I hear." Leigh leaned closer, meeting Fiona's gaze directly. "And Micheline has given her blessing."

Ewww. Creepy. Wisely, Fiona kept these thoughts to herself. Everything Micheline Anderson did had a reason. So what hidden motive might be behind her using Fiona as bait for her son?

"You're a beautiful woman, Fiona," Leigh continued, not noticing. "But honestly, you present yourself as stern and serious and strong. Men don't like that sort of thing, you know."

Resisting the urge to gape at the other woman, Fiona widened her eyes instead. "I'm proud of being strong," she said quietly. "And any man who doesn't like that doesn't need to be hanging around me."

Her comment had Leigh giggling. "You're so funny." Even though Fiona hadn't been joking. "Now sit still and let me show you how to enhance what the universe gave you."

Fiona sighed. Why not? If this was the worst thing that happened to her while here, then she'd take it.

Though she already knew how to apply makeup, it'd be interesting to get Leigh's take.

She sat unmoving while Leigh, humming tunelessly under her breath, applied foundation, blush and powder before moving on to her eyebrows. Fiona didn't balk until Leigh came after her with a pair of spidery-looking false eyelashes.

"Please." Fiona held up her hand to ward her off. "How about we just use mascara?"

"They're magnetic," Leigh explained, as if that made all the difference in the world. "I just put a little bit of special eyeliner on you and they'd attach right to it."

"No, thank you." Keeping her tone polite, Fiona shook her head. "I have some great mascara that I'd prefer to use instead."

Leigh heaved a disappointed sigh, but she put the lashes back in a box. "Fine. You won't look as dramatic, though."

Fiona nodded. "I understand." She did suffer through letting Leigh apply three painstaking coats of mascara.

"There you are," Leigh finally cooed. "Look at yourself and see how stunning you are."

Half curious, half dreading it, Fiona strolled into the bathroom to take a peek in the mirror. As soon as she caught sight of herself, she froze. Leigh was good, she had to admit. She'd used the makeup to highlight Fiona's cheekbones and make her eyes appear huge. Even her lips, painted a reddish-purple color, appeared plumper, more sensual.

In short, she didn't look like herself at all. In fact, Fiona thought, if anyone at the Bureau were to see her like this, she'd get laughed out of the building. But thankfully, she wasn't in the office—she was undercover.

No one would see, she reminded herself, willing her heart rate to slow. Since here she'd been playing a role, she might as well embrace a new look along with it.

"Well?" Leigh demanded, poking her head in the door. "What do you think?"

"I love it!" Fiona enthused. "I don't even recognize my face. You're amazing."

Leigh smiled at the compliment. "See, I told you with a little work you'd be gorgeous. Now all you have to do is get Jake Anderson to look at you and he's a goner."

"I see." Though Fiona didn't. "I'm still not sure—"

"Failure is not an option," Leigh cut her off, her normally breezy tone turning emphatic. "I need you to get super close to him, as close as possible." Unexpectedly, she pulled Fiona in for a hug. "And then since we're BFFs now, you can tell me everything about it."

Fiona hugged her back, pretending to be hugely grateful for the other woman's friendship. Her cover had just gotten even more perfect. "Of course I will. You don't know how long it's been since I had a real friend."

Leigh's bright blue eyes got a little misty at that. Either she was a master actress, or her emotions were easily swayed. "I'll always be here for you, girlfriend," she declared. "Now let's go downstairs and wait for Micheline's son to arrive."

BATTLING A STRANGE mixture of anger, hope and frustration, Jake Anderson finally turned onto the long driveway leading to the AAG center. He hadn't seen his mother in over two decades, and really hadn't cared to. Now, at forty years old, part of him couldn't help but wonder if his seventeen-year-old self's perception of her might have been slightly tainted by his youth.

Nah, he didn't think so. Micheline Anderson might be beloved by her thousands of followers, but inside she was a monster to the core.

And, if she was to be believed, now dying of some rare form of fatal cancer. Somehow, she'd tracked him down and called him, tearfully begging him to come see her so they could reconcile before she left this earth. What kind of a man would he be to deny the woman who'd given birth to him his presence in the last moments of her life?

The sad thing was, he didn't believe her. From his earliest recollection, his mother had done nothing but lie.

When he'd escaped her clutches right after graduating high school early, he hadn't bothered to change his name, since Jake Anderson seemed so common. He'd worked hard, managed to erase the scars of his past and built a life for himself. After putting in several years as a ranch foreman, he was now the proud owner of a small but growing property of his own, a couple hours north of Mustang Valley.

He didn't know what Micheline had planned, but he knew for certain he wanted no part of it. He'd go visit her, stay a couple days and get out. Hopefully untouched and unscarred.

Pulling up to the building, he parked and got out of his truck. Though he'd seen photographs of the place in a few newspapers, he allowed himself to admire its clean, woodsy lines. Welcoming and neat, the renovated ranch house seemed the perfect place to allow Micheline to ply her trade.

None of his business, he reminded himself. Still, every fiber of his being clenched in dread as he forced himself to walk through the front door.

Blinking at the change in light, he suddenly came face-to-face with the most beautiful woman he'd ever met. Wide, dark eyes met his, and a graceful hand came up to push back silky black hair away from her face. He couldn't help but let his gaze roam, from her slender shoulders to her full bust and narrow waist.

"Excuse me," she said, her voice throaty and sexy as hell. "Can I help you?"

"Yes." He managed to rapidly collect his wayward thoughts. "Sorry. I'm Jake Anderson. I'm here to see Micheline." Damned if he could bring himself to call her his mother.

She blinked and extended her hand. "Oh. Welcome. I'm Fiona Smith." She used her fake name rather than real since AAG had tech experts. "I was asked to show you around until Micheline's schedule clears enough so she can see you."

Figured. He suppressed a flash of resentment. Micheline couldn't even bother to make sure her afternoon was open enough to see her own son.

For a moment, he seriously considered turning around, getting back into his truck and heading home.

But then Fiona took his arm and leaned close, bringing a tantalizing feminine scent with her. "Please," she whispered, distress shining in her eyes. "I'm new here. Showing you around is the first task I've ever been given. I don't want to fail at it."

What could he do but go with her? Still, she might be attractive, but what kind of person could she be if she belonged to his mother's cult?

She led him down a long hall into a large room dominated by a huge stone fireplace. A fire blazed cheerfully, despite the relative warmth of the Arizona day.

People were seated on various couches or at tables, some reading, a few talking, and he even saw one or two playing a board game or doing a puzzle. Almost, he thought, as if he stood in the lobby of some fancy hotel.

He eyed them as he passed, trying for casual but wondering if he'd be able to see something on their faces or in their eyes that might reveal what had made them ripe for Micheline's indoctrination. When Jake had been younger, she'd talked about someday starting her own church. In fact, she'd managed to create her own group of followers.

He wanted no part of it.

Fiona continued on, her hips swaying as she led him to a door on the far side of the huge room. Just as they reached it, an overly made-up young blonde woman rushed over.

"Hello there," she murmured, looking him up and down, her predatory manner reminding him so much of the way his mother used to act that he nearly took a step back. "I'm Leigh Dennings, a welcome coordinator here at the AAG. And the reigning Miss Mustang Valley," she chirped.

Not sure how to respond to that, he settled on "Congratulations."

"Thank you." She smiled sweetly at him before turning her attention to Fiona. "If you need anything, anything at all, just ask someone at the reception desk to call me and I'll be right there."

Fiona nodded. "Will do." She checked her watch. "Do you have any idea what time Micheline will be available?"

Good question. Eyeing Fiona, Jake waited to hear her answer.

Leigh shrugged. "I know she's booked solid all afternoon. I'm sure she'll be out here as soon as she can."

"You know what?" Jake decided he'd had enough. "Take me to her. Right now."

"I… I don't think she'd appreciate me doing that," Leigh stammered, eyeing him as if he'd suddenly sprouted a pair of horns and a tail. Fiona, on the other hand, looked at him with what he'd swear was approval. In fact, she appeared to be struggling not to laugh.

"I don't care," he told Leigh. "Not only is she the one who called and asked to see me, but it's been years. If today is not a good day, then I'll be heading home and you can tell her if she really wants to see me, she's welcome to make the drive to my place." Which he knew she'd never do in a million years. Micheline preferred to remain in her place of power.

Still staring, Leigh finally nodded. "Give me five minutes," she said and then rushed off.

Both he and Fiona watched her go.

"I take it your relationship with your mom is strained," Fiona drawled. She sounded completely different than the nervous, uncertain acolyte she'd resembled a few minutes ago. Was it because Leigh was gone?

"Strained doesn't even begin to describe it," he replied, flashing her a sideways grin.

Her dark eyes widened, and then she grinned right back at him. "I like you." She jerked her thumb over her shoulder. "Here comes Micheline. Give 'em hell, cowboy."

Stunned, he barely managed to collect himself in time to turn and watch as his mother barreled toward him, her high heels clicking on the wood floor.

"My boy," Micheline boomed, causing more than a

few heads to turn. She held out her arms, clearly expecting him to rush into them.

Since he didn't want to cause a scene, though he stayed in place, he allowed her to hug him, hoping the grimace on his face looked more like a smile than it felt.

"Let me look at you." Pulling back, Micheline made a show of pretending to take in every detail of his appearance. "Wow, son. Forty sure looks good on you." The slight edge in her voice told him how little she liked the idea of having a child so old.

Already bored, Jake thanked her. "Is there somewhere private we can go and talk?" he asked.

To his disbelief, she actually checked her watch, a flashy designer thing that cost more than several head of cattle. "I don't live too far from here," she mused, considering. "But I've got a magazine crew arriving in thirty minutes to do a photoshoot and feature on me for *Mindful Living* magazine." She shook her head, sending her artfully styled blond hair swinging around her perfectly made-up face. "I know." She brightened. "We can chat in my office."

Chat. He'd driven all this way so she could squeeze out thirty minutes to chat with him.

"Follow me." Without waiting to see if he would, Micheline spun around and marched off in the direction from which she'd come. Leigh trailed along after her.

Fiona put her hand on his arm, as if she understood exactly what he was thinking. "I don't know what's going on here," she said. "But maybe it wouldn't hurt to give her a shot."

Jaw clenched, he nodded.

When they reached Micheline's office, the double mahogany doors were wide-open. Jake stared as he realized several other people were already there. In addition to his mother, Leigh and Fiona, a big blond guy with a crew cut and a physique that screamed *bodyguard* stood with his arms folded.

Moving with all the grace of a queen, Micheline sailed around to the other side of her massive desk and settled herself in her luxurious leather chair. "Have a seat, Jake," she said. "And then we'll talk."

Instead, Jake took his time looking around the room, taking care to make eye contact with every single one of them. "Could we have some privacy?" he asked the room at large.

Fiona actually took a step toward the door before apparently realizing no one else had moved. They all looked to Micheline, clearly waiting for her approval.

An expression of shock crossed her face. But then she slowly nodded. "Everyone out."

"Even me?" the muscular guy asked.

"Yes, Bart," Micheline said, smiling. "You can stand guard outside my door." She looked at Jake, one perfectly shaped brow raised. "He's my bodyguard."

"I figured."

As soon as the door closed, Micheline came around the desk and took Jake's arm. He didn't jerk away, but he felt himself tense up even though he knew better than to show any weakness around her. He let her lead him over to a small, overstuffed couch in a little sitting area to one side of her office.

"Sit." She patted the space next to her. "When I'm gone, all of this will be yours."

He didn't bother to hide his distaste. "I don't want it. Any of it. Micheline—" damned if he'd call her *Mom* or *Mother* "—you said you were dying."

"Yes." She looked down, hands twisting in her lap. "Stage-three bone cancer. I'm not sure how much time I have left."

"Tell me about your treatment," he asked. "I assume you're doing chemo and some sort of radiation?"

Grimacing with distaste, she waved her hand. "I don't want to talk about any of that right now. We'll have plenty of time for that later. How long are you staying?"

He didn't have the heart to tell her he had planned on heading home in the morning. The less time he spent under her roof, the better. The things he'd witnessed her do to others when he'd been a boy still made him shudder. He'd seen her order beatings when someone defied her and once, he seriously wondered if he might have witnessed her disposing of a body she'd murdered. As for himself, he guessed he'd been lucky that she'd pretended he didn't exist.

"I'm not sure," he replied instead. "I definitely don't want to intrude on your busy schedule." Said without even a hint of sarcasm.

Micheline's expressive face fell. "I have so much to make up for with you," she mused. "Before…you know." She waved her hand vaguely.

By that, he deduced that she didn't want her assistants, or whatever they were, to know about her cancer. None of his business, he thought. "The question is," he said, deciding to be blunt, "are you going to have time? It's clear you're insanely busy."

Eyes narrowing slightly, she regarded him. While he waited for her answer, part of him wished she'd just dismiss him and let him go. Another part, a tiny kernel of the child he'd once been, hoped she'd put him first for once.

"Can you give me a couple of days?" Micheline pleaded. "Too many people depend on me for me to just drop everything. If I can tie up some loose ends and delegate a few things, I'll be free to spend a day or two with you. Will that work?"

This from a woman who hadn't ever seemed to care if her own son was lonely. And when he'd craved a father figure, she'd told him coldly that she had no idea who his father had been.

"We'll give it a shot," he responded, his expression as neutral as his voice. "I've got people taking care of my livestock. Let's play it by ear and see how it pans out."

Was that surprise that flashed across his mother's face? Surely not, especially when she let out a cry of pure joy and wrapped him in a hug. "Thank you, Jake. Thank you. I promise you won't regret it."

He couldn't shake the feeling she was playing a part. But then again, what did he know? He hadn't seen her in years. Maybe she'd changed. Doubtful, but who knew?

Micheline released him, pressing a button on a walkie-talkie on her waist and summoning Fiona and Leigh back in. A moment later, the door opened and the two women entered. Micheline turned to Fiona and smoothed her face into a benevolent look. "I'm entrusting him into your care," she said, patting the younger woman on the shoulder. "Looking after Jake is to be your only task while he's here, and he's to want for nothing, you hear?"

Slowly, Fiona nodded. "Yes, ma'am."

Micheline and Leigh exchanged a look. Jake wasn't sure what it meant, but it clearly made Fiona uncomfortable.

"Are you all right with that, Jake?" Micheline asked.

Glancing up, he saw both Fiona and Leigh watched him expectantly. He had no idea why it mattered, but he suddenly didn't want Fiona to think him heartless.

"That's fine," he replied.

"Perfect. Fiona, be your best you and take good care of my son," Micheline reiterated, taking Leigh's arm and sailing away.

Chapter Two

Be your best you. AAG's stock phrase and one of many catchy little sound bites Micheline fed like pap to her followers. They set Fiona's nerves on edge. She swallowed, willing away her embarrassment and hoping Jake didn't pick up on his mother's underlying message. Did Micheline and Leigh seriously think she'd fall into bed with Jake simply because the head of AAG wished it?

Undercover while undercover could be a tricky thing.

Luckily, Jake appeared to be oblivious. He watched his mother go, his hard expression at odds with the hurt she could swear she saw briefly flit in his gaze. His broad shoulders and narrow waist filled out his western shirt well and the way his brown hair had started graying at the temples gave him a look of distinction. But his compelling blue eyes were what attracted her the most. Despite his guarded manner, they glowed with warmth.

"What now?" he asked, noticing her staring.

Improvising, since she truly had no idea, Fiona figured she'd first need to find him a place to stay. "Let me get you a room. I imagine you need some time to freshen up after your long drive."

"That sounds great." Jake glanced around. "Will I be staying here or somewhere else?"

Crud. Though Fiona had hoped she would, Micheline hadn't mentioned letting him stay in her house. Despite decreeing that he'd be bunking in the center, Fiona couldn't imagine a mother wanting her son to stay elsewhere. Still, she knew better than to offer up something that might be wrong. "As far as I know, you'll be staying here with us. But let me check with Leigh. She's one of Micheline's right-hand people."

He nodded. "Thanks."

Fiona fingered the walkie-talkie Leigh had given her earlier. Taking a deep breath, she thumbed the unit on, bringing it up to her mouth and murmuring Leigh's name.

"On my way," Leigh said. A moment later, she appeared, striding through the room with her usual exuberant self-confidence. Her silky blond hair gleamed, and her long, perfectly toned legs flashed beneath the hem of her short skirt.

When she reached them, Leigh flashed Jake a flirty smile before turning her attention to Fiona. "How can I help?"

Tamping down an irrational flash of jealously, Fiona briefly wondered why Micheline hadn't chosen Leigh to fix up with her son. This thought stung so badly that Fiona wondered at herself. He might be handsome as all get out, but her job came first. Centering herself, Fiona managed a smile. "Since Jake is going to be staying a few days, I thought I'd find out where he's—"

"I've had a room prepared for him," Leigh interrupted with a small laugh. "Right across the hall from yours, as a matter of fact."

It took an effort, but Fiona managed to appear happy about that news. A quick look at Jake reassured her that he didn't appear to notice Leigh's innuendo. Thank goodness, because the last thing Fiona needed was fighting off a man who believed he was entitled to anything solely due to being Micheline's son, even if he really wasn't.

Though so far, Jake seemed the opposite. Almost as if he too saw through all the BS. Nah. She knew better than to make quick assumptions about anyone, most particularly someone related to this cult.

"Here," Leigh chirped, batting her false eyelashes. "Take this." She handed Fiona a one-hundred-dollar bill and a card key similar to the room keys used by hotels. "The two of you go out to dinner tonight, on Micheline, of course. There are several excellent restaurants nearby. Enjoy yourselves and get to know one another." She simpered prettily. "And if you need a recommendation, please let me know."

Then, with one more pointed glance at Fiona, Leigh sashayed off.

Every male in the room watched her go.

Except Jake. When Fiona looked up, she caught his gaze fixed on her. Her lips parted, and her heart skipped a beat. "What?" she asked, hating how breathless she sounded.

"I'm just wondering at the difference in my mother's choice of aides," he said, shrugging. "You and Leigh are like night and day."

If only he knew. Handing him the hundred-dollar bill, she flashed an impersonal smile. "If you follow me, I'll show you to your room."

He stared at the money as if it was tainted. "I don't want this," he said, holding it out. "Please. Take it."

Instead, she looked up at him, frowning. "Why not? Micheline is your mother. I don't feel comfortable accepting her money."

"Neither do I." Once more, he thrust the money toward her, his jaw clenched. Again, she ignored it.

With a grimace, he tossed it on the floor. Horrified, she eyed it, torn between not wanting to be wasteful but also not wanting to let him win. Finally, she couldn't stand it anymore, so she retrieved it and jammed the bill into her pocket.

"Let me show you to your room." She turned and walked away, not bothering to look behind her to make sure he followed. When she reached the second-floor hallway, she headed toward her own quarters, stopping right outside the door. Checking the room number on the card key, she saw he was indeed directly across from her. This knowledge caused her stomach to swoop alarmingly, since under any other circumstances she'd be teasing him about sneaking into each other's room.

"Here you are." She used the card to unlock and open the door. "I'm right there," she said, pointing at her door. "Knock if you need anything."

Following her inside the compact space, he looked around with interest. "Not bad. Not what I expected, but still…"

She dropped the card key and the hundred-dollar bill on the dresser. "I'll see you later," she said, her voice as stiff as her spine.

"Wait." He caught her arm. She tensed, not sure what she expected but hoping she was wrong. When she glared at him, he released her. "Sorry. But please, can we talk a minute?"

"Sure." Aware crossing her arms would be a defensive posture, she kept her hands down at her sides. "If you want to know where I want to go for dinner, it doesn't matter. I'll eat whatever you're in the mood for."

"I don't want to talk about dinner." He gestured to the room's lone chair. Once she'd taken a seat, he sat down on the edge of his bed. Elbows on his knees, he studied her.

"Why are you here?" he asked, the intensity in his voice matching his eyes. "Leigh, I can understand. But you? You seem like a levelheaded person, someone who considers her options carefully and deliberately before making a choice. What made you choose to join the AAG?"

Her cover story stuck in her throat. For whatever reason, she couldn't lie to him, this handsome man she'd just met and barely knew. Something about him… He appeared to be the first genuine person she'd met since arriving at AAG, though she really didn't know enough about him to reach that kind of a conclusion. She settled for a shrug instead of telling her story.

"You know this is a cult, right?" he continued, his expression fierce.

Making sure to act alarmed, she made a sound of indignation. "Do you truly expect me to sit here while you say bad things about AAG? Your mother is practically a saint."

He laughed at that. "You clearly don't know her, then." He held up both hands in a defensive posture as she deepened her frown. "Never mind, Fiona. I didn't mean to upset you. Forget I said anything."

She nodded, careful and cautious. Still smiling, he looked at her, rugged and masculine and the sexiest damn cowboy she'd ever met.

"I'm looking forward to having dinner with you later." He jumped to his feet, dusting his palms off on the front of his jeans. "But right now, I'm going to get my bag from my truck, shower and unpack, and maybe even take a quick nap."

Considering him, she stood. Ignoring the insistent tug of attraction she felt when she looked at him, she nodded. "I'll see you later, then," she said, her voice clear and steady.

He followed her toward the main entrance. As she turned to walk away, he called her name. "Fiona."

Her heart skipped a beat. "Yes?"

"Seven tonight?"

"I'll be ready," she said, her heart racing for absolutely no reason whatsoever.

Back in her room, she shook her head, making a face at herself in her mirror. Now was definitely not the time to be acting like a teenager with a crush. Especially since putting her and Jake together was something Micheline wanted to do. That alone made Fiona want to do the opposite.

In her five years working in the Phoenix FBI office, she'd been jockeying for a prime undercover operation like this one. She'd known in advance of coming here what kind of woman led the organization. She'd spent hours prepping, learning everything she could about Micheline Anderson and the AAG. Naturally, she'd also read quite a bit of material on Micheline's estranged son, who actually was Ace Colton.

For all intents and purposes, Jake appeared to be the

polar opposite of the woman he apparently still believed to be his mother. As if when he'd left home, he'd asked himself in every situation, what would Micheline do, and then done the exact opposite. Of course, that made sense. Jake wasn't Micheline's biological son.

He led a quiet life, running a small cattle ranch north of here. At first, Fiona had suspected Micheline had asked him to visit with the intention of bleeding him dry, but judging from bank records, every penny Jake made went right back into his ranch. He wasn't exactly flush with cash.

Unlike the head of AAG, who spent money as if there wouldn't be a tomorrow. Which explained why Micheline was behind in her personal income taxes and appeared to be struggling to juggle all her bills. She booked speaking engagements and even organized a few crowd-funding events, lining her pockets with donations, fees and contributions from people desperate to live their best lives. Despite that, she managed to stay cash poor.

Fiona planned to take her down. She wouldn't rush, she'd be careful, her methods above reproach. But she would stop her. The money laundering was bad enough, but her some of her investment schemes had bilked a lot of people out of cash.

During her training at Quantico, Fiona had learned to trust her instincts. Her gut told her that Jake wasn't involved in Micheline's scams, ongoing or pending. As far as Leigh, who appeared to honestly believe in her boss and her mission, Fiona thought the young woman might have been blinded by what she viewed as altruistic behavior. Either that, or Leigh was a very good actress.

Intelligence had indicated Micheline had something

big coming up, though no one had been able to learn what exactly it might be.

Before taking this assignment, Fiona had gone over every possible scenario with her colleague Holden St. Clair. He'd recently spent some time undercover investigating a killer who targeted beauty pageant contestants—the same beauty pageant Leigh Denning had won. He'd even fallen for, and gotten engaged to, a contestant—a distant Colton cousin named Isabella. Appearances were definitely deceiving when it came to Micheline and her people. No one had known the prodigal son would return, but she'd been prepared just in case. She hadn't expected Micheline to try and push them together or her own, visceral reaction to Jake's rugged masculinity. In the past, Fiona had been drawn to more clean-cut, law enforcement types. Jake, with his wavy brown hair and easy, relaxed attitude, seemed the exact opposite.

Cowboys had never been her type. Until now, apparently, when she needed to stay focused on her job—digging up information that would expose Micheline. Maybe it wasn't too late for some of these poor, deluded people.

At least Jake appeared levelheaded and unwilling to put up with any nonsense. Yet one more thing she liked about him.

Whatever Micheline was plotting involved Jake and, to a lesser extent, Fiona. Not for one second did Fiona believe Micheline had cancer. She'd lied to get her son to come visit, and she lied to her followers, not just seeking donations, but stripping people of their entire savings by getting them to invest in her schemes. While gathering proof of this, as well as investigating allegations of money laundering, the Bureau had been unable to find even one recent instance where Micheline had visited a doctor—any kind of physician at all. Not a general practitioner and certainly not a specialist like an oncologist.

Thinking of the Bureau had Fiona grabbing the untraceable cell phone she'd been issued when she'd taken this assignment. She had a text from Holden, saying he had news and to text back when she could talk. They'd settled on a basic sort of code in case someone else managed to get ahold of her phone. If she texted back anything but the number 1, he knew not to call.

She texted 1 and waited. A moment later, her phone rang.

"Big goings-on at Colton Oil," Holden said. "Seems Micheline paid them a little visit recently. She's still claiming she's dying from stage-three bone cancer."

"Okay." Since this wasn't news, Fiona waited. She also had to be careful what she said, just in case someone might be listening in via a hidden bug or recording device in her room.

"She told Ainsley Colton and Ace Colton about her son Jake Anderson's upcoming visit," Holden continued.

"Yes, he's here now. He got in today."

"Wow. Then things are about to get really interesting. Does he know? I mean, rumors have swirled about a Colton baby switch for months."

"He doesn't appear to know, actually," Fiona responded. "He's never mentioned anything about Micheline switching babies in the hospital when both Ace and Jake were newborns." If Micheline had done this, she might be guilty of additional crimes, too.

"That's really odd, since the entire Colton family

does, and they raised Micheline's birth son, who grew up as Ace Colton. My fiancée, Bella, has gotten closer to Marlowe throughout all of this, and of course I'm old army buddies with Spencer, and they shared this with me."

"Then what game is Micheline playing?" she asked.

"That's for you to find out," Holden replied. "How are you and Jake getting along?"

Rubbing her now aching temples, Fiona sighed. "For whatever reason, I felt an instant connection to Jake."

"Micheline instructed you to cozy up to him?"

"Yes. We're going to dinner tonight, on her."

Holden laughed, a short bark of sound. "Have fun with that. Remember, stay out of trouble."

Ending the call, Fiona stashed the phone back in her pocket. Its compact size made it almost undetectable, and she kept it on her at all times. She wouldn't put it past Micheline and her crew to periodically search her room.

Replaying the information Holden had given her, she kept circling back to Jake. Did he know? Could that possibly be the reason he'd stayed away all these years? Right then and there, she knew she had to do what Micheline had asked of her—get close to Jake and find out exactly what kind of information he had.

ALL THE WAY to his car, Jake gave himself a mental tongue lashing. Fiona Smith might be one of the most beautiful women he'd ever met, but she certainly didn't need rescuing. As an adult, she'd clearly made a conscious choice to join his mother's "self-help" group. He barely knew her and did not have the right to try and change her mind. However, that didn't stop him from wanting to.

Hefting his bag over his shoulder, he gave a quiet groan. He'd never been able to resist attempting to right a wrong, especially when said wrong involved children, animals or women. Micheline was a parasite, preying on vulnerable people, using them for her own ends and twisting their minds. He couldn't stand to see Fiona meet that sort of fate.

Since he didn't intend on being here long enough to have time to persuade her, he figured he'd sound her out at dinner tonight to ascertain her true thoughts about the AAG. One thing he'd noticed in particular was that many members didn't even seem to be aware it *was* a cult. If he could get her to admit that, she might be agreeable to talking to one of his friends who worked to deprogram cult members. It was worth a shot.

Back in his small room, which seemed just as antiseptic and impersonal as that of any chain motel, he walked to the window and pushed aside the curtains. Instead of a view of cement and parking lots, he saw a lush garden filled with vibrant flowers of every color. A large metal bench made an inviting place to sit, and he could have sworn he saw a koi pond on the other side of the bench.

For just an instant, he allowed himself to enjoy the restful beauty of it all. And then he remembered who had most likely arranged that lush garden, and why. Micheline would do anything—anything—to get what she wanted. She'd move people around like chess pieces, manipulate their emotions and their surroundings, as long as she thought it would benefit her in some way. She cared nothing for the wreckage she left in her wake.

Collateral damage, she'd always said, as if the wording made it right. The garden no doubt played some role in her schemes. She never did anything without a reason.

At thirteen, he'd come to the realization that if she found a way to use him, she would. As a kid, he'd been forced to charm elderly couples into investing with his mom, aware his mother only wanted their money. Back then, she'd marketed herself as a skillful investor, but secretly priding herself on taking every cent of people's life savings. She also lured in a rotating crop of men in her personal life, all wealthy, training Jake to make them all feel as if she might be a doting mother and a wonderful girlfriend. Of course, once she'd managed to use them, she'd dump them and move on to another, uncaring that her young son might have just been happy to have a father figure around.

At seventeen, having seen far too much of the awful things she did to people, he'd taken off before she could.

Shaking his head, he reminded himself not to focus on the past. Yet, even now, with his mother claiming to be dying, he had difficulty believing anything she said. In fact, he couldn't help but suspect she had an ulterior motive for wanting him to be here. She never did anything without a reason, usually one that benefited her.

He took a hot shower and then stretched out on his bed with the intention of dozing. But images of a doe-eyed woman with a sleepy smile had him tossing and turning. He finally abandoned the idea of a nap and decided to go for a walk instead. Might as well explore the AAG headquarters and grounds.

Managing to slip through the lobby unnoticed, he headed in search of an exit that went to the back and the garden area he'd viewed from his room. To his annoyance, Micheline's overly chipper minion caught sight of him and made a beeline for him, her heels tapping a staccato beat on the floor.

"There you are!" Leigh beamed at him as if she felt so delighted to see him. "Where are you going?"

He explained he'd decided to tour the premises, which appeared to distress her.

"Alone?" she asked, her tone appalled. "What happened to Fiona? She was given the task of escorting you anywhere you wanted to go."

"I told her I wanted to take a nap," he clarified, not wanting to cause trouble for Fiona. "She has no idea that I've even left my room."

"I see." Still frowning, Leigh thumbed her walkie-talkie and spoke a few words into it. When she met his gaze again, she'd smoothed out her expression. "Fiona will be here momentarily."

With an effort, he kept from groaning out loud. "I really didn't want to disturb her," he said.

Leigh's brightly painted lips widened into a smile so false, it made him want to grimace. "For the time that you're here, Fiona is to devote herself completely to you. Micheline has given her that assignment, and it's in her best interest to make sure she does what she's asked to do."

Was that a threat? The words seemed to indicate it was, though Leigh's vacuously pleasant expression told him she wouldn't see it that way.

Fiona rounded the corner, hurrying toward them. The first sight of her caught him like a punch in the stomach.

Dark eyes troubled, she swung her gaze from him to Leigh. "I'm so sorry I wasn't here to help you," she began. "I had no idea."

"Why would you?" he asked, watching her for the slightest indication that she might be afraid. There. That slight tremble in her lush lips. So help him, if Micheline dared enact some sort of punishment on Fiona, he'd have her hide.

Leigh watched Fiona, her eyes narrowed, her expression hawkish. Suddenly, he realized what he had to do. "I apologize," he said, softening his tone. "I give you my word I won't go anywhere without letting you know."

Fiona locked gazes with him. Finally, she gave a quick nod. "Whew. Glad we got that sorted out."

"Me, too," Leigh chirped. She patted Fiona lightly on the back and then marched away, her task clearly completed.

"What was that about?" Jake asked. "Did I get you in some sort of trouble for going off without you?"

"Of course not." Her small flash of a smile contained no humor. "I imagine your mother is just overly concerned with making sure you have a good time."

"That has to be it," he agreed, even though he knew damn good and well it wasn't. "I saw a beautiful garden area from my room. Would you take me there?"

Though she gave a confident nod, she leaned in close. "I'm new here, so I'm not exactly sure what you're talking about. But unless you want me to call Leigh, how about you and I try to find it on our own?"

The warmth of her breath tickled his ear, sending a shiver down his spine. Her scent intoxicated him. Resisting the urge to reach out and touch her hair, he managed to agree. "No Leigh. You and I will just wander around until we find it ourselves."

"We'll just go out back. Since your room faces that way, I'm sure we can manage to happen upon it." She shrugged. "I've only been outside a couple of times, but I remember how to get back to that walled-off area. I'm sure that's where the gardens are."

It turned out she was right. They followed a pebbled stone pathway bordered by lush plants and flowers. When they turned one corner of the building, he saw the bench he'd spotted from his window.

"Wow." Fiona stopped short, one hand to her chest. "I can't believe I never knew this was here."

He took a seat on the bench, gesturing her to sit beside him. Moving gingerly, she did, leaning back and stretching her legs out in front of her. She sighed. "This is nice."

Chancing a glance sideways at her, he admired the way her dark hair gleamed in the sun. *Sensual*, he thought of her expression, and then pushed the thought away. Not going there. With her eyes half-closed, she actually appeared relaxed, no longer vibrating with tension.

Because of this, he allowed himself to let go of some of his own stress. He hadn't wanted to come and he didn't like being here with the knowledge that his mother somehow was manipulating him, but for this small moment in this peaceful garden, he could release all that.

They sat for a few moments in companionable silence. He liked that she didn't feel compelled to fill the silence with chatter. Again, he found himself wondering what it was about this woman. One look at her and he'd known immediately that he wanted to get to know her better. She fascinated and intrigued him, made him ache in ways he hadn't since he'd been a teenager. Of course he'd dated, but he'd never allowed himself to get serious. After all, he didn't want to take a chance on loving someone like his mom.

Yet here he was, fighting his attraction to this woman who clearly didn't understand the evil behind the head of AAG's smiling façade. Fiona seemed too innocent, too trusting.

And the thought that she was under Micheline's thumb galled him. Clearing his throat, he broke the silence. "Tell me, what appeals to you most about AAG?" he asked.

Slowly, she opened her eyes and focused on him. "I like the idea of evolving," she said, the answer seeming to come easily. "Of becoming the best person you can be."

Micheline's stock phrase. *Be Your Best You.* She'd developed it when he'd still been a teenager, living with her. If she'd even once thought her behavior to be the best version of herself, he shuddered to think of what the worst might be.

"Is that what you think Micheline and Leigh are doing?" he asked, keeping his tone mild. "To me it seems like they're awfully concerned about money. Even more than truly helping others."

She blinked. "We all have to find ways to use the talents we've been given," she said, once again parroting his mother. "The AAG has to have an influx of cash to support itself. All Micheline is doing is taking her talent for helping others and soliciting donations to keep us going." She shrugged. "You honestly can't blame her."

He could and he did, but knew better than to say that out loud. Did Fiona honestly believe that crap?

Though he knew he'd probably get nowhere, he'd

hate himself if he didn't at least attempt to help save her. "Are you aware that many people consider AAG a cult?"

Something—Surprise? Dread?—flashed in her eyes. "Many people?" she asked, her tone dry. "That's kind of vague. Who exactly do you mean?"

Unable to help himself, he covered her hand with his. "What I'm trying to say is that I know someone you could talk to, if you want help trying to make sense of all this. He's a therapist who specializes in this kind of situation."

She'd gone absolutely still, her beautiful eyes still fixed on him. *"This kind of situation?"*

"Cults," he finally admitted. "He deprograms people who've been indoctrinated into a cult."

Though she looked down, he could have sworn her mouth twitched in the beginning of a smile.

He squeezed her hand once before releasing her. "You don't have to decide right now. All I ask is that you think about it. There'll be no cost to you—I'll take care of all that. And if you need a place to stay, I've got that covered as well."

When she finally met his gaze again, her face had gone expressionless. "Thanks for your kind offer," she said. "But none of that is necessary. I'm fine where I am. Right now, at this point in my life, this is where I need to be. I belong here."

Her words made his heart ache. "Fiona, I know we've just met, but I'm attracted to you. The thought of you under Micheline's thumb is…unpalatable to me. Please, at least say you'll think about it."

"I need to get ready for dinner," she stammered, the heat appearing to simmer in her eyes matching what thrummed in his blood.

He opened his mouth and then closed it. With a curt nod, he pushed to his feet and turned to head inside and up to his room. "Just knock when you're ready to go. I'll be there waiting."

She didn't follow.

All the way back to his room, he cursed his impetuous words. She must think him a complete idiot. He definitely felt like one. He couldn't help but wonder if Fiona might run to Leigh or Micheline and tell them what he'd offered. That would definitely be…interesting, to say the least.

Back in his room, he checked in with Tom, the hand he'd pegged to run his ranch while he was away. Though he hadn't expected any trouble, he couldn't help but feel relief to hear that everything continued to run like clockwork in his absence.

Though he only planned on staying two more days at the most, he went ahead and unpacked his suitcase, hanging his clothes up in the closet. Wherever they ended up going for dinner tonight, Western shirts, blue jeans and boots would have to work, since that's all he had.

He turned on the television to kill time and watched the evening news, glad of the sense of normalcy in a place that felt anything but.

The tap on his door came just as the news program ended. He shut the TV off and opened his door.

Fiona stood there, wearing a form-hugging dress of pale yellow and a pair of killer stiletto shoes. Somehow, she managed to look both virginal and sexy as hell. His body responded immediately.

"Are you ready?" she asked, clearly unaware of the effect she had on him.

"I am." If he could walk. "You look...amazing."

Instead of smiling, she grimaced. "Thanks. Leigh picked this dress out and brought it to me, along with the shoes. Micheline bought it. Your mother told her that yellow is your favorite color."

He gaped at her for a moment, and then everything clicked into place. "Did Micheline ask you to get close to me?" he asked.

She blinked. "Yes," she finally answered, surprising him with her honesty. "For whatever reason, she thinks you and I would be a good match."

This both infuriated him and intrigued him, even without knowing his mother's reasoning. "Then you know what? You and I ought to give her a good show."

"Excuse me?" Clearly startled, Fiona eyed him. "What do you mean?" A slow, sultry grin spread across her face as his words sank in. "Are you saying we should...pretend?"

Careful to keep it casual, he shrugged. "If you're up for it, sure. I'm not planning to be here that long anyway, so..."

Slowly, she nodded. "Okay. I think that's a great idea." Again, she flashed that smile, lighting up her dark eyes. "It's easier since you're so hot."

"Hot?" It took a moment for him to understand. "You think I'm hot?" The thought was so unbelievable it made him laugh. He realized she'd already begun playing her role. He held up a hand before she could respond. "No need to explain. I get it. And for the record, I find you hot, too." She didn't need to know he truly meant it.

They exchanged grins. Again, that pull. Leaning toward her, he found himself fighting the urge to kiss her.

Later, he thought. When necessary to help with their acting. Fiona didn't need to know how much he'd enjoy it.

If only he didn't get the sense she was hiding something.

Chapter Three

Fiona loved the idea of playing along with Jake to fool his mother and Leigh. And who knew, Micheline might be so pleased with her apparent success with Jake that she'd accidentally reveal something that might help the FBI build their case against her.

And, since Fiona always tried to be honest with herself, the notion of getting all up close and personal with the sexy cowboy made her entire body hum.

Even if Jake did happen to believe she needed a deprogrammer's help to get her out of the cult. He'd simply have to continue to think that. She had no choice in the matter, at least until she had enough evidence to secure an arrest.

As they strolled arm in arm through the now-crowded lobby, she felt as if she floated in her pretty dress and heels. With her chosen career, she rarely if ever got to dress like this. And the appreciation she'd seen glowing in Jake's blue eyes made her feel feminine and beautiful. In her line of work, if she wanted to be taken seriously—and she did—she'd learned to underplay her feminine side. She couldn't even remember the last time she'd dressed like this.

"They haven't yet rung the dinner bell," Fiona mused.

"You should see these people move when they do. They all jostle for a good place in line. It's amazing and sometimes slightly scary to watch."

Jake nodded. "What kind of food do they serve here?"

"It depends." She shrugged. "I think they mostly try to keep it healthy." She grinned. "Though everyone seems happiest when they have pizza night."

When they reached his truck, she stopped and studied it, letting him see her appreciation. "Latest model Ford F-250," she mused. "With a lift kit, custom wheels and a bed cover. Not at all what I expected."

He unlocked the doors. "I'm almost afraid to ask, but what did you expect?"

"A farm truck." She got inside, running her hand over the soft black leather. "You know, big and kind of beat-up. Not a beautiful new truck like this."

"You sound as if you know a lot about trucks," he said, pushing the start button.

"All vehicles, actually." She smiled slightly. "I'm a bit of a car nut. I've been that way ever since I was a preteen. My dad worked for a dealership in Phoenix, and he sometimes let me go to work with him."

Jake nodded. "Does your family still live there?"

"Yep." Sticking to the truth, without elaborating. Less chance of slipping up, or giving herself away.

He waited a heartbeat and then nodded. "Where to?"

"Do you like sushi?" She braced herself for him to decline. Even before she'd gone inside AAG, she never could find anyone willing to eat sushi with her.

"Sometimes." He shrugged. "Only if it's really great. Is there a good sushi place around here?"

Nearly humming with anticipation, she nodded. "There is. Turn left on Fifth Street."

When they reached Purple Sushi, she barely restrained herself from bouncing up and down in her seat like an excited child. "It's been so long since I got to have sushi," she said, not bothering to hide her glee. "Thank you so much for agreeing to come here."

Eyes gleaming with amusement, he watched her. "I'm guessing AAG doesn't ever serve it."

Just like that, she sobered. "No, they don't." She supposed she should thank him for reminding her of the reality of her life right now. She couldn't let her love for a good tuna roll make her forget the entire reason she was here in Mustang Valley.

"Don't." He lightly touched her shoulder.

"Don't what?"

"Dim your joy just because I mentioned AAG," he said.

Since she couldn't tell him that wasn't all of it, she simply nodded and got out of the truck.

Once they were shown to a booth near the back, a waitress came and gave them menus and took their drink orders. Fiona stuck to water while Jake ordered a beer.

"It's been so long since I had sushi, I'll let you order for both of us," Jake said, pushing his menu away.

She narrowed her eyes. "Have you ever even *had* sushi?" she asked.

His sheepish grin was answer enough. "I'm game to try it," he said. "Since you're such a big fan, it can't be all that bad."

This made her laugh. "You know what," she mused. "I like you."

"I like you, too." He studied her for a moment. "I just can't help but wonder what my mother's motivation is for wanting us to get together. She never does anything unless it's going to benefit her in some way."

Here was where she should rush to Micheline's defense, as any good little disciple would. But right now, Fiona didn't have the heart. She just wanted to enjoy her meal and the company. She'd go back to her role once they'd returned to the AAG center.

Right now, she just wanted to enjoy a couple of good sushi rolls and the company of the handsome cowboy sitting across from her.

Instead of responding to Jake's statement, she smiled at the waitress, which brought her over to see if they'd decided. Fiona ordered an assortment for them, wanting to give Jake a chance to sample several of her favorites.

Through it all, Jake sipped his beer and watched her, his expression contemplative.

Once the waitress had gone, Fiona eyed Jake. She wanted to see if she could find out how much he knew. "Since we're getting to know each other, what's the deal with you and your mother? Is it true you haven't seen her for years?"

"Yep. All true." He eyed her. "I'm sure you probably won't agree with me, but Micheline is not a good person."

Now they were getting somewhere. "Why do you say that?" she asked mildly, clasping her hands on the table in front of her.

Instead of answering, he leaned across the table, his intense stare locking on her. "My turn," he said. "What made you decide to join AAG?"

"They found me roaming the streets," she said simply. "They offered me a place to stay and a hot meal. They were kind to me when no one else was. I owe them for that."

He took another sip of his beer, clearly considering what he should say next. She could tell he badly wanted to talk to her about leaving the cult, getting some help. While she found this admirable—hell, it was something she would do herself were the situations reversed—she couldn't tell him the truth and risk blowing her cover.

Luckily, their food arrived. Happily, she eyed everything, enjoying the colorful artistry of the two elaborate sushi towers. Jake eyed them, too, his expression a mixture of curiosity and confusion. "Do we eat those?" he asked. "It seems a shame to mess up the artwork."

This made her laugh. "It kind of does, doesn't it? Just wait until you taste it."

They passed the serving platters around, taking samples of each. She waited for Jake to try one, wanting to see his reaction when he had his first bite. In her experience, people either loved or detested sushi. She had to see in which camp Jake would fall.

He chose a crab roll. "Good choice," she said, nodding in approval as he popped it into his mouth.

Chewing slowly, he appeared to be savoring the taste. He swallowed and inclined his head. "That was pretty good, actually."

"Only pretty good?" she challenged. "Try the California roll. Most people like that one."

"Why aren't you eating?" he asked instead.

"I wanted to see your reaction." Shrugging, she

began to help herself to her own plate. “Fresh,” she managed, speaking around mouthfuls. “So, so delicious.”

Together, they finished off all the food she’d ordered. To her delight, as he sampled various rolls, Jake ate with gusto.

“Dessert?” the waitress chirped. They both shook their heads.

After paying the check with Micheline’s hundred-dollar bill, they walked out to Jake’s truck in a food-coma silence.

“I enjoyed that,” he said, smiling at her across the seat.

“So did I,” she responded.

“Clearly.” He made no move to start the truck. “Before we head back, I wanted to talk to you about the AAG. Did you happen to do any research before you joined them?”

Though she knew where he was going with this, she pretended not to. “No. I needed help, and they offered it. Right now, I owe them a debt, and I’m working to repay it.”

When he started to speak, she held up her hand. “Please. I can see that you have issues with the organization. But don’t project them onto me. I promise you, my head is clear. I completely understand what I’m doing. Okay?”

After a moment, he nodded. “Okay,” he agreed. “Let’s head on back. Just promise me one thing?”

Brows raised, she waited.

“If you ever need help, no matter what time of the day or night, you’ll call me.” He reached into the center console, extracted a business card and handed it to her. “This is my ranch, but my cell phone number is on here, too.”

Accepting the card, she slowly nodded. "Thanks," she said. If he noticed she made no promises, he didn't comment.

As they turned onto the long driveway leading to the AAG ranch, the tall streetlamps Micheline had installed came on.

Though the sun had begun to sink below the horizon, the sky had not yet fully darkened. This, the gloaming, was Fiona's favorite time of the day. Spectacular skies that seemed to go on forever, the way the sky lit up in swirls of orange, pink and red.

Once he'd parked, they were walking from the back lot toward the house when movement behind one of the large storage buildings caught her eye. Two men, one of them a college-age kid, making her wonder if he was a brand-new recruit or the target Leigh had mentioned Fiona working with. She saw only a quick blur of movement, though it was enough to convince her something had gone wrong.

"Just a sec," she told Jake, pulling free. "I need to check something out." Without waiting for him to answer, she strode away, cursing the high heels.

Halfway up the grassy hill, she said the hell with it and yanked them off. Grateful for the mild Arizona weather, she dropped her shoes. Now barefoot, she broke into a run.

As soon as she rounded the corner, she saw the college kid, down on the ground huddled into a ball, arms up in a defensive posture to protect his face. The older AAG member, a stout, bald man with a mustache, kicked and pounded on the younger guy.

"Stop," Fiona ordered, her hands clenched.

Instead, the assailant smirked at her, one arm up in

the air, halfway to throwing another punch. "Make me," he said, sneering.

Aiming low, Fiona charged him, twisting at exactly the right moment and taking him down with a kick behind the knees. He lurched forward, bloodshot eyes wide with surprise, as she came back around with a second, well-placed blow, sending him face-planting in the dirt.

Slowly, he climbed to his feet, warily eyeing her.

Fiona rounded on him, hands up, glad for all those martial arts classes she'd taken as part of her FBI training. "Ready for round two?" she asked, her voice cool, even though she was vibrating with adrenaline.

Scrambling up to his feet, the bad guy shook his head.

"What's your name?" Fiona demanded. "I want to give it to Micheline so she can make sure you face appropriate punishment."

For the first time, stark fear shone in his face. "Please don't tell her. She'll put me in one of the cells. Let me just go pack my stuff and clear out of here."

"Cells?" Fiona cocked her head. "What cells?" she asked. Maybe, just maybe, she was about to learn something new. "I don't know what you're talking about."

But he'd already begun backing away, his large stomach shaking. "I can't," he stammered. He turned without another word and ran away, heading toward the same parking lot where Jake had left his truck.

Jake. She spun around to find him eyeing her as if she'd suddenly sprouted horns. Just then the kid groaned and staggered to his feet.

He had a bruised lip and a purpling under his left eye, which was swollen shut. Blood still ran from his nose, though he tried to wipe it away with the back of his hand. Standing, he swayed slightly as he studied Fiona with his one good eye.

"Are you okay?" Fiona asked.

"I think…so." Flexing his arms, and then his legs, he eyed her. "I don't think anything is broken."

"Luckily. What on earth happened?" she demanded.

"Thank you for helping me," he managed, wincing as his fingers came into contact with a large gash on his cheek. "I came out here for a smoke, and he caught me." Smoking was definitely not allowed at AAG. "He took my e-cig away, and then he demanded I pay him one hundred dollars to keep quiet. Once I told him I didn't have that kind of cash on me, he just started whaling away on me."

"Come on." Fiona slipped her arm around the kid's slender shoulders. "Let's get you to the infirmary and see if they can patch you up."

CLEARLY FORGOTTEN, JAKE trailed along behind Fiona and the battered kid, turning over what he'd just seen in his mind and trying to make sense of what he'd just seen. Quiet Fiona had fought the guy like a badass. Mulling this over, he waited outside in the hallway while Fiona talked to the person inside the area that apparently served as the AAG medical center.

When Fiona finally emerged alone, she seemed surprised to find Jake still waiting. "Oh," she murmured, her eyes widening. "I'm so sorry. I had to fill out a report while I was there, so Micheline can review it."

Micheline. Everything centered around the most avaricious, self-involved, evil woman he'd ever met. Sometimes he wished he could purge his veins of her blood.

Shaking his head, he focused once more on the slender woman standing in front of him.

"Do you have a moment to talk?" he asked, his tone clipped, though he struggled to keep from showing any emotion.

"Sure," she replied, her easy tone at odds with the quick flare of panic he caught in her eyes. "Let's go for a walk."

"Good idea." Away from the AAG center and any possible cameras or recording devices. No doubt she knew he planned to ask her what was going on and wanted to make sure no one else overheard.

She definitely wasn't what Micheline and the others believed her to be. He couldn't help but wonder what kind of explanation she'd give.

Side by side, not touching, not speaking, they strode out the front door. This time, instead of heading around back to that secluded little garden, she led the way down the driveway. By now, dusk had settled in. Soon it would be full dark.

"Well?" he finally demanded, when it seemed she didn't intend on speaking.

"Well what?"

"Who are you?" Stopping, he crossed his arms. "And don't say some random homeless woman who was found wandering the streets. I saw how you took that guy down earlier."

"Why can't I be both?" she asked, her tone reasonable. "You never asked about my past. How I became homeless, what the circumstances were leading up to my change in lifestyle. Isn't it obvious that at some point, I took some martial arts classes? Yes, and it was before I became homeless. Thank you for not asking. All you ever wanted to focus on was the AAG."

Stunned, he swallowed. Because damned if she wasn't right. He'd been so blinded by the need to get her away from the cult that he hadn't taken the time to try and get to know her as a person. Of course, he'd only just met her earlier in the day. And he recognized her deflection as a way to avoid answering his question.

"I just got here," he protested. "And yes, of course I'm going to focus on what's right in front of me. I'm not planning on staying long. There'd be plenty of time to get to know you and your reasons once I got you away from this craziness."

"Why do you even care?" Her direct look challenged him. "As you said, we barely know each other. Maybe it just so happens that AAG is exactly what I've been searching for my entire life. The one place I fit in. Has that ever occurred to you?"

He blinked. Damn if she wasn't good at deflecting. He had no patience for games like this. All his life, he'd been a straight-shooting kind of guy. Micheline's opposite. Naturally, his mother would choose to surround herself with people she could manipulate. Sadly, as much as he hated to admit the possibility, Fiona felt she belonged here, no matter what he thought of her reasons.

Maybe she was right. What business of his was it whether she chose to stay with his mother? Yet every single time he glanced at her, his heart turned over in his chest. He'd never felt such a strong tug of attraction, such a powerful urge to spend time with someone. And yes, to get to know her better, in every way possible. Too bad he wouldn't have enough time to do that.

Since it seemed clear that continuing to press her wasn't going to work, he decided to let it go. For now, maybe even forever. It depended on how long he actually stayed.

"Sorry." He grimaced. "It's been a long day. I woke up on my ranch this morning and…"

"Now you're here, right in the middle of a bunch of drama." She touched his arm, the light touch of her finger sending a shiver through him. "It's still early, though. We have a few seminars that run at night if you'd like to attend one of those."

So earnest, so sincere. Even though she had to know attending an AAG seminar ranked among the very last things he'd ever want to do.

"No, what I'd like is to see my mother," he said. "I just need a few minutes of her clearly precious time. I'm intending on going back home tomorrow."

Fiona eyed him, her face blank. "Let me check with Leigh," she began.

"Not necessary," he interrupted. "I'll just take myself to Micheline's office and see if I can catch her myself."

Full of righteous indignation that he hadn't had to work too hard to manufacture, he stormed off in the direction where he'd met his mother earlier.

The heavy wooden doors were closed this time. When he tried to open them, they wouldn't budge. Locked.

Rattling the handles one more time for good measure, he turned. "Frustrating."

"I'm sorry," Fiona said, her voice as calming as her serene gaze. "I haven't heard back from Leigh yet, but I know Micheline keeps an impossible schedule."

"This is ridiculous." He glanced at his watch. "She

tracks me down after so many years of no contact, informs me she's dying—which I'm not sure I believe, by the way—so I drive all the way down here, and now she disappears. I might as well go home tonight."

A slight widening of Fiona's eyes was her only reaction. "Let me see if I can track down Leigh," she said, her voice still soothing. "Please. I'm not sure how well it will go for me if I lose you the very first night of your visit."

Masterful manipulation from Fiona, he thought. In fact, he nearly complimented her out loud. She intrigued him, this woman who fought like a ninja but made herself appear quiet and docile in order to remain under the radar. Unraveling her mysteries nearly made him want to stay a couple of days at least.

Nearly.

Except the one thing he could not stomach, thanks to his mother, was a liar. He avoided them like the plague. And the more time he spent with Fiona Smith, the more he realized she wasn't on the up and up. If he had any common sense, he'd go pack his suitcase right now and get the hell out of here. In fact, he'd go do that right now. The sooner he'd left this place in the dust, the better he'd feel.

Then he made the mistake of glancing at Fiona. She studied him, her gaze warm, her lips parted. Desire short-circuited his brain. "Don't do that," he rasped.

"Do what?" Picture of innocence.

"Look at me as if you want to eat me up." His body stirred—hell, more than stirred. Rock hard, in an instant.

She took a step closer to him. His mouth went dry. His heart thudded in his chest.

"Common sense be damned," she said before wrapping herself around him and pulling his head down for a kiss.

The instant she pressed her mouth against his, heat flared, consuming him. Openmouthed, he lost himself in the taste of her, the lush curves of her body molded against his.

When she finally stepped back, they were both breathing hard.

"I think you ought to stick around awhile," she murmured, the heat in her eyes matching the one in his body. "It'll be…interesting, to say the least."

Chapter Four

The kiss had not gone as expected. Despite her initial intention to distract him, there had been nothing casual about it. Fiona had been warring with herself against the sensual lure of the man ever since she'd first laid eyes on him.

She'd acted completely on impulse, trusting her instincts. But what she'd thought would be merely a bit of a tease, a lighthearted flirtation, had erupted into an incredibly passionate kiss that had left her weak at the knees, her body aching in all the right places. Despite it being against every rule of undercover work, if Jake had asked right then and there, she would have been sorely tempted to tumble into his bed with him.

Luckily, he hadn't asked. Most likely he'd been as shocked by the raw force of that kiss as she had been. She had to wonder if that, coupled with when he learned about being switched at birth, would be enough to make him stick around a few more days.

Though part of her wanted to keep Jake here for purely selfish reasons, Fiona also sensed that his presence was somehow integral to whatever Micheline had planned. The FBI had set up a case file after receiving several complaints about the AAG swindling people out of their life savings. They'd learned of intricate financial schemes, fraudulent investments, and even potential money laundering. Then a former cult member had shown up claiming Micheline might be planning something big, something awful, hinting that it could end multiple lives. This had been the catalyst for the Bureau sending Fiona in undercover. She'd been tasked with not only obtaining proof of Micheline's swindling, but finding information about what exactly the AAG leader planned to do. If it was something that would harm innocent people, Fiona was to neutralize the threat.

After getting to know Micheline, Fiona would do whatever she could to gain the older woman's trust. Jake had unwittingly offered to help her out there by asking her to pretend to be a couple. If only he'd stay just a few more days. Right now, the AAG leader had proved to be both busy and evasive. Fiona had only managed to spend a few moments with her. She spent more time with Leigh than anyone else. Close, but not close enough.

And now Micheline couldn't seem to make time for the son she'd summoned home, even if only to reveal the truth about his parentage.

Honestly, though, Fiona couldn't blame Jake for considering leaving. She didn't understand what the hell kind of game Micheline was playing by avoiding him. As far as Fiona could tell, Jake had no idea he'd been switched with Ace Colton. Was that why Micheline didn't want to spend time alone with him? Was she planning on revealing the truth? Did she dread seeing his reaction?

This entire scenario puzzled Fiona. Jake had left home over two decades ago, and he and Micheline hadn't spoken the entire time. Not even once. Whatever had happened to send Jake running must have been awful, but why had Micheline made no effort to reach him until now? Did she intend to involve him in whatever big thing she had planned? And where did the Colton family come in?

Fiona sighed. While this wasn't her first undercover assignment, it definitely was the most complex. And getting more and more so with each passing day.

At least she thought she'd been able to convince Jake to hang around at least one more day. Not her finest moment, but even so, she hadn't been able to stop thinking about that kiss.

Which she needed to do pronto. She had to be sharp and focused in order to complete the job she'd come here to do. Unfortunately, the single kiss had only made her want more. So much more. She couldn't help but wonder if Jake felt the same way.

Just as she'd decided she might as well get ready to go to bed, her walkie-talkie chimed. Leigh was summoning her to her suite. Somehow, Fiona managed to keep from groaning out loud. She kept her voice cheery as she agreed to head that way.

Exhaustion warred with tension as Fiona trudged down the long, carpeted hallway toward Leigh's suite. Leigh had been given a deluxe suite, which included an anteroom she used as her office.

After a soft tap on the elaborate iron and wood door, Fiona waited. A moment later, Leigh bade her to enter. When Fiona stepped inside, feet sinking in the plush carpet, Leigh remained seated behind a massive oak desk that had been polished to a high sheen.

"Micheline is very pleased with you." Beaming,

Leigh wasted no time on pleasantries. "You saving Theodore Royce III has worked very much in our favor."

"Who?" Fiona blinked. Whatever she'd expected Leigh to say, it hadn't been this.

"The new recruit you kept from getting beat up." Leigh drummed her long, perfectly manicured, hot-pink nails on the desk in front of her. "And now I've been informed Ron Underhill tried to attack you. Rest assured, Micheline has made sure he has been dealt with."

Cell, Fiona remembered. Underhill had been worried about being taken to the cell.

"How?" Fiona asked. "What did she do to him?"

Leigh waved her question away. "That's not any of your concern. What matters is that Theodore is overwhelmingly grateful. He now trusts you completely." She smiled. "This process usually takes much longer. You've saved us quite a bit of time."

To do what? Uneasy now, Fiona waited to hear the rest of it.

Still smiling, Leigh continued. "Theo was visiting here today because he's that struggling freshman at Mustang Valley College I mentioned you helping earlier. He, like many of our members, is searching for something more. For the first time in his young life, his wealth hasn't bought him happiness. AAG has offered him assistance. We can help change all that."

"We can?" Fiona knew where this was going. The thought made her queasy, but she managed to appear eager.

"Yes. It's what we do, as you know. Help him become his best him." She sighed, still smiling prettily, and brushed her hair away from her face. "Micheline is offering him entry into her new, specialized, individual courses. He will get a discounted rate of one thousand dollars for each of his first classes—how to judge worthy friends, how to choose a significant other, how to know if your parents are really not in your corner, and so on. Micheline will help him attain honest selfhood."

"Wow." This was all Fiona could manage to say. She wasn't sure exactly how many classes they'd get poor Theodore to take, but it sounded as if they planned to help relieve him of somewhere in the vicinity of ten thousand dollars.

Her comment made Leigh laugh. "Wow is right. What an opportunity for him." She winked. "Of course, those are only the first tier of courses. Once he's ready to move up a level, the price will also increase to five thousand dollars each."

Though Fiona nodded as if she was on board with the entire thing, inside she seethed. This kind of thing—AAG taking advantage of the young and uncertain or elderly and infirm—made her furious. Which of course, she couldn't let show.

"We'd like you to be the one to discuss this with him," Leigh continued, her voice smooth. "It should be a breeze, a shoo-in for your first networking task, since he already views you as his savior." Her smile faded, her gaze sharpening. "What exactly did you do to get Underhill off him?"

"Underhill? Was he that big bald guy?"

"Yes." Leigh shook her head. "He outweighs you by like a hundred pounds."

Praying there hadn't been security cameras, Fiona grimaced. "I'm not sure. It all happened so fast. He came at me and I twisted away. He got off balance." She shrugged, hoping she sounded modest and frightened. "It was awful. I was so lucky. Maybe he's seen me with you and knew Micheline was going to find out about what he'd done. Either way, he ran off." She took a deep, shaky breath.

No frown creased Leigh's perfect forehead to indicate she might suspect Fiona might be lying. Of course, around here, falsehoods were the flavor of the day.

"Anyway," Leigh finally continued. "We're going to set you up with a visit to Theo tomorrow. He's still in the infirmary, so you can stop by to visit and check on him. That's when you'll bring up the custom plan Micheline has developed for him." She rummaged through a small stack of papers, extracted one and passed it over to Fiona. "This is a list of all the classes we think would benefit him."

"Okay." Swallowing back nausea, Fiona accepted the paper. While this sort of thing was not in any way illegal, because Micheline gave people exactly what they paid for, it was unethical.

"Sit." Gesturing at the antique French chair across from the desk, Leigh gestured at an open wine bottle and two stemless glasses. "Would you like a glass of wine?"

Though she took a seat, Fiona politely declined. The last thing she needed would be to dull her wits around Leigh.

Leigh pouted at Fiona's refusal but poured herself a large glass. She took a deep sip and sighed. "Well, then, tell me how you and Jake are getting along. The last time I saw the two of you, you seemed very chummy."

"Chummy." Fiona pretended to consider the words, finally allowing herself a slow, sultry smile. "I guess you could say that."

"Good, good!" Leigh all but clapped. "Was it hot and heavy?"

Fiona nodded. "Honestly, I now believe in love at first sight." She looked down, swallowing hard, hoping she wasn't coming off as overly dramatic. "I think Jake does, too. I know it's sudden, but I'm pretty sure he feels the same way."

Watching her, Leigh took another deep drink of wine. "That's perfect. I'm absolutely thrilled and beyond happy for the both of you. Believe me, Micheline will be as well."

Which meant they hoped to use her connection to Jake as leverage. While she still had no idea what exactly Micheline might be planning, or even if it was a singular event, since the revelations had started leaking about Ace Colton, she imagine Micheline's jig was nearly up. That's why she couldn't shake the feeling that it would be very bad, truly awful. Catastrophic, even. A chill snaked up her spine. As long as she could get Leigh and Micheline to consider her as part of their inner circle, she stood a chance to stop the AAG.

Overexaggerating a yawn, which she covered with her hand, Fiona sighed. "I'm sorry, but I'm exhausted. It's been a crazy, long day. Though I'd love to stay and chat longer, if you don't mind, I'd like to take myself to my room and get ready for bed."

"Sure, go ahead and get some rest." Still smiling, Leigh poured herself a generous second glass of red wine. "I'll talk to you in the morning."

As she walked back to her room, Fiona wondered if it was too late to stop by Jake's room and warn him. Her heart skipped a beat as she pictured him getting up from his bed, wearing only a pair of boxers low on his hips, his hair mussed and his sleepy eyes warming with heat at the sight of her.

Professional, she reminded herself. She needed to maintain her distance.

Though her steps slowed in the hall outside her room, with his right across the way, she forced herself to continue on inside her own space and close the door.

She caught sight of herself in the mirror, flushed and breathing fast. Turned on. "Not now, Evans," she cautioned herself, sotto voce. Continuing on into the bathroom, she washed the makeup off her face and brushed her teeth. She rummaged around in her dresser drawer, pulling out the old, soft T-shirt she often slept in.

Finally, she crawled between her sheets and clicked off the light.

The next morning, she got up early and meditated for her usual twenty minutes before showering. After drying her hair, she made a valid attempt to duplicate the makeup style that Leigh had used, but finally scrubbed it all off and redid her face in her usual, understated way.

In the cafeteria, she had her usual yogurt and fruit, along with a cup of strong coffee. She liked getting up this early, as it often turned out to be the only time she had to herself. Neither Leigh nor Micheline ever showed their face before eight. Fiona imagined they were still asleep at five thirty. She'd always been a morning person and, despite not having a concrete agenda, she liked to be ready for whatever tasks they might throw at her.

She poured herself a second cup of coffee and carried it outside to the front porch. Her favorite time of the day, no matter the season, was before sunrise, when the birds gradually came awake and the nighttime creatures went silent.

Peaceful. In a career like hers, she needed to steal small, steadying moments when she could. She took a sip of her coffee before heading over to one of the large rocking chairs.

About to sit, a sound, a blur of motion to her right had her swinging around, almost too late. A large shape launched itself at her, sending her coffee cup flying. It shattered on the wood porch.

At least her hands were free. She crouched, instinctively taking a defensive position. Large man, clumsy. Familiar, too. She launched herself forward. The top of her head caught her attacker in his large stomach, hard enough to knock the breath from him. The guy from yesterday, she realized. Ron Underhill.

Wheezing as he rasped for air, he stumbled, nearly going down. He grabbed the porch railing to pull himself up, still trying to get air. If she followed through right now, she could take him out quickly.

Instead, for some reason, she hesitated a bit too long. Long enough for him to catch a second wind. He pushed himself up, rounding on her, gulping in air. "Bitch," he snarled, still panting. "You're going to pay for what you cost me."

Damn, she wished she had her firearm. Since she didn't—couldn't, since packing heat would completely blow her cover—she'd have to take this guy down with her bare hands. Which might also blow her cover, though she had no choice.

Moving fairly fast for a guy with so much bulk, Underhill tried to rush her again. Too slow, though. Right before he reached her, she twisted, just enough to use her shoulder to knock him off balance. A swift kick took his legs out from under him, sending him crashing hard into the rail. He yelped in pain.

"Stay down," she ordered. "Don't make me hurt you."

"What the hell?" a voice said from the doorway. Jake, his voice as hard as his gaze. He stepped forward, eyeing her as if she'd donned a superhero costume. He might have been able to convince himself that what he saw her do yesterday had been a fluke, but twice would really be stretching it.

Several other men pushed their way out behind him, crowding around her, forming a protective circle between her and Underhill. At first, she thought they were protecting him from her, but then she realized they believed they were doing the opposite.

As if she needed their help. Since she needed to stay in character, undercover, she managed to arrange her face in what she hoped was a terrified expression. "Don't let him get away," she urged. "He attacked another new member yesterday, too."

Bart Akers pushed his way through the group. "Fiona?" he asked. "Are you all right?"

She simpered up at the brawny blond security man. "I'm better now that you're here."

Bart grabbed Underhill and hauled him to his feet as if he weighed nothing. "You're coming with me."

"Not to the cells," Underhill pleaded. "Let me go and I promise I'll clear out of here. You have my word that you'll never see me again."

Ignoring him, Bart shoved his hands behind his back

and secured them with a set of metal handcuffs. Randall Cook, the AAG center's handyman, asked if he could help. He and Bart were good friends, and they both worshipped Micheline and Leigh.

"We'll take care of him now," Bart said, dipping his chin at Fiona. "Are you sure he didn't hurt you?"

"Yes." She smiled sweetly, relieved none of them—with the possible exception of Jake—had seen her fight Underhill. Even then, she had no idea how much Jake might have seen. "You got here just in time."

SHE FOUGHT LIKE a professional, with deadly, precise skill.

Watching silently as the security guard took the man away, Jake debated what exactly he'd say to Fiona. Who clearly wasn't at all what she seemed. They'd started to have a discussion about this yesterday, but he'd gotten nowhere. Damned if he'd let her snow him again.

"Whew," she said with a sigh, smiling up at him. "I'm sure glad Bart and the others got here in time."

"Are you?" Keeping his voice level, Jake eyed her. "You didn't appear to need any help. In fact, you looked like a pro to me."

She grinned, as if she didn't notice the tinge of betrayal in his tone. "Thanks," she replied. "Still, I'm glad help arrived before things got out of hand."

He shook his head, keeping his voice low and steady. "Either you level with me, or I'm out."

Clearly stunned, she eyed him. "I… I'm not sure what you mean."

"Cut the crap," he said. "You aren't who you pretend to be. Who are you and what are you doing in AAG?"

"I'm Fiona Smith," she replied. "And I've already told you my story."

Teeth clenched, he glared at her.

She glared right back.

Stalemate. Fine. "I'm done." Turning, he started to walk away.

"Wait." She caught at his arm. "I can't tell you."

"Can't? Or won't? I don't have time for this, Fiona. You know what? I've been worried because the last thing I wanted to do was be attracted to a woman who is in a cult, for Christ's sake. Not just any cult, but my mother's."

"Ouch." Wincing, she gazed deep into his eyes. "Are you really that attracted to me? We've known each other one day."

Ever honest, he gave her the truth. "I was. But not now. The one thing I refuse to deal with is a liar. Having Micheline for a mother drove that point home."

She winced again. "Please. I just need a little more time."

"For what?"

"To decide if I can trust you." Though her voice came out small, the fierceness of her expression had him wondering.

"Trust me?" Stunned, he looked away. "This coming from someone who puts their faith in a con woman. I don't understand, Fiona. Please, explain."

Something that looked an awful lot like desperation flashed across her expressive, beautiful face. "We all have our reasons for doing what we do. What's yours?"

Again, no explanation. Since he didn't appear to be getting anywhere by being direct, he decided to bite. "I don't know what you mean," he said. "My reason for what?"

"Right." She snorted. "I want to know why you're going along with pretending Micheline is actually your mother."

"Unfortunately, she *is* my mother," he said slowly, wondering if she'd completely lost her mind.

Something in her stunned expression told him the truth.

"She isn't?" He shook his head, as if by doing so he could clear it. "Micheline isn't my mother. Damn, what did that awful woman do now?"

Fiona looked as if he'd punched her in the gut. Shocked and worried and maybe even about to get sick.

"You didn't know," she whispered, looking around as if to make sure they weren't overheard. "Damn it, I'm so sorry. You really didn't know."

Because he felt like he needed to sit down, he did. Walked to the edge of the drive and sank down onto the manicured lawn.

"Micheline's really not my mother?"

She shook her head. "No."

"Seriously," he mused. "All these years..."

Fiona remained silent.

While he realized what she'd done by dropping this bombshell on him, as a distraction it sure as hell worked. For a moment. He wasn't even sure if he believed her.

"I'm not sure whether to feel relieved or what," he said. "But first, you sure as hell better tell me what you know. After that, I want the truth about you. All of it."

She sat down next to him, tucking her legs under her gracefully. "Micheline switched you at birth with another baby. No one really knows why."

Though his head had started to ache, he nodded encouragingly. "What other baby?" he asked, his voice a rasp.

"Ace Colton. You're really a Colton." She took a deep breath. "And Ace is actually Micheline's biological son."

"Ace Colton? Of Mustang Valley's founding family? *That* Ace Colton?"

"Yes." She took a deep breath. "Honestly, I didn't intend to shock you. I thought you knew."

"Not really." He shook his head. "Despite the way everyone in Mustang Valley reveres them, the Coltons are almost as self-serving as Micheline."

Fiona sighed. "Not really. Not even close."

Jake let himself digest this for a few seconds. Then, his natural skeptical nature kicked in. "And you know this how?"

"Apparently, Micheline marched into Colton Oil and confirmed it for them recently. The family tried to keep it under wraps, but some of the news—of a baby switch—leaked. No one knows yet what her motive for doing that was."

Again, he wondered where Fiona got her information. When he asked her, she simply sighed. "Word gets out. People talk."

"People? Are you telling me Micheline has someone working inside Colton Oil?"

"That I don't know for certain. But it's possible."

"Anything is possible," he drawled. "As to why she'd do something like that, Micheline has a reason for everything she does. I'm sure we'll all find out soon enough."

"Most likely we will," she agreed, the picture of innocence.

"Don't think I haven't noticed that you've been avoiding answering all of my questions about you. Finding this out is a hell of a big distraction, I'll admit." Grimacing, he shook his head. "But I'm still not planning on letting you off the hook."

She shrugged. "I don't blame you. But you have to understand, I can't always give you the information you're asking for."

"Why not?"

The sun had just begun to rise above the horizon, bathing them in a warm, orange glow. Despite the bright light, he couldn't read her expression as she stared at him.

"I just can't," she finally said. "As I said, I'm not sure how much I can trust you."

This earned a bitter chuckle from him. "Micheline's son who *isn't* her son? The one who, despite every awful thing I've seen her do, still came running back when she said she was dying of cancer." He shook his head, allowing the familiar bitterness to fill him. "That actually explains a lot. As a kid, I always wondered why she never seemed to love me." Even now, saying that out loud hurt. "I wonder what her end game is then. She's probably not even sick. Even before I left, I wondered how much of that was real."

"I agree," she murmured. "She seems remarkably healthy to me."

"I'm thinking it's all tied into whatever scam she's running now. It's always been about two things with her. Power and money."

Once more, she nodded.

Narrowing his gaze, he focused back on her. "You've dropped a hell of a bombshell on me with no warning."

"I'm sorry," she said, sounding sincere. "But I figured you'd want to know."

"It's a lot to process," he admitted. "And I will, just later. Now, enough about me. Who are you, really? I'm sure you'd hate for me to go to Micheline with my concerns."

Her eyes narrowed. "You wouldn't do that."

"Wouldn't I?" Bluffing, but she'd never know. Jake knew he excelled at bluffing. He made a hell of a poker player.

Her hard swallow told him he'd succeeded.

"Jake, I want to tell you the truth. Really, I do."

"But?" he prodded.

"But I can't take a chance of jeopardizing…everything."

He opened his mouth, intending to press again, but she held up her hand.

"I keep my ears open," she said, offering up a halfhearted shrug. "You'd be surprised at the kind of things you can learn when people find you invisible."

"Uh-huh." With his arms crossed and his expression skeptical, he let her know he wasn't buying it. One, two, another heartbeat while he waited for her to say more.

When she didn't, disappointment knifed through him. "That's all you got?" he asked. "The best you can do?"

He could have sworn he saw a twinge of guilt in her face, but she managed to smile. "That's it. I wish I had more."

He shook his head. "That's too bad. That tells me that you're more like Micheline than I realized."

The insult made her gasp. "In what way?" she asked.

"You're a liar, just like her. I can put up with a lot of things, but I refuse to deal with a liar."

Back stiff, he turned and walked away.

Once inside his room, he locked the door. He dug out his laptop, powered it up and did a search for Ace Colton. Quite a bit turned up.

First, he pulled up the picture. Though they were both forty, the ousted CEO of Colton Oil looked nothing like Jake. But then, why would he? They weren't related. Instead, Jake realized he could actually see traces of Micheline in the other man's face. There, in the chin, maybe even the nose. While the other man's appearance seemed fashionably casual, he also exuded an aura of comfortable wealth. Because as a Colton, Ace would have been brought up wanting for nothing, especially love.

Except Ace Colton had been accused of trying to kill the man he'd believed to be his father. And, even worse, the fact that he wasn't actually a Colton had made the news. Ace had eventually been cleared and the actual attempted killer had been caught. Still, something like that had to leave scars.

Slightly queasy, Jake couldn't help but wonder what kind of life he might have had if Micheline hadn't taken it upon herself to switch babies. He couldn't help but want to know her reasoning.

He'd never know now. With four decades already under the bridge, he supposed the Colton family might be content to simply leave things the way they were. Though a simple DNA test would be able to prove or disapprove Micheline's story.

In that instant, Jake realized he wasn't going to be able to go home, not just yet. He wanted to meet Ace

Colton. He assumed the other man would be just as curious about him, especially since Ace already knew about the baby switch.

Decision made, he grabbed his keys and left. To his surprise, no one intercepted him or tried to stop him.

He first drove to Colton Oil, but when he reached the parking lot, he realized Ace probably was too high up in the corporate ladder for Jake to simply walk in and expect a meeting. Still, he'd come this far. It couldn't hurt to try.

Once he'd killed the engine, he stared up at the building. If things had been different, he would have been comfortable in this place, known. Now, while he might have been a Colton by blood, since Ace had been ousted as CEO, they were both strangers here.

Inside the modern, industrial structure, which had been decorated in an upscale Western theme, he walked over to the huge reception desk and asked to see Ace Colton. He'd read in the local paper that Ace would be there today to meet with the board.

The young woman behind the counter looked him up and down before pushing her fashionable eyeglasses up. "I'm sorry, but he is no longer employed here."

"I understand. But I'm aware he's in the building and I really need to talk to him."

Expressionless, she studied him. "Do you have an appointment?" she asked politely.

"No," he drawled, leaning in confidentially. "But I have a feeling he'll be open to seeing me. Why don't you check, if you don't mind."

Though she sniffed, the corners of her pink-painted lips fought a smile. "Your name?"

"Jake Anderson."

She froze. Her eyes went wide. "Yes, of course," she said hurriedly. "I'll just let him know you're here."

Turning away, she quietly spoke a few words into the phone. When she hung up, she dipped her chin and pointed toward the elevator. "Second floor. He's expecting you."

"Thank you." As Jake started for the elevator, the doors opened. Ace Colton stepped out, a guardedly optimistic look on his handsome face. Jake froze, swallowing hard. He wasn't sure how to act, what to think. In fact, his first instinct was to back the hell away and claim this entire situation must have been a colossal mistake.

Ace, however, apparently had other plans. "You must be Jake," he said, shaking hands. "I heard you were in town and I wondered when we would meet."

Jake nodded, somewhat at a loss for words. "Is there somewhere we can go and talk?" he asked. "Somewhere private?"

"My thoughts exactly," Ace replied. "Since it's way too early to go to a bar, how about we grab some coffee at Java Jane's?"

"Sounds good." Though Jake had expected this meeting to be awkward, to say the least, Ace's relaxed, casual demeanor had a way of dissipating any tension.

"Do you mind if I drive?" Ace asked, jingling a set of keys.

"That depends," Jake responded. "Whether I have to cram myself into some kind of sports car or not. I have a really nice truck."

After a second, Ace laughed. "It's a Porsche. Does your truck have a lift kit?"

"Yep." Jake grinned back at him. "F-250. Custom

everything. It's new. I special ordered it, and I'm pretty proud of that truck. This drive here was the first road trip." Plus, though he'd never admit it out loud, driving would help him regain some semblance of control in an admittedly crazy situation.

Ace pocketed his keys. "I'm in. Lead the way."

He whistled when he caught sight of Jake's pickup, the paint gleaming in the sun. "Nice."

He actually liked this guy, Jake thought. "Thanks."

They drove a couple of blocks. Ace pointed out the coffee shop on the right, and they parked. Neither man got out immediately.

"Are you as weirded out by all this as I am?" Jake asked.

"Yeah," Ace said. "I've got to tell you up front, I've never liked Micheline. But this, this takes the cake."

"That makes two of us," Jake replied, not bothering to keep the bitterness from his tone. "Let's go inside."

Side by side, the two men walked into the crowded coffee shop. "What'll you have?" Ace asked. "I'm buying."

"Just coffee," Jake answered. "Thanks." He looked around, impressed by the cleanliness and warmth of the place.

"Here you go," Ace said, handing him a coffee. "Now to find a place to sit."

Jake grimaced. "I've scanned the entire place. There are no empty seats."

"There's another room in the back. Follow me." Moving with the confidence of a local, Ace led the way through the crowd. They passed through a doorway into a smaller, less crowded room. "Perfect." Ace made a beeline for a couple of overstuffed armchairs near the window. "My favorite spot."

They sat. Jake studied Ace, making no effort to hide it. And Ace, in turn, studied him back.

"So *she* summoned you home to tell you the truth?" Ace finally asked.

"Micheline? No." Jake took a drink of his coffee. "She still hasn't told me. She tracked me down to tell me she had cancer."

"Do you believe her? She said something about that when she stopped by Colton Oil."

"I'm not sure," Jake admitted. "I swear she seems desperate now, closer to being truly mentally ill than I've ever seen her. Of course, it's been twenty-three years since I left home. Obviously, she must have deteriorated in all that time."

"Twenty-three years? Wow." Ace whistled. "Your life must have been hell for you to take off at seventeen."

His life. The life that should have been Ace's. "I wouldn't wish it on you, man," Jake said. "None of this is your fault, or mine. I'm still reeling with the knowledge that I'm really not related to that b—" He broke off, realizing Micheline was actually Ace's biological mother. "She's crazy," he finally amended. "Truly delusional."

"Great, just great." Glum now, Ace gazed out the window with a contemplative expression. "That means it runs in the family."

Just as Jake was searching his mind for how to respond to that, Ace laughed. "This is so messed up." He eyed Jake. "You know you're going to have to take a DNA test. I did, and it confirmed what we already know."

"I figured. And I will. But you should know, I'm not

after anything. I like my life. I've worked hard and own a small ranch north of here. If anything, I'd just like to get to know your family. *My* family, too, I guess."

Ace met his gaze. "That can be arranged. I'll just need a little time to get them used to the idea. Everyone is still in shock."

"I can understand that," Jake said. "I'm in the same state myself."

Clearing his throat, Ace nodded. "I'm sure you've read about me being framed for attempted murder. I was exonerated and the actual gunman was caught."

"I did." Jake wasn't sure what else to say. "That must have been tough."

"It was." Ace eyed him. "You do understand, once all the smoke clears, you'll most likely be able to assume a position on the Colton Oil board. You could even move to the Triple R if you want."

"I have my own ranch," Jake answered quickly. "But thank you. What about you? What will you do now?"

Ace grimaced. "I might start an energy consulting firm but that is still up in the air. I suppose at some point, Micheline is going to want to spend some time with me, too, and get to know me. Though she hasn't cared for forty years, so why would she care now?"

"Don't take it personally," Jake advised. "That's just the way she is. She cares about herself and only herself."

"But what about all those people who belong to AAG? Surely by now, at least some of them would have noticed she isn't what she seems."

"You'd think." Jake took another deep drink of his coffee. "But they see what they want to see. And Micheline is a very good actress. However, I'd still like to know why she switched us as infants."

"Me too." Ace sighed, also sipping his coffee. "Tell me about yourself," he urged. "I know we're not really related, but I feel like we could be brothers."

Though Jake preferred not to talk about himself, he complied. Ace Colton was surprisingly easy to talk to.

"I'm sure you've read about what happened to me," Ace said.

"When your—*our*—father was shot?"

"Yes." Ace nodded grimly. "I was framed for that. As if I'd ever hurt Payne. Luckily, they caught the guy who did it, a man who had a real grudge against my dad. But they suspected me because we all heard the news that I'm not really a Colton, at least by blood. That little bit of knowledge got me ousted from the board of Colton Oil and Dad and I got into an argument."

Jake winced. "Ouch. Though I know it's not my fault, I feel like I should apologize."

"No need." Ace waved him away. "My life is still good. I know my family—*our* family—still loves me, even if we don't share the same blood. I even recently learned I have an adult daughter from a long-ago relationship. Her name is Nova and she's pregnant. Which means I will soon be a grandfather."

"Wow. At our age?"

This made Ace laugh. "Yes. I'll be a young, hip grandpa." He leaned forward, his expression going serious. "Now tell me what it was like being raised by Micheline."

"Well..." Jake tried to think of a way to sound diplomatic. Then he decided the hell with it. Ace deserved to know the truth. "She's an awful woman," he said bluntly. "And always treated me like an afterthought or an unwanted pest. Which now makes sense. I ran away from home when I was seventeen and never looked back."

"Yet you returned now," Ace pointed out.

"She found me and made contact, claiming she has cancer." Jake shook his head. "Despite everything, she was my mother. Or so I thought. So I came back. Now, I'm glad I did. I always wanted a large family, with brothers and sisters."

"Well, you've definitely got that now."

"I do."

"I don't remember you from school," Ace pointed out. "Which seems weird."

Jake grimaced. "Micheline kept me home. She signed me up to be home schooled, but I mostly learned by myself. Luckily, I wanted to learn, so I was able to not only keep up with what everyone else was doing, but I graduated early."

"That's amazing."

Enjoying the camaraderie, Jake and Ace continued to share stories, talking and laughing until Ace's phone buzzed.

"My secretary is texting me," Ace explained. "I need to get back to the office. But I'd really like to get together again, soon." He handed Jake his phone. "Put your contact information in and I'll text you, so you can do the same."

After Jake dropped Ace off at the Colton Oil parking lot so he could retrieve his car, he couldn't stop smiling. Maybe something good would come out of this entire mess after all. He'd always wanted a brother. And family. The prospect of meeting them all was enough to make him decide to stick around Mustang Valley just a little longer.

Chapter Five

Considering Jake's words, aware he believed her to be as big of a fraud as Micheline, hurt more than it should have. Fiona wrestled with her conscience as she paced her small room. Being undercover did mean she had to play a role, and the most important thing here was her mission. Though she'd like nothing more than sharing the truth with him, in the end she couldn't risk Jake blowing her cover. There was too much at stake, including her professional reputation.

More importantly, if Micheline ever learned the feds were on to her, she might move up her timetable for whatever awful thing she had planned. They'd be caught unaware, and innocent lives could be lost. Fiona had no choice but to continue on playing the part of a fully indoctrinated cult member, no matter what the personal cost. Still, she ached for Jake. While she knew he would have eventually learned the truth, the fact that she'd been the one to unleash it on him, even accidentally, really bothered her.

Deep cover sometimes involved forgetting who you really were. So far, she hadn't achieved that level, and in this situation, she doubted she ever would. First, she wouldn't be here that long, and second, in a cult allowing oneself to actually be indoctrinated could be dangerous. Due to her intensive training, she honestly felt as if she was doing a good job of pretending. So good that Micheline and Leigh appeared to completely trust her. Everything she'd worked so hard to achieve appeared to be going forward exactly as she'd planned.

And then she'd met Jake. Talk about bad timing. One look from his blue eyes and she turned into a puddle of want and need. While she'd been attracted to other men, the way she felt about him was different. Stronger, more intense. As if she craved him with more than just her body.

The foolish, romantic notion made her scoff at herself. She'd never been a believer in sappy things like soul mates or love at first sight. This had to be simply an issue of overactive hormones or pheromones—something easily explained by science. Whatever the explanation, she couldn't stop thinking about him. Part of her hoped he would follow through on his threat to leave so she wouldn't constantly be tempted. The rest of her—*most* of her—wanted to throw herself into his arms and let passion take her where it may.

Not merely foolish. Dangerous. She'd need to be careful. Walking a fine line between her undercover persona and herself would be difficult, but not impossible. The knowledge that Jake hated liars shouldn't bother her, but it did. Far too much.

Jake already suspected something, though. Since she sensed the strong attraction went both ways, she figured he'd be easily distracted. Judging by the way they'd both reacted to the kiss, they'd both enjoy any distractions she decided to throw his way.

He probably wouldn't be a problem for too much longer, anyway. She knew he planned to go back home really soon, especially if his mother—who wasn't really his mother—continued to dodge him. Fiona couldn't blame him for wanting to put Mustang Valley in his rearview mirror. His entire childhood had turned out to be a lie. He'd built another life, his own life, far away from here. Once he'd gotten to know his new family and explored his options here in Mustang Valley, naturally, he'd want to get back to the familiar reality of his home, his ranch, even if just to put his affairs there in order. Unless Micheline found a way to stop him. Which Fiona wouldn't put past her.

After the incident with Underhill, Fiona had known better than to go look for Jake. After all, he'd made his feelings clear. She wished it didn't bother her so much—really, she barely knew the man, so it shouldn't—but it did. A lot.

Sighing, she twisted her hair into a neat ponytail and got dressed in her dressier day clothes. She wasn't sure what Leigh had scheduled for her, but she knew she was supposed to go to the infirmary and coerce a young man who'd just been beaten for no reason into signing up for a bunch of expensive classes.

For this odious task, she chose a different cheery yellow shift dress than the previous night's and tan heels. Bright colors helped lift her spirits. While she hated the thought of doing what they wanted her to do, it helped if she separated her true self from the person she had to be here. Cultist rather than FBI agent.

Her heels clicked as she walked down the hallway on the way to the infirmary. Perched on the edge of one of the massive sofas in the lobby, Leigh nodded and gave her a thumbs-up sign as she passed.

Fiona managed to smile back.

When she reached the infirmary, she stopped by the front desk. "I'm here to see Theodore."

Barely acknowledging her, the middle-aged attendant gestured toward the back. "Room three."

Here went nothing. Taking a deep breath, Fiona went to the back.

Theodore looked up from his phone when she entered. "Hey," he said, pushing up his wire-rimmed glasses. "They promised me someone was coming to take me back to campus. Is that you?"

"Why not?" Secretly relieved, she gave him a genuine smile. "How are you feeling today?"

He shrugged, dragging his fingers through his curly hair. "Embarrassed. I came here thinking it would be different than college. But it's not. It all sucks. Just once, I'd…" Stopping, he shook his head, his brown eyes earnest. "Never mind. I should be thanking you for helping me instead of complaining."

"You're welcome," she said. "If you're ready to go, I can drive you back to campus. We can talk along the way."

Since he was already dressed, he hopped down off the bed. "Sounds good. Let's do it."

She walked him out, half expecting the woman at the desk to stop them. Instead, she waved them past, still not looking up from whatever had her engrossed.

"It's a romance novel," Theodore confided, once they'd exited the room. "She reads them 24/7." He shrugged. "Whatever makes her happy."

This made her laugh. "You're a good guy, Theodore Royce the third."

Hearing her say his full name made him wince. "Just call me Theo. You're Fiona, right?"

"Right. Are you okay to walk to the back parking lot, or would you prefer I swing by here and pick you up?"

"I can walk," he hurriedly told her. "That guy didn't do anything to my legs. I have a couple of bruised ribs, though. You know, I still have no idea why he was even messing with me."

"Money," she replied. "He thinks you're rich, so he figured you could pay him."

"Rich doesn't mean stupid." He actually sounded indignant.

She took that as encouragement. Hopefully, he'd see through the sales pitch she was about to try to use on him.

They got into her vehicle, a government-issued sedan that, despite being painted maroon, still managed to look like an undercover police car. She waited until they'd pulled out of the long driveway before making her first attempt.

"I heard you might be interested in attending our self-enlightenment program," she began.

"Maybe." He shrugged. "I was, I mean. But now after what happened, I'm thinking there's nothing that can help me."

"Help you with what?" she asked, genuinely curious.

When he glanced at her, for a moment he let her see his misery. "I'm not doing well in school. I don't mean academically, because I'm good there. I just can't seem to make friends or get dates." He swallowed hard. "I'm lonely."

Damned if she could actually try to indoctrinate this poor kid.

Theo didn't seem to notice her indecision. "Anyway, Leigh told me about the classes. They sound intriguing. And the price isn't too bad, either." He glanced at her, almost shyly. "I really want to learn how to become the best person I can be."

It's all a load of BS, she really wanted to tell him. Of course, she couldn't, so she simply pressed her lips together and tried to think of some kind of noncommittal response to give.

Luckily, it didn't appear one would be needed. Theo continued to talk, evidently relieved to unburden himself. "I like the idea of knowing how to choose friends," he mused. "So far, all I've met are people who just want to use me. And the idea of learning how to choose the right significant other—that blows my mind."

She nodded, keeping her gaze on the road, not trusting herself to speak.

They reached the campus, and Theo directed her to his dorm. When she pulled up in front and put the car in Park, she turned to look at him. "Maybe you should just focus on your studies," she suggested quietly. "You're a freshman. Give it time, and you might be surprised at how seamlessly you'll eventually fit in."

"But what if I don't?" His slender form radiated tension. "That's easy for someone like you to say. I bet when you were my age, you didn't have these kinds of problems."

His comment made her laugh. "You'd be surprised," she told him. "I was scared and shy and homesick. I mostly hid in my dorm room the first semester." Of course, that had been when she hadn't found her true calling: law enforcement. She'd started out taking business classes, until a chance lecture had piqued her interest. From there, she'd gotten her degree in criminal justice. Applying to Quantico had been a no-brainer next step.

Squeezing his shoulder, she hoped he took her words to heart. "I promise you, it gets easier. Just give it time."

"I'll try." Opening the door, he got out of the car. "And I'll think about trying one of the seminars."

"You do that." As she watched him walk away, relief flooded her. Along with anger at Micheline and her machinations. Freshman college students, new to living on campus and away from home, were particularly vulnerable. The idea that Micheline wanted to milk them for money infuriated Fiona. At least Theo had given her something to say when Leigh asked her how it had gone. He'd said he'd think about it. And using a version of the truth was always the best option when undercover.

When she arrived back at the compound, she sat in her parked car for a few minutes, watching the yard staff do their thing. Finally, she got out of her car and strolled inside.

Almost instantly, Leigh appeared, making Fiona wonder if the other woman had been watching for her.

"Well?" Leigh demanded. "How'd it go?"

"He said he's going to think about it."

Leigh pursed her bright pink lips together. "You'll give him a day. Then I want you to start pressuring him. At least get him to sign up for the first seminar. Most times, that's all it takes. One class to open their eyes to the boundless possibilities we can lay out in front of them."

It took an effort not to roll her eyes. "Okay. I'm guessing you have his phone number?"

"Of course," Leigh purred. "I'll text it to you. I want you to call him first thing in the morning."

Fiona nodded. "Will do." She eyed the other woman. Leigh always seemed to be posing for something, as if she carried her beauty queen title into every second of her existence.

"Jake went out today, too," Leigh said, flipping her blond curls over her shoulder. She looked around the room before pinning her sharp gaze on Fiona, clearly watching for a reaction.

Not sure how to respond, Fiona said nothing.

"I think he was looking for you before he left," Leigh continued.

This got Fiona's attention. "Was he? Did he specifically say that?"

"Well, no." Leigh giggled. "Not in so many words. But it was pretty obvious. He was wandering around the first floor as if he was looking for something or someone. I'm guessing that most likely was you."

"Or Micheline," Fiona put in. "She still needs to meet privately with him."

"How do you know she hasn't?" The unrelenting, fake cheerfulness in Leigh's voice had Fiona clenching her teeth.

"Has she?"

Leigh tittered. "No. She's really very busy."

"I'm sure Jake is, too. As a matter of fact, he mentioned something about leaving soon."

Just like that, her words managed to wipe the smile off Leigh's face. "He can't," she said flatly. "Do whatever you have to, but make him stay."

"Why?"

Leigh blinked. "Are you questioning me? Seriously?"

"Yes." Crossing her arms, Fiona regarded the younger woman steadily. "I am. I need to understand why it's so important that Jake stay when it's clear Micheline doesn't find him a priority at all."

Just like that, all traces of friendliness disappeared from Leigh's face. "That is not for you to question, do you understand?" She waited a beat for Fiona to respond. When she didn't, Leigh repeated the question. "Do. You. Understand?"

The fury in Leigh's voice overrode Fiona's own innate stubbornness. Slowly, she nodded. She rearranged her expression, hoping she appeared abashed, even though inside she was seething.

"Good. Now." Leigh reached out and touched her shoulder, all friendly and confident again. "I want you to go look for Jake. Hang on him, bat those pretty brown eyes of yours, lay it on thick, do whatever you have to, but get him to stay." She paused to take a breath. "I'm counting on you. Micheline is counting on you. Heck, the entire AAG is counting on you."

That big? Deliberately, Fiona widened her eyes. "I'm honored," she whispered. "I'll do my best not to disappoint anyone."

"See that you don't," Leigh snapped. Then, softening her tone, she told Fiona how much Micheline valued her presence. "We all do," Leigh said, her earnest expression as intense as her tone. "We're committed to helping you become the best you."

"Of course," Fiona murmured, bowing her head. "And I promise that I won't let you down."

She couldn't help but catch Leigh's self-satisfied smirk as she turned away.

Head down, Fiona made it to her room. After closing the door, she debated taking a second shower, as if by doing so she could wash some of the icky feeling off her. She'd known coming in that she might be called upon to do things she considered unethical. She simply needed to do a better job of reconciling herself to being Micheline and Leigh's obedient little cultist.

The message had been clear—do whatever you have to do. They wanted her to seduce Jake. Hell, the thought sent a shiver of pure longing all the down her spine. One time, she thought wryly, where doing Micheline's bidding would actually be pleasurable.

Only Jake himself—knowing how betrayed he'd feel if he learned she'd used him—made following through on her orders difficult.

Enough, Fiona told herself sternly. She'd known this assignment wouldn't be easy. Time to pull on her big-girl panties and do what she had to do.

Oddly enough, as Jake drove back toward the compound, the first person he wanted to talk to was Fiona. A member of Micheline's evil little cult. Proof that he still was thinking with the wrong head.

Still, so much had changed in his life, and he had no one he could discuss it with.

Except Micheline, he reminded himself. Micheline knew. She'd always known. And for whatever reason, she'd let him grow up believing he was an only child and that she was his mother.

A family. He actually had a real family. For the sake of his own sanity, he couldn't allow himself to think about the missing years, the lost love. That would come later. Right now, he could only focus on the fact that he wasn't related in any way to that horrible, awful woman

Micheline. He felt kind of sorry for Ace, who had to be bummed at the knowledge that he carried her tainted genes. Jake had spent years trying to shed the rot he'd worried he'd carried deep inside, at a cellular level. Now, the colossal relief of knowing he didn't nearly overwhelmed him.

Still stunned at the news, he suspected it would take a long while to shed the full weight of the false past he'd believed to be his.

Back at the AAG center, Jake strode through the lobby, keeping his gaze fixed straight ahead. He didn't want to talk to anyone, least of all Micheline or one of her minions. Including—despite the way his heart skipped a beat at the thought of her—the beautiful Fiona. Uninterrupted, he went straight to his room, where he closed and locked the door.

Another man had lived the life he should have had. And Jake, growing up among all the suffering that he had told himself had been character building, was in reality a Colton.

Even so, he wouldn't wish his childhood on anyone. Especially Ace. Once, he'd even thought he'd seen Michelle kill someone and dump the body, but he was young and it was dark and he could not be sure of what he saw. Ace would never know how lucky he was to have been spared that.

Sitting on the edge of his bed, Jake reflected on the unexpected ease of the meeting today. Ace had been a hell of a nice guy. Odd how sometimes you met someone and felt that instant bond, as if they could be almost a brother—definitely friends.

Of course, Jake had felt the same way about Fiona, except stronger. That instant flash of connection. He groaned out loud, hating the way his thoughts always seemed to return to her. Even now, he still craved her. A woman enthralled by a cult run by the evil woman who'd raised him.

Thinking of all this made his head ache. So much had changed in his life in the last twenty-four hours. He needed to try and focus on that, instead of on something that could never be. No matter how much he might want it.

He was a Colton. Ever since he could remember, he'd heard stories about the powerful Colton family. They were a large, close-knit family and involved in everything, from ranching to oil. Here in Mustang Valley, they were spoken of with a kind of affectionate reverence. Truthfully, on the outside looking in, Jake had always assumed their success had to be due to the same kind of machinations that Micheline employed. Just the short time that he'd spent with Ace, hearing the other man's obvious affection for the Colton family, had made Jake begin to realize he might have been wrong.

And now he, too, was a Colton. Not that he planned to hang around long.

A soft tap on his door startled him out of his reverie. He immediately tensed, thinking maybe Micheline had finally sought him out. Bracing himself, he turned the knob and blinked. No Micheline, but the woman who haunted his every waking moment. Fiona.

"Hi." Her uncertain smile cut straight to his heart. "I'm wondering if we could talk."

She wore another formfitting yellow dress and sexy high-heeled shoes. Forcing himself to think before he spoke, he swallowed hard. He knew better than to let her into his room.

"May I come in?" she asked.

He stepped aside and let her in.

"Thanks." She appeared restless, uncertain. She strode to his window, her long legs made even more shapely in her heels, and twitched aside the curtain to peer out.

Though she kept her back to him, he couldn't seem to tear his gaze away from her.

Finally, she turned. "I came here to apologize," she said, her voice as miserable as her expression. "I shouldn't have told you about being switched at birth that way. I honestly suspected—hoped—you already knew."

Surprised, he shook his head. "I had no idea. It came as a hell of a big shock to me."

"I see that now. Anyway, I know what you think of me, and I couldn't bear to have you hold this against me, too." She swallowed hard, drawing his gaze to her slender throat. "I'm sorry, Jake. Really sorry."

Though every instinct urged him to take her into his arms, he didn't. Even now, he suspected she might be playing him, acting on Micheline's orders or something.

His lack of reaction appeared to be what she'd expected. "Take care, Jake. It was good to meet you."

He let her get halfway to the door before reaching out. He didn't grab her—no matter how badly he wanted to haul her up against him and kiss her senseless. Instead, he touched her shoulder, a mere brushing of his hand as she passed.

But it was enough. Enough to make her stop short, turning to look at him.

"Let me help you, Fiona," he heard himself say. "You don't belong here, not with these people. I can set you up with the therapist I mentioned who specializes in deprogramming."

Her gaze searched his face. "Why?" she asked. "What do you get out of it? It's been my experience that no one does something for nothing."

"I want to help you, nothing more. I can let you stay on my ranch—your own room—if you need a place to stay." He let her see some of his inner turmoil in his expression. "I can't bear to see someone like you under Micheline's power."

"So that's it then. You want to get back at Micheline for what she did to you."

"No. Of course not." Considering, he amended his statement, adding in the truth. "Well, I would like to see her pay for what she's done. Not to me, but to others. A nice jail cell with a sentence of twenty to thirty years would do nicely, though."

After a startled look, Fiona laughed. Really laughed, the sound infectious and honest and going straight to his gut. "You really mean that, don't you?"

"I do. And I'm also serious about getting you help. You're too good for this place, Fiona."

He expected her to argue or protest, to make excuses or to flat out deny. He didn't expect her to wrap her arms around him and pull him in close for a kiss.

A kiss that seared his soul and stopped all rational thought. As their lips moved together, his heart pounded in his ears, and his body moved, too. Involuntarily pressing his huge arousal into her soft curves.

She let out a sound, a moan of desire, of need. Then, as he fought to gather up the willpower to pull away, she matched him movement for movement. Tongue, hands and that curvy, soft, sexy body that he so badly wanted to sink into.

Damn he wanted her, so badly the need for her made him shake. But still, he held himself back, unable to keep from wondering if this wasn't yet another soul-crushing trick ordered by Micheline.

Did it matter? Yes. Fiona had to be here of her own free will, not at the behest of AAG.

"Wait," he muttered, even as his body contradicted his words. Somehow, he managed to put enough space in between them to enable his head to clear. "I need to know. Did Micheline or Leigh ask you to come here and..."

She hesitated, just long enough to give him his answer.

"Sorry, but no." This time, he wrenched himself free. Despite his arousal, he moved to stand on the other side of the bed, using it as a physical barrier between them. "You're clearly not in your right mind. I won't take advantage of you like that."

Staring at him, she blinked. "I promise you, I'm in my right mind. No one is forcing me to be here."

"You still didn't answer my question. Were you asked to come here and..."

"Get you to stay by using whatever means necessary?" She sat down hard on the edge of the bed, dragging her hand through her long, thick, dark hair. "Yes. Leigh used those exact words with me a little while ago."

His heart sank. The rest of him still had not registered the stand-down order.

"But that's not why I'm here," she breathed, her eyes locked on his. "I'm here because I'm incredibly attracted to you. I want you, Jake Anderson. Nothing more than that."

Every part of him wished he could believe her. He cleared his throat, willing away his unrepentant arousal. "Leave with me," he told her, desperate to give her one more chance. "Let me take you away from here, get you some help. Then we might revisit this."

"I can't." Her sensual mouth twisted. "I can't leave. I have a very real reason for being here."

"Then tell me."

She shook her head and pushed to her feet. "Come with me," she said, holding out her hand. "Let's walk outside." She pointed to her ear, then gestured around the room as if to say she thought someone might be listening.

He wouldn't be surprised.

Looking down at himself, he sighed. "I'm going to need a minute before I can walk anywhere."

Though she nodded, the way she eyed him, as if she wanted to gobble him up, made losing his arousal even more impossible. Tearing his gaze away from her, he moved into the bathroom. He might need a cold shower, but hopefully it wouldn't come to that.

Briefly, he considered taking matters into his own hands, just to regain a measure of control. But because he really, really wanted to lose himself in Fiona, he settled for the quick cold shower.

When he finally emerged again, she still waited.

"I'm good," he said, aware she'd no doubt heard the shower.

"Then let's go." And she took his hand.

Of course, his body jolted again when she slipped her slender fingers into his hand. Ignoring it, he concentrated on putting one foot in front of the other, well aware that somewhere Micheline or one of her people would be watching.

Outside, he took deep gulps of the dry, fresh air.

They walked in silence, and Fiona didn't speak until they'd rounded a curve in the drive and put the house out of view. She stopped, tugging on his hand to make sure he did, too. Gazing down at her upturned face, for one heart-stopping moment he thought he might kiss her. But he remembered why they'd come out here, and didn't.

"I'm deciding to trust you," she said, her expression both vulnerable and earnest. "If you betray my trust, for whatever reason, know that you'll put numerous lives at risk, not least of all my own."

Not sure if she was being overly dramatic or her words were really honest, he simply nodded for her to continue.

She took a deep breath. "I'm really not sure I should do this," she mumbled. "But here goes. I'm an undercover FBI agent. I'm investigating the cult and Micheline."

It took a few heartbeats for her words to even register. Shock. Then, thinking of the way she'd fought, understanding.

"You're serious?" he finally asked.

"Yes. That's why I can't leave. And why I don't need to go see a deprogrammer. Micheline is planning something big, something awful, though we don't yet know what. In addition to that, we've received numerous complaints about her swindling money. Lots of money."

"You *are* serious," he repeated, shocked and stunned

and overjoyed all at once. "That means you really aren't a brainwashed cultist."

"No, but I'm here to play one."

Just then he realized the chance she'd taken, trusting him. She'd risked her entire mission—maybe even her life—by trusting him. That was huge. Beyond huge.

He reached for her and she met him halfway.

As their lips met, he realized he'd just gained another reason to stay a bit longer. Now that he knew Fiona wasn't actually brainwashed, he could allow his burgeoning feelings full reign. And if Fiona planned to take Micheline and her cult down, he wanted to be here to see it.

Keeping the kiss short, he broke away. "Let's go back to my room."

"And finish what we started?" One brow arched, she smiled.

But it was the vulnerability still lingering in her dark eyes that undid him. "Yes," he said, grabbing her hand.

Chapter Six

Telling Jake made her feel as if a heavy weight had been lifted from her chest. She could breathe again, move again and let herself make love honestly again. Micheline and Leigh be damned.

I've jeopardized my mission, a little voice whispered inside her head. But no, she'd carefully considered. Jake had wanted to get her out, away from these people. There was no way in hell he was in with them. Especially after what Micheline had done to him.

They raced through the front door, through the lobby, earning more than a few curious stares. Instead of the elevator, they took the stairs, running up the steps hand in hand.

Once inside his room, he secured the door by putting the desk chair under the knob. When he turned, the raw need blazing from his face took her breath away.

"Come here, you," he said, holding out his arms.

Without hesitation, she went to him and wrapped herself around him.

"It's okay," he told her, nuzzling her neck. "I'm going to stay a little longer and help you."

She pulled him down to her, meeting his mouth with

hers. Not only to silence him, but because she needed to kiss him as much as she needed to breathe.

This time, as they came together, tasting, touching, allowing the craving to blossom, she felt her eyes sting with the beginning of tears. "Please give me your word that you won't reveal what I've told you. I know you won't, but I just need to hear you say it."

"Don't," he told her, wiping a stray bit of moisture away with his finger. "I give you my word, you won't regret this."

That made her smile. "Put it off any longer and I might prove you wrong."

With a shout of laughter, he kissed her again, deepening the kiss until her head swam and her knees were weak.

"Too many clothes," she mumbled against his lips. "Off with them."

Again he chuckled. "Patience." He reached for her shirt. She batted his hand away.

"You first. I want to see you naked."

"Okay." Keeping his gaze locked on hers, he slowly unbuttoned his shirt. Once he'd removed that, he went for his belt.

"Let me," she demanded, tugging the buckle open. When she undid his jeans and went to pull down the zipper, his erection surged free.

"Careful," he rasped.

"Hot damn." Slowly pulling his boxers and jeans down past his hips, she couldn't take her eyes off him.

"Boots," he said, choking on the word. He dropped back onto the bed, groaning as she knelt in front of him, pretending to be going for his feet. Instead, she grazed her lips over the engorged head of him and then she took him into her mouth. All of him, deep. He tasted like man and salt and sex.

Moving slowly, she relished the power of her taking him that way. In and out, falling into a rhythm and feeling her own body throb.

"Enough." He pulled her up and off him, pushing her back against the mattress. "While that was…extremely pleasurable, I want to be inside you."

Grinning up at him, she reached for him. "I want that, too."

"Wait." He grabbed his jeans, located his wallet and removed a condom. Once he'd managed to pull it over his arousal, he went back to her and kissed her again. Deep and fierce, his hands coaxing her back to life, his erection huge against her belly.

Slowly, she opened her legs and guided him to her.

One push and he filled her. Completely. For a heartbeat or two, he held himself utterly still, letting her body adjust to his size. "You're so damn wet," he groaned.

"You're so damn hard," she shot back, thrilling to the way his body pulsed at her words.

She arched her back, anticipating his next stroke, and moved to meet him.

They moved together, fast and furious, a crashing crescendo of desire and need. So raw, so instinctively honest, so…good. When she felt the beginning starburst of release building, she cried out. Her body clenched around him, and she gripped him tight while she shuddered from the strength of her climax.

A moment later, one final push and he joined her.

They clung to each other, damp and sweaty, the sweet, musky scent of sex filling the air.

"Wow." Totally drained, she rested her head against his shoulder. "That was…"

"Good," he finished for her, kissing the top of her head. "Amazing. Unbelievable. Should I go on?"

Smiling, she shook her head. "You understand what they're going to think?" she murmured, turning her head so that her mouth was pressed against his ear. "That I seduced you in order to get you to stay. Did it work?"

His quick bark of laughter made her wiggle and raise her head to look at him.

"Yes," he responded, kissing the tip of her nose. "Though honestly, now that I've met Ace Colton, I was planning to stick around awhile anyway."

Stunned, she eyed him. "You met Ace? When?"

"Earlier today. After I learned about my true parentage, I drove myself over to Colton Oil. Even though Ace no longer is CEO, I'd read in the local paper that he would be there for some kind of meeting, so I went in and introduced myself. We hit it off. He's a hell of a nice guy."

Unannounced, uninvited, Jake had simply shown up and asked to meet the man with whom he'd been switched at birth. She had to admire his bravado.

"And he met with you?" she asked, just to be clear.

Jake tilted his head. "Yes. You sound surprised. Don't you think he had to be curious, too? Naturally, he'd want to meet the man whose life should have been his."

She let her gaze roam over his rugged, handsome face. "You don't sound bitter. I don't know that I wouldn't be, if I were in the same position."

"Maybe a little," he admitted, lifting one bare shoulder. "But it's forty years in the past. There's nothing I or anyone else can do to change things. All we can do is move forward, one day at a time."

Admirable. She didn't know that she'd be able to be so sanguine if she were in his position.

He kissed her again, a quick press of his lips against her temple. "He's going to introduce me to the rest of his—of my—family," he said, his eyes drifting closed. "That should be interesting." He tightened his arms around her, pulling her in close.

Nestling into his embrace, she marveled at the myriad of complex emotions swirling around inside her. In the space of twenty-four hours, her entire situation had completely changed. On the one hand, as far as Micheline and Leigh were concerned, she'd been a good little cult member and done what they wanted by getting Jake to stay.

On the other, by revealing herself to Jake, she could have placed the entire undercover operation in jeopardy. Her gut twisted at the thought. But as she gazed at Jake's rugged profile, she just knew her trust wouldn't be misplaced. He wasn't a part of the AAG. Even before learning of his true parentage, he'd been destined for other things. He had his ranch, a life he'd built from the ground up. Soon, he'd have a new family to get to know. The machinations of Micheline Anderson and her merry little cult would figure very little in his world. Especially once he'd left here.

For Fiona as well. Once she'd completed this assignment, she'd go back to her job working out of the Phoenix office and her tidy little apartment downtown. Until her next assignment. Then this time she'd spent here in Mustang Valley would become nothing but a memory.

For now, she wanted to simply revel in the moment. She'd learned a long time ago to enjoy the happy moments when she could. Because in the crazy world she worked in, she knew they were few and far between.

She must have fallen asleep, because when she opened her eyes again, someone was trying to open Jake's door. Quietly, but clearly attempting to get the stuck door to open.

"Jake!" she whispered, nudging him with her elbow. He came awake instantly, and she held her finger to his lips to keep him silent.

Once more, the intruder rattled the door. The chair Jake had wedged under the knob held. Slowly, Jake sat up. "Who's there?" he asked, his voice stern.

"It's Micheline," a familiar voice answered back. "I think it's time we had a chat."

Talk about timing. Fiona's first instinct was to panic. How embarrassing! Her second had her burrowing deeper into the covers, thinking letting the cult leader find her here might not be a bad thing. After all, as far as Micheline was concerned, Fiona had simply done what she'd been told.

"Let her in," she murmured to Jake, keeping her chin up though her cheeks were hot.

One brow raised, he asked her if she was sure. When she nodded, he pushed himself off the bed, stepped into his jeans and, after zipping them, he answered the door.

"Micheline." He stepped aside, allowing her to see into his small room.

Fiona waved, just to make sure Micheline saw her.

"Oh." Micheline took a quick step back. Fiona had to stifle a smile.

"Sorry. I was busy." Jake dragged his hand through

his hair. "Maybe you should have considered calling first."

"I didn't know you had company," Micheline responded, sounding a bit tense. Translation—her spies hadn't informed her that Jake was with Fiona. "But I had a cancellation, which meant a couple of hours opened up in my schedule. I thought we could get together and talk."

Jake glanced over his shoulder at Fiona before gesturing toward a chair. "Come on in. Have a seat. We can talk here."

Micheline didn't move. "Alone," she clarified. She cut her eyes to Fiona, pasting an utterly false beatific smile on her perfectly made-up face. "Fiona, honey. Would you please go on back to your own room?"

"Of course," Fiona replied, dipping her chin. "I'll need to get dressed first."

"What if I want her to stay?" Jake asked, crossing his arms. "Fiona and I have become very close. She can hear anything you want to say to me."

Interesting. Fiona watched Micheline, curious to see which way this would go. On the one hand, Fiona was supposed to do whatever the cult leader wanted. On the other, Micheline would want to placate her son. Especially if she ever revealed the truth of his birth to his face. She had no way of knowing Jake already knew.

Or did she? Fiona frowned, looking down to hide it. She'd long suspected the presence of cameras and/or recording devices, which was why she'd made Jake go outside to discuss her true identity. She generally tried to be super careful with what she said, but perhaps Jake had not.

"Fiona can stay," Jake repeated when Micheline didn't respond.

Micheline ignored him, walking over to stand at the side of the bed and peering down at Fiona. "Honey, my son and I need to have a private, personal conversation. Would you mind going back to your own room?"

Mindful of the role she had to play, Fiona nodded. "Of course." She wrapped the sheet around herself, got out of bed, grabbed her clothes and hurried to the bathroom to dress.

When she emerged a few seconds later, she flashed a shy smile at Micheline and hurried for the door.

Before she could exit, Jake grabbed her arm. "Wait."

She shot him a look, hoping it conveyed a *don't ruin this for me* statement. Evidently it did, for he let her go.

"Thank you, sweetheart," Micheline purred as Fiona slipped out the door.

Outside in the hall, Fiona paused to catch her breath. Part of her wanted to rush back in and stand with Jake. But if she wanted to continue to play the obedient little cult member, she couldn't. Whatever Micheline wanted, Jake would have to deal with it alone.

BRACING HIMSELF ONCE the door closed behind Fiona, Jake turned back to face Micheline. He thought about making it easy on her and telling her he already knew, but why should he? Plus, she'd want to know where and when he'd found out, and how. Which would hurt Fiona and her mission.

Crossing his arms, he eyed the woman who'd raised him and said nothing.

"You don't have to look so angry," Micheline chided. "This is our chance to make up for lost time."

"Is it?"

"Yes." She reached out, clearly meaning to either hug him or squeeze his shoulder.

Neatly, he stepped away. If she touched him, he wasn't sure he could manage to conceal his revulsion.

Tilting her head, she considered him. "Why'd you leave all those years ago?" she asked quietly.

One of her tricks had always been to counter a question with another question instead of an answer, so he employed that now. "Did you even look for me? I was seventeen years old, out there on my own. Do you have any idea what kind of horrible things can happen to a boy that young?"

"Did they?" she asked. "I mean, did terrible things happen to you?"

Question after a question. He realized they could keep this up until the morning. "What do you want, Micheline?" he asked tiredly. "First you call me up and tell me you're dying, then you seem dedicated to avoiding me. Now all of a sudden, you've got something important to say. Why don't you just spit it out?"

Another woman might have decried the hardness in his voice or tearfully demanded to know what she'd done to deserve his apathy. Not Micheline. Either she already knew or she simply did not care. Jake would bet on the later. Or maybe even both.

"Fine," she sighed, her tone more annoyed than apologetic. "You're not really my son."

"What?" He snapped his head up, summoning back his first reaction when he'd learned the news. Shock and disbelief.

"It's true. We're not blood related. I switched you

with another infant at the hospital when you were a day old."

Pretending shock seemed anticlimactic. Instead, he settled on rage. "Why?" he asked. "Why would you do such a thing?" Maybe now she'd give him some answers.

"I should have just given my baby up for adoption," she mused, still avoiding his question. "There was this other infant who wasn't doing so well. *You.*"

Confused, he eyed her. "So you traded your healthy child? That doesn't even make sense." But then, knowing her, he realized it did. "You thought I was going to die, didn't you?" Horror filled him—fury, too.

Micheline, being Micheline, merely shrugged. She didn't even have the grace to try and appear ashamed. "To my surprise, you didn't. You thrived. The other baby started out sickly, but he did, too. *My* baby. I was able to keep tabs on him, because he became part of the most prominent family in Mustang Valley. My birth son is a Colton now. While you…" She let her gaze travel over him. "Clearly never felt any connection to me at all."

No remorse. No apologies. If anything, she seemed to be gloating. Horrible, awful woman.

When he'd been a child, he'd wondered what was wrong with him that his own mother couldn't seem to love him. As he'd grown and come to realize what kind of person Micheline actually was, he'd reckoned her lack of maternal instincts were a blessing in disguise. Despite that, he still carried scars from his younger years. This was one of the reasons he'd continually shied away from relationships: his fear of allowing any woman to hurt him the way his mother had.

"Do you even have cancer?" he asked abruptly. "Or was that sob story a ruse to get me to come home and see you?"

She narrowed her eyes. "How could you think such a thing?"

Again, not answering his question. "Because I know you. Do you or do you not have cancer?"

"I do," she finally replied, though she dropped her head to avoid meeting his eyes. "I'll be starting treatment soon."

"What treatment? Chemo? Radiation?"

"Yes. Both of those." She sighed heavily. "Instead of focusing on me, don't you want to know the name of the man who grew up with the life that should have been yours?"

Right for the jugular. She was a real piece of work, that Micheline. "You already told me. A Colton."

"There are a lot of Coltons all over the country," she countered.

"Sure." All he wanted now was to get her out of his room. "Who is it?"

"Ace Colton." Triumph rang in her voice. "He's one of the most valuable members of that powerful family."

Valuable. Odd choice of words. But sadly appropriate, since she always made sure Jake knew his existence held no value for her.

Be Your Best You. Her catchy little meaningless phrase flashed into his mind.

A flash of rage went through him, so strong he had to clench his hands into fists. He wanted to lash out, to tell her what he thought of her, and on top of that, how he felt about this, the ultimate betrayal.

Instead, he did none of those things. Partly because

he suspected she wouldn't care and partly because he really wanted to know what she planned to do now.

Swallowing, he looked down at his feet, taking deep breaths and stuffing his anger back deep inside. When he felt he could speak normally, he raised his head to find her watching him, her expression both gleeful and yet somehow full of pseudo-concern. Even here, alone with him, she still felt the need to continue to play a role.

"Why tell me this now?" he asked.

"I'm dying," she replied, injecting a note of pathos into her tone. "And I'm trying to right the wrongs of my past."

Coming from anyone else, anyone but her, he might have believed that. After all, that was exactly the kind of thing a rational, caring human being might do in their final months or years of life. But this was Micheline. He might have been gone from her life for the last twenty-three years, but he knew damn well she hadn't changed. Not one bit.

"The truth, Micheline," he prompted, letting some of his exhaustion show. "What's your angle?"

At that, she drew herself up. "I don't have an *angle*, as you so charmingly put it. I run one of the largest self-help organizations in Arizona. People look up to me, and I help them. I *help* them, Jake. Not hurt them. Because of me, thousands of people are becoming their best selves."

Ugh. If he heard that tired old phrase one more time.

"Are you afraid the baby-switch story will get out?" he asked, watching her closely. "If your followers learned what you did, maybe they wouldn't follow you."

That made her laugh. And laugh. So long and so hard tears streamed down her cheeks. Finally, she got herself together, grabbing a tissue off his dresser and dabbing at her face. "Not likely," she managed.

Since he didn't have a response for that, he simply jerked his chin in a reasonable facsimile of a nod. About to tell her to get out, he closed his mouth when she spun around on her expensive high-heeled shoes and strode to the door. "Take care, Jake." She fluttered her fingers. "I'm sure we'll talk again. I'm guessing you're sticking around awhile, since you and Fiona appear to have a thing going on."

"Maybe," he allowed. "But if I do decide to leave, I'll make sure and have one of your minions inform you."

"Minions!" She tittered, though her eyes remained hard. "How quaint. And really, you should give it a few more days. Things are just about to get really interesting around here. And you might be able to play a big part in it."

And then she left, shutting him in his room with a decisive click of the door.

He wanted to throw something, break something, toss back a shot or two of whiskey. Instead, he thought of Fiona, with her lush body and huge brown eyes. Though she too had lied to him, she'd had good reason. She had a mission, a task, and if there was anything he could do to help her accomplish it, he would. He wanted to dedicate his life to bringing Micheline down. Helping Fiona, who seemed as different from Micheline as night from day, would help expunge some of his bitterness and maybe even help him heal.

Things were about to get interesting around here, Micheline had said. Which meant Fiona was right—the cult leader had something planned, though he didn't know what, only that it appeared to involve him. And maybe even the Coltons.

Too drained to do anything but stay in his room, Jake tried to call Fiona, but she didn't pick up. He wondered if she'd been summoned by Micheline. Still, she was the last thing he thought of before he drifted off to sleep.

Ace Colton called right after breakfast the next morning. "The family would love to meet you," he said. "Payne was just released from the hospital. He's a bit weak, but he's eager to get to know you. Would you be available to come by the house for dinner tonight?"

"I'd love that," Jake replied.

"Perfect." Ace's voice turned serious. "I'll brief you a bit ahead of time. All the Coltons are trustworthy—the siblings, the triplet cousins—but Selina Barnes Colton, my father's ex-wife, is not to be trusted." Here he gave a small, self-conscious chuckle. "I guess I should have said *your* father's second wife. Selina is my ex-stepmother and is on the board of Colton Oil. She's a witch. At least Dad had the sense to divorce her. Genevieve is much nicer. Whatever you do, don't trust Selina. Just watch out for her, okay?"

"That I can do," Jake said. "I've read a little about all of them. As for Selina, I have some experience with women like that. I was raised by one."

"Ouch." Ace went silent for a moment and then continued on. "Anyway, even though it's going to be a huge family get-together, I don't want you to feel uncomfortable. I can try to get them to scale it back some. Payne got really excited and went overboard, despite barely being out of the hospital. Genevieve loves big parties. Though she's been invited, Selina is grinding her teeth."

"You know, I'd rather just meet your immediate family right now, if that's all right with you," Jake admitted. "It's already a lot to take in. Meeting the extended family right off the bat might be too much." Overwhelming, actually. Still in shock, he'd prefer to take this in small doses, a few people at a time.

"Thank goodness." Relief rang in Ace's voice. "At least now I might stand a chance in hell of reasoning with Payne. Oh, and if you want to bring a date or a friend, that's fine, too."

Jake immediately thought of Fiona. Would she want to go, or was it too much, too soon? Though they'd made love, they barely knew each other. He guessed it would depend on whether or not a dinner with the Colton family fit into her mission. "I'll let you know," he said. "What time do you want me to be there?"

"How about seven?"

"Sounds good. I'll text you if I decide to bring someone."

"Ah, you've got to ask her first."

"Exactly." Smiling, Jake ended the call. He wouldn't exactly blame Fiona if she begged off going. Still, it didn't hurt to ask.

Chapter Seven

As soon as she rose the next morning, Fiona showered and rushed through her makeup and getting dressed. At any minute, she expected either Leigh or Micheline to summon her and quiz her about her developing relationship with Jake. After all, the cult leader had walked in and found Fiona in Jake's bed.

When nothing happened, it almost felt anticlimactic. She guessed Micheline had seen enough to feel confident Jake would stay.

Fiona thought of Jake. Of the way his hands had felt on her skin, how his body had filled hers, how they'd fit together so well. While she wasn't usually prone to poetic, flowery thoughts about sexual mechanics, Jake had made her body sing.

Pleasantly sore, she wondered how he'd act around her now. Would things be strange? She hoped not. While Micheline's dramatic entrance had made for an awkward ending to a wonderful night, she hoped Jake could get past all that. Privately, Fiona considered him the best part of this entire undercover assignment.

She pushed away her thoughts and made her way to the cafeteria for breakfast. Since only a small group of AAG members lived at the house full-time, the meals were set up buffet style. After grabbing a couple of spoonfuls of scrambled eggs, she took two slices of bacon and a muffin, filled her cup with coffee, and took a seat.

Jake appeared just as she took her first sip. He looked happy, she thought, watching as he went through the line and got his own breakfast. He made his way directly to her table.

"Mind if I join you?"

Her heart leaped at the sight of him, but she managed to keep her expression cool. "Have a seat."

Jake mustn't have been a morning person, either. She got it—most days she preferred not to have to speak to anyone until she'd downed a least one cup of coffee. They ate together in companionable silence, and it wasn't until they both finished their meal, when he offered to get her a refill, that she felt cheerful enough to initiate friendly conversation. "That'd be great, thanks."

"Cream and sugar?"

"No." She made a mock face. "Just black."

"Good choice."

When he returned a moment later, he placed both their coffees down on the table. "Do you want to hear what Micheline had to say last night?"

Immediately, she glanced around them, giving her head a tiny shake. "Not here," she mouthed.

"My bad," he mouthed back. "I forgot."

Curiosity won out. She pushed to her feet, taking another sip of her hot coffee. "Do you want to go for a walk? This is the best time of the day for that, as far as I'm concerned."

Taking the hint, he got up, too. "Sure."

Side by side, they took a leisurely stroll through the

mostly empty lobby. Fiona made a show of gazing adoringly up at him.

Outside, he grinned. "You can stop with the adoring looks now."

"Who says I want to?" she quipped.

This made him laugh.

They continued on down the long, winding driveway. A small gravel path led to several of the maintenance sheds. Impulsively, Fiona took it.

"Where are we going?" Jake asked. "Are those storage buildings?"

"Yes, but we're not going that far." She looked around, taking care to make it casual. "I have no idea where they might have cameras hidden. I just want to make sure we don't have eyes on us."

"Paranoid much?" Jake teased. "Surely, Micheline doesn't have the entire grounds wired."

She shrugged. "Probably not. And I have to be paranoid. I can't take a chance on blowing my cover."

As they neared the largest maintenance shed, she spied a security camera mounted just under the roof. "Come here," she murmured, keeping her back to it. "Don't look, but I've spotted a camera. Give me a kiss so we can make it seem like we snuck off somewhere private to make out."

Again, that flash of a sexy grin. "Gladly."

He pulled her in close. The moment his mouth covered hers, the lighthearted mood vanished. Passion, white-hot and fierce, flared instantly. For a moment, just that second in time, she allowed herself to give in to it, to him.

"Keep that up and we'll be doing a lot more than

making out," he warned, the rasp in his voice matching the heat in his eyes.

"You're right." She took a deep breath, trying to steady herself. "I don't know why, but with you, I always get carried away."

Shaking his head, he yanked her close and kissed her again.

When he finally moved back, they were both shaking.

"Okay," she said, taking his hand and leading him back toward the driveway. "Tell me what Micheline had to say after I left your room last night."

Just like that, his smile vanished. Fiona actually felt awful for being the one to make it go away.

"Basically, she told me the truth. She switched me with another infant in the hospital. She even went so far as to tell me why."

Something in his voice… "Do I want to know?" she asked.

"Why not?" His mouth twisted. "She took me because one baby was sickly and the other wasn't and she wanted her child to be raised a Colton heir. ."

"Ouch." Wincing, she squeezed his hand. "She's a horrible person, but we already knew that. Still, that must have been hard to hear."

"It was. No matter that I know she's not related to me in any way by blood, despite being well aware of how awful and soulless she is, that still hurt. Made me wonder if all during my childhood, she might have been plotting to kill me and make it look like an accident."

Though she wouldn't have put it past Micheline, she kept that thought to herself. "Well, at least one good thing has come of this," she said instead. "You've got an entirely new family to get to know."

"True." He eyed her, his expression clearing. "Speaking of them, Ace invited me to dinner tonight. He said it would be okay to bring a plus-one. Would you like to go?"

"Me?" Her initial reaction was to refuse. First off, all they knew about her was that she was a member of AAG. Secondly, this was Jake's time, and why would the Colton family want an outsider to bear witness to what would surely be an emotional and touching reunion?

But then she realized maybe Jake might need her support.

And that trumped anything the Colton family might want.

"Yes, you." Leaning in close, Jake brushed a kiss on her cheek. "Up to you, no pressure. But I wouldn't mind having someone in my corner while I'm there. It's going to be awkward, no matter how you put it."

Just as she'd thought. He *needed* her. "I'd love to go," she responded. "It'll be fun."

He laughed again. "I wouldn't go that far. But it will be interesting, that's for sure. Meet me in the lobby around six thirty?"

"Perfect." Her phone chimed. She checked it and groaned. "That's Leigh. I'm being summoned. I'm guessing she'll want to go over my progress in convincing you to stay. I wish I knew why that's so important to Micheline. What part does she have planned for you to play?"

"I don't know," he replied. "If I can, I'll try to find out. In the meantime, I'm going into town to do some exploring. I'm guessing you won't be able to break free to go with me."

She tapped her phone. "It doesn't look like it. Enjoy your day and I'll see you tonight."

They walked back toward the house together, but instead of going inside, Jake veered off toward the parking lot and his truck. She stood in the drive and watched him go, waving once when he turned around to look back at her.

Inside the house, Fiona headed immediately toward Leigh's suite. To her surprise, no one answered when she knocked on the door. She tried the knob. It was locked. Now what?

She dug out her phone and texted Leigh. I'm here. Where are you?

Almost immediately, a text came back. I got called into a meeting. We'll have to reschedule later. There are a couple of good seminars starting up right now. Go learn.

Ugh. Attending another class ranked up there among things she'd avoid at all costs if possible. She responded with a smiley face emoji, aware that was vague enough that she couldn't be accused of lying later.

Now that she'd made it seem like she'd be occupied the next couple of hours, she could do some exploring. Ron Underhill, the man who'd been busted for attacking Theo, had mentioned something about cells. The stark terror in his expression meant they weren't a good place. Did Micheline have her own prison or holding cells somewhere on the property? Since Micheline acted like queen of her own little kingdom, Fiona wouldn't be surprised to learn the other woman meted out her own form of justice. Not just illegal, but if Fiona could obtain proof, it would be further grounds to not only arrest Micheline, but to shut the AAG down.

Though it was generally rare to find a house with a basement in Arizona, she had to wonder if Micheline had thought it worth the cost to have one. After all, if one were going to have prison cells, what better place to put them than underneath the house? Like dungeons in old castles.

Though she'd seen nothing to indicate this might be the case, the first thing she decided to look for was a door leading to a stairwell. She figured it wouldn't be anywhere obvious or easy to get to, which ruled out the common areas. Maybe near the kitchen or the laundry area.

Generally, no one but the workers entered the kitchen, but when she pushed through the double doors, moving purposely as if she belonged there, no one stopped her. Which was good, because the best excuse she'd been able to come up with had been to say she'd gotten hungry and wanted to rustle up a snack.

After passing through the entire kitchen, which, with its gleaming stainless steel equipment, resembled something found in a high-end restaurant, she emerged in a small hallway. Since she could now smell detergent and fabric softener, she guessed the laundry room would be down that way.

Why not? She might as well check it out since she'd come this far.

Sure enough, the next door on the left opened to a large laundry space, again more reminiscent of a hotel than a private home. Of course, the AAG center did house around twenty guests, plus maybe ten to fifteen staff members, though most of the workers made the drive in from town each day.

About to turn around and head back the direction from which she came, she realized the hallway didn't end after the laundry room, as she'd first supposed. A small hallway, an alcove really, sat on the right, just past it. And at the end of this, a door marked No Entrance.

Which meant it was probably kept locked.

Just in case, she tried the handle. To her surprise, it turned.

Glancing around her—she didn't even see any of the usual cameras she'd noticed everywhere—she opened the door and slipped inside.

Cement walls. And a concrete staircase, leading down. Still wishing she had her pistol, she began slowly descending the stairs, moving as quietly as possible.

Heart pounding, Fiona tried to imagine what she might find. A medieval-type torture chamber? A clean, gleaming modern prison? Or something in between?

At the bottom of the stairs, she encountered another door. Thick steel and windowless. This one was locked.

On the off chance that someone might have been careless, she stood on tiptoe and felt along the top of the door frame, hoping to find a key. No such luck.

Still, the mere fact that there was space under the house was worth looking in to. There had to be another entrance, she thought. Having only one way in and out would be unsafe, to say the least.

Turning, she retraced her steps. This time, when she went through the kitchen, she snagged a small bag of vegetable crisps from the pantry. One of the workers frowned at her but didn't comment.

She'd have to figure out another way to access the

basement. Underhill's comments—and his very real terror—had made her curious to learn what other dark secrets Micheline might be hiding.

In downtown Mustang Valley, the well-decorated store windows and clean store fronts made Jake realize how much the locals loved this town. It also made him realize how seldom Micheline had let him leave. Even when he was a small child, she'd rarely taken him out in public. He'd actually believed that was normal until he'd learned from classmates about their celebrations.

Now that he knew Micheline had never really loved him, he had a better understanding of why his childhood had been so bleak. He knew now not to take it personally, but he wasn't sure how else to handle it.

Focus on the present, he reminded himself. He hoped and prayed the FBI could bring Micheline and the AAG down. And more than anything, he wanted to be there when it happened.

Once more, he pondered Micheline's actual plan. Was she trying to turn her cult into its own religion, make herself into the next prophet, sent by a higher being to tell her followers what to think and how to live their lives? Did she plan to delve deeper, beyond her Be the Best You seminars into something else?

He shook his head. Since he was sticking around here for a while—exactly how long, he hadn't yet decided—he hoped he could be there when Micheline was arrested and charged. She'd gotten away with so much over the years. Even before he'd left home, he'd been pretty sure he'd witnessed her hiding a body that one time.

Thoroughly exasperated with himself, he decided to put all thoughts of the woman who'd switched him at birth out of his mind. He needed to prepare himself mentally to meet the people with whom he should have been raised. The idea filled him with a crazy combination of anticipation and dread.

Ridiculous, if he thought about it. At forty years old, he'd overcome the handicaps of his past and knew he had an easygoing nature. Generally, he had no difficulties making friends. None of what had happened was his fault. In fact he, as well as the Colton family, was a victim in all this.

But would Payne Colton view it that way? From what Jake had read about him, the man wasn't someone who took well to being crossed. Surely, Payne wouldn't blame Jake for any of this.

Despite the mental pep talk he gave himself, he still felt nervous as he got ready to meet Ace's—*his*—family. He wasn't sure how they'd react to him now, with so many years gone by, especially after learning that all along, their true son had been living with a megalomaniac narcissist. *Their true son.*

He swallowed, the thought a bitter pill. Then he considered how Ace must feel, knowing his entire life had been one big lie. No matter what angle one came at the thing from, it all sucked.

A quiet tap on his door coaxed a reluctant smile. Fiona. Though they'd planned to meet in the lobby, she must have changed her mind and decided to come fetch him instead. He truly considered meeting her one of the best things about this visit.

Opening the door, he stared. She grinned at him, her long, dark hair swirling around her shoulders. She wore a silky white dress that clung to her figure and simple silver and turquoise jewelry.

"Well?" she asked, twirling slightly as she stepped inside his room. "Will this do?"

"You look amazing," he told her, leaning in for a quick kiss. "Let's go."

As usual, they made a show of strolling through the common area, hand in hand.

Once they were in his truck, she sighed. "This place is starting to get on my nerves. But you're not going to believe what I found. There's a basement under the main building."

She went on to describe a staircase with a door at the top and the bottom. "I couldn't get through, since the bottom door was locked."

"What do you think is on the other side?" he asked, backing out of the parking spot and driving down the long driveway.

"Well, when they dragged Underhill away, he started going on about cells, as in prison cells. I'm trying to see if perhaps Micheline has her own personal prison. Or torture chamber."

"I wouldn't put it past her." In fact, the more he considered, the more he believed Fiona was right. "I'll help you look for the other door," he said.

She eyed him. "It might be better if we look separately. There's much less chance of being discovered that way."

"Maybe," he allowed. "But it's also an easier explanation if we're caught. We can simply say we were looking for a private place to have a little fun."

This made her laugh, the sound light and feminine and making his heart squeeze. He needed to remember to be careful around this woman. The intensity of the feelings she aroused in him equaled how badly he could get hurt.

Following the directions on his phone GPS, Jake drove through town and into the country, heading toward the mountains. On the way, they passed a huge wrought iron gate that barred entrance to a gated, clearly wealthy enclave. "I've never been in there," he murmured. "Until I began researching, I would have thought that would be the kind of place a Colton would live."

"Payne Colton is a rancher," Fiona said. "He and all of his family live at Rattlesnake Ridge Ranch. I've never been there, but I've seen lots of pictures. It's a gorgeous place, made to look like a luxurious guest ranch overlooking the Mustang Valley mountains."

"I'm aware, but how do you know all this?" he asked, curious.

She laughed. "Research. I had to do quite a bit of reading about Mustang Valley before I took this assignment."

They continued on, his GPS letting him know he still had about ten miles to go. The flat countryside seemed greener, maybe owing to the more fertile soil as they neared the high desert and the mountains.

Here there were what Jake thought of as ranchettes—wealthy people with luxurious homes and land who wanted to dabble in ranching or farming. He saw a smattering of horses, a few cattle, even a herd of goats, their glossy coats gleaming in the bright sunshine.

"This is beautiful," Fiona said, clearly impressed. "If I had money, I'd live someplace like this."

"Me, too," he replied absently. According to the GPS, they were nearly there.

She gave him a curious glance. "I thought you did. I swear you or someone told me you had your own ranch."

This made him laugh. "Oh, I do. But it's a real working ranch. Not all fancy like these."

"I'd love to see it someday," she said, surprising him.

Before he could figure out how to respond, the GPS announced they'd arrived at their destination. Ahead of them sat a home, surrounded by fenced fields. In the distance was an actual cattle ranch, with huge, fancy white barns, more fenced pastures and animals dotting the hillside. This place made his own small ranch look like nothing. He couldn't help but wonder what it must be like, running this kind of operation. He supposed he would have known, had not Micheline switched him and Ace.

"Wow." Jake slowed. "This is amazing. I wonder how much acreage they have."

"I believe I read thousands of acres," she said. "That's why there are no other houses after this one."

Gripping the wheel tightly, Jake turned into the long driveway. "Three stories and multiple wings." He shook his head. "This makes the AAG center look like a summer camp."

His comment made Fiona laugh. "Yes, it definitely does."

A huge gate marked the entrance to the ranch. Three *R*s were inset right in the center. "Rattlesnake Ridge Ranch," Fiona said. "I wonder if they really have a problem with rattlesnakes."

"That wouldn't work with livestock," Jake told her. "I'm sure they took care of getting rid of them."

"Maybe." Fiona shrugged. "But even if they wiped out the entire snake population one year, they couldn't ever completely eradicate them. Especially if they were so numerous the ranch was named after them."

"Annual rattlesnake roundup." Jake squinted into the sun. "That's what I'd do, anyway. And judging from the looks of some of those cattle, he's got some high-value herds here."

"Of course." Grinning, Fiona gestured at the expansive land, the stunning house, the quality fencing. "I mean, what do you expect for a Colton, right?"

He nodded. The Colton name had always been synonymous with luxury, the kind of lifestyle many in Mustang Valley wished they could emulate. Jake's research had revealed the family was not only wealthy, but kind. They participated in numerous charities and quietly helped many who were less fortunate. The more he learned about them, the more he realized they were to be admired.

Driving slowly, he finally pulled up close to the house. In addition to the driveway, there were separate garages with their own parking areas. He decided to park his truck there. They could walk up to the house.

They got out of the truck. As she walked to him, Fiona gazed around her. "Just think," she murmured, squeezing his shoulder. "If things had been different, you would have grown up here."

He grimaced, refusing to acknowledge the ache her words caused inside him. Not just the ranch or the riches or even the Colton name, but the idea of family, people who would stand by your side no matter what. Something he'd never had and never believed he would. "Probably so. I can't imagine. I've never seen a ranch like this."

"I wonder if this is why you became a rancher. Maybe it runs in your blood."

"That's a very real possibility." He didn't let on that that, too, hurt him. He'd never known the truth of his past, his heritage, his family. Now at long last, he might finally get some glimpses of understanding of some of the factors that had contributed to making him the man he was today.

Side by side, they walked up to the front door, and he pressed the doorbell, wondering if there would be servants.

Ace himself answered the door, grinning. "Welcome," he said, clapping Jake on the back.

"This is Fiona Evans," Jake said. "Fiona, Ace Colton."

She held out her hand, but Ace pulled her in for a hug instead. Eyes wide, she made a face at Jake over Ace's shoulder, making him smile and breaking up some of the tension coiled inside him.

"Come on in," Ace invited.

When they stepped into the foyer, a delicious smell drifted their way. Mexican food, Jake thought. His favorite.

As they walked inside, Fiona's heels clicking on the wood-look tile floors, he caught sight of several people gathered in the kitchen. His heart jumped into his throat.

Some of his unease must have shown on his face.

"Relax," Ace murmured. "It's all good. Just my dad and my brothers and sisters, along with their significant others." He gave a self-conscious laugh. "Correction, *your* brothers and sisters. I managed to get them all to come to dinner on short notice. Please understand, my father—*your* father—just got out of the hospital."

He glanced toward the kitchen. "He's still a bit weak, though don't let him know I said that. He prides himself on being strong."

"I remember hearing about that," Fiona interjected. "He was shot, wasn't he? I'm so glad to hear he's on the mend."

Jake glanced at Ace. Payne had been shot and in a coma at the very same hospital where Jake and Ace had been switched at birth. Ace had actually been accused of shooting him after it was discovered he wasn't Payne's son. As Ace had told him, the real killer had been caught, but Ace had lost his job as CEO of Colton Oil since the company's bylaws stated the company's CEO had to be a biological Colton.

Enduring all of that must have been hell. Jake couldn't help but admire Ace for making his way through it so well.

"Are you ready?" Ace asked. "They're all eager to meet you."

"Likewise," Jake replied, pretending his stomach wasn't clenched into knots. As if she knew, Fiona slipped her arm through his, offering her physical support.

Then the introductions started. An older man with silver hair moved slowly over, leaning on a cane. "Damn bandages," he muttered. He stepped forward, his gaze intense as he shook Jake's hand. This must be his father, Payne, with his latest wife, Genevieve, standing slightly behind him, her expression both concerned and friendly.

His *father*. Jake had never figured he'd even know his father's name, never mind meet him. Wary, a bit uncertain, Jake eyed the older man, not sure what to say or how to act.

Before Jake and Payne could even exchange words, the older man enveloped Jake in a gruff, partial hug. "Sorry, I'm still a bit sore," Payne said. "We've known about your existence a good while now, though we had no idea who you'd turn out to be. You don't know how good it is to finally meet you."

"Same here," Jake replied.

Ace clapped both men on the back. "First we all got an anonymous email, letting us know I was switched with another infant in the hospital. Next, some guy named Jace Smith claimed to be the Colton baby that was switched." Ace shook his head. "This must have infuriated Micheline, because she eventually waltzed into our office and announced she'd been the one to do it and she alone knew who was the missing Colton heir."

Spoken without a single note of rancor or bitterness. Again, Jake couldn't help but admire the man.

"I'm almost glad I was in a coma for most of this," Payne said. When he raised his head to look into Jake's face, Payne's eyes gleamed with unshed tears. "She's a piece of work, that Micheline. I wish you could have met Tessa," he said, his voice breaking. "Your mother. You look so much like her. She died from lung cancer years ago, when all three of her children were young. She was kind, loved animals and had a big heart. She was an amateur photographer, always with the camera. Pretty damn good at it, too. She would have been thrilled to meet you."

Rummaging in his pocket, he pulled out a wallet and extracted a creased photograph. "This was her, holding who we thought was Ace in the hospital. She had no idea any of this ever happened."

Accepting the snapshot, Jake's breath caught in his chest. His mother had been beautiful, with long, dirty-blond hair and a kind, expressive face. *Tessa.* The woman who'd carried him, birthed him and lost him, had never known her baby had been switched. And now she never would. Jake couldn't believe she was dead. Ace must have forgotten to mention that. Jake nodded, struggling to find the right words. To his surprise, tears stung the backs of his eyes, too. "She's lovely," he managed, passing the photograph back. "I would have loved to meet her."

"I would have liked that as well," the old rancher said. Turning slowly, he eyed Ace and beckoned him over. "You're both my sons, no matter what. Please understand that."

Ace smiled. "Thanks, Dad." He raised his head and sniffed the air. "That food smells insanely good. When are we going to eat?"

"Let Jake meet the others first," Payne chided, seemingly oblivious to the way his current wife continued to glare at his back. "Come on, Jake. Let me introduce you and your lovely friend to the rest of the family."

Grabbing Fiona's hand, Jake followed his father. He met his full sister Ainsley, an attorney for Colton Oil, and her fiancé, fellow lawyer Santiago Morales. Next his brother Grayson, a first responder who kept his arm around his date, Savannah. Then his younger half sister, Marlowe, a pretty blonde who said she was the current CEO of Colton Oil, her fiancé, Bowie, and their baby son, Reed. Her twin Callum, a muscular man who said he worked as a bodyguard, appeared with his live-in love, Hazel, and her daughter, Evie. Hazel was a chef and had prepared their dinner this evening. Ace's daughter Nova, visibly pregnant, smiled shyly while her beau, Nikolas, shook Jake's hand. Rafe Colton, Payne's adopted son, was there with his fiancée, Detective Kerry Wilder, and so were Marlowe's and Callum's brother, Asher, and his love, Willow, with their baby daughters. Jake also met a petite, slender woman with reddish-blond hair named Sierra Madden, Ace's girlfriend. Triplet cousins Spencer, Bella, and Jarvis Colton—along with their respective partners, Katrina, Holden, and Mia, plus Mia's son, Silas—were also in attendance.

Selina, Payne's second wife, had apparently declined to attend, as Jake saw no sign of her.

By the time the introductions had finished, Jake felt better. He'd give himself a fifty-fifty shot at remembering the names, but everyone seemed kind and easygoing.

"Time for dinner," Genevieve announced, her soft voice matching her large, kind eyes. They all traipsed after her to a large formal dining room. Inside, an amazing Western-style, cedarwood table had been set with plates of every color. The decor seemed like a mix between Western and a Mexican fiesta. Elegant, yet homey. He liked it a lot.

"Fiestaware," Fiona breathed. "My favorite."

"There are place cards on the table," Genevieve continued, her formal tone softening some as she looked at the twins. "I know Hazel has prepared an amazing meal for us tonight."

With much scraping of chairs, they all sat down to

eat. Looking around at his new family, a sense of peace settled in Jake's heart. These, he thought, were his people. Someday he might be able to sit at this table and feel as if he belonged here. Tonight would be the start of something good.

Chapter Eight

"You know what? I don't want to go back to the AAG center," Fiona murmured, her head resting comfortably on Jake's broad shoulder, after dinner. "That was some seriously good company. And the food…" She rolled her eyes, even though he couldn't see. "Wow. Just wow."

"Better buckle up," he advised, smoothing her hair away from her face. The husky note in his voice heated her blood. "You know as well as I do that we both have to go back."

He was right. After all, they couldn't sit in the Colton ranch and make out like a couple of horny kids in the front seat of his truck. With great reluctance, she slid back into the passenger side and fastened the seat belt. "Did you enjoy yourself?" she asked.

"Yeah, I haven't tasted carne asada that good outside of a pricey restaurant," he replied.

She glanced up at him. He stared straight ahead, his concentration on the road as he drove, but there'd been a hint of remoteness in his voice. As if he'd shut down to avoid dealing with what surely had to be a tangled web of emotions.

Her phone pinged, indicating a text. Can you talk? Holden texted.

"I need to make a call," she told Jake. "Work related. It'll just take a second." Then, instead of texting Holden back, she punched in the number to call him.

"What's up?" she asked.

"Not much," he answered, his tone cheerful. "I wanted to check in with you and see if you've learned anything new."

"I might. That depends." She told him about the basement and the possibility of cells or a jail of some sort under the house. "I'm working on trying to gain access," she said. "They also had me working on some poor college freshman, trying to get him to sign up for seminars at a grand a pop. They prey on people who are desperate enough to try anything."

"True. Unfortunately, as long as their victims receive what they were promised for their money, it's not a crime."

"I know. But there's more, though I don't have concrete evidence yet. Our intel is correct. Micheline is planning something big, though I haven't been able to learn yet what it might be. I'm trying really hard to gain the welcome coordinator's confidence."

"Leigh?"

"Yep. And they've assigned me to get close to the son in order to get him to stick around." She shot a quick glance at Jake, who continued to watch the road, though she knew he was listening.

"What's he like?" Holden asked.

"Jake? Oh, he's all right," she replied, grinning. "He's easy on the eyes, so that helps."

"Well, that's good, I suppose. As long as he's not another one of those crazy cult members." Holden sounded amused. "Keep me posted if anything changes."

She promised she would and ended the call. "My colleague," she explained. "I try to keep him updated periodically, but I can only do it when I'm not at the center."

"Makes sense." He eyed her thoughtfully. "Is it hard to play your role?"

"Sometimes," she admitted. "Especially when I have to do something that's abhorrent to me, like try and fleece a young college student. But I know it's for the greater good in the end. Once we get enough information to arrest and convict Micheline, I'll be proud of myself for doing my job so well."

"I'll be looking forward to that day, too."

A thought occurred to her. Crazy, maybe. But she could use all the help she could get.

"Maybe you should play along, too," she said, not sure how he'd receive this idea.

As she'd expected, Jake shot her an incredulous look. "Play along how?"

"Well, clearly Micheline needs you for some part of her plan. What if you were a willing participant?" When he started to speak, she held up her hand. "Hear me out. As you know, Micheline is all about two things. Money and power. If you can convince her that you crave those as well, she might be willing to let you in on her little plan."

"The woman switched me with another baby at birth." The flat note in his voice and the tight set of his jaw spoke volumes. "Why would she care what I want?"

The more she considered, the more she liked the idea. "If it benefits her, she'll care a lot."

"No." Just that. Nothing more.

"I understand." She shrugged. "I'll admit that I'm disappointed, too, but I get it. Sort of."

As she'd suspected it might, her response earned her another sharp, sideways glance.

"It'd make your skin crawl," she continued. "I know it does mine. Everything that woman stands for is the opposite of my own beliefs."

"But if in the end, what you do helps keep her from hurting other people, it's worth it," Jake finished for her. "No need to pile it on any thicker. I get it. I'll do it. Or at least try. What do you suggest?"

Now it was her turn to eye him. "Tell her you want to meet with her. Refuse to take no for an answer. Then, when you do, tell her you want something in return for all the grief she's caused you. Play it by ear. I guarantee she'll relate."

"Oh, she'll relate," he said, his voice grim. "Greed is one of her highest motivators."

Fiona nodded. "Remember, don't do anything that will put you in any sort of danger. But if you can get her to think you're completely on board, and she might stand to gain financially, then you might be able to learn something important."

"Why not?" he said. "It'll keep me from getting bored, plus I'll feel as if I'm actually contributing toward Micheline's downfall."

He spoke without rancor, his tone matter-of-fact. She wondered what all he'd seen in his seventeen years with a woman who'd never wanted him and certainly hadn't loved him. She considered it a small miracle that Jake had grown up relatively unscathed.

"Did someone help you?" she asked. "After you left home? Seventeen is awfully young for a kid to be on his own. Did you even have any money?"

"Actually, I did. Micheline had me homeschooled, so

I didn't have any friends my own age. I started working at Burger Barn when I was sixteen. Micheline didn't know. By then, she was already busy starting up her foundation." He grimaced. "The people I worked with—other teens mostly—were my first real friends. Despite the temptation to party with them, I saved every penny I made. Because I already had a plan. I also managed to keep it hidden from Micheline. If she'd found it, she wouldn't have had any qualms about taking every cent."

"That doesn't surprise me," Fiona remarked.

"Yeah. And I did have help. I used some of my money to buy an old motorcycle. I headed north, figuring I'd keep going until I found a place that felt right."

He went quiet for a moment, clearly lost in his thoughts. "I was driving through this small ranching town when I saw someone toss a kitten from a car window. I pulled over, and the little thing was still alive, though injured. I picked it up and drove to the veterinary clinic I'd just passed." He shook his head. "They were amazing. The vet, an older man named John Letcalf, rushed the kitten into emergency surgery to repair a broken jaw. They let me hang out in the waiting room and gave me a drink and some chips. I think they knew..."

Watching him, her heart swelled. He'd been through so much.

After a moment, he continued. "In the end, Dr. Letcalf fixed the kitten and promised to find it a home. And he offered me a job and a place to stay." His voice had gone rough. "If not for him and his wife, I don't know what would have happened to me."

Fascinated, she nodded. "So you worked at the vet clinic?"

"No. Actually, he and his wife lived on a ranch. He

hired me on as a ranch hand. It was a big enough place that the hands had their own bunkhouse. I learned everything I know today about cattle ranching from that job. Believe me, it wasn't anything near as fancy as the Coltons' operation, but was a profitable, working cattle ranch."

"Is that the same one you own now?" she asked.

"No. Dr. Letcalf's wife got dementia. He retired, sold the veterinary clinic to two of his partners. His son took over the ranch. He let me stay on, but I knew it would be only temporary. When one of the neighboring ranches went up for sale, I bought it. It's much smaller—only a couple hundred acres—but works for me."

"I'm impressed." She smiled at him. "Let me guess. You saved up every penny you made working for Dr. Letcalf."

He nodded. "You would be correct. I wasn't able to pay cash for the place, but I had more than enough for a hefty down payment. Still, Dr. Letcalf had to cosign for me. I had no credit history at all."

Unable to resist, she reached over and touched his arm. "Still, you overcame tremendous odds and made something of yourself."

"Thanks." He glanced at her, making her wish it wasn't too dark to read his expression. "What about you? What's your story?"

"I grew up in Phoenix. My father was a police officer and my mother a teacher. I was an only child. I had a basic, boring, wholesome childhood." She swallowed hard. "It was great, actually. Until the day my dad was killed by a drunk driver. Life changed in an instant."

"I'm sorry," he said.

She nodded. "Thanks. After that happened, I focused

my entire life's purpose on becoming a cop. When I got to college, I took criminal justice classes. The FBI recruited me right after graduation, and here I am."

"That's impressive, too," he told her.

"Maybe. I always wished my dad were alive to see what I've done with my life."

"I'm sure he knows. What about your mother?"

"Oh, she's proud, though she can't really relate. She retired from teaching and keeps busy with a bunch of volunteer work. She still lives in the same house I grew up in, though she's remarried."

They turned down the long drive leading to the AAG Center.

"I wonder how she came up with this idea," Fiona mused of the AAG. "Even her catchphrase is kind of general, as if she couldn't think of anything better."

"She was working toward something like this even when I was a young child," Jake said. "Because she truthfully believes everyone else is an idiot, she always used short, catchy sound bites." He shrugged. "It seems to have worked out for her."

"Yeah." Fiona shuddered. "But try sitting through seminar after seminar, hearing *Be Your Best You* over and over. Now, whenever someone says it, I fight the urge to be sick."

He laughed. "Well, we're here. You'd better get ready to put your game face on."

"I'm ready," she said, though she was reluctant to get out of the car. "What about you? Are you sure you're up for this?"

Slowly, he nodded. "I like that you're giving me the option of saying no. But I really want to help, even if every time I have to be nice to that woman, I want to vomit. It helps to know you can relate."

"Oh, can I ever." She got out of the truck, waiting for him to join her. Together, they walked back toward the house. When he took her hand, interlacing his fingers with hers, warmth blossomed inside her. Right before they reached the front porch, she turned to face him. "Good luck with Micheline."

"Thanks. I might even go look for her tonight."

AS IT TURNED OUT, Jake didn't have to go through all of the trouble of badgering Micheline for a meeting. She appeared at his door moments after he got in himself. *Good.* After meeting his family and seeing the ranch, he now understood what all she'd taken from him. At least Payne had survived. Jake felt bad enough that he'd lost the opportunity to meet his late mother. He was grateful he'd have the chance to get to know his father.

Now, he braced himself for the confrontation about to come. At least she knocked this time.

"Micheline?" He didn't have to pretend to be surprised. "What are you doing here?"

"I've been waiting for you to come back," she said. "A little birdie told me you paid a visit to the Rattlesnake Ridge Ranch."

Which meant she must have already spoken to Fiona across the hall. "I did," he replied. "I can't believe that all of that could have been mine. My little ranch is nothing compared to that spread." He glared at her, keeping his expression hard. "You owe it to me to help me figure out a way to get part of that place. They view me as an outsider and likely always will. Since you switched me with Ace forty years ago, it's on you to make sure I'm not cheated out of what's rightfully mine."

Mouth slightly agape, she stared at him. "How do you suggest I do that?"

Instead of answering, he crossed his arms.

She crossed the room, going to his small window and pushing aside the curtains. "I may have an idea or two," she said thoughtfully. "But as I'm sure you've already guessed, I'll want a cut."

"A cut?" This was the tricky part. "Why would I give you anything? You're the one who basically ruined my life."

"If you want my help, you've got to be willing to pay," she snapped. Then, softening her tone, she continued. "Look, I'm pretty sure there's a way we can work together, but it's got to be mutually beneficial."

Boom. Slowly, he nodded, though he kept his jaw tight. "I'm listening."

She began to pace back and forth, making the short distance in a few strides, as if standing at the front of one of her packed lecture halls. "You have something of value now, Jake. Yourself. You're one of them, a Colton. They don't want to lose you again. We just need to figure out a way to make them understand they owe you. All those years when they were raising someone else's child..." She stopped, gazing off into the distance, her eyes slightly unfocused.

It took an effort, but Jake managed to refrain from shaking his head. An act. He'd seen her play this one before. Maybe her persona had become so ingrained in her, she couldn't help but carry on with her role-playing. She probably no longer remembered how to be honest or human. "You know some guy tried to pass himself off as the baby who was switched."

"I heard. Payne Colton mentioned him. Jace Smith."

"Yeah. He thought he could pull his own con. Little did he know that I was Luella Smith."

"That's your real name?" He couldn't help but gape.

"Micheline Anderson is who I am." She shrugged, the movement both elegant and weirdly frenetic. "He went away finally. I'm sure the Coltons must have asked for a DNA test."

"I've been waiting for them to ask me to take one," he said.

"Go ahead and take it. I guarantee it will confirm you are a Colton. I should know."

"I will. The sooner I can prove my identity beyond a shadow of a doubt, the quicker I can get what I deserve."

Too much? Conscious of holding his breath, he forced himself to exhale. Meanwhile, Micheline watched him with narrowed eyes and flat expression.

"Let me think about it," she finally said. "Once I devise a workable plan, I'll let you know."

Which meant she hadn't fallen for it. She didn't believe him. Maybe she knew him better than he gave her credit for.

He dipped his chin. About to tell her it sounded good, he reconsidered. "I thought you already had some sort of plan," he said.

Her blank stare didn't fool him. "Why would you think that?"

"I don't. Maybe because you so badly wanted me to stick around for a while. I knew there had to be a reason."

She blinked, a rapid fluttering of her false eyelashes.

One of her tells, which meant she was about to straight up lie.

"Don't." One hand forestalled her. "I've had enough of your BS. Just give it to me straight."

"Fine. How would you like to become not only CEO of Colton Oil, but a multimillionaire?"

Though these were all things he could get on his own, he decided to play along to see where she might be going with this. "I'm listening."

"Let me work on it." Confident again, she reached out and touched his arm. It took every ounce of self-control he possessed not to flinch away from her.

"Make it worth my while," he said. "And I promise I'll make sure it's worth yours."

With a smile and a brusque nod, she spun on her heels and left his room, closing the door firmly behind her.

After she'd gone, he debated taking a long, hot shower. Even pretending to go along with her made him feel unclean, like no amount of soap or water could wash the stain away.

Instead, he found himself crossing the hall to stand outside Fiona's room. He tapped lightly, in case she'd fallen asleep. A second later, she opened the door with the wild hair and wide-eyed yet sleepy look that he found sexy as hell. She still wore the outfit she'd put on to have dinner at the Coltons and hadn't yet washed her makeup off.

"Did I wake you?" he murmured.

"No," she lied. "I might have just closed my eyes for a minute or two." Stepping aside, she gestured at him. "Come on in."

He did. Once she'd closed the door, he took in her

room, a carbon copy of his but in reverse. Odd how a few items here and there could make her space so feminine. She'd clearly made an attempt to decorate, which for some reason surprised him.

"It's not much, but I tried to make it feel like home," she said, correctly interpreting his thoughts. "I mean, why not? I knew I was going to be living here, after all."

"Micheline just left," he began.

Fiona quickly shook her head, one finger against her lips to quiet him. She moved forward, wrapping herself around him. "Not here, not now," she murmured, so quietly he had to strain to hear it. And then she kissed him.

Instantly aroused, he let himself drown in her, the contradictions of her athletic yet soft body, her sensual nature and the air of innocence she managed to maintain despite no doubt having seen things that would give grown men nightmares.

She was wild yet restrained, beautiful and smart and the most interesting woman he'd ever met.

Still kissing, they helped each other get rid of the clothing that stood between their skin. Naked, eager, they rushed to press their bodies together once more.

Later, much later, he held her in his arms as she dozed, wondering how the hell he was ever going to be able to let her go.

Waking in the early morning, Jake gathered his clothing and crept back to his room. Good thing he did, because no sooner had he gotten out of the shower than Micheline knocked on his door.

He couldn't help but remember how he couldn't even get her to talk to him when he'd first arrived.

"Here." She shoved a cardboard cup of coffee at him

as she breezed past. "Drink up. I want you awake when we hammer out the details."

Details. At any second, he expected her to whip out a contract for him to sign.

Taking a sip of his coffee, he eyed Micheline fidgeting near the doorway. The coffee—whatever it was—tasted rich and expensive. It certainly wasn't what they served in the lunchroom or the lobby. "What is this?" he asked, making sure his appreciation showed in his voice. "It's amazing."

"I have it flown in from Jamaica," she said, drinking deeply of her own mug. "My own personal blend."

Noting the way her hands shook, he wondered if she was on something. Or perhaps, *off* her meds. He had no idea what she might be taking or for what. One thing was for sure—he didn't believe she was doing anything for her supposed cancer.

Finally, she stopped moving long enough to perch on the single chair. "I've thought about several possible scenarios," she began. He couldn't help but notice the way her pupils seemed enlarged. Definitely drugs, he thought. Though what kind?

He took another drink of the rich coffee, allowing himself to savor it. "Go on," he replied, his tone neutral. He realized how little Micheline truly knew about him. Did she really think he'd go to such lengths to avoid the work of getting to know his family?

"You could sue the Coltons," she announced. "They owe you for all the years of lost benefits. I bet they would have paid for you to go to college. And your rinky-dink little cattle ranch—they probably would have bought you a much nicer one. You should take them to court and make them pony up. I bet they feel so guilty, they won't even fight you."

Was she high? Because that was the craziest bunch of nonsense he'd ever heard her utter.

Remembering Fiona's advice, he swallowed back an incredulous response. Instead, he pretended to consider Micheline's words.

"I'm not sure that would work," he finally allowed. "I'd become their enemy. I want power and influence, as well as money. That can only be gotten if I'm part of them, not against them."

She narrowed her eyes at him before sipping again on her drink. "That takes time, which is the one thing I don't have an overabundance of. I need to get my hands on a lot of cash fast."

"Why?"

The disgusted look she shot him made him want to smile, though he managed not to.

"Because I don't have long to live," she snapped. "Are you honestly that stupid?"

He locked his jaw, breathing deeply, summoning up enough self-control so he didn't snarl something equally rude back at her. Old habits apparently died hard. Instead, he arranged his features into what he hoped would be a suitably abashed expression. "Sorry. I guess I just don't like to even imagine the possibility of you being gone."

Instantly gratified, Micheline preened. "I *knew* you hid your attachment to me," she gloated. "I never could understand how you made yourself stay away so long. You must have missed me terribly."

Talk about wanting to gag. He managed to make himself nod.

"You may be right," she admitted, jingling multiple bracelets on one of her arms in a repetitive motion that set his teeth on edge. "I'll need to think on it. Now that we're working together, if any good plans occur to you, be sure and discuss them with me immediately."

"Of course I will."

"Good." She pushed to her feet, finally stopping the noise. "I'll be working mostly out of here the next week. Let Leigh know if you need to see me."

"Will do." He held back his sigh of relief until she was actually gone.

At the doorway, she spun around so fast, she staggered. For one awful second, he thought she might go down. Instinctively, he moved to catch her, but she managed to grab on to the door frame and catch herself right before he reached her. Her coffee, however, slipped from her grasp and spilled all over the floor.

"Are you all right?"

She lifted her head and met his gaze, her lips pulling back from her teeth in what he supposed she thought was a smile. "I'm fine." With that final lie, she shook her head and pointed to the spilled coffee. "Make sure you clean that up."

Once she'd gone, he grabbed one of the extra bath towels and mopped up the mess. Luckily, the AAG center provided maid service, so he knew someone would change the towel out later that day.

Wow. Eyeing his own coffee cup, he carried it over to the sink and poured the rest of it out. Quite simply, he'd lost his taste for Micheline's expensive coffee. In fact, he wasn't even sure he could eat breakfast.

One thing was for sure—he now had a newfound respect for Fiona and her ability to do her job and somehow manage to maintain her sanity.

He decided he'd go across the hall and see if Fiona needed some help waking up.

Just the thought had his body instantly hard.

The soft tap on his door startled him. Had Micheline come back? He swore under his breath and went to the door.

Fiona stood there, barefoot, wearing a T-shirt and tiny shorts, her eyes huge. "Mornin'," she said, her husky voice stirring up all kinds of trouble inside him. "May I come in?"

Instantly, he stepped aside. Barely had the door clicked shut behind him than they were wrapped up in each other's arms.

They shed what little clothing they had on quickly, still kissing. Skin to skin, they fell together onto his bed. One thrust and he buried himself deep inside her. Instantly, she convulsed, her body caressing his. So warm, so tight, enough to drive him mad.

Somehow, he managed to hang on to his rapidly shredding self-control. Once her shudders had subsided, he began to move. Slowly at first, but as momentum built, he abandoned all attempt at restraint.

Each time they came together, it was fireworks and trumpets: crazy stuff he'd never really believed in. They fit perfectly, and though they hadn't known each other very long, lovemaking felt instinctive. Somehow, he felt he knew just what to do and how to do it to take her to the edge of the cliff and beyond. And as for her…just one touch, one look, one kiss and she sent him over the moon.

After, sated and content, they lay in each other's

arms. He propped himself up on one elbow and looked at her.

"What?" she asked, peering up at him through drowsy eyes.

"You're beautiful," he mused. "And special." Taking a deep breath, he decided he might as well go for it. "I'm falling in love with you."

She froze. Then, refusing to look at him, she slowly edged herself out of his arms. "Don't," she said.

Whatever reaction he'd expected, it hadn't been this. "Don't what?"

"Don't ruin this." Still, she wouldn't look at him. He felt the awful weight of her words settle in heavy in the pit of his stomach.

When she finally turned to meet his gaze, her expression stern and full of resolve, he knew what she was going to say before she even opened her mouth.

"We're good together, true. And I like you, Jake Anderson. I like you a lot." She reached out her hand to touch him. He jerked away.

"Don't be like that," she urged, her voice soft. "We're good together. I know it as well as you do. But I need to focus on my life here, becoming my best me. You know what I mean. Until I do that, I won't be able to—"

"I get it." He cut her off. Ever conscious of the probability of someone listening. Two could play that game. "What if Micheline *herself* wants you to be involved with me?"

Her eyes widened. "She does." She sounded confident. Certain. "At least that's what Leigh told me. I'm not sure what her motivation is, though. I'm sure it's something nefarious."

"We'll see about that," he muttered, more for the benefit of anyone listening than anything else.

"Jake. You don't mean that."

"You're right," he responded immediately. "But there's one thing you should know about me. I don't give up easily. I know beyond a shadow of a doubt that we can have something special."

She nodded, her expression sad. "It's just bad timing," she began.

Since his chest already hurt, he knew he didn't want to hear anymore. Not right now. Not for a good while. Hell, maybe not ever.

A horrible revelation hit him. Was Fiona using him to help her make the case against his mother? Again, he didn't have to wonder if she could actually be this deceitful. Micheline had long ago set the bar for that.

He needed to shut down the emotions swirling through him, and quickly. If he'd truly been such a fool, he'd deal with it later, when he could go off somewhere and lick his wounds.

Grabbing up his clothes, he dressed hurriedly, without looking at her. "Take care, Fiona." He crossed to the door without a backward glance, opening it and stepping aside so she could pass. "I'll be seeing you around, I'm sure."

Chapter Nine

She'd done the right thing, turning Jake down, Fiona thought. Even though right now, it didn't feel like it. She truly believed this, beyond any shadow of a doubt. But then why did her heart feel as if it was breaking? Why did the backs of her eyes sting and her throat feel like it had closed up?

The vulnerable look in Jake's eyes, the hope turning to pain, killed her. He'd eyed her steadily, as if he knew the truth no matter how much she might deny it. But how could he, when she didn't even know it herself? The only thing Fiona knew for certain was her job. Over the years, she'd built a reputation as someone reliable, someone who didn't make mistakes. She'd already made a huge one by revealing her mission to Jake. She couldn't compound that by making another one.

Rule number seven of the undercover handbook: don't get seriously romantically involved with someone. Male agents had casual flings all the time. She'd definitely heard the stories.

Since Micheline herself had, for whatever reason, wanted Fiona to get close to Jake, everything had seemed to naturally fall into place. A little fun, some mind-blowing sex and no one got hurt. Except now apparently, Jake had.

When she'd allowed herself to give in to the insane attraction she felt toward Jake, she'd never expected this. The absolute certainty that he could definitely be the one. Even worse, she wasn't sure she could trust the feeling. How much of it was due to the role she played while undercover here at the AAG center? If she'd met him during her regular, normal life, working from the FBI field office, and they'd gone on the usual dates at trendy gastropubs or bars, would things have ignited so quickly between them?

She didn't know. For that reason alone—okay, that was only one of the reasons—she had no choice but to focus on the mission. When all of this was finally over, the case wrapped up in a neat little bow, maybe then she'd have the luxury of finding out if what she and Jake had might be real.

Leigh buzzed her a few minutes later, summoning her to her suite. Instantly alert, Fiona told her she was on her way, glad to have something to focus on besides the mess she'd made of things with Jake.

When she got to Leigh's hallway, she realized Leigh stood in the doorway, waiting for her. The other woman practically buzzed with excitement.

"Come in, come in," Leigh urged. "There's a lot going on today, but Micheline asked me to speak to you specifically."

Fiona followed her inside. "About what?" she asked, wondering if she'd be called on the carpet for her rebuff of Jake. While she knew they listened in on her, if Leigh brought this up now, it would be tantamount to admitting her room and Jake's had been bugged.

"Take a seat." Leigh gestured toward a pair of antique chairs near her fireplace. Idly, Fiona wondered how many of the rooms in this place actually had fireplaces. Not too many, she'd bet.

Fiona sat.

Instead of sitting next to her, Leigh bounced around the room. In place of her usual fashionable high heels, Fiona noticed Leigh was barefoot. And so hyped up, she couldn't stay still.

Drugs? Fiona wouldn't have thought Miss Mustang Valley was the type, but who knew. If Micheline had ordered her to take something, no doubt Leigh would have obeyed. Though why?

Increasingly alarmed, Fiona repeated her question. "What's going on, Leigh?"

"I've just been enlightened," Leigh exclaimed. "And it's like a giant lightbulb just turned on. I can see much more clearly now, and everything is so beautiful."

"Did you take something?" Maybe not pills. Maybe she'd eaten peyote or smoked mushrooms in some sort of bizarre ceremony Micheline had organized.

"Of course not." Rather than indignant, Leigh appeared distracted. "I'm hyper because I've got a lot on my mind."

Fiona nodded, pretending she understood. Better to say nothing and simply wait Leigh out.

"Micheline sometimes gives me private lessons," Leigh finally said. "She and I were talking about a new philosophy she came up with. It was sent to her in a dream."

With difficulty, Fiona kept from rolling her eyes. "What is it?" she breathed instead, leaning forward and hoping she looked intensely interested.

"What if—" Leigh's earnest expression seemed at odds with her giant dangling feather earrings swinging furiously every time she took a breath. As usual, the beauty queen had dressed more like a fashionable coed than a competent employee, minus the shoes. "—to be our best selves, we must die and be reborn?"

Religion? Or something else, something darker? Every instinct on alert, Fiona slowly nodded. "I'm listening," she said. "That seems intriguing. What exactly do you mean?"

"I know that sounds like a religious teaching," Leigh continued. "But when they say 'born again,' they mean it figuratively. I'm speaking literally."

Still not sure where the other woman was going with this, Fiona eyed her. "When you say..."

"Yes. Death." Excitement flashed in Leigh's eyes. "What if we must die so we can be reborn as our absolute best selves?"

Horrified, Fiona decided to treat this statement as if she thought Leigh might be joking. "You first," she said. "I happen to like being alive."

"Think of it," Leigh continued, clearly deciding to pretend she hadn't heard Fiona. "A covenant, between all of the AAG and Micheline. All of us, crossing over at once. Imagine the news coverage. And then, imagine the shock when we're all reborn."

Like the Jim Jones thing at Jonestown. Mass suicide. It took every bit of acting skill Fiona possessed not to reveal her complete and utter horror. Then, her FBI training kicked in.

Details. She needed more details.

"Sounds like you already have a plan," she managed,

the tremble in her voice coming naturally. "How long would we have to prepare?"

"No plan." Though Leigh demurred, Fiona didn't believe her.

"Are you sure?" Fiona pressed. "I mean, if we're going to do something like that, I'd like to know as far in advance as possible."

Though Leigh hesitated, she finally grinned. "It's still in the planning stages," she allowed. "A lot depends on money. Micheline is trying to work out those details."

"Now I'm really confused. What does money have to do with any of this?"

"Think, Fiona," Leigh chastised. "We have quite a few wealthy members whose families might pay handsomely to keep their loved ones alive."

"Like a ransom?" *Think* indeed. "What good would money be, though, if Micheline was dead?"

"Dead?" Shuddering dramatically, Leigh shook her head. "Micheline has no intention of dying and being reborn. Why should she? She has no need. As our leader, she's already the best version of herself she can be."

Fiona shouldn't have been surprised, but... Seriously. How did Micheline get her followers to believe this nonsense? "What about you, Leigh?" Fiona asked softly. "Are you already your best self?"

With a sly smile, Leigh used one hand to push back her hair. "What do you think? Not only am I Micheline's right-hand woman, but Miss Mustang Valley. How much better could a person get?"

Typical. Let the others do the crazy stuff. Those in charge, or close to the leaders, got off with a free pass.

Despite the flash of anger that shot through her with

Leigh's statement, Fiona nodded. "Okay, humor me. I'm really trying to understand. What does that mean? Only Micheline's top people get to avoid the whole 'let's get reborn' thing?"

Some of her bitterness must have shown in her voice. Leigh cocked her head. "Worried, are you? I don't know, but if I were you, I'd be busting my tail to prove myself an invaluable member of the AAG. Maybe then you, too, could avoid that fate."

That fate. Almost as if Leigh knew exactly what Micheline would be asking her followers to do. Almost as if she were an accessory to murder. She wondered how someone like Leigh would fare in prison. Not too well, she suspected.

"Anyway, keep this between us for now," Leigh ordered. "We're not ready to roll it out yet. Micheline still has a lot of planning to do."

Though Fiona wanted to ask what would happen if any of the members, such as herself, declined the whole die-and-be-reborn experience, she didn't want to blow her cover. The devout groupie she'd been playing would probably do whatever Micheline asked.

"Thank you for telling me," Fiona enthused. "I'm so honored."

"You should be." Leigh beamed at her. "How are things going with Jake?"

"Hmm." Noncommittal, Fiona grimaced. "He's wanting to go too fast," she said. "I need to focus on my studies."

"He's falling for you? Perfect!" Clapping her hands, Leigh jumped up and down. "Micheline will be so excited!"

"Why?"

"Why not? Come on now, Fiona. Show a little enthusiasm. You are rocking this assignment." She peered at Fiona, considering. "You know, this might just be enough to distract Micheline from your failure with Theodore. He never returned any of our calls about scheduling some seminars."

Good. Even though Fiona hung her head as if ashamed, inwardly she rejoiced.

"You must do better," Leigh chided. "That assignment was handpicked for you by Micheline herself. If you don't watch it, she'll be sending you out to campus to troll for your own students."

Fiona nearly snapped her head up at that. She definitely didn't need to get sent somewhere outside the AAG center. That would defeat the entire purpose of her undercover assignment.

"I'll try harder with Jake," she responded meekly. And she would. Jake had agreed to work with her. He would simply have to figure out a way to separate emotion from the job. Especially since Leigh had hinted at mass suicide.

"See that you do." Smiling again, Leigh looked Fiona up and down. "Maybe you need to dress a little bit sexier, you know?"

Startled, Fiona shook her head. "I don't have—"

"Oh, that's right," Leigh interrupted. "You only had the clothes on your back when we rescued you and took you in." The subtle reminder wasn't lost on Fiona, who managed to nod and look embarrassed.

"No problem," Leigh continued on cheerfully. "I'll have some things sent over. You must keep Jake Andrews interested enough to stick around. Micheline really needs him to be here at least ten more days."

A time frame. Though inwardly she perked up, Fiona took care not to reveal anything of her interest. "Ten days, huh? I'll figure out something."

"See that you do." Turning to her computer, Leigh clicked her mouse and began to read whatever she had on the screen, clearly dismissing Fiona.

JAKE SAW FIONA coming across the lobby, and his entire body tensed. Judging by her purposeful stride and the intent look on her beautiful face as she headed his way, she wanted to talk to him. He braced himself against the hopeless rush of attraction and waited.

"Do you have a minute?" she asked, her curt tone pitched low. "For a walk outside?"

He shrugged, deliberately casual. "Sure. Why not?"

When she slipped her small hand into his, he couldn't prevent his instinctive initial reaction—shock. But then he tightened his fingers around hers.

Neither spoke until they were several hundred feet down the driveway. "What's going on?" he asked finally.

"I just got out of a meeting with Leigh." She shook her head. "I'm to do whatever it takes to keep you around here at least ten more days."

As she'd probably known he would, he picked up on the time frame immediately. "Ten days? What's going on in ten days?"

"I don't know for sure," she said slowly. "But judging from what Leigh was hinting at, it's not going to be good."

He waited while she eyed him, clearly trying to decide what to say.

"Mass suicide." Her voice hardened. "But with a

catch. From what I understand, she's planning to ask for payment from their families in order to save some of the wealthier members' lives. How she plans to explain this to her followers, I have no idea. It's crazy."

Jaw tight, Jake grimaced. His stomach turned at the thought of the depths to which the woman he'd once believed to be his mother was capable of sinking. "No surprise there. The lure of money has always been her motivator. All the rest of it comes secondary. Micheline is one of those people who doesn't care what she has to do to pad her pockets. Even murder, apparently."

"But this will be too blatant. She'll face charges. A full bank account won't do her any good in prison. And the feds will probably freeze her bank accounts." She shook her head. "If she's looking for notoriety, this will get her that. But the risk of getting caught is really high. I'd think it outweighs whatever monetary gain she'd stand to get."

"Unless she has a plan," Jake said, unable to keep from wanting to hold her. "And believe me, Micheline *always* has a backup plan."

"I've got to find out what it is." Rubbing her temples, Fiona sighed. "Jake, I know we had…words earlier. But you did agree to help me, and right now I need your help. I was basically told to turn up the heat with you. Leigh is even going to send me over some more revealing clothes to wear."

His heart skipped a beat at the thought of what she might wear. "We can work together," he said, keeping his voice level.

"Can we?" Her gaze found his. "We'll have to act as if we're really into each other."

"Act?"

This teasing question earned a smile from her.

"We've got that covered," he continued. "We'll continue on as before. And I promise I won't bring up anything about—"

"Feelings," she said, slightly breathless. "Not now, not yet, okay?"

Yet. That single word made him happier than he should have been. Proof once a fool, always a fool. "Sounds good." Still deliberately casual.

"Thank you." Her frown showed him her thoughts had already turned elsewhere. "If I'm going to find out exactly what Micheline has planned, I'm going to have to push. Try to get closer. The only way she'll trust me enough to—"

"Stop." Unable to help himself, Jake brushed a kiss across her lips. "I know you'll do whatever you have to do in order to stop her. But know this. Micheline trusts no one but herself. Not even that perky coordinator of hers."

"Leigh."

"Right, Leigh." He kissed her again, lingering this time. "Leigh might think she knows everything that's going on, but I guarantee she doesn't. Micheline will probably leave her twisting in the wind, holding the bag."

Swallowing hard, she nodded. "Kiss me again," she demanded. "In case someone is watching."

Wisely, he swallowed back a chuckle at her justification and covered her mouth with his.

For a moment, just a brief heartbeat or two, nothing else existed but the two of them.

When they finally broke apart, they were both

breathing heavily. "You are a hell of a distraction," she told him.

"You needed to break your focus. You were on the verge of—"

"Panicking?" Interrupting, she shook her head. "Maybe. Maybe not." Professional Fiona had returned. "The more I hear about this, the messier it gets. I like clean cases, all wrapped up in tidy bows. Of course, the vast majority of them aren't anywhere close to being like that."

"And I can promise you this one will never be." He let his gaze roam over her, allowing himself to reveal his very masculine appreciation for her sensual femininity. She blushed, which fascinated him, and cleared her throat.

"How much longer are you staying?" she asked, not even bothering to try and pretend her question was casual. He liked that about her.

He laughed. "Oh, I'm not going anywhere until this is over. No way could I go back to the ranch without seeing how this all ends. I've got people in place running things for me. Plus, I'm really enjoying getting to know the Coltons. They're really good people."

"They seemed like they were," she agreed. "Much better than the family you formerly believed was your own."

"True." Cocking his head, he eyed her. "What are your plans for the rest of the day?"

"I'm going to do some exploring. I need to find out what's in the basement."

"Now?"

"Why not?" She shrugged. "The longer we wait, the closer we get to whatever horrific event Micheline is planning. I just need enough evidence for an arrest. Failing that, at least enough to obtain a search warrant."

"I'd think you already would have enough evidence," he commented. "Especially with her asking you to fleece a college student."

"I wish. While that was unethical, at least in my opinion, it wasn't illegal. She offered him a service—self-improvement classes and counseling sessions—for payment. No, I need more than that."

He could prove nothing about his "mother" without evidence, he realized, and even if he could, he'd only been speculating as to the end result. While Micheline might have acted in an unsavory manner, he had no idea if she'd committed any actual crimes. Gut instinct said yes, but hunches didn't stand up in court.

Fiona bumped him with her shoulder. "Earth to Jake. What's going on in that mind of yours?"

He shook his head. "I get what you mean about needing evidence. I'm just trying to come up with the best way to obtain it."

"I just wish I'd managed to get deeper into Micheline's inner circle," Fiona commented. "But Leigh tends to act as a very effective deterrent. No doubt that's why Micheline keeps her around."

"Micheline has a certain type she goes for," he said. "Underneath all that outward self-confidence, I'm willing to bet Leigh is a very insecure person. Maybe even has mommy issues, which is a role Micheline is happy to fill for her."

"Interesting analysis." She gave him a considering look. "And actually very good. You're probably right. Let's go back."

Still hand in hand, they strolled toward the entrance and into the lobby.

"One of Micheline's goons is headed our way. Her security detail, Bart."

"Ugh." She made a face. "Something about that guy gives me the creeps."

"I'm sure that's the reason Micheline hired him."

Bart continued sauntering toward them, smiling a smug smile, as if he enjoyed knowing how people reacted to him. When he reached Fiona, he stopped, raking his gaze up and down her.

Fiona's jaw tightened, but she didn't react. Jake knew she wanted to, though. Only the fact that she played a role undercover prevented her.

"What's up?" she asked, her voice cold.

"Just doing my rounds. I thought you were supposed to be in Happiness 101," he said, referring to the popular seminar going on right now in the auditorium.

"I've already done that one," she replied, her bright smile so false it made Jake's teeth ache. "I'm actually about to go do self-reflection and then journaling."

Bart yawned, not bothering to hide his bored expression. "Sounds like fun. Keep after it." And he sauntered away.

"He's up to something," Fiona declared. "Not sure what. If I wasn't afraid of getting caught, I'd follow him."

The idea of what a man like Bart might do to a woman like Fiona if he had her alone and up against a wall made Jake cold.

While he knew better than to suggest she take a pass on that one, he also knew he should distract her. "I want to kiss you so damn bad," he said, telling the truth.

Lifting her chin, she challenged him with her gaze. "What's stopping you?" she asked.

So he kissed her, right there in the lobby of the AAG center, for all the other guests—and cameras—to see.

DROWNING, FIONA THOUGHT. From the instant Jake's lips touched hers, everything else disappeared. For a few seconds, she kissed him back, allowing herself to get lost in the taste of him, in the feel of his hard body pressed against hers.

But then, as all good things must, she knew it had to come to an end. She had a job to do, after all.

"Whoa," she teased, stepping back and hoping the entire lobby couldn't see how hard she was breathing. "Potent stuff. But I really need to stay on track and get back to work. I want to try and find the cells."

Blue eyes dark, he nodded. "Then let's look," he said. "Do you want to split up or search together?"

This—the ability to go with the flow and make a move when required—was one of the things she loved about him. Wait—*loved*? Surely not. She hadn't known him long enough.

But yet…

Shying away from any deep thoughts about her emotions, she reminded herself to focus on the job. Her mission mattered the most right now. She could sort out her feelings about Jake later, just like they'd agreed.

"Let's split up," she said. "I still think if we do it that way, there's less likelihood of us getting caught."

"Maybe. But I'd rather we stick together. That way if trouble comes, we face it side by side. We have each other's backs."

"Too obvious," she argued. Before she could say another word, her walkie-talkie buzzed. She glanced at it, saw Leigh was once again summoning her and sighed. "I'm really getting tired of this thing. I've got to meet up with Leigh again. Go ahead and start searching without me if you want. I'll touch base with you later."

"Sounds good." He leaned in and kissed her cheek, surprising her. She had to actively fight the urge to turn her head so that her lips met his.

"Please be careful," she said instead, already moving away.

On the way to Leigh's suite, she wondered if the continued summons made the younger woman feel more powerful. She didn't remember Leigh doing this so much before—usually they'd run into each other somewhere around the center. Maybe that meant Fiona had been shifted to a position of greater trust.

After tapping on Leigh's door, she stepped inside.

"There you are!" Leigh smiled at her. "Close the door and come in."

Fiona took her time complying. Finally, she turned and faced Leigh, who remained seated behind her massive desk. "What's going on?"

"We have another plan," Leigh announced, her voice high-pitched with excitement. "Micheline wanted me to discuss it with you."

Instead of playing her usual role—which was to mimic Leigh's enthusiasm, Fiona crossed her arms and shook her head. "Why doesn't Micheline discuss it with me herself?"

As expected, Fiona's comment had Leigh narrowing her eyes. "Listen to you, Miss High and Mighty," Leigh snarled. "I think you are getting way too big for your britches. Why would you even think Micheline would need to discuss anything with you personally?"

Fiona blinked. While she'd expected a put-down, she hadn't anticipated this level of vitriol. Despite that, she stuck to her guns. She could always quickly back down if things escalated too fast. "If what she wants me to do is important enough, I'd think she'd want to tell me herself."

"I'm her messenger." Mouth tight, Leigh spoke angrily. "I can't believe you of all people are acting like this. After all we've done for you."

How much to push? Fiona debated. She wanted to get on an inside track with Micheline, but she really couldn't take the risk of alienating Leigh.

"I'm really not trying to cause trouble," Fiona responded, her tone conciliatory. "I just feel like these days Micheline is distancing herself from me—from us. When I first got here, I saw her a lot more. She coached me personally. Now, if she has anything to say to me, she has you do it. I miss her."

Leigh's hard expression softened. She even got up and came around her desk to place her hand lightly on Fiona's shoulder. "I get it, really I do. But Micheline is really busy. She's even been communicating with me via email lately. I haven't even seen much of her, and I'm her trusted employee."

Interesting. Email. "When was the last time you actually saw her in person?" Fiona asked.

"Don't worry about it." One flip of her hand dismissed Fiona's question as Leigh went back behind her desk and took a seat in her leather office chair. "Micheline has another job for you. When she finishes firming up the details, she'll need it carried out right away."

Leigh took a deep breath, pausing as if for dramatic effect. "You should know, this plan involves the Coltons."

Instantly alert, Fiona nodded. "What about them?"

"First, I need to ask you a possibly delicate question. Is there any chance you could be pregnant with Jake's child?"

Floored, Fiona simply stared. "Um, I don't know. I guess." Though she took her birth control pills religiously and Jake had used condoms, she supposed there was always a very small, remote chance. Unlikely, but still…

"Perfect." Beaming, Leigh fiddled with a stack of gold bracelets. "Micheline might need you to pretend to be pregnant."

"What?" Fiona felt sick again. Was there no end to the horrible things Micheline would ask her to do? "Would I have to tell Jake that, too?"

"Of course. Even better if you can convince him to play along for a cut."

"A cut of what?" Fiona asked, though she suspected she already knew. Heaven help her if Micheline wanted to try to sell the Coltons a mythical baby.

"Money. Duh." Leigh rolled her eyes. "Micheline hasn't unveiled the rest of her plan to me yet, but trust me when I say there will be lots of cash involved."

"Doesn't that ever bother you?" Fiona asked. "All the emphasis on money? The purpose of the AAG is supposed to be helping people figure out how to be the best versions of themselves. I don't understand why Micheline is so fixated on—" She almost said *extorting people for cash*, but stopped herself just in time.

"It takes lots of money to keep this place running,"

Leigh snapped. “Everything Micheline does is for the greater good. Everything.”

Leigh’s fervent defense of a con woman seemed par for the course. Fiona figured Leigh didn’t even realize she was in a cult. Oddly enough, most of the people she encountered here shared the same lack of awareness. She found this both strange and unnerving, a testament to Micheline’s powers of persuasion.

“Anyway,” Leigh continued. “For now I need you to simply convince Jake that you’re carrying his baby. We won’t do anything else until Micheline decides for sure what course of action to take.”

No sure what else to do, Fiona nodded her agreement. This assignment just kept getting weirder and weirder—and more and more dangerous.

Chapter Ten

Watching Fiona walk away, Jake hoped he didn't wear his heart on his sleeve. She was beautiful, his Fiona. *His?* When had he started thinking of her that way? He didn't know—didn't actually care. Despite her declaration that she couldn't do a serious relationship right now, he knew there would come a day when all the obstacles were gone. He understood that the way he felt about her was the sort of thing that only came along once in a lifetime. The trick would be to make her realize that, too.

After all this was over.

The intrigue, the drama, the danger that seemed to swirl around Micheline like a storm over the desert. He couldn't wait to see her arrested, brought down. And hopefully before she hurt anyone else in the process.

Remembering what Fiona had said about the door to the basement, he deliberately wandered over toward the kitchen, figuring he could claim hunger and the urge to find a snack as an excuse. But before he even made it halfway across the lobby, the beefy guy who acted as Micheline's bodyguard intercepted him.

"Micheline would like a word," Bart said, his tone

and aggressive stance indicating the subject wasn't up for debate.

Following the guy, Jake wondered why Micheline just didn't simply have a meeting with everyone at the same time—him and Fiona and Leigh. Instead, she apparently had Leigh meeting with Fiona separately. He had to wonder why. Maybe she had some plan to pit them against each other. But of course, only if it benefited her.

As he walked into her office, she greeted him with a huge smile. "I hear congratulations are in order," she cooed.

Since he had no idea what she might be referring to, he simply waited.

"I'm surprised you're not more excited," she continued.

Clearly, she was going to make him ask. "About what?"

"Becoming a father!" The gleam in her eyes chilled him to the bone. "How thrilling!"

Becoming a...what? Still trying to process her words, he didn't immediately respond. Just stood staring at her, as if waiting for her to laugh and say, "Just kidding."

Except she didn't.

Her smile faded. "Oh dear. You didn't know."

He hid the rough flash of anger. Though he was 99 percent sure Micheline was acting out another one of her scams, he decided to play along. "You mean Fiona? She can't be pregnant. She'd tell me if she was."

Micheline's smug expression had him gritting his teeth. "She's afraid. That's why she hasn't said anything to you. She's meeting with Leigh right now to discuss her options."

Sure she was. More likely getting her script from Leigh as to how they wanted her to play along. Games. Micheline always had several balls in the air at once.

He needed to become better at playing this game. Still, it had only been a few days since he and Fiona had slept together. There's no way she or anyone else could know whether she was pregnant yet.

"It had to be someone else," he said, proceeding to outline his reasoning. Micheline watched him closely, the gleam in her eyes letting him know she had expected this reaction. How could she not have, with the statistical impossibility of the scenario she'd mentioned?

"Most likely." Micheline shrugged. "Does that matter to you? Are you going to dump this poor, homeless woman and let her fend for herself?"

"Maybe." He crossed his arms, aware he'd be more believable if he stuck to his guns.

"Very well." The malice in Micheline's smile chilled his blood. "I'm guessing you're more like me than either of us realized."

A statement which she damn well knew would virtually guarantee to make him do the opposite.

"Damn." Walking over to the couch, he allowed himself to drop down and sit. Covering his face with both hands, he thought furiously, trying to figure out how he should react. "You know I'd never abandon her. But why wouldn't she come to me first?" he asked, his voice breaking. "She knows how I feel about her."

"And how is that?" Micheline's tone sounded cool and disinterested, even though he knew damn well she wasn't.

Hell, he didn't know how Fiona did this. He already felt queasy, and now he was actually going to bare his soul to one of the most narcissistic women on the planet. "I'm falling in love with her."

"You are?" Yep, that was pure glee. She didn't even bother to keep that particular emotion in check. "Then I know you'll want to do the right thing for her."

Slowly, he raised his head. "Which is?" Was she going to insist he marry Fiona?

"Help her find the baby the best home."

Though he should have known better, disappointment flooded him. For all of three seconds. "Oh? You don't want me to marry Fiona and promise to support our baby?"

The incredulous look she gave him let him know how far off base she believed he'd gone. "Of course not. Your child could have all the luxuries in life that you missed out on."

Though warning bells—hell, *sirens*—were blaring inside his head, he kept his face expressionless. "Do go on."

"He or she should be brought up among the wealthy, the cultured. People of his own blood."

He stared at her, hard. Hoping at least a hint of his revulsion leaked through in his glare. "You want to give my child to the Coltons." A statement rather than a question.

She laughed. Micheline actually laughed, causing him to grind his teeth and clench his jaw as well as his fists. "Not *give*," she said, shaking her head. "More like *sell*."

Sell. What the actual… He could only imagine what Leigh and Fiona were now discussing. A fake pregnancy, along with a completely illegal and unethical and just plain despicable act: selling a baby that didn't even exist to *his* family!

Worse, he knew Fiona would want him to pretend to go along with it. But he suspected Micheline would know something was up if he did. She understood him at least that well.

"Why would you do that?" he asked, hoping he sounded reasonable. "The Coltons are my actual family. Any child born from my blood is already theirs. Why would you think they'd be willing to pay *you* anything?"

If she noticed the emphasis he put on the word *you*, she didn't react. "Because if they don't pay, I'll make sure the child will disappear."

Horrified, he didn't even try to hide it. "You'd kill my baby?" he demanded.

She held up both hands. "I didn't say that. The decision will ultimately be up to Fiona. She might decide to give the baby up for adoption."

Fictional, he reminded himself. There actually wasn't a baby. Yet. Maybe never.

"Or keep it," he growled. "Fiona would make a damn good mother. Jeez, Micheline. You never change."

His disparaging comment didn't appear to faze her. "I am consistent," she agreed proudly. "Plus, you need to understand where Fiona is in her life. She's only been here less than a month. We picked her up homeless, living in the streets. She has become part of our family here at AAG."

About to storm out, he remembered—just barely—that he had a role to play, so he restrained himself. "I want to talk to Fiona first," he said. "Since this is our child, the decision really should be between the two of us first."

Her smug smile told him she believed she had Fiona in her back pocket. "Of course. Take your time. I'll check in with you tomorrow."

As soon as he left her office, he went in search of Fiona. He saw her in the lobby, helping one of the elderly AAG members get settled with a book.

"Do you have a moment?" he asked, keeping his tone polite. "To take a short walk outside?"

Gaze searching his face, she nodded. "Are you comfortable?" she asked the old woman, pulling up the light blanket and tucking it in around her waist.

"Fine, dear. You go for a walk with your nice young man."

Fiona blushed but she didn't correct her. "Let's go," she told Jake. "I can't stay long. I've got a few more tasks I need to handle here at the center."

Though he could barely contain his impatience, he managed to wait until they were out the door, down the porch steps and halfway down the driveway.

"Is there something you forgot to tell me?" he asked, his voice harsh. "I met with Micheline just now. She said you were talking to Leigh."

"About the pretend baby?" Though she spoke without inflection, pain and anger flashed in her eyes. "And Micheline's strange scheme to sell him or her to the Coltons?"

"Exactly!" He expelled his breath in a sigh, hoping to release some of his tangled-up emotions. "This is a new low, even for someone like her."

"I agree." Her calm voice acted like a balm upon his rage. "Of all the things I've had to do while here, this is the absolute worst."

"Because who would do that? Who would actually

sell their own child?" He realized part of the reason this bothered him so much was due to his own circumstances. Micheline had switched him with another baby and actually hoped he would die.

"You do know the baby isn't real, right?" Fiona asked, touching his arm. "I'm not actually pregnant."

He blinked. "I know."

"Do you? Because you sound uncertain."

Considering, he finally nodded. "Probably because Micheline talked like you really were. In fact, I'm pretty sure her henchwoman Leigh probably told you to lie to me and say you really are pregnant."

"She did at first, but then she kind of left it open. She even mentioned offering you a cut of whatever they rake in."

He didn't bother to hide the disgust that filled him. "More proof that Micheline never really knew me. Because if she had even the slightest clue who I am, she'd know I'd never abandon my child the way she did me."

"Come here," she said. "Right now." And she tugged him into her arms, holding him tight.

Just like that, all the frustration and impotent rage drained away.

"You can do this," she continued, her arms still wrapped around him. "*We* can do this. Just think of the end result."

Micheline behind bars. "You're right," he said, raising his head. "I guess I let emotion get the better of me. She's such a—"

Fiona kissed him then, midsentence, midbreath. Kissed him as if she were dying and he might be her last hope for survival.

After a moment, he relaxed enough to kiss her back.

This woman, he thought, even as he drowned in sensation. The scent of her, the feel of her, the taste of her filled him with both yearning and the certainty that she was the one. Even if she didn't know it yet.

WITH MICHELINE PLOTTING and scheming, Fiona had a suspicion that events might occur along an accelerated timetable. Which meant if she was going to locate these cells or whatever might really be in the basement, she needed to do it quickly. She hadn't seen Underhill either, so either he'd been dismissed or Micheline had locked him up.

If the inner door remained locked, then she had to locate the key. She decided to stake out the laundry room. Eventually, someone had to go into the basement. She'd watch from there and see. Most likely, whoever had basement duty would have been given the key for their shift, but she also wouldn't have been surprised to see they stashed it somewhere close to keep things simple. After all, they'd probably figure no one would want to break *in* to the basement, only out.

Luckily, even though the center had maids who picked up the laundry every week, Fiona had enough clothes to pretend to be doing her own laundry. While she felt quite certain this would be frowned upon, at least she'd have a credible excuse if anyone caught her. She bundled them up and stuffed them in a large tote, hoping this would help keep them hidden from view, and trudged downstairs, through the lobby and past the kitchen to the laundry room.

She'd finished her first load and moved it to the dryer when she heard male voices coming down the hall. Two of them, and it sounded like they were arguing. She moved to the dryer closest to the doorway and bent over to shuffle around her clothes inside it, hoping that way she'd be mostly hidden.

"It's your turn to sleep down there," one of the men said. "I had that duty all of last week, and I did it."

"I really don't want to," the other guy replied. "After the lights go out, it's creepy as hell."

"Then leave them on."

"I tried that. It's still creepy down there."

"Tough." A rattle of metal, like a full key chain.

Fiona took a chance and raised up enough to peer around the doorway. Both men had their backs to her now. One big man, with close-shaven hair and broad shoulders. The other held a large key chain and appeared to be trying to extract one of the keys from it.

"I need to give you this," he said. "It's impossible to get off this thing."

"Keep it. Harley told me a couple of weeks ago where he kept a spare key hidden."

"Out here?" Man Number One sounded outraged. "Why would he do something so stupid? Those brainy types never have any common sense."

"No, not out here," Number Two replied. "In the laundry room. No one would think to look there."

Fiona's heart stopped. Damn it. She glanced around. No place to hide. If they came in here to retrieve the key, she was busted.

On the other hand, she'd know where the key had been stashed.

Holding her breath, she braced herself for the two men to appear. Luckily, she had her laundry, so she continued to slowly place one wet clothing item at a time into the dryer.

"Here it is!" the first guy announced, all triumphant. "I got it off the chain. The key is your responsibility now."

A moment later, she heard the solid metal door open. Once the men went through, it clanked shut behind them. And then she heard the sound of the dead bolt clicking into place as they locked it.

Damn. It had been left unlocked last time. She could only hope the key fit both locks. It must, since they'd discussed one key rather than two.

Getting to her feet, Fiona looked around. Somewhere inside this laundry room, a spare key had been hidden. All she needed to do was find it.

Aware that at least one of the guards, if not both, would eventually return, presumably after completing their check on things, she started searching. First, she checked all the obvious places—inside the linen cabinet, on the shelf near the detergent and fabric softener, and behind the bins used to pick up the dirty towels. No sign of a key.

Think. It had to be someplace easily accessible but still well hidden. If the guard was too lazy to carry a key around with him, he wouldn't want to expend a lot of effort to get it.

The folding table. She checked underneath. Sure enough, someone had glued a small plastic pouch near the front corner. Inside, she found a metal key.

Triumphant, she slid it into her pocket and went to check the dryer. Since her stuff was still wet, she left it there for now and strolled on out and back to her room. She'd come back and retrieve it later.

The key. She had the freaking key. Inside her room, she closed the door. Keeping it in her pocket—because she still wasn't sure if there might be a camera here or there—she debated not only where to hide it, but whether to show it to Jake.

While she appreciated his help, the FBI wasn't in the practice of endangering innocent citizens. Going down into the basement could be considered hazardous, therefore she didn't think she should involve him. Best to go it alone.

Now to figure out when. Clearly, the place was well guarded at night, since the two men had talked about having to sleep there.

It would have to be during the day. From what she'd seen, the guards left periodically, whether to have a meal or just take a break. She'd need to time everything perfectly, so she'd need to learn when the guards left. Patience, she reminded herself. She'd keep an eye on the hallway and make notes whenever she saw guards leaving or arriving.

Satisfied with her plan, even if it was going to take a few days, she decided to focus on Leigh and, by proxy, Micheline.

Micheline's latest scheme—inventing a fake baby and then trying to sell it to the Colton family—seemed sloppy. Especially for someone usually so meticulous with details. She seemed to be all over the place, at least judging by what Leigh passed on. Schemes of a mass suicide, extorting money from the Coltons, milking impressionable college students: all indicated Micheline was ramping up her attempts to increase her fortune.

Why? What had changed? All along, the AAG had continued to churn away, staying just under the radar of law enforcement. They were widely perceived as charlatans and well-known for bilking people out of their life savings, but due to not only the lack of complaints, but the fact that people received services such as seminars and self-help classes, as well as books, no actual charges had ever been filed.

In fact, until the Mustang Valley Police Department had received several calls from worried relatives believing their family members' had not only lost their savings in her schemes but that their lives might be in danger, law enforcement had considered their hands to be tied. And then, when an informant had mentioned money laundering, the FBI had gotten involved.

Now this—rumors of something big, something dangerous about to occur had Fiona feeling the pressure. Though undercover stings often were long, drawn out affairs, she knew she couldn't let anyone die if there was a way to prevent it.

She went for a long walk by herself and called Holden while she was out. Once she'd outlined Micheline's latest scheme, he whistled. "Are you sleeping with him?"

Though she flushed with embarrassment, she kept her voice steady. "I am. It's a long story."

"Ok." To his credit, Holden didn't judge. "Though selling a baby is definitely a crime, considering what other misdeeds we think she's committing, or about to commit, that's small potatoes, though."

"True," she agreed. "I don't even know if she'll actually follow through. But it's the first time I've actually witnessed her doing something that could constitute an actual crime. Yet."

"Just wait and watch," he said. "And be careful."

"Always. I did figure out a way to get into the locked basement. I've just got to get the timing right. Who knows what I'll find down there? Since she has the place heavily guarded, it might be something interesting."

"Heavily?" Holden sounded skeptical. "As far as I know, she only has two men working security detail out there."

"Really? The way they talked, there are at least three. Who are they?"

"I'll text you pictures," Holden replied. "One of them is Randall Cook. He's thirty-nine, tall, thin, a bit of a sad sack. Brown hair, brown eyes. He's been at the center for four years, working as a handyman. Worships Micheline and Leigh."

"Who's the other?"

"Just a sec." Holden clearly riffled through some papers. "Micheline's bodyguard, Bart Akers. Big and brawny with a blond crew cut."

"I've seen him around," she said. "Met him even."

"He and Randall Cook are good friends. If Micheline has anyone guarding whatever is in the basement, those two would do it."

"What about the third guy?" she asked. "They mentioned him hiding a key."

"No idea. The only other male in Micheline's inner circle is in custody. Harley Watts. He's a tech geek, and he does a lot of dark-web work for Micheline. He sent the initial email about Ace not being a biological Colton to the Colton Oil board. So far, he's not talking." He snorted. "He appears to think Micheline hung the sun and the moon."

"There's more than a few like that out here," Fiona responded. "I honestly don't get it. Nothing I've seen in Micheline's character should inspire that kind of blind loyalty. Even her teachings are pretty lame."

This comment made Holden chuckle. "Yeah, but clearly not everyone feels that way."

"Well, if there are only two guards, that will make this much easier to manage," she mused.

"Maybe so. But again, take no chances."

"I gotcha."

"And don't involve Jake Anderson in that. It's too dangerous," he advised.

"I wasn't planning on involving him. It's bad enough that Micheline lied and told him I was pregnant with his child."

"She's reaching for straws. But why the sudden, desperate need for money?" he asked.

"That's what I'd like to know." She thought for a minute. "Though I'm sure you've already done this, can you have someone check out her financial records again? Look for any huge payments she might have made. Or any large purchases."

"Will do. And keep me posted if you happen to learn anything more about this possible mass suicide she's planning."

Fiona agreed. If she had concrete evidence of something that horrendous, Micheline could be charged with attempted murder. The trick would be to stop her before anyone got hurt.

After hanging up, she turned around and went back inside.

Staking herself in the lobby initially seemed simple. She had no official scheduled duties, other than the multitude of seminars she was supposed to attend. While she still tried to show up periodically for one or two, for the most part she skipped out on them. The constant repetition gave her a headache.

But that afternoon, every time she got into position so she could see if anyone emerged from the hallway near the kitchen, either Leigh called her with a task or someone in the lobby needed her help.

Finally, she got a rare Micheline sighting. Even better, the cult leader was accompanied by her bodyguard, the big goon who'd been one of the two men going into the basement.

"What's up?" Jake said behind her, startling her. "Watching Her Highness move among her subjects?"

The analogy made her smile. "Yep."

"Is it me, or does she seem a bit off?" Jake commented. "Look at how jerky her movements are. And her eyes seem a bit…wild."

Without being too obvious, Fiona watched Micheline. From this distance, she couldn't hear what the other woman was saying, but Jake did have a point. If she'd been anyone else, Fiona might have thought she was drunk or on something. And who knew, she might very well be. That would definitely explain the sudden, desperate need for cash. Or even worse, Leigh's strange statement about death and rebirth. She shuddered at the thought.

"Maybe it's her illness," Jake said, just a hint of sarcasm in his voice. "Though I really don't think she's actually sick. That's the problem with people who constantly cry wolf. It's hard to know when to believe them."

Ever mindful of potential cameras or listening devices, Fiona made a sympathetic face. "Cancer is hard. So is the treatment. If she's started chemo…"

Though Jake made a face, he didn't comment. Instead, he jerked his head in Micheline's general direction. "She's headed this way," he said.

"Great," Fiona mouthed, before plastering what she hoped was a worshipful smile on her face. "Micheline," she gushed. "It's so great to see you!"

Micheline nodded, as if acknowledging the compliment. "Leigh mentioned you were feeling a bit…left out. Since I wanted you to understand how much I value you, I decided to put aside some of my very valuable time and chat with you. How are you feeling?"

"Fine," Fiona began, and then realized Micheline was asking because of the imaginary pregnancy. "I haven't had a chance to get down to the medical center and pick up the prenatal vitamins yet, but I'll do it today."

"Good, good." Now Micheline turned and faced Jake. "And you. Now that you've had a little bit of time to reflect on this, have you come to any decision about your involvement with this baby?"

Fiona could see Jake trying to figure out something diplomatic to say. "He and I are still discussing this," she interjected. "Jake wants to get married and move away to live on his ranch. I'm trying to convince him that our child deserves so much more."

Spoken like a true, brainwashed believer. It took everything Fiona had not to gag on the words. While she knew in reality she was definitely not pregnant, the idea of handing over a baby to strangers for money was abhorrent. And even if Micheline was successful in extorting the Coltons, Fiona didn't think it likely that she'd get a whole lot of cash.

"I want to talk about the new thing you're working on," Fiona said boldly. "I'm interested in learning about what's involved with being born again."

Micheline looked from Fiona to Jake and then back again. Her mouth worked, but no sound came out. Judging by her confused expression and frown, she had no idea what Fiona meant.

"Like in church?" Jake asked, clearly hoping to prod the conversation along.

Instead of answering, Micheline just smiled. "Stay tuned for details," she said, and then moved away, her bodyguard moving right behind her.

If he was here, that meant the other guy must be down in the basement. If the place was kept guarded at all times, which Fiona now doubted. Micheline simply didn't have the staff for that. Which was good as far as giving her more time to explore the area once she figured out the guards' schedule.

"That was weird," Jake mused. "She really seemed disconnected and unfocused."

"I'm sure it's just because she has a lot going on," Fiona offered, ever conscious of her role. "It's a heavy responsibility being the spiritual leader for so many people."

"Not to mention being overly involved in decisions for an unborn child that may or may not actually be born."

Fiona winced. "Don't talk about our baby like that," she said, putting her hands protectively over her still-flat stomach. "Come on, Jake. I know all of this is a shock, but you must know Micheline has our best interests at heart." She cut her eyes over to the lamp on the decorative table near them. She'd long ago spotted the tiny surveillance camera mounted there.

Giving a small nod, Jake grimaced. "I need some time alone to think." He shook his head and walked away, leaving her alone in the lobby once again.

Chapter Eleven

Though he'd assumed Fiona would come after him, Jake wasn't too surprised when she did not. This situation could go from bad to worse, and she needed to be on top of her game in order to deal with it. Honestly, he couldn't blame her.

He wasn't usually a gut instinct kind of guy, but he couldn't shake the feeling that something major was about to go down. Whether it was Micheline's bizarre attempt to ransom off Fiona's imaginary baby or something else, he had no way of knowing. Plans had been set in motion, the FBI had Fiona undercover and hopefully by the time the smoke cleared, the woman who'd raised him was going to go down.

For that, he could definitely manage to pretend to be something he wasn't. He'd never be as good at it as Fiona, but she'd probably had training and years of practice.

Despite being constantly aware Fiona had to play her role, he had to admit doing it himself creeped him out. But then he'd always prided himself on being an up-front, straight-shooting kind of guy. He didn't like games, he'd never aspired to become an actor and playing along with Fiona was the first time he'd ever done anything like this. He hoped he never had to again.

He caught sight of Micheline's bodyguard, Bart Akers, talking earnestly to the center's handyman, Randall Cook. Despite the difference in their appearances—Bart clearly worked out and exuded confidence, while Randall appeared to slouch his way through life—the two men appeared to be good friends. Jake studied Randall carefully. Though Jake had seen the thin, mopey guy lurking around, he'd never actually had a conversation with him. Whatever Randall and Bart were discussing must have been important, judging by Bart's frequent, emphatic hand gestures and Randall's defensive posturing.

Finally, the handyman walked away, head down and shoulders bent. Bart stormed off in the opposite direction. Jake made a split-second decision to follow Randall, just for the hell of it. Since Randall appeared lost in his own thoughts, Jake doubted he'd even notice.

To Jake's surprise, Randall headed toward the huge kitchen area. Where Fiona had mentioned the door that went to the basement was located. Interesting. Maybe Randall was headed there right now. Jake wondered what would happen if he followed him. If and when the handyman noticed him, Jake could come up with some spur-of-the-moment story explaining his presence. He figured since Randall knew Jake was important to Micheline, he'd be safe.

Randall wove through the equipment, neither looking at nor acknowledging any of the other employees. Walking confidently, Jake followed. Randall never looked over his shoulder or indicated any awareness of being followed. Several of the kitchen workers glanced up as they passed, but no one commented. Proof that they were used to Randall coming and going. Jake assumed that meant that they simply believed he was with Randall, who remained oblivious.

Worked for him.

Out of the kitchen finally, and into a short, narrow hallway. They passed a laundry area with several industrial-size washers and dryers. Randall stopped at a metal door and dug in his pocket for a key ring. He then proceeded to curse under his breath as he tried various keys until he finally located one that worked.

After opening the door, he slipped inside, letting it slam shut behind him. Jake rushed forward and grabbed the knob, bracing himself for the sound of a dead bolt being engaged.

It didn't happen. Either Randall didn't plan on being inside too long, or it never occurred to him that someone might want to follow him. Either way, Jake decided it was too good of an opportunity to miss. He couldn't wait to see Fiona's face when he told her.

Cautiously, Jake opened the door. Once inside, he carefully closed it, taking care to make as little sound as possible. He found himself in a well-lit staircase, with metal steps and a handrail. This seemed awfully institutionalized for a private residence, but who knew what Micheline actually used the basement for.

Basement. Who in Arizona even had a basement?

Moving down the metal stairs as quietly as possible, he wasn't surprised to find a second door at the bottom. This was the one Fiona had gotten to as well, only to find it locked. However, judging by Randall's attitude, Jake figured this time it wouldn't be. Turning the handle, he found he was right.

Now came the hard part. Since he had no idea what the layout might be on the other side of that door, he couldn't judge how exposed he'd be once he stepped through. He'd have to do some fast talking if discovered, that's for sure.

He took a deep breath, pulled the door open and stepped inside. And found himself blinking at the bright fluorescent lighting.

At first glance, he might have thought he was inside a large animal shelter. Rows of tall cages, roughly eight by six feet, lined one wide hallway. The sharp ammoniacal tang of urine mingled with disinfectant stung his nose.

What the…?

He took a step. The first few cages were empty. But then he caught sight of the occupant in the next one and froze. A man, beaten and bloody, barely conscious, lay on the concrete floor. His clothes were ragged and filthy, stained with blood and dirt and bodily waste.

Stunned, Jake stood in front of the cell, trying to make sense of what he saw. A moan came from the next cage up, drawing his attention. The occupant there—female—peered up at him with sunken eyes, her long hair tangled and dirty, her body all bony angles, as if she'd been starved for weeks.

Beyond her, he caught sight of yet another person—prisoner? As he went to head that way, pain exploded in the back of his head, and he went down.

WHEN JAKE OPENED his eyes again with a pounding headache, it took a moment for him to realize where he'd ended up. He lay on a cold, cement floor and there were metal bars. A locked cell.

Hell. Micheline's basement.

Gingerly, he felt the back of his head, unsurprised to find a large and painful lump. Obviously, Randall or someone had come up behind him and clubbed him hard enough to knock him out. And now they'd locked him up in a cell, just like all the other poor souls he'd spotted earlier.

It would be okay, he told himself. Micheline would put a stop to this. She needed him for her little scheme with the Coltons.

"Hey," he called out, pushing himself up to his elbows and wincing at the blinding pain in his head. "Where are you? Show yourself."

But no one—not Randall or Bart or anyone else—appeared. None of the other prisoners even responded, as if they'd grown used to hearing unanswered pleas for help.

For the first time, a small prickle of dread went through him. How often did Micheline's hired men make their rounds? Judging by the condition of the others, not on a regular basis. Jake remembered Fiona saying something about Randall spending the night down here. That could be good or bad, depending on how one looked at it.

Fiona. He started to groan out loud, but even that small sound made his aching head throb. They'd had a disagreement. She might not be looking for him at all for hours, maybe days.

His only hope was Micheline, of all people. Even the thought made his head hurt worse.

WHEN HER WALKIE-TALKIE BUZZED, Fiona gritted her teeth and considered tossing the thing into the nearest arrangement of silk flowers. Leigh again, of course. Summoning Fiona once more. Almost as if she might be testing Fiona to see how much she could take before breaking.

Obediently, Fiona trudged to Leigh's suite. Knocked on the door, waited for Leigh to tell her to come in and then went inside.

This time, instead of waiting behind her desk, Leigh stood just a few feet from the door.

"About time you got here," she said crossly. "I'm swamped, and I don't have time to wait for you."

Instead of responding that she'd come as soon as she'd been called, Fiona apologized.

"Here." Leigh handed her a stack of leaflets. "I've got a job for you. There's going to be a Gathering."

"A what?" Juggling the papers, Fiona barely managed to keep from dropping them.

"A Gathering." Leigh high-fived the air. "It's a big deal. Micheline is inviting all of her fans and followers. We've been working nonstop making sure the mailers go out. We're also doing mass emails, but these are for the older folks who might not have access to computers."

Intuition tingling, Fiona looked down at one of the fliers and started to read. She looked up at Leigh, hiding her alarm. "Is this…" She licked her lips, her heart racing. "Is this going to be the born-again ceremony? The big one?"

"It just might be." Leigh practically sang the words, though her heavily made-up eyes were still cold and calculating. "I'm so excited!"

Fiona pretended to share in Leigh's fake joy. Meanwhile, her insides were jumping. She had to find out the actual plan and then not only come up with a way to stop it, but surefire proof that Micheline was the instigator. Once she had, she could call Holden and have a team brought in to carry out the arrests.

Leigh would be going down, too. The beauty queen might be naive, but so far she'd done nothing but go along with her boss's unethical, moneymaking schemes. And since she'd appeared to sanction the mass murder—as long as she herself didn't have to die—Leigh would also be charged.

But there was more, and like the excellent FBI agent she knew she was, Fiona wanted to find it. The existence of some sort of basement cells, where people were being held prisoner without rights to a trial or hearing, would clinch it. She had to figure out a time and get herself down there.

"What are you waiting for?" Leigh sniped. "Is there something else you need?"

"What do you want me to do with these?" Fiona asked, holding up the leaflets.

"Take them to campus and put them up, pass them out, whatever you have to do in order to get more people to come. College kids love the idea of stuff like this."

Feeling queasy again, Fiona nodded. "Will do."

"Get going," Leigh ordered, shooing her away with one hand. "We're short on time."

Fiona clutched the papers to her chest and hurried toward the door. Only when she'd gotten in the front seat of her car and locked the doors did she take the time to thoroughly read one.

This Friday. The date jumped out at her. All of this would be going down in less than a week. Which meant Micheline would have to try and sell off the mythical unborn baby before her followers committed mass suicide.

It was going to be a busy week. Fiona started the car and drove to a local office supply store. There, one could rent the use of a paper shredder. Fiona paid her money and began rapidly shredding the documents. She kept back three copies, but she didn't want to take a chance on any of these getting in the hands of a single student.

Once she'd finished, she drove over to campus, parked and got out. Just in case Micheline had installed a GPS tracker on her car.

She spent a good half an hour walking around after stopping in the campus bookstore and picking up some fliers advertising a concert by a local band. These she tacked up on bulletin boards and telephone poles. If anyone had followed her to make sure she'd completed her task, unless they stopped and looked at the posters, it would appear she had.

Then she drove quickly back to the AAG center. Maybe if she could get in unnoticed, now would be the perfect time to check out the basement.

First, she needed to make sure both Bart and his friend Randall were elsewhere in the center. Walking with purpose, she strode through the common area as if she had an urgent task, looking for them.

She found them in the dining hall, sitting together and chowing down on hamburgers. Which meant there wouldn't be a time better than right now.

Heart pounding, she rushed through the kitchen, out the back door and down the hallway by the laundry room. The first door was locked, but her key fit. After gaining entrance, she made sure to lock it after her, just in case.

Clattering down the metal steps, she reached for her weapon, which of course she didn't have. Habit. But she sure did wish she'd found a way to arm herself, at least while down here. Bottom line—she didn't feel safe. She could fight and she could run, but she had no recourse against a man with a weapon. And she'd seen the side piece Bart carried in a shoulder holster. As for Randall, she doubted he even knew how to use a pistol.

The second door was also locked. No surprise there. Once again, her key worked. She took a deep breath and yanked it open, stepping inside. Out of reflex, she carefully locked it behind her and pocketed her key.

Then and only then did she turn and allow herself to process what she saw before her.

During her time in the FBI, she'd paid many a visit to jails and prisons. This place, with its row of metal cells and strong urine smell, appeared to be an attempt to recreate that, though on a much smaller scale. There was only one long row.

Underhill had begged not to be taken to the cells. Now she knew exactly what he'd meant.

The first two cells were clean and empty. In the third, a huddled pile of clothes looked eerily familiar. She hoped—oh, how she hoped—there wasn't a person underneath.

As she moved closer, her heart in her throat, she realized exactly who she saw lying in a mess of blood on the concrete floor. Jake.

She must have gasped or made some other sound of disbelief, because he raised his head. His face—his handsome face—was now so swollen he was barely recognizable. Swollen, bruised, his split lip combined with blood—so much blood—made him look like something out of a nightmare.

"Jake." Her heart broke. How the hell had he gotten in here? And why? "Who did this to you?"

But he'd lost consciousness and slumped back to the floor. And of course, his cell door was locked.

She tried her key, even though she guessed it wouldn't work. It wasn't even the right size.

"Jake," she whispered. "I'm going to go get you some help."

A moan from the next cell had her squinting. She took a hesitant step toward the sound, stopping short when she realized Underhill was the next prisoner. He'd been beaten, too, though not as badly nor as recently as Jake. Beyond him, in yet another cell, she saw what appeared to be an extremely emaciated woman.

Micheline, she thought, battling back a flash of fury. Micheline had done all this. Maybe not personally, but no one in the AAG center acted without her orders.

She pulled out her cell phone, intending to call Holden. No signal. Of course. But she could still use the camera. Photographic evidence would go a long way. She snapped pictures of everything—the setup, the cells and the prisoners themselves. Twice she tried to text them, but with no signal, they wouldn't go through.

Jake still hadn't moved, though she thought she could see his chest rise and fall as he breathed. "Please stay alive," she murmured and spun around to go.

Hands shaking, she unlocked the first door, barely remembering to lock it again before rushing up the stairs. She fumbled with the key and dropped it. Telling herself to breathe, to stay calm, she bent over and picked it up. As she straightened, the dead bolt turned and someone on the other side shoved the door open, right into her. Unprepared, she stumbled backward and grabbed for the handrail, barely stopping herself from falling down the stairs.

Bart came slamming through the door, expression hard. The instant he saw Fiona, he pulled his pistol. "Keep your hands where I can see them," he ordered.

The irony of the situation wasn't lost on her. But she was too worried about Jake to care a whole hell of a lot what Bart thought. "Go get Micheline," she demanded. "Or Leigh. Or both of them. Right now."

His upper lip curled in a sneer. "I don't take orders from you. And with you sneaking around in places where you don't belong, you don't have a lot of bargaining power."

"I don't care." With a pistol pointed at her, she didn't want to make any sudden moves. Especially since she didn't know what kind of training Bart might have had.

"Does Micheline know Jake is in here?" she asked, softening her tone somewhat. "He's been badly beaten. He needs to get immediate medical care."

"You don't say," Bart drawled. "I'll get right on that." He gestured with his gun. "Now you, move back down the stairs. Keep your hands where I can see them at all times."

Would he shoot her? For the first time, she wondered if Bart and Randall were running their own little shop of horrors down here without Micheline's blessing.

Somehow, knowing what she did about Micheline, she doubted that. "You can't hurt me," she said, infusing her voice with way more confidence than she felt. "Micheline needs me too much to lose me."

"Does she now?" Judging from his snide smirk, he doubted that.

"Call her and see." Fiona decided to brazen this out. "Call her right now. I've had just about enough of this. Jake is hurt and—"

Moving so swiftly she didn't have time to react, he shoved her hard, sending her tumbling down the metal stairs. It happened so fast, a split second in which one moment she'd been whole and the next, her entire body screamed with pain.

She'd broken her ankle, she thought, though since she could still move her legs, she hadn't broken her neck. Though she could have. Or her back. Bart had pushed her, knowing full well she'd be badly hurt, maybe even paralyzed, and he hadn't cared.

Calling on her own inner strength, she grabbed the handrail at the bottom of the stairs and hauled herself to her feet. Excruciating pain sliced through her when she tried to put her weight on her right ankle, which meant definitely broken.

"You tried to kill me." She didn't have to feign disbelief. "What the actual hell?"

"No," he drawled, coming about halfway down, his weapon still aimed at her. "If I wanted to kill you, I would just shoot. But…" He took another step, bringing him closer. "I know Micheline will likely want you alive, just like your boyfriend. Though she won't give a rat's ass what kind of condition either of you are in."

"But she will," she informed him. "She needs the baby I'm carrying to leverage what influence she has."

"Baby?" Momentarily fazed, he eyed her. "Right."

"I'm serious," she protested.

He ignored her. One more step, then another, until

only a matter of feet separated them. He waved the gun in a way that made her consider snatching it away from him. If she'd been able to stand on both her feet, she might have tried. As it was, all she could do was glare at him and hope he didn't pistol-whip her.

"She won't care if I have some..." He licked his lips, pupils darkening. "Fun."

Horrified, she realized what he meant. He planned to rape her. "Not in this lifetime," she snarled, catching him by surprise. "I promise I will fight you," she said, letting him see the steely resolve in her eyes. "And you might be bigger than me and stronger than me, but I will hurt you. In more ways than one." She bared her teeth in a savage smile. "In fact, you're probably going to end up having to kill me before I'll let you lay one hand on me."

He took an inadvertent step back before he caught himself. "Move," he ordered. "There's a cell down there calling your name."

By now the pain had become so intense perspiration broke out on her forehead. She could barely hobble on one leg.

"The cell," he repeated. "Now."

Since she didn't have a choice, she did as he said. Once she'd made it inside, he slammed the door shut and locked her in. "Slide me your phone," he said.

"No." She stuck out her chin. "There's no service here anyway."

"Slide. Me. Your. Phone." He gestured toward Jake. "If you don't, I'll make sure and hurt your boyfriend even more than he already is."

Judging by the anticipation in his face, he actually hoped she'd refuse. Disgusted, she reached into her pocket, pulled out her phone and slid it across the floor to the edge of the bars.

"Thank you." Pocketing it, he smiled. "Enjoy your stay," he said, mocking her. And then he turned and clomped back up the stairs, slamming and locking the door. Now alone, she sank down to the floor and removed her shoe. Her ankle had swollen and turned black and blue. Examining the rest of her aching body, she took a quick inventory. She had various other cuts, scrapes and bruises, all caused by her fall, but as far as she could tell nothing else appeared to be broken.

On the other side of her, separated by a low metal partition, Jake moaned. Her stomach twisted, even as her own throbbing pain made her nauseous. Bart had pushed her down the stairs, but who knew what he or Randall had done to Jake.

Her only hope—oh, the bitter irony—was that Bart would contact Leigh or Micheline and they would order her to be freed, along with Jake. Jake needed medical treatment immediately. Her broken ankle wasn't life-threatening. Whatever they'd done to Jake might be.

Hours passed, how many she had no idea. She'd relied on her phone for checking the time, so didn't even own a watch. The throbbing in her ankle seemed to intensify by the minute, and no matter how she shifted her position, she couldn't seem to lessen the pain. No more sounds came from Jake's cell, which worried her. She even tried calling his name several times, but he never responded.

Damn. If anything had happened to him, she'd bear full responsibility. She should have urged him to get out, to go back to his ranch, to stay safe. But she'd let the attraction blazing between them distract her. Now, she hoped neither of them had to pay the consequences of her foolishness.

Foolishness. Was it, though? They hadn't known each other very long, but she couldn't imagine going through another day without him in it. He had to be all right. He had to be. She refused to accept any other outcome.

Finally, she managed to doze, though the slightest movement brought stabbing pain and she'd wake, perspiring and disoriented. Though she'd seen others locked up here, the absolute silence wore on her as heavily as some kind of sensory deprivation torture. She, who'd never been the slightest bit claustrophobic, began to feel acutely aware of the size of her small cell.

She understood what they—the AAG, Micheline or just Bart and Randall—had going here. A prison of sorts, where offenders were locked up without legal representation or access to a fair trial. Inhuman and cruel treatment, including beatings and starvation, denying medical care and who knew what else.

There was no telling how much time had passed when Fiona heard the clunk-click sound of the dead bolt unlocking. She tried to push herself to her feet, but her swollen ankle screamed in protest, so she abandoned that idea. She couldn't even manage to get to her knees.

Bart came through the door, followed by Micheline. Fiona's intense relief at seeing Micheline faded at the furious expression on the older woman's face. Micheline moved forwarded, holding something in her hand, brandishing it like a weapon. As she stopped outside Fiona's cell, Fiona realized Micheline held her cell phone, the one Bart had taken from her right before locking her up.

At least, Fiona thought, the phone was a burner. She

kept nothing stored on it, with the exception of Holden's number.

"You little idiot," Micheline spat. "What the hell were you doing snooping around down here?"

Fiona said the first thing that came to mind. "I was looking for Jake. We had a fight, and he was upset. I wanted to make it up to him."

"Jake?" Micheline turned and looked at Bart, who nodded. "Why didn't you mention that Jake was here, too?"

He shrugged, his expression mulish. "I honestly didn't think about it."

"Or you didn't want her to know what kind of shape he's in," Fiona interjected. "He's pretty beat-up, Micheline. He needs medical attention right away."

Micheline rounded on Bart. "You idiot. What did you do to him? Right now, Jake is a valuable commodity. You'd better not have messed that up."

"I didn't do anything to him," Bart replied, his tone sulky. "Randall caught him snooping around down here and hit him a few times with a baseball bat."

Fiona gasped. "No wonder he looks so bad."

"Show me," Micheline demanded.

Bart led her a few steps down the row, stopping in front of Jake's cell.

She cursed. "Get him up to the medical area immediately."

"But…" If Bart even briefly considered arguing, he clearly changed his mind. "Yes, ma'am. Right away." He used his walkie-talkie to call someone—probably Randall—and then nodded. "I'll get him moved out immediately."

A moment later, the door opened, and Randall hurried through. He kept his head down, refusing to make eye contact with anyone. Judging by the extreme submissiveness of his posture, Fiona wondered how it could be possible for him to beat anyone. But then again, some of the most horrible crimes had been committed by the least likely individuals.

"You two." Micheline pointed. "Get Jake up to the medical area right now. See that he gets treatment. And Randall, don't you ever beat one of my guests without checking with me first, understood?"

Randall mumbled something that sounded like agreement and nodded. Then Bart unlocked Jake's cell, and he and Randall hefted Jake up between them, half carrying, half dragging him along.

"No way is he going to make it up those stairs," Fiona called out, worried out of her mind. Even her own pain faded into the background as she tried not to imagine the damage to Jake's already broken body if the two men tried to drag him up metal stairs. Even worse if they failed or dropped him.

Bart shot her a poisonous look, but when Micheline agreed with Fiona, his expression changed.

"Get a stretcher and a couple more men to help you," Micheline directed. "He's already in bad shape. The last thing I need you to do is kill him. He's important to one of my plans."

Of course, Fiona thought grimly. Micheline didn't care about Jake, despite having raised him since birth. She only wanted him whole so she could still use him to try and bilk the Coltons for money. And Fiona had to put a stop to that, somehow. No matter what.

Chapter Twelve

Previously in his life, Jake had been kicked by a horse, gored by a bull, and crashed a motorcycle, but he'd never hurt like this. Since he'd lost consciousness after the first blow, his assailant must have simply kept on beating him, just for the hell of it.

Judging by the way he felt, the weapon of choice had been either a crowbar or a baseball bat or along those lines. He had a pretty good idea that more than one bone had been broken, and judging by how much it hurt to breathe, two or three ribs. Or more. He couldn't tell. His entire body felt like one giant throbbing mess of pain.

He jolted awake when someone—two men—lifted him under his arms and tried to drag him out of his cell. Silently screaming, he mercifully blacked out and knew nothing else until he woke up in some kind of hospital bed.

Which meant at least they'd let him out of the cell. But taking him to a hospital? Risky on Micheline's part. One of his eyes was too swollen to open, but he used the other one to try and figure out his location.

Not a hospital, he realized. He wasn't hooked up to any machines, for one thing. And the room didn't have that sterile feel of most hospitals.

Then where? Dimly, he thought he remembered Fiona saying something about a medical area at the AAG center. Of course—Micheline wouldn't take a chance on him telling anyone what had happened to him.

But did they have the resources to patch him up? He knew he needed an ER, a skilled physician and some medicine. At least the pain seemed to have subsided, which meant most likely he'd been given some sort of drugs. He felt…good, actually. Yep, definitely drugs.

Lifting one arm, he realized someone had bandaged his chest. Which would definitely help with his ribs.

He wanted Fiona. Would they tell her where to find him? And if they did, would she even visit? The thought made him frown. He could swear he'd heard her voice, down there in the basement. Had he hallucinated it, driven crazy by pain and wishing for the one person who might be able to make him feel better?

Once again, he must have drifted off. When he opened his eyes again, his mouth felt dry and his stomach empty. Moving his head slowly, he looked for a nurse or an attendant, hating the way the entire world seemed to move drunkenly along with him. Vertigo, which meant strong medicine.

An older woman with a bright smile appeared in his line of vision. She adjusted his bed, raising him into a half sitting, half reclining position, and handed him a paper cup with ice water in it.

"Drink slowly," she advised. "Give your body a chance to get used to fluids."

Accepting the cup, he took a sip, resisting the urge to down the entire thing. Since his mouth was so dry, he took a few ice chips and let them melt on his tongue.

For one absurd moment, he caught himself wishing he had a living mother. But since he didn't, he figured it must be whatever drugs they'd given him that made him entertain such crazy thoughts.

Carefully, he set the cup back down on the metal tray and closed his eyes.

He must have drifted off to sleep. The next thing he knew, someone brought in a plastic food tray and placed it near his cup. "Soft foods only," the smiling attendant told him. After she'd left, he glanced around the room, only to see he was alone.

"Fiona," he croaked, as if by saying her name he could somehow summon her.

When she didn't appear, he shook his head at his own foolishness, then winced as the room spun and dipped alarmingly.

Once he felt steady again, he opened his eyes and gingerly reached for the covered plate. Inside he found a bowl of lukewarm chicken soup and a container of green Jell-O. Slightly nauseated, he went ahead and tried a spoonful of soup.

It tasted delicious. Surprised, he tried another. Before he knew it, he'd finished the entire bowl.

After he ate, he dozed. He knew there was something important he needed to do, but he couldn't seem to muster up the knowledge of what it might be. Instead, he let himself sleep. He figured he'd probably remember once he'd gotten some rest.

Fiona. Jake came awake with a start. His entire body hurt. Even breathing made him shiver with pain. Which meant the drugs had worn off. But at least his mind wasn't befuddled.

Fiona was in some sort of trouble. He tried to think,

to remember if she'd been with him when he'd descended into the basement to find Micheline's prison.

No. She hadn't. But then why did he remember hearing her voice? He thought back, wincing as he recalled Bart and Randall trying to pick him up, thinking he could somehow walk up the stairs. And then Fiona had insisted he wouldn't be able to, so Micheline had asked them to get a stretcher.

Fiona had been there. How? And why? He doubted Micheline had brought Fiona down there to show off her prison. Plus Leigh would have been there, and he didn't remember hearing Leigh's voice.

Which meant…what? Had Fiona been taken prisoner, too? Had they—Randall or Bart—beaten her, too? Fury heated his blood. So help him, if either of those fools had touched one hair on her head, he'd make them regret it.

He had to go check on her. Glancing around, he saw he'd been hooked to a single IV, though the hanging bag had gone dry. His painkillers, no doubt. There didn't appear to be any kind of machines monitoring him. Taking a deep breath, which brought on so much pain he broke out in a sweat, he tried to push himself up on his elbows.

Not happening. Not today, his broken body screamed.

Still, he persisted. Damned if he'd lie here and rest while Fiona suffered. He had to get to her or, even better, figure out a way to bring in reinforcements.

There had to be someone in the FBI he could call. But first, he had to get out of this bed and find a phone.

Finally, after several excruciating attempts, he managed to sit up enough that he could press the button to electronically adjust the bed. Now, with back support, he could sit, and hopefully the pain levels would subside enough for him to try to get up from the bed.

A quick glance under the sheet made him realize he wore no clothes, not even his underwear. He didn't see them anywhere in the room, either. Guessing they'd been bloody due to his beating, he imagined his captors had tossed them in the trash somewhere or incinerated them.

There had to be something he could wear. Even a hospital gown would be better than wrapping a bedsheet around himself and trying to walk down the hall. Though he would if he had to. Once he made it back to his room, he could grab a change of clothes and check on Fiona.

His phone. He could simply call her, and once she answered, he'd let her know where to find him. If only he had his phone.

Evidently, they'd taken that, too. Glad he'd password protected the thing, he took a fierce kind of pleasure knowing they wouldn't be able to use it. Unless they pressed his thumbprint on it while he was unconscious, which was entirely possible.

"Looks like you're going to live."

Jake looked up. The same attendant from earlier stood in the doorway, eyeing him.

"It appears so," Jake replied. "What's the prognosis?"

"Since they wouldn't take you to the hospital for X-rays, I can't be entirely certain, but I think you have a couple of bruised or broken ribs. It looks like whoever beat you kept the blows centered there. You're lucky, because they could easily have taken out a kneecap or an elbow. You've got a lot of bruises and cuts, but as far as I can tell without X-rays, nothing else seems to be broken."

Jake nodded, wincing at the pain this caused. "My head?" he asked. "No fracture? They clubbed me in the back of my skull to knock me out. It still hurts like hell."

Coming closer, the woman smiled. "You have a pretty big gash there, so I'm guessing that's the source of your pain. And your nose doesn't appear to be broken, surprisingly. Initially, I even thought one of your cheekbones was fractured, but it's not."

The lackadaisical approach to medicine floored him. Something of his thoughts must have shown on his face, because she frowned. "Look, I'm just an RN. I'm supposed to be treating colds and strep throat and the occasional infected cut. Not something like this." She waved her hand at him. "I demanded you be transported by ambulance to the ER. You looked terrible and I wasn't sure you'd make it. They wouldn't let me call 911, so I did the best I could."

"They?" he asked. "Meaning Micheline."

Slowly, she nodded. "And Leigh. I've seen far too much of this kind of thing lately. Now that I know you're stable, I'm quitting. I can't work for people like this."

If they let her leave, he thought, though he didn't say it out loud. He wouldn't be surprised if she didn't end up in a cell down in the basement, too.

"You called?" Bart's voice, startling both of them.

Suddenly, the nurse wouldn't meet Jake's gaze. "Yes. He's well enough to be transported back to his cell."

"What?" Jake tried to push away from the pillow, but the blinding pain knocked him back instead.

"I'm sorry," the nurse said before lifting a needle and giving him a shot in the arm. Everything went black after that.

AFTER JAKE HAD been taken away on a stretcher, Micheline turned to face Fiona.

"I don't know what I'm going to do with you," she said, her gaze cold. "You got yourself into this mess. Maybe I should see how you plan to get yourself out of it."

Dammit. Micheline couldn't abandon her now. Not when everything seemed so close to coming to a head. Fiona decided she might as well throw caution to the wind. She'd beg if she had to. "I only took your advice," she said, well aware of how much Micheline liked having her ego stroked. "I decided to let Jake think I wanted to marry him. I followed him, and when I saw him come down here, I got curious."

Expression impassive, Micheline shook her head. "Have you never heard the cliché expression about curiosity killing the cat?"

"Please, help me. I think my ankle is broken." Fiona lifted her leg so the older woman could see her swollen limb. "I'm sorry I came down here, and I swear it won't happen again. Would you please have someone take me for medical attention?"

Instead of answering, Micheline made a show of studying Fiona's phone. "This is an odd choice for a cell phone," she mused. "A disposable one, the kind people who aren't on the straight and narrow path might use."

"Or people with limited funds," Fiona pointed out, shifting slightly and then wincing from the pain. "As you know, I've been homeless. That phone was all I could afford, and even then it was a stretch. I prepay my minutes and rarely text." Luckily, she routinely deleted both her call history and text messages. Nothing would show if Micheline did a cursory search of the phone. A fact Micheline probably already knew. She wasn't the type to leave anything to chance.

"I'm not really tech savvy," Micheline continued. "But luckily, I have someone in my employ who is. He was able to go into your phone and retrieve deleted text messages and contacts. Plus he showed me all the pictures you took of my little holding area down here."

Fiona blinked. She knew better than to say anything. It was entirely possible Micheline could be lying, hoping to draw Fiona out.

"Are you working with the FBI?" Micheline asked. "Because I see quite a few texts and calls with Holden St. Clair, who as I'm sure you are aware, happens to be an FBI agent who spends quite a bit of time here in Mustang Valley. He also is dating Bella Colton."

Heart racing, Fiona didn't respond. Her cover was well and truly blown. Not only that, but she had a broken ankle and had been locked up in a basement cell. No one knew she was here, not even Jake, who'd been so badly beaten, he probably didn't even know his own name.

"As you might remember," Micheline continued, "the AAG will become internationally famous as of this Friday, when all my followers will ingest the substance that will kill them, so that they may be born again." A slight smile played over the older woman's face as she took in Fiona's shock and dismay. "I've decided to have you go first. I'll livestream it to social media so that everyone—including your friend Jake—can watch you die."

"But what about the Coltons and my baby?" Fiona asked, her hand cradling her nonexistent bump protectively.

"That plan was too flawed. I've decided to simply

ransom Jake to them." Her smile looked more like a baring of teeth. "He's the real Ace Colton, after all. Their flesh and blood. I'll just make sure they understand that you have convinced him to die so he can be born again. I have someone inside the Colton organization handling this for me right now. If they want him to live, they'll need to deposit ten million dollars in an offshore account. I'll also require a private plane and pilot."

Which meant that Micheline didn't need Fiona anymore. Then the rest of what she'd said sank in. "Why say that I'm the one who convinced Jake to die?" Fiona asked, wincing as she shifted her weight and made her ankle throb even worse. "Why involve me in that plan at all?"

Micheline laughed, the trilling sound grating on Fiona's nerves. "I want them to hate you," she said. "That way, no matter how this shakes out, they won't attempt to save you."

How this shakes out. Picking up on that, Fiona decided she might as well go ahead and ask. "You aren't planning to stick around and see for yourself, are you?"

"Of course not. I'll be long gone, to some sun-kissed beach and my ten million dollars, plus whatever else I can rake in from other families desperate to save their loved ones. My name will go down in history while I enjoy my new, carefree life." Micheline's smug tone had Fiona clenching her teeth.

"You honestly don't care how many people you kill?"

Micheline shrugged. "Honey, if they're that stupid, I'm doing the world a favor." She checked her watch. "I'll leave you to your cell and your pain. Remember, if it gets too bad, we can end it all a little bit early."

With that, Micheline spun on her stylish heels and

marched away. Fiona heard her climbing the metal stairs and opening and closing the door.

"She's gone," a familiar voice said. Underhill. "Welcome to the cells. By the time you've been here awhile, starving and with your broken bones untreated, you'll probably beg her to let you drink the poison."

"Is that what you plan to do?" Fiona shot back. "Do you really want to go out that way, Underhill? Death by poison can be very painful."

Silence. Clearly, his goading didn't extend to thinking that far ahead.

Her ankle's throbbing made Fiona nauseated. She tried various positions on the concrete floor. While getting comfortable would be impossible, she'd settle for whatever caused the least amount of pain. Then and only then did she allow herself to close her eyes and try to rest.

Sometime later—she had no idea how long—the sound of the door opening at the top of the stairs caused her to jerk upright. The sudden movement brought a stab of agony, but she pushed through it. Alert, she listened. She knew she had to come up with some sort of plan of action in case Micheline or Leigh showed up and tried to get her to ingest some sort of toxin.

Two voices, both male. Bart and Randall. She'd need all her strength if Bart tried to hurt her again. She couldn't allow her pain to distract her.

They'd been the ones who'd taken Jake away on the stretcher. Did that mean they were bringing him back? Surely not. If anyone had ever needed to go to the hospital, Jake had.

Much cussing ensued as the men slowly made their way down the stairs. Fiona managed to prop herself up into a sitting position so she could see. Sure enough, one of the men appeared, moving slowly since he carried one half of the stretcher.

Finally, they made their way to the bottom of the stairs. Jake lay, still unconscious, on the stretcher.

At least he appeared to have been cleaned up. Worried sick, Fiona watched as they carried him back to the empty cell he'd occupied before. Setting the stretcher down, one man unceremoniously rolled Jake out and onto the floor.

"Is he alive?" Fiona asked, drawing the attention of both Bart and Randall.

"He is," Bart answered, his smirk and leer making her skin crawl. "He'll probably be around long after you're gone. He's way more valuable to Micheline than you'd ever be."

Randall laughed at this, pushing his glasses up his nose. The other two men simply stood there, expressions bored, waiting until they were given the okay to leave.

"Come on," Bart finally said, when she didn't give him the reaction he'd evidently been waiting for. "We're done here. Let's go."

They clomped back up the stairs and left, locking the door behind them.

Damn. Scooting across the concrete floor, she tried to peer around the dividing wall separating her cell from Jake's. But she couldn't.

"Jake," she said, raising her voice. "Wake up."

"We're all awake now, lady," Underhill complained. "Would you mind keeping it down? I'm trying to get some sleep back here."

"Wouldn't you rather get out?" she countered.

"Hell yes, but how do you think you're going to manage that? Even if you could get out of the cell, there are two locked doors between this basement and the main house. If by some miracle you were able to make it through those, there are cameras everywhere between there and freedom. They'd grab you before you made it anywhere near an outside door."

Wisely, she didn't share the fact that she possessed a key to the double doors. "You'd be surprised at what I can do," she said instead.

Underhill laughed and didn't reply. The other prisoner, the poor woman in the last cell, didn't make a sound at all.

As the hours passed, Fiona would have thought the pain from her broken ankle would have subsided. Instead, it seemed to intensify. She'd never broken a bone before, and how badly it hurt came as a shock.

Finally, she drifted into a kind of uncomfortable doze. But every movement, no matter how small, brought a sharp reminder of her now swollen and black-and-blue ankle. She'd had to take off her shoe earlier, and now even her sock felt too tight.

When the door at the bottom of the stairs opened, she pushed herself up onto her elbows, muffling a groan at the pain. No way did she plan on letting Bart catch her unprepared.

Instead of one of Micheline's male henchmen, Leigh came through the door, striding directly to Fiona's cell. She stood a few feet back from the bars, as if she thought Fiona might reach through and grab her.

Fiona spoke first. "Please tell me you're here to get me medical help."

Instead of answering, Leigh just stared, frowning.

The look of distaste on her perfect features made Fiona's skin crawl.

Not knowing how to react, Fiona settled for refusing to break eye contact. Simply staring back, she wondered how long this would go on.

Finally, Leigh shook her head. "I have just one question," Leigh said, her cold tone dripping disdain. "Why? Why would you do this to us? After all we did to help you? We took you in, set you on the path to becoming a better you, and you betray our trust? *Why?*" Her voice rose with the final sentence.

So much drama. With a Herculean effort, Fiona managed not to let her face reveal any expression. "Leigh, are you aware you're part of a cult?"

Leigh's face contorted. "AAG is *not* a cult. I wish everyone would stop saying that. We do so much good, helping people—"

"Find their best selves," Fiona finished for her. "I know, believe me. Cut the nonsense, Leigh. You need to strip the blinders off your eyes and sit down and take a long, hard look at what you're a part of. If Micheline goes through with this little born-again gathering she's planning, you'll be an accessory to multiple murders. Do you honestly think she's going to stick around to see the results of the horror she's unleashed? Do you?"

Something—Fiona wasn't sure what—flitted across Leigh's expression. Realization, maybe? Fiona could only hope.

But immediately, the stubborn, intractable look came back. "Everything Micheline does is for the good of the AAG."

This time, Fiona refused to let a comment like that slide past. "Is it now? Do you truly believe asking your followers to commit a mass suicide is a good thing? Bilking confused and lonely college kids out of their money with a bunch of false promises, is that a good thing? Tell me, Leigh. Honestly. Tell me some real and true good things the AAG has done."

Leigh opened her mouth to speak. And closed it. When she finally did offer up her thoughts, her tone carried way less confidence. "What about our seminars? We help people feel good about themselves. We give hope, often to those for whom there is no hope left."

"Reciting from the leaflet?" Fiona asked dryly, moving just enough to set off more throbbing in her ankle. She sucked in a breath, trying like hell to ignore the pain, but perspiration broke out on her forehead just the same.

"What do you want, Fiona?" Leigh dropped all pretense of her gung-ho attitude. "What's your angle in all of this?"

"I want it to stop, that's all. The taking advantage of innocent people, the bogus seminars, the baby switching and now extorting for money. Most of all, I don't want a bunch of misguided people to keep being bilked out of their life savings with some vague promises of a better version of themselves."

Leigh recoiled. "Is that really what you think of us?"

"I'm locked up in a basement cell with a broken ankle," Fiona replied. "From what I saw, Jake was beaten to within an inch of his life. Even though he's back in the cell next to me, I still don't know if he's received any kind of medical care. How about you let a doctor take a look at my ankle, maybe put a brace or a boot or a cast on it? Then maybe I'll be a tiny bit more inclined to think better of you."

But Leigh had already started backing away, eyeing Fiona as if she was something she'd found living under a rock.

Once Leigh had gone, Underhill chuckled, a dry, rasping sound. "She's never going to believe the truth," he said. "None of them do. That's why Micheline picks them. She knows how to zero in on the neediest ones."

"What about you?" she asked, genuinely curious. "Why work here?"

"I needed a job," he said. "They hired me for security. It was a decent gig, until I got greedy. When I realized what kind of moneymaking scheme Micheline had going here, I decided to try and get some of that cash for myself. I'd been pretty successful at it for a while, shaking down the newbies."

"Until I caught you."

"Yeah." He went quiet for a moment, and then started coughing. "She didn't like me beating up that kid. I was just shaking him down for cash. You turning me in was a death sentence, you know."

"Why?" she asked. "You don't think she'll let you go?"

He laughed, or tried to. It turned into a bout of coughing. "Nobody gets to leave here. This is Micheline's death row. Anybody she throws in one of these cells knows too much to ever see the light of day."

A chill skittered down Fiona's spine.

"Most die of something else. Like you, with your broken bone. Maybe infection will set in. Me, I got some kind of cold that moved to my chest. Bronchitis now, maybe. Eventually pneumonia. They don't treat you for anything. Hell, they barely even feed you, and some of the slop they bring isn't even edible."

"Except Jake," she pointed out. "They took him for medical help."

"Yes, they did. Which means Micheline has some use for him. Otherwise, she'd have left him there to rot in his own blood." His next fit of coughing left him gasping for air.

The bleakness in Underhill's voice gave Fiona pause. The FBI would be looking for her, she knew. However, they wouldn't be aware anything had gone wrong until it was too late. She had to figure out a way to get out of here on her own. She had to stop Micheline's rebirth gathering before it was too late for all the poor souls she'd managed to dupe.

Chapter Thirteen

When Jake next stirred, he swore he heard Fiona's sweet voice, calling his name over and over. Dream? Or reality? Opening his eyes, he tried to sit up and the entire room spun. What the…? Then, everything that had happened came rushing back. Whatever had been in that shot that woman had given him had done a number on his equilibrium. Among other things.

Where was he? Squinting, he tried to make out his surroundings. Sore and nauseated, he realized they'd taken him back to his small cell down in the basement.

"Jake, are you okay?" Fiona's voice, sounding as if it was coming from the cell next to him, which most likely meant he was hallucinating, too.

"Jake?" Her voice broke as she tried again. "Please, answer me."

He frowned, not sure if what he heard was genuine or a product of his drug-addled imagination. "Fiona? Is that really you? What are you doing down here?"

"It's me," she replied. "And they locked me up right after they beat the crap out of you. I've been trying forever to wake you up."

It took him a moment to process her words. Locked up. Fiona had been put into a cell, too. His gut clenched.

"I was so afraid they'd killed you," she continued. "Especially when you wouldn't respond no matter how many times I called your name."

"They drugged me. Not sure with what. How long was I out?" He glanced around, taking in the off-color artificial lighting. "I imagine it's hard to tell time down here."

"It is. The lack of natural lighting makes it impossible to even guess if it's day or night." She sighed. "Still, I'd have to say you were unconscious for several hours. What did the nurse say? How do you feel?"

He told her everything that had occurred while he was up in the sick bay, or whatever they called it here.

"Micheline came to see me," she said. "She's decided not to go with the fake-baby plan after all. She says she has someone inside Colton Oil who is going to tell them that I've convinced you to join in on the mass suicide. She'll offer to stop the scheme if they wire ten million dollars to an offshore account."

"Ten million?" He winced. "That's a lot of money. And why is she making you out to be the bad guy in all of this?"

"My cover is blown. She wants to make damn sure the Coltons won't want to rescue me. She even said something about making me be the first one to die."

Heart racing, he cursed. "We've got to get you out of here."

"My ankle is broken," she said, her voice steady, which made him love her even more. "They won't let me have any medical attention, so even if I could unlock this cell door and crawl my way up the stairs, I'd be moving so slow even a grandmother with a walker could catch me. I'm pretty sure escaping is out of the question."

"Then what?" he asked. "What's the plan?"

"I don't have one," she finally admitted. "Of course, I'd love it if the FBI magically realized I was in trouble, but honestly, by the time that happens, it will be too late. The Gathering for Rebirth is Friday."

"How many days?" he asked.

"Two."

"Two days?" Horrified, he tried to push past the mind fog from whatever drug they'd given him.

"Yes. And they've got something like seventy-five people signed up. My only hope is Leigh. She came down here to question me after Micheline. Leigh's gullible and a bit naive. I pushed her to really think about what she was doing. Though she still denies that she's involved in a cult, I'm hoping she'll take a long look at what's going on and figure it out."

In another cell, someone started to laugh, a raspy, wheezing sound that quickly turned into a breath-choking cough.

"That's Underhill," Fiona explained. "The guy who was beating up the college student. Apparently, Micheline locked him up here and he got sick."

"Really sick," Underhill clarified, in between bouts of gasping for air. "I think I have pneumonia. In fact, I'll probably be dead before she even gets a chance to force me to drink her poison."

"I believe him," Fiona said quietly. "He sounds pretty ill. And that poor woman in the back cell. I wouldn't be surprised if she isn't already gone."

Jake felt in his pants pockets. No phone. Of course they'd taken it.

"There's no cell service down here anyway," Fiona said when he told her. "Believe me, I tried. If I could have called out, the FBI would already be storming the place."

Still trying to clear the last of the cobwebs from his brain, he thought for a moment. "There's got to be a way out of here," he finally said, wondering why he seemed to be slurring his words. "We've simply got to come up with a plan."

Fiona didn't respond. He could guess what she must be thinking. They were both injured, and even if they could figure out a way to unlock their cells, they wouldn't get very far.

While he knew Fiona well enough to know she'd put up a hell of a fight when they came for her, that broken ankle would hinder her abilities.

A wave of dizziness hit him, so strong he had to close his eyes and lower his head in case he passed out.

He must have briefly lost consciousness, because the next thing he heard was Fiona's voice, once again calling his name. He tried opening his mouth to answer, but he couldn't get his vocal cords to respond. Instead he found himself sliding back to the dark oblivion. He wanted to fight but didn't seem to be able to summon up enough strength.

DESPITE JAKE'S WORRYING lack of response to her requests for him to answer her, Fiona refused to give up hope. Most likely, whatever drugs they'd injected into Jake were causing his lapses from consciousness. She refused to consider the very real possibility that the severity of his head injury might be the cause. She knew head wounds were prone to bleeding a lot, so Jake's definitely could have looked worse than it actually was.

They were in dire straits, but she had to believe

they'd make it out. She wasn't about to die, not now, especially not at the hand of a narcissistic psychopath like Micheline. Holden would try to reach her and when he couldn't, realize something was wrong.

Time locked up in her cell passed slowly, but her best guesstimate would be that at least one day had passed since they'd brought back an unconscious Jake. He seemed lucid now, though he still slept a lot, which worried her. From what she'd been able to see, he'd received some sort of head injury, and with a lack of any real competent medical attention, that could go south fast.

At least her ankle had stopped swelling, though the pain remained at an eight out of ten. She could only hope moving around on the broken bone didn't make it worse, but since she had little choice, she kept it off the floor as much as she could.

At least Micheline had put little toilets and sinks in the corner of each cell. Trying not to think of what might be on the floor, Fiona crawled back there only when strictly necessary. Mostly, she lay with her back to the wall, facing the front of her cell, so she could at least be ready whenever they came for her.

As if she'd summoned someone, the door finally opened. Luckily, it was Randall rather than Bart. As usual, he seemed awkward and uncomfortable, barely able to make even the smallest bit of eye contact.

"T-minus twenty-seven," he announced to no one in particular.

Twenty-seven what? Hours?

"Are you talking about the mass suicide?" Fiona asked, deciding to be direct rather than talking in euphemisms.

Randall flinched. "Wow. I'm not sure I'd call it

that, but yeah. The Gathering for Rebirth is in twenty-seven hours."

"Are you going to take part in it, too, Randall?" Fiona asked, holding on to the bars as she struggled to stand. She finally managed to get up, using only her uninjured leg, keeping the broken ankle up off the floor.

He didn't answer. Still avoiding eye contact, he busied himself with checking some storage bins on a long, metal table.

"You don't seem to be the gullible type," Fiona pressed. "More of a thinking man, at least that's how I see you. Why would you want to ingest poison, just because some egotistical blowhard of a woman told you to?"

Randall snapped his head up at that. "Don't talk about Micheline like that," he ordered. "She's a good person."

"Is she? Are you aware that she doesn't even intend to be anywhere near here when all her poor followers die? She'll be hoofing it to the Caribbean, along with the ten million dollars she asked the Coltons to wire her."

"What?" Randall blinked. "No, you're wrong. She's going to pass out the elixir herself. She told me so."

"Really? Because when she visited me, she made it clear that she planned on bugging out of here long before the big gathering went down. She'll leave the rest of you holding the bag, Randall. If you live, you and Bart and Leigh will be accessories to murder. You'll spend the rest of your lives in prison."

Slowly, he shook his head. "Micheline wouldn't let that happen. She promised to always take care of us."

Before Fiona could respond, Randall's walkie-talkie squawked. At the familiar sound, Fiona instinctively looked for hers, but it had apparently been taken when they'd grabbed her cell phone.

Randall pressed the button and answered. "Code red, code red," Bart screamed. "Get up here now!"

"What the…?" Randall paled. He glanced at Fiona, then took off running for the stairs. Judging by the way he slammed the door, he'd left it unlocked.

"Too bad we can't get out of our cells," Jake said. "I'd love to see whatever is going on up there."

"I can only hope it's law enforcement," she muttered. "Who else could cause Bart to react like that?"

Due to the double set of steel doors, no noise from the house above reached them.

"I hate not knowing what's going on," Jake finally said.

"Me, too," she admitted.

She'd barely gotten the words out of her mouth when the door smashed open, so hard it slammed into the wall.

"FBI," a voice hollered. Holden St. Clair.

While she had no idea how they'd known to come here, the relief made her legs go weak. "Down here," she yelled. "They have me and three others locked up in individual cells."

The sound of more feet clattering down the stairs. Three more FBI agents, two men and a woman, came in, walking Randall and Bart, both in handcuffs, in front of them.

"We're going to need medical assistance," she told Holden once he'd retrieved the keys from Randall and unlocked her cell.

"How badly are you hurt?" Holden asked, pulling her to her feet and letting her lean on him.

"Broken ankle," she said. "But Jake has a head injury and probably broken ribs. There are two others in cells that way." She pointed. "The man most likely has pneumonia, but it's the woman I'm really worried about."

Holden nodded, signaling one of the other agents, who went back upstairs so he could call for help. Assisting Fiona so she could walk, they went to Jake's cell and unlocked it. Immediately, Fiona went to him.

"Are you okay?" she asked, falling to her knees next to him.

Attempting to smile at her, he nodded. "A bit woozy. Slipping in and out of consciousness. But I'll survive."

"Wait here," Holden ordered. "I'm going to check on the other two."

A moment later, he returned. "The man with the pneumonia is very ill. I'll have the paramedics take him out first."

"What about the woman in the last cell?" Fiona asked.

Slowly, Holden shook his head. "She didn't make it. No idea how long ago she died, but she's gone. I double-checked to make sure. She has no pulse."

Fiona didn't bother to hide her fury. "Micheline did this. When she's charged, you need to add this woman's death to the list."

"Oh, we will." Grim faced, Holden glanced from her to Jake, who remained woozy. "Luckily, we caught Micheline just as she was about to leave. She seemed stunned that we actually had a search warrant. And we've rounded up her closest followers, including Miss Mustang Valley."

"Leigh." Fiona nodded. "I warned her. I refuse to feel sorry for her now."

"We've got a full search going on of this entire building. We got a tip that all the poison Micheline intended to feed her followers had been delivered."

"A tip?" Fiona eyed him. "Is that how you found us?"

"As a matter of fact, yes. Dee Walton, Payne Colton's administrative assistant, called us. Apparently, Micheline asked her to not only extort her boss but to join in the mass suicide." He shrugged. "Pretty hard to believe, but she claimed she'd never realized she was part of a cult until then."

"I get it," Fiona said. "I tried to talk to Leigh about that, and she refused to believe the AAG is a cult. I'm not entirely sure why."

"Micheline had honed the fine art of brainwashing," Jake said. "She's always been good at convincing others to do what she wanted."

"The paramedics are here," one of the other FBI agents announced. "We've got enough ambulances to transport all four of the injured."

"One is already deceased," Holden informed him.

The agent winced. "Also, we need someone to make a statement to the other AAG members. They're demanding to know what's going on."

"I can do that," Fiona said. "Most of them know me anyway." She looked from Holden to the other agents. "I'll just need a lot of help getting up the stairs."

With one agent on each side, leaning on them heavily and hopping on one foot, she made it out. Someone located a wheelchair and brought it to her.

"We've asked them to gather in that amphitheater in the back," the female agent said. "My name is Bonnie. If you'd like, I can push you there."

Grateful, Fiona accepted her help.

When she was wheeled into the large arena where Micheline had held her most intense seminars, the noisy room gradually fell quiet as people realized she was there.

She wouldn't have thought addressing these people, with whom she'd interacted on a daily basis, would be so difficult. Heart in her throat, she looked around, seeing their open, trusting faces, bracing herself for the disbelief and disappointment that was sure to follow.

Since she couldn't stand to reach the microphone on the podium, Bonnie unhooked it from the stand and brought it down to her.

Fiona swallowed, looking out at the group assembled, making eye contact with as many people as she could. "Good afternoon, everyone," she said. "Many of you know me as one of the AAG's newest recruits. In reality, I'm an FBI agent who has been working here undercover." And then she told them why. All of it, leaving out nothing.

As she spoke, she saw the ripple of shock and disbelief spread through the crowd. Many expressions turned mutinous, as if the instant she stopped speaking, they meant to stand up and accuse her of spreading falsehoods about their beloved Micheline.

She wrapped things up with the worst transgression of all—the born-again gathering, a blithe name for a horrible mass suicide. "We believe Micheline had a secret, offshore bank account, blackmailed the Coltons for ten million and had ordered a private plane to take her somewhere, likely in the Caribbean, like Grand Cayman. At this point, we can only speculate as to her reasons for doing such a thing. She is currently in FBI custody and facing numerous criminal charges."

At this last sentence, the room erupted in sound. Shouts of denial, some cursing her, calling her names. Some people cried, wailing loudly as if grief stricken, now that the woman they'd revered as a prophet had been proven false. There would be some, Fiona knew, who'd discount what she'd told them, who'd refuse to believe even the slightest stain on Micheline's character.

There wasn't anything she could do about that. All she could hope for was in the coming days, as the story played out on both the local and national media, the doubters would come to a gradual realization that maybe everything wasn't exactly as it had seemed in the AAG. She wondered if they'd ever truly understand how close they'd come to losing their lives. Would they someday look back on all this and wonder how they could have been so foolish?

Since the entire AAG center was now considered a crime scene, she'd pleaded her case and would be allowed to stay and work out of the room she'd been occupying while working undercover. Which was good, since the alternative would have meant going back to the field office and trying to work remotely.

She'd done well. Micheline had been stopped, pure evil taken down. Her supervisor had commended her and this would look good in her file.

As always when a case concluded, there were statements to make and reports to fill out. But first, she had to get her ankle looked at. Holden drove her to the same ER where Jake had been taken.

Jake. Just thinking about him had her stomach doing somersaults. More than anything, she wanted to explore a relationship with him, to see if the hot intensity of these feelings might do well as a slow simmer. She hoped he felt the same way.

X-rays proved conclusively that her ankle had been fractured. They gave her a pill for the pain, along with instructions not to drive for twenty-four hours. Then the doctor put a boot on her foot and handed her crutches, urging her to see an orthopedic surgeon as soon as possible.

"I want to go check on Jake," she told Holden, who only rolled his eyes, though he agreed to accompany her.

Jake had been admitted, she learned. Though they cited HIPAA laws and refused to release any information about his condition, she got his room number.

Moving awkwardly on the crutches, she and Holden rode the elevator to the third floor. She hobbled slowly down the seemingly endless hall, brushing off Holden's repeated attempts to help. "There," she said, relieved when she finally saw his room number.

Moving as quietly as crutches would allow, she went inside. Jake lay unconscious in the hospital bed, hooked up to an IV and various machines. He seemed pale, she thought, hobbling over to stand at the edge of his bed. His head hadn't been bandaged, so she took that as a good sign.

"You really care about this guy, don't you?" Holden asked quietly.

She nodded. "It caught me by surprise, but yes. I do."

"Does he feel the same way?"

"I think so." She gave Holden a tiny smile. "I'm hoping to get a chance to find out."

"Let's get you back to the AAG center," Holden said.

"You need to rest, and I've got to get back to work. There's a lot of evidence to process."

With one last lingering look at Jake, Fiona turned to go.

THE EFFICIENCY AND competence with which the medical personnel checked him out made Jake's head ache even more. While he drifted in and out, they took X-rays and blood, examined and cleaned his various wounds and abrasions, and hooked him up to an IV drip to provide him with fluids and who knew what else.

He couldn't tell how much time had passed—it could have been minutes or hours or days. Though no one had any idea what kind of drug he might have been given, they told him they were monitoring him to make sure he would be all right until it left his system.

Comforting, those assurances. Now all he wanted was Fiona. He was dimly aware of hearing that various Colton family members had stopped by to check on him, and he remembered seeing Fiona's face once or twice.

During one of his more lucid moments, he tried to locate his cell phone, intending to call her. But after a frantic search in his bed linens, he remembered the phone had been taken from him.

Surely, she'd come to see him as soon as she was able. Clinging to this certainty, he allowed himself to slide back into the darkness, even though he didn't want to miss seeing her.

When he next opened his eyes, he felt more like himself. Surrounded by the steady beeping of medical machines, he sat up slowly, bracing himself for pain. Instead, he felt only a dull ache.

And the fog had left his brain, which meant the drugs had finally been flushed from his system. He stretched, tentative with his movement at first, then gradually allowing himself more confidence.

A doctor finally stopped by, letting Jake know he was actually in pretty good shape, all things considered. Aside from several messed-up ribs—bruised, not broken—he had a concussion and some nasty cuts and bruises. They'd been more concerned about the drug they'd injected into his bloodstream. Though the FBI had seized control of the entire AAG center, including the medical facility area, analyzing everything they'd found was going to take time. And since he clearly appeared to be recovering, that had removed any level of urgency in them getting rush results.

Once the doctor left, Jake sat back in bed, relieved. Now that all of this was finally over—Micheline had been arrested, the empire she'd built on lies and scams in the process of being dismantled—Jake had thought he'd feel more…satisfaction? Relief?

Instead, he couldn't help but feel sorry for all the innocent lives Micheline had ruined, including his own. He'd bet a lot of her followers still refused to believe that they'd been duped. He'd seen it over and over growing up. Somehow, Micheline managed to make people believe in her.

Not anymore. Though he wouldn't put it past her to try and start up some kind of cult following in prison once she got there.

Hell of a situation. And to think he almost hadn't come back. Just that tiny, remote possibility that Micheline might have really been dying of cancer had been enough to lure him in. And as usual, everything she'd done had been calculated as to how it could benefit her.

Now, Micheline's reign would finally be over. And a lot of the people whose lives she touched would never be the same.

For him, a few good things had come of it all. He'd not only learned his true identity, but he'd met Fiona, the woman he suspected he could love. And he'd finally gotten started getting to know the family he should have grown up with.

"Hey, there." Ace Colton strolled into the hospital room, almost as if Jake's thoughts had summoned him. "Glad to hear you're going to live," he said, smiling.

Jake found himself grinning back at the other man. "Me, too," he said. "For a while there, I wondered."

Ace pulled a chair up next to the hospital bed and took a seat. "At least it's just a concussion, not a skull fracture. Fiona was really worried, you know."

Simply hearing her name brought warmth to Jake's heart. "How is she?" he asked.

"I was worried about her, too." Ace smiled. "Luckily, she won't have to have surgery on that ankle. They put her in a soft cast inside a boot. She's been up here twice."

Jake groaned. "She has? I wish someone would have woken me so I could have talked to her. How much time has passed?"

"Two days," Ace informed him. "Sorry, man."

"Do you have any idea when Fiona is coming back?"

"Oh, she's here now. I drove her. You should see her getting around on that knee scooter." Ace smiled. "She hates it."

"You would, too," Fiona said, wheeling herself into

the room. "Good news, Jake. You're being released to go home today."

Home. For him, that would be his ranch, 120 miles to the north. Way too far away from Fiona.

Something of his mixed emotions must have shown on his face.

"You can stay with us," Ace invited. "One of our guest bedrooms is yours for as long as you need."

Relieved, he thanked the other man, then eyed Fiona. "What about you? Where are you going?"

"I'll be hanging out at the AAG center for a few more days, gathering evidence," she said, smiling. "I'd love to see you when I'm not working, if you'd like."

Ace laughed, startling them both. Jake realized he'd managed to briefly forget the other man was there.

"I have an idea," Ace said. "How about we have you over for dinner again, Fiona? Everyone enjoyed meeting you last time."

"Sounds great." She rolled over to Jake's other side and leaned in to kiss his cheek. If Ace hadn't been there, Jake would have turned his face toward her for a real kiss instead.

He could have sworn disappointment flashed across her expressive face.

"I'd better get back to it. I've got work to do," Fiona told them. "I wrote my number on a slip of paper, Jake. Use the room phone and give me a call once they have you sign discharge papers. They said it would be later this afternoon. I'll see who I can finagle a ride with."

"Will do."

"I can give him a ride," Ace volunteered. "Since he'll be coming to the Triple R anyway."

"Perfect." With a jaunty wave, Fiona wheeled herself out of the room.

After she'd left, Ace turned back to Jake. "My dad's assistant is beside herself," he said. "When Dee finally realized the truth about Micheline, she took it hard."

"At least she did the right thing and notified the authorities. Fiona said it was awful when she told the AAG members, too. Apparently, most of them didn't want to learn the woman they'd idolized had feet of clay."

Ace regarded him steadily. "We would have paid the money, you know. If it came down to that."

"What?" Jake stared. "Ten million? That's a lot of cash. Surely, you didn't believe I'd be foolish enough to even consider ingesting poison in some bizarre attempt to die and be reborn."

"Of course not. Dee let us all in on Micheline's scheme. Did you know when they caught her, she had a one-way ticket to Grand Cayman? That must have been where she set up her untraceable bank account. She would have disappeared by the time her followers started to die."

Shaking his head, Jake winced as a quick flash of pain hit him. "I don't know what's worse. The fact that she'd actually talked a bunch of gullible people into dying for false hopes and promises, or that she intended to leave them alone while they did it."

Ace grimaced. "I can't believe I'm actually related to her."

"My condolences," Jake replied. "Believe me when I say I know how it feels. At least neither of us will have to deal with her again. She'll be locked up for the rest of her life, most likely."

"I think so," Ace agreed. "I hear there are so many charges."

They talked about a few other things, including Ace's desire to show him around Colton Oil. "I used to be CEO there," Ace said, his tone rueful.

"This all has been a lot to deal with."

"True. But one good thing came of it. I met the woman I'm going to marry. You met her. Sierra. She was a bounty hunter looking for me."

"Wow." Jake tried to wrap his mind around that. "She doesn't look the slightest bit dangerous."

For whatever reason, this caused Ace to laugh. "Oh, she is, believe me," he said. "She's the best thing that ever happened to me."

Jake nodded. He could definitely understand that. Because Fiona was exactly the same to him. Glancing over at Ace, he realized meeting his new family and getting to know this man, in particular, ranked right up there too.

Chapter Fourteen

Getting around on the knee scooter was a royal pain. Though she had to struggle not to show her frustration, Fiona found the entire process way too cumbersome and slow. Patience had never been one of Fiona's virtues, and though it was something she constantly tried to work on, she realized twenty minutes into trying to navigate through life on one knee that she still had a long way to go. It didn't help that this broken ankle had happened at the worst possible time—the biggest bust of her career.

Micheline Anderson was going down. Though the FBI already had enough to charge her with to put her away for years, especially with Ainsley having direct experience of Micheline's Marriage Institute, Holden working with Spencer, and Spencer already investigating the AAG with Katrina, they wanted more. Fiona did, too, with a furious sort of passion that consumed nearly every waking moment. Because she wanted justice. Retribution for what Micheline had done to Jake Anderson, one of the finest men Fiona had ever known. And for all the poor, gullible or desperate souls she'd taken in with her quasi-affirmation hocus-pocus. The college students she'd swindled, the elderly people who'd gladly handed over their life savings and everyone in between. Including the Colton family, who'd suffered their share of bizarre events already. Learning their eldest son and heir wasn't actually related by blood had to rank up there as one of the worst. Having Micheline try to extort them for ten million dollars must have been the final straw.

Righting injustice had been one of the main reasons she'd chosen a career in law enforcement. The training she'd received at Quantico had underscored her certainty that she'd been born for this kind of work. Taking this undercover assignment had been more difficult than she'd expected, especially since so many of the things she'd been expected to do went deeply against her beliefs. She was glad it was over, happy that they'd been able to end it with an arrest and numerous, serious charges.

And because of it, she'd met Jake. While they hadn't known each other very long at all, the connection they'd made hinted at the possibility of a long and happy future as a couple. If she allowed herself to be optimistic—something she rarely did, since she considered herself a realist—she'd come to believe he might just be the one. Once this case was closed, she planned to take some time off and find out.

Meanwhile, the formidable fact-finding machine that was the FBI had gotten hard at work obtaining information. The AAG center swarmed with agents. Since they'd obtained a far more detailed search warrant, the Bureau had brought in teams, who all conducted an intensive search. This went on from sunup to sundown. As soon as one team left to get some rest, another showed up to take their place.

For her part, Fiona tried to stay out of their way. Though she hadn't been removed from the case, she hadn't been assigned to a particular team, either. The special agent in charge allowed Fiona and Holden to stay and do as they pleased, as long as they didn't interfere with anyone else. Fiona had claimed Leigh's suite as her own search area and took a certain satisfaction in taking apart the room piece by piece.

Thus far she'd found nothing substantial. But then, Leigh clearly had been coached not to leave any kind of paper trail. She'd kept only a few paper files—one with handouts touting the miracle seminars that AAG offered, and another with printouts and newspaper clippings regarding her Miss Mustang Valley win. The rest had to be stored on a computer or in the cloud.

Fiona itched to get a look at her laptop. But of course, she'd had to turn the computer over to the FBI's IT department, who would thoroughly examine its contents. Right now, she was kneeling on the floor going through the bottom drawer of a mostly empty filing cabinet, just hoping Leigh had been careless one time.

A quiet tap on the door made her look up. Holden St. Clair stood in the doorway, eyeing her. "Did you find anything?" he asked.

"Not really." Struggling to pull herself up without putting weight on her ankle, she gratefully accepted Holden's help getting on her knee scooter. "I have to say, I'm really disappointed. I honestly believed Leigh knew a lot more secrets than she let on. Now I'm wondering if Micheline kept her mostly in the dark and told her only what she wanted her to hear."

"I wouldn't put it past her," Holden replied. "Micheline was a master at manipulating people. And Leigh

Dennings seemed a naive and trusting sort. By the way, speaking of her… Leigh has been asking for you. She keeps saying she doesn't belong in jail. She's been telling everyone who will listen that you will vouch for her character."

Momentarily taken aback, Fiona shook her head. "She's wrong. I gave her the opportunity to get out before it all hit the fan. I asked her to do the right thing. She refused. She left me lying in the tiny basement cell, injured, determined not to hear anything bad about Micheline or the AAG. She made her choice. Now she's going to have to live with it."

"I agree." Holden walked around the room, one brow raised. "She decorated this place like a Pottery Barn store," he said.

His comment made Fiona laugh. "Good analysis. Stylish, cozy and expensive." She eyed the other agent. "What about you? Is there something you're not telling me?"

"That's why I'm here now." Holden flashed a quick smile. "We've got some new information," he said. "A while back, we rounded up a guy named Harley Watts. He did all of Micheline's dark web work and took care of helping her set up a new identity for when she took off. Once he'd had a little taste of jail, he said he was willing to talk if the prosecutor would hammer out a plea deal."

Fiona perked up. "Did you get that worked out?"

"We did. And let me tell you, it was worth it. This Watts guy bugged Micheline's office. He recorded everything and hung on to it all. Once he told us where to find it, we sent a couple of agents over to get it. We've got people listening to it all now. My hunch says we'll have a ton of evidence of even more crimes. Enough to put Micheline away for a long, long time."

"I'd like to see the transcript when it's finished," Fiona said. "I want to throw the book at that woman."

"I agree. Anyone awful enough to plan for all her followers to commit suicide needs to go away for a long, long time." Holden shook his head. "It never ceases to amaze me how people can be so evil and yet manage to convince so many others to believe in them."

"At least we got her." Her knee had started aching, as it usually did when she spent too much time on the scooter. "I'd better get back to it."

"Let me know if you need any help," Holden replied, turning to go. "And please, give me a holler if you find anything good."

Even though she privately didn't think she would at this point, Fiona agreed. Back to work, she told herself, but she remained on her knee scooter rather than lowering herself to the floor. What she really wanted, she realized with some disbelief, was to be with Jake. This seemed so out of character for a woman whose work always, always came first, she had to sit still and consider.

She really had it bad for him. Jake was never far from her thoughts. She found herself wondering at odd moments during the day what he might be doing right then, if he felt okay, how his new Colton family was treating him.

Pushing thoughts of him away, she returned her focus to where it belonged right now—her search. She'd give Jake a call later, once she was off duty.

THOUGH JAKE HAD wondered if he'd feel awkward, walking into the huge house at the Triple R felt almost like coming home. Part of that feeling might have been the warm welcome everyone gave him, from Payne and his wife, Genevieve, who actually hugged him this time, to Ainsley, Grayson, the twins Marlowe and Callum, as well as Asher, and a host of other family members. Jake did wonder how Ace had managed to coordinate everything, but he definitely appreciated their kindness.

"I feel like one of the family," Jake mused to Ace after Ace had shown him his room.

Ace laughed. "You *are* one of the family," he said. "Actually more than I am."

Studying the other man, who appeared both confident and relaxed, Jake decided he might as well ask, especially since they were all going to be in such close quarters. "How are you feeling about all this, Ace? I definitely don't want to be encroaching on your..."

"Territory?" Ace grinned even wider. "You couldn't. They love me like a son. Hell, I *was* their son for forty years. I still am. As are you, now. Believe me, the Colton family has enough room in their hearts for one more." His smile faded. Stepping forward, he clasped Jake's shoulder. "I never, ever want you to feel uncomfortable or awkward around any of us, understand? None of what happened was your fault."

Slightly embarrassed, Jake nodded. "I know. I just wondered if it felt weird."

"Yes, of course it does." Ace released him, going to the window and pulling aside the drapes so he could see out. "At first, I questioned my own identity. I mean, Micheline is a pretty awful woman. Anyone would have issues learning they were actually related to her."

Now Jake had to laugh. "I know, believe me. I lived with that for forty years. It was hell."

Ace's cell phone rang. Glancing at the screen, he glanced at Jake. "Sorry, I need to take this." Answering, he walked out into the hallway to listen.

Jake placed his suitcase on the bed, debating unpacking. He decided he might as well. He hadn't brought a lot of clothes since originally he hadn't planned on staying long. Since then, he'd bought a few things, but he really needed to go shopping again. Maybe he and Fiona could make plans to do that when she was off work.

"Wow." Returning, Ace grinned at Jake, his expression both bemused and excited. "I'm officially a grandfather."

"What?" Stunned, Jake eyed the other man. Since they were the exact same age, he could hardly imagine. "I didn't even know you had kids."

"One—I just found out, to be honest. Her name is Nova. She just gave birth to her daughter, Clara, with her boyfriend, Nikolas, by her side." Ace shook his head. "He's a great guy. The baby isn't even biologically his, but he loves Clara so much, he's planning to raise her as his own daughter." A single tear leaked from one eye. Ace wiped it away with one finger. "I knew her due date was coming up, but I wish someone had called me when Nova went into labor."

"Congratulations." Jake held out his hand.

Ace gripped it, still grinning. "I've got to head up to the hospital. I want to see my granddaughter. And make sure Nova is doing okay."

"How about I take you?" Jake offered. "You seem a bit too shook up to drive."

Expression still a potent mixture of joy and bewilderment, Ace shook his head. "Thanks for the offer, but I'm fine. Just a bit…overcome, I guess." He snapped his fingers. "I need to stop and get some flowers or something. A teddy bear for the baby. I'll see you later back here."

He started to walk off, but then turned. "Oh, before I forget, Ainsley is planning a get-together so the entire family—cousins and all—can meet you. Bring Fiona, too, of course. I'm sure Ainsley will get you details as soon as she finalizes everything."

Ace rushed off, still muttering to himself under his breath.

After unpacking, Jake debated going into town alone and doing some shopping. But since buying clothes was a task he despised, he decided to wait and see if Fiona wouldn't mind joining him.

He wandered downstairs, still feeling pretty self-conscious, thinking he might go out to the barn and check out the horses. With Ace gone and the rest of the Colton family busy with their jobs or their daily routines, the massive house seemed empty.

As he headed into the kitchen to see if he could rustle up another cup of coffee, he found Payne sitting alone at the kitchen table. The older man still appeared weak, though he seemed to be gradually recovering.

"Pull up a chair," Payne invited, his fingers wrapped around a steaming mug of his own coffee. "Grab a cup. I just made a fresh pot."

Jake did. The coffee tasted strong, just the way he liked it.

Payne talked mostly about generalities, the ranch, his livestock and how much he loved Mustang Valley. Genevieve drifted in, wearing yoga clothes, smiled at Jake and kissed Payne's cheek before drifting back out. "I'll be home in an hour or so," she said, and left.

She'd barely left for her yoga class when Payne

leaned forward, his intense gaze fixed on Jake. "I'm going to have to ask you to take a DNA test you know."

Jake nodded. "I've expected that. And I've already done one and sent it in. I'm just waiting on the results. Honestly, I don't blame you. That's the only way to make sure."

"Good, good." Payne exhaled, clearly relieved. "We'll get that done as soon as possible. That way there's no room for doubt."

"I agree." Jake smiled at the older man.

"So many years wasted. All because of that awful woman."

Fighting the urge to apologize, Jake nodded instead. "I really appreciate how welcoming everyone here has been."

"Welcoming?" Payne's brows rose. "Son, even though we don't have the DNA results, I can tell you're one of us. It might have taken you forty years to find your way back, but you're a Colton. Don't you ever forget that."

"I won't." Feeling absurdly relieved, Jake took another drink of his coffee. "I just wish I could have met my mother."

"Me, too. I loved your mother," Payne said. "I've been married three times. Tessa's been gone just a little over thirty-five years, but I've never stopped missing her."

Jake nodded. "You seem happy now, though. Genevieve seems nice."

"Oh, she is. And I am happy," Payne declared. "The only relationship mistake I ever made was marrying Selina. And now I can't get away from her. Damn woman is even on the board at Colton Oil."

Jake wasn't sure how to respond to that, so he simply sipped his coffee and said nothing.

"Wait here." Getting up slowly, Payne disappeared for a moment. When he returned, he carried a large, faded photo album. "Come into the living room," he said, leaving his cup on the table.

Jake did the same. Payne grunted, lowering himself onto the couch. "Sit beside me. This is a photo album, one of many. Though Tessa was the photographer in most of the others, all the pictures in this one were taken by other people, so she's in them. Let's take a little walk down memory lane."

Once Jake had taken a seat, Payne opened the album. There, in the first photograph, a beautiful woman smiled at the camera, her face alight with love. She held a baby in her arms, whom Jake guessed must have been Ace. He felt a pang, well aware that this might have been him. Though he'd never wish to take that experience away from Ace, he couldn't help but feel envious. Not once in his forty years had he known a mother's unconditional love.

Payne turned the pages slowly, giving Jake time to study each picture. In all of them, Tessa's love of her family shone through. She positively glowed with it.

And there, on the last page, Tessa and Payne. Gazing into each other's eyes.

Swallowing hard, Payne closed the book. "Still gets me," he said. "Even after all these years. She was a good woman."

"Thank you for sharing that with me," Jake told him. "I really appreciate it."

"No problem." Payne yawned, covering his mouth with his hand. "Sorry, son," he said. "I need to go lie down. Colton Oil has a board meeting this afternoon, and I need to rest up for that."

The way Payne casually called him *son* made Jake's chest ache. He managed a nod. "A nap sounds like a great idea," he said. "Do you need any help getting to your room?"

"No, thanks." Payne waved him away. "I'm getting stronger bit by bit. The walk will do my legs good."

As Payne pushed to his feet, Jake did, too. "At least let me walk with you. It's always good to have company, just in case."

"Am I that wobbly?" Payne shot him an amused grin. "Don't answer that. You're not much better yourself, you know. Come on then. You can escort me to my room."

Once they'd reached the doorway, Payne turned and put his hand on Jake's shoulder. "I know I can never make up to you all the years we lost. We can only move forward. You understand that, right?"

"I do."

"You're welcome to attend the board meeting this afternoon," Payne said. "As my guest. I think it will do you some good to learn about our company." And he went inside his room, closing the door without waiting for Jake to answer.

Jake took himself outside, slowly walking the grounds around the ranch. The Triple R was well maintained in addition to being beautiful. He admired the livestock, their coats gleaming with health, took in the clean barn, the outdoor ring with its freshly raked surface. Pride of ownership shone here, making him miss his own ranch. Though not nearly as large or prosperous as the Triple R, he'd worked damn hard to get it and keep it running. He'd built it from the ground up, and while the ranch was still a work in progress, it was his.

Turning slowly, he took it all in. The massive house, designed to blend in with the landscape. The barns, the acres of fenced pastures and the mountains in the distance. This place was now part of his life, too. He couldn't imagine simply returning to his ranch and never seeing the Triple R or the Colton family again.

Or Fiona. The thought of going back to his old life—where he'd been a rancher with no real family—made his gut hurt. These people, each and every one of them, were important to him. Especially Fiona. He could see himself spending the rest of his life with her.

He'd simply have to figure out a way to make this work.

Ace arrived back home shortly after lunch. He sent Jake a text asking if he could meet him in the kitchen. Since Jake had been thinking about rustling up something for lunch, he texted back that he was on his way.

When he reached the kitchen, he found Ace munching on a sandwich. "I had the chef make one for you," Ace said, sliding the plate toward him, along with a can of diet cola.

"Thanks." Grateful, Jake pulled up a chair and dug in.

The two men ate in silence. When they'd finished, Jake eyed the man he'd come to think of as his brother. "How was your grandbaby?"

Ace's eyes sparkled. "Beautiful. Smaller than I imagined, but I'm told that's how newborns are."

"I can only imagine," Jake replied. "Want to do something this afternoon?"

"We're having a board meeting today," Ace said,

his tone apologetic. "Since you might someday be part of this company, I thought you might want to sit in."

"Payne invited me earlier, and I've been thinking about it. Won't they mind?" Jake asked. "The rest of the board?"

"Nope. I've already cleared it with them. And since I'm no longer CEO, I'll just be there as an observer anyway."

Jake shrugged. "Sounds good." He shifted his weight from one side to the other, trying to stretch and wincing at the sharp stab of pain. "As long as I can sit down. My ribs are really hurting me."

"There are chairs." Grinning, Ace checked his watch. "You have just under thirty minutes to get cleaned up and ready to go. Did you bring a suit?"

"A suit?" Jake looked at him as if he'd suggested going in costume. "I only own one suit that I wear to funerals or weddings. It's hanging in my closet back home at my ranch."

Ace laughed. "I don't think we're the same size, but I've probably got a pair of slacks and a dress shirt you can borrow. And I'll let you choose the tie."

The slacks were a little loose, but a belt took care of that. The shirt felt a little tight, though it would do. Since Jake and Ace had completely different shoe sizes, Jake had to wear his best set of boots. He chose a dark blue, nondescript tie.

When he made it downstairs, Payne was also waiting, since Ace would be driving him as well. He smiled when he saw Jake. "Glad you decided to come," he said, leaning on an elaborately carved cane. "Ace wanted me to use a wheelchair, but I'm perfectly capable of walking."

"As long as you promise to use that cane," Ace interjected. "The last thing you need right now is a fall."

Payne shook his head, but he didn't argue.

This time, they were taking one of Payne's vehicles, a large, black Mercedes. Ace drove, and Payne took shotgun, leaving Jake to ride in the back. He didn't mind. He was just glad they were letting him participate.

Ace dropped Payne off at the front entrance before parking in a spot marked Reserved for P. Colton. "I used to have my own spot," he commented. "I'm really hoping that the reason Payne asked me to come today is because he's planning to ask the board to give me my job back. Especially since I was cleared of any crime."

Jake had read up on how Ace had been accused of shooting his own father and gone on the run. "Makes sense," he agreed. "That must have been hell."

"It was a nightmare. But the one good thing that came out of it made it all worthwhile. I'd never have met Sierra otherwise."

They walked inside. Ace nodded to the receptionist before striding to the elevator. He punched the up button, and the doors immediately opened.

"Are you nervous?" Ace asked.

"Not really. I thought I might be, but I'm actually looking forward to seeing how these kinds of things work."

"They're never boring, that's for sure." The doors opened and they stepped out. "Come on."

Several people were already seated at a long, highly polished wooden table. Jake recognized Payne and Selina, Ace's ex-stepmother, along with Marlowe, Ainsley, and Rafe. Jake was glad he'd met them.

"Ace," Payne boomed. "I'm glad you're here. And

welcome, Jake. So good to see you." As if he hadn't ridden in with them.

All of the others echoed his welcome. Except Selina, who simply eyed him with one brow raised.

Once Ace and Jake had taken seats in a grouping of chairs away from the table, Payne got down to business.

"I called this meeting the minute my doctor released me to get a little work done," Payne said. "I want Ace reinstated as CEO, if the board will vote to rescind the blood Colton clause. If not, I will dismantle the company."

Several people shifted in their seats, but no one dissented.

"We'll take this to a vote. All those in favor, raise your hands and say aye."

One by one, every single person at that table raised their hands and agreed. Save one. Selina. Mouth tight, eyes flashing, she pushed to her feet.

"Don't you see what he is doing?" she cried. "Each and every one of you? He's going to take away your birthrights and give it to that no-good son of his. Even worse, Ace isn't really even his! He's not a Colton by blood. I see no reason why he should be allowed to have anything at all to do with this company. Stand up for what is right," she entreated. "Because this is absolute nonsense."

No one spoke. In fact, they all sat frozen, appearing uncomfortable, watching Payne for his reaction.

"You're finished, Selina," Payne said. "I'm ousting you. From the board, from the company and our lives. I want you to go to your office, pack your things and get out of my building. I'll have my attorneys draw up papers immediately with your severance package."

Instead of surprise, fury darkened her eyes. "You won't dare, Payne Colton. Because you know damn well I'll reveal your little secret. The one I've kept for way too long. It will destroy you." With a self-confident smirk, she dared him to contradict her.

Payne took a deep breath. Jake saw the barest hint of nerves in the way the old man's fingers trembled. But he lifted his chin and met Selina's gaze. "Go ahead. My family has already been to hell and back, and we're still strong. We've survived everything else, and we'll damn sure survive you and the blackmail you've levied against me for years."

"You'll be sent away to prison for life," she warned. "And you'll never see that precious family of yours. Remember, there's no statute of limitations on murder."

Murder? Jake started. Next to him, he heard Ace suck in his breath.

"It was self-defense," Payne declared, looking around the room. "I swear to you."

Selina snorted. "He told me he shot and killed a man at the mansion during his marriage to Tessa. Turned out the guy was a well-known enemy of his and he was afraid to report it, so he buried the body himself and told no one."

"When was this?" Ace asked.

"Thirty-five years ago," Payne replied. "You first three kids were small. It was right before Tessa got sick and died."

A long time to carry such an awful secret, Jake thought. This entire thing felt intensely private, and Jake really wished he were somewhere else—anywhere else instead of there.

"I'll give you twenty-four hours to change your

mind," Selina announced. "If I don't hear from you before then, I'll go to the police. And I know exactly where you buried the body, remember? I'm sure the Mustang Valley Police Department will happy to re-open a cold case like this, especially with such a high-profile killer."

Snatching up her designer alligator-skin briefcase, Selina sailed out the door. She paused at the last moment and turned. "You can all go to hell," she said. A moment later, she roared off in her Porsche. They all wanted to cheer that she was finally out of their lives, but the gravity of her accusations made that impossible.

Only once she'd left did Payne's impassive expression crumble. "I'm so screwed," he said, covering his face with both his hands. "Everything she said was true, except it really was self-defense."

Ace went to him and clasped his shoulder. "There's got to be a way to prove that. We'll do whatever it takes."

"I'll help, too." Jake pushed to his feet and joined Ace. He exchanged a troubled look with the man he'd come to regard as a brother. "Somehow, we'll figure something out."

Chapter Fifteen

After the meeting broke up, Jake and Ace collected a visibly shaken Payne and left Colton Oil. The somber mood felt heavy, much different than the one they'd driven out with. As they drove back to the Triple R, Jake watched the two in the front seats, worried. Neither man spoke much, each lost in his own thoughts.

"Mustang Valley sure is a dramatic place," Jake finally said, hoping to lighten the mood.

Ace shot him a surprised look, but then he smiled. "It has been lately," he agreed. "So much craziness going on, we could be an episode of one of those television soap operas."

Once they arrived at the ranch, Jake went up to his new digs and called Fiona. Rather than sit around and brood in the unfamiliar room, he wanted to find out what time she'd be finished with work. Maybe they could go out for dinner or take a walk.

"I'm just wrapping things up now," she said, sounding delighted to hear from him. "Since it's too early to eat yet, maybe we can figure out something else to do."

The husky invitation in her voice made his body stir. "I'm on my way to pick you up," he said. "I'll be there in ten."

As he pulled up in front of the AAG center, he knew for him, the rustic beauty of the huge house would forever be tainted. Micheline might be safely behind bars, but he'd always feel her presence in this location. Always.

The instant Fiona climbed into Jake's pickup, she somehow knew that something had gone wrong. "Are you all right?" she asked sharply.

He told her all about his visit to Colton Oil, the board meeting and Selina's threats.

Fiona frowned. "If this is true and he really did kill someone and hide the body on the Triple R, it's not going to look good, to put it mildly. Self-defense is his only hope."

"But how would he even prove that?" Jake asked, refusing to allow the utter hopelessness of the situation to creep into his voice. "That was long before the days of modern technology. It would simply be his word against the evidence."

Fiona didn't comment. He figured he knew why. Sometimes, if there was nothing good to say, it was better not to speak at all.

"I just learned I had a father," he said. "I've barely even begun to get to know him. If he goes to prison now..." He couldn't finish the sentence. Since his mother had died so long ago, he'd never get the chance to develop a relationship with her. The Coltons were the family he'd never known he had.

"Are you sure you're in the mood for company?" she asked. "If you'd rather have some time alone, I get it."

Incredulous, he shook his head. "I need to be with you. I was hoping we could go for a long walk. Fresh air helps me think. There are a lot of trails out at the Triple R, if you don't mind going back to the ranch with me."

"Trails?" she asked. "Do you ride? I'm betting Ace wouldn't mind loaning us a couple of horses. The Triple R has some amazing riding trails, or so I've heard. We could ask one of the ranch hands."

He liked that idea. If his still-healing ribs could take it. Which, as long as they kept the pace slow, he felt confident they could. Before he could think too hard about it, he pulled over to the shoulder of the road and dialed Ace's cell. As soon as he relayed his request, Ace agreed.

"We've got several horses we use just for taking guests on trail rides," he said. "I'll have Jarvis or one of the ranch hands get them saddled up for you two. He can give you some info about where to go. Sierra and I would join you, but we've already made other plans. We'll be going out in about an hour." He gave instructions as to where they should go and promised to have the horses brought up and ready immediately.

"Thank you so much," Jake said. "We should be there in about ten minutes or so."

"Perfect. When you pull in, drive straight to the big white barn. The horses will be tied up inside. When you're done riding, a couple of the ranch hands will come get them."

Ace hung up. Jake passed along all he'd said to Fiona while he drove.

"I haven't been riding since I was a teenager," Fiona said. "Is it weird that I'm really looking forward to this?"

"Not at all." He smiled at her, right before they turned onto the road that led to the Triple R. The enormous house sat high on a hill, surrounded by acres of fenced land and well-maintained barns and storage sheds. A beautiful and prosperous ranch, with the mountains as scenic backdrop. Sometimes he wanted to pinch himself.

All the years he'd missed… But then again, he wouldn't wish his actual childhood on anyone, especially not Ace.

"I wonder if my mother liked to ride," he said. "It feels awful not to know anything about her, other than the photo album Payne shared with me."

"Maybe you should ask Ace to share some of the photos she took," she suggested. "Didn't Payne mention she was some sort of amateur photographer? If so, I bet there are a ton of pictures. You might see a lot of her in the way she framed her images."

Her insight made him love her even more. Swallowing past the sudden lump in his throat, he nodded. "Good idea. I'll ask him later tonight or tomorrow."

When they drove around to the barn and parked, Jake saw that Ace had been true to his word. Two ranch employees waited with two horses, already saddled.

But just as Jake and Fiona got out of the truck, the sound of several vehicles driving too fast on the gravel road had them turn to look back in the direction from which they'd come.

Several Mustang Valley patrol vehicles pulled up in front of the house. Jake cursed. "Selina must have gone to the police." He took off running, then remembered Fiona couldn't keep up due to her knee injury. Instead, he motioned for her to get back in the passenger seat, and they drove back.

They reached the house just as Ace opened the door.

Clearly dressed for his night out, he wore a dark blue suit and tie. He glanced back at Jake and Fiona before focusing on the police. "Can I help you, Officers?"

"We have a search warrant." The man in front ceremoniously handed it over, waiting while Ace read it.

"You want to search the house?" Ace asked, clearly taken by surprise.

"No." The detective, an older, graying man, scratched his head. "Sorry, but we're just going to do some digging on your property."

Digging. Jake met Ace's gaze and swallowed. Fiona took his arm and held on tight.

"Have at it," Ace finally said. Sierra came up behind him, her expression troubled. Behind her, Ainsley frowned. Ace filled them in. Then they all stood watching while the police officers got in their cars and drove over to a small, unused pasture near the edge of the property.

"Exactly where Selina told them to dig," Ace said. "Payne showed me the spot earlier."

"Hush," Ainsley chided sharply. "I'm putting on my attorney hat now. No more discussion of any of that, do you hear me?"

They all nodded, even Jake. The more time he spent around these people, the more welcome they made him feel. Like part of the family. *His* family.

Though everyone wore the same worried expression, they all clearly didn't want to look away. Side by side, they kept watching. Standing on the sidewalk, near the circular drive, with a clear view of all the activity taking place below them.

Only Payne was absent. He'd taken to his bed shortly

after the confrontation with Selina, worried that he was too newly recovered to deal with so much stress.

"This is too much," Ainsley finally muttered. "Let's go back inside. They'll come and tell us if they find anything."

Not *if*, Jake thought. But *when*.

"Come on." Ace punched his arm, a light, brotherly type of gesture. "When Ainsley speaks, the rest of us listen."

Which earned him a glare from his attorney sister.

They trooped back into the kitchen, got cups of coffee and took seats around the large table.

The knock on the door came exactly thirty-seven minutes later.

"I'll get it," Ainsley said. No one argued.

A moment later, she returned, her face ashen. "They found a body. They're going to arrest Dad."

Of course everyone insisted on standing in solidarity when the police read Payne his rights. Though the older man kept muttering that it had been self-defense, he didn't argue. Instead, he held out his hands for the cuffs, his expression resolute.

"We're going to beat this," Ace reassured him.

But how? Jake wondered silently. Right now, all they had was Payne's claim, no proof. And his actions after killing the man pointed more toward someone guilty.

Once the police had driven off with Payne, Ainsley had immediately gotten on the phone, rustling up help from Santiago, who specialized in criminal defense. "He'll meet them at the jail," she announced once she'd ended the call. "Meanwhile, we've got to get busy finding some sort of proof to back up Dad's claim of self-defense." She eyed Fiona. "Is any of this your area of expertise?"

Slowly, Fiona shook her head. "Not really. But I'll do everything I can to help you."

Ainsley nodded. "Jarvis had done quite a bit of searching the property already. At the very least, he can tell us where not to look."

"We need to find proof," Ace declared. "There's got to be something. We'll just have to find it." But how were they going to do that? No one asked the question out loud, especially not Jake. He'd barely spent any time with his birth father, certainly not enough to understand what made Payne Colton tick.

Ace, on the other hand, was an open book. Despite his previous plans with Sierra, he canceled them, saying he wanted nothing to distract him from focusing on clearing Payne. Talking to him, Jake could see hints of the ruthless CEO he'd once been, though he'd clearly mellowed. He was also leaner than he'd been in the old photographs Jake had seen online.

"Don't you think if Payne had evidence to back him up, he would have produced it by now?" Fiona asked softly.

Though Ainsley shot her a quick look, she nodded. "My thoughts exactly. Unless he isn't aware that there even *is* evidence."

And there might not be. Jake knew better than to voice this thought out loud.

"There's got to be something we're overlooking," Ace announced, pacing the length of the kitchen and back. "It's got to be right there in front of us. Got to be."

"Sometimes when you try too hard to find something, it stays just around the corner of your vision," Jake pointed out. "We need to take a break, look at something else for a little while. Maybe then, something will come to us."

At first, Ace shot an impatient look his way. But then he apparently reconsidered. "You may be right. How about this? Earlier, you were asking for information about your birth mother. Payne stored all of her photography stuff and her journals in one of the unused bedrooms. When we were younger, we all spent some heavy-duty time in there, going through the pictures. I think it might help you get a feel as to what kind of woman she was."

Jake nodded, feeling a flicker of interest. "I'd like that," he responded quietly. "Plus it might be a good distraction right now." He turned to Fiona. "Want to come?"

"Sure."

Sierra chimed in that she'd take a look, too. "I've always been a huge photography fan."

"You guys go," Ainsley said, waving them away. "I've got some case law I want to study before I head downtown to see what I can do to get a judge to allow me to get Dad out on bond."

Instantly, Ace declared he wanted to go, too.

"We'll see," Ainsley replied, not appearing convinced. "Actually, I think it would be better if I just went. We want to try and keep this small, quiet and contained. Since I work with these people, I'm the best candidate. I promise to fill everyone in as soon as I know anything."

Ace looked like he wanted to argue, but he clearly thought better of it.

"Now shoo." Ainsley returned her attention to her book. "I've got a lot of ground to cover in a short period of time."

FIONA AND SIERRA followed the two men down a long hall, up a flight of stairs and into another part of the house. She couldn't help but admire the way the decor and furniture worked together and looked both elegant and comfortable.

Her heart ached for this family. They'd been through so much already, and now this. So many people erroneously believed the simple act of being wealthy ensured an easy life. In Fiona's opinion, great wealth seemed to bring even greater challenges.

Ace paused at a closed door, turning to face the rest of them. "No one is usually allowed in here," he said. "Dad keeps this room as sort of Tessa's shrine."

Jake glanced over his shoulder at Fiona, who shrugged. "Maybe this isn't the right time," Jake said, looking as if he wished he were anywhere else but there.

"It's the perfect time," Ace responded. "Honestly, I think Dad would want me to show you this. We'll let Ainsley do her thing, clear our heads and go back to brainstorming in a little while."

"I thought you and Sierra had plans." Jake tried again. Fiona wasn't sure why he appeared to be so hesitant.

"We canceled them." Ace raised a brow. "Do you not want to learn about Tessa? Sorry, it never occurred to me to ask first."

Fiona moved to Jake's side and took his arm, offering her silent support.

"Naturally, I want to learn about my birth mother."

Jake's tone was wry. "Actually, I ache for it, with every fiber of my being. But my birth father has been arrested, might be charged with murder and has been hauled off to jail after recently awakening from a coma and being released from the hospital." He shook his head. "Honestly, Ace. After reading up on everything on the internet, I found himself wondering if the Colton family had been cursed."

Ace's mouth twisted. "I hear you. If not cursed, we've certainly had a rather spectacular run of bad luck." He eyed Jake. "Say the word. If you don't want to do this right now, we won't."

Fiona found herself holding her breath. She caught Sierra watching Jake, too, a similar look of anticipation on her face.

Jake turned and caught Fiona watching him. "Let's check it out. I think we could all use a small distraction right now."

Small distraction? Either way, Fiona breathed a sigh of relief. Personally, she thought Ace was right. If they all sat around wringing their hands and bemoaning Payne's fate, they'd have trouble thinking up any kind of solution.

Ace turned the knob and opened the door. He flipped the light switch, and they all stepped inside.

It wasn't a bedroom, as Jake had expected. Instead, the room appeared to be some sort of studio, with photographs rather than paintings.

There were trays of negatives, labeled by date, and a neat row of photo albums stood on one long shelf. Her favorite prints had been blown up and hung on the wall, the subjects ranging from landscapes to people and animals. They were all good, some spectacularly so. One or two made Jake catch his breath.

"She really was talented," Fiona breathed, catching at Jake's arm. "I'm surprised she didn't have a career as a professional photographer."

"Remember, some of these were taken over thirty-five years ago," Ace interjected. "Think about how different things were when we were kids. Since there are two entire photo albums filled with baby pictures of me, Ainsley and Grayson, I'd venture a guess that most of these pictures are at least thirty-six years old, many older."

Jake stood frozen, taking it all in. Still holding his arm, Fiona moved them forward. "Look," she said, pointing. A couple of vintage cameras sat in a glass-fronted cabinet. She spied a Pentax, a Nikon and even an ancient Polaroid.

"Back when everyone used actual film," Ace said. "Since photographers often have to take tons of shots to get one good one, I imagine she burned through a lot of film." He pulled open a drawer. "See. Here's a bunch she hadn't developed yet."

"Interesting." Jake came closer. "Did she have her own darkroom?"

"Yep. In the closet." Ace walked across the room and opened the door. "We were all too young to remember, but I'm betting this entire area was off-limits to us kids."

Fiona hung back, letting Jake set the pace. She could only imagine how he must feel, seeing his real mother's art—an expression of herself—for the first time.

As Jake picked up one of the albums and began leafing through it, Ace's phone chimed. "It's Ainsley," he said. "She'd like us all back downstairs right now."

With what could have been a sigh of relief, Jake placed the photo album back on the shelf. They all filed out, Ace carefully closing the door behind them.

Ainsley waited, tapping her foot impatiently, making a drumming sound with the heel of her shoe. "One of my colleagues is at the jail, waiting to see Dad. He's trying to expedite a bail hearing so we can get Dad home before he gets sick."

"Can we go see him?" Ace wanted to know.

"Right now, they aren't allowing any visitors other than his lawyer," Ainsley replied. "If we can get bail set, we'll be able to post bond and bring him home."

Impressed with the younger woman's efficiency and optimism, Fiona kept her mouth shut. In her experience, the legal system moved at a snail's pace and wouldn't be hurried along by anyone. She could only hope that in this case, Ainsley was right.

Sierra offered to give Fiona a ride back to the AAG center, most likely because she felt as out of place as Fiona did. Fiona accepted, kissing Jake on the cheek and asking him to keep her posted.

The two women kept the chatter light and inconsequential on the drive. Fiona had met a bounty hunter or two in the past, and Sierra did not fit her preconceived notions of individuals in that profession at all.

Once they reached the AAG center, Sierra dropped her off and waved a cheerful goodbye. As she got out of the car, Fiona impulsively turned. "You and I should get together sometime when things aren't this crazy," she said. "Talk over a drink and get to know one another."

Sierra grinned. "I'd like that. Let's plan on it."

As they'd all feared and as their cousin Bella had warned them, the story hit the newspaper the next day.

"Body Found on Rattlesnake Ridge Ranch!" the headline screamed. "Prominent citizen Payne Colton arrested and charged with murder."

Fiona's stomach clenched when she read the story. Selina had gone ahead and leaked the information to the paper. It didn't escape Fiona's attention that since the woman had clearly known about this for years and helped cover it up, she could also be named as an accessory. Though Fiona wouldn't put it past her to have worked up some sort of plea agreement in advance. Fiona itched to check in with the Mustang Valley Police Department and see what she could learn, but felt doing so officially would be unethical since the FBI wasn't involved in the case at all.

She just needed to put her head down and work. The sooner they'd gone through every square foot of the AAG center, the better case they'd have built against Micheline.

Still, the day crawled slowly past. Fiona helped catalog and bag evidence, trying to keep her mind on the task despite being unable to stop thinking about Jake.

She must have pulled out her phone a dozen times with the intention of calling Jake. Each time, she reconsidered. No doubt he, and the entire Colton family, were already aware of this. She needed to wait until he called her. He'd found himself in a unique and awkward position, just getting to know his new family while under the shadow of a major investigation.

When he finally called, he wanted to know if she'd like to come over and look at Tessa's photographs with him again. "I'm going to spend a couple hours in there tonight, and I could use your professional help?"

This surprised her. "Professional? What do you mean?"

"Going through things," he replied, making her wonder if he deliberately chose to sound vague. "I'm more of an outdoor guy, not a paper pusher. Just the thought of trying to see my mother by flipping through tons of photographs is overwhelming to me." His voice softened. "Plus, I'd like to see you. I'd enjoy your company."

She laughed. "I'll be there in twenty minutes. Do you want me to bring anything?"

"Just yourself. We'll grab dinner here. Ace had the cook make a bunch of sandwiches since everything is so crazy right now. They're stored in the fridge."

"Is Payne out yet?"

"Not yet. Ainsley is up there now posting bond. She said she's not leaving until she has him with her."

"I really like her," Fiona told him.

"Me, too. I really hit the jackpot when it comes to family," Jake said. "Both Ace and I got lucky. See you soon."

She hung up, thinking she'd also lucked out in meeting him. While she didn't know where this relationship might be going, she couldn't wait to find out.

Chapter Sixteen

After ending the call, Jake walked downstairs and went out to sit on the front porch and wait for Fiona. He'd felt weird all day, as if there was something vitally important he'd managed to overlook. Though he had no idea what that might be or even what it might relate to, he'd learned from past experience that sitting outside in nature and clearing his mind often helped him figure out a solution to whatever problem he had.

The Triple R had several oversize rocking chairs on one side of the house. He took a seat in one, taking in the breathtaking view of land and livestock and mountains. A sense of calm, of peace, stole over him. With all the recent turmoil, it felt good to sit and breathe, to simply *exist*.

In one of the pastures below him, a horse reared up, kicking up a clump of dirt before taking off running, tail streaming high behind him. Soon another horse joined him, and then another, galloping just for the sheer joy of it.

By the time Fiona pulled up, driving a government-issued dark sedan instead of the old junker she'd used before, he felt calm and centered. And hopeful—more hopeful than he'd been in forever.

"Hey!" He stood, moving down the steps to greet her. The instant she swung her long legs out of the car, he pulled her close and held on tight. "You smell good," he told her, trying to identify the scent and failing.

"Lavender and vanilla body lotion," she said, smiling up at him.

He kissed her then, unable to help himself. Right there, on the front porch of the Triple R, where anyone could see. When they finally broke apart, they both were breathing heavily.

"Whoa, cowboy," she said, smiling.

"I've missed you," he replied, aching to kiss her again. "Let's go inside."

She slipped her slender hand in his. Together they walked through the front doors.

"It's sure quiet in here today," she commented. "Are you the only one home?"

He liked that she used the word *home*. It wasn't yet, but he knew it could be if he wanted. The entire family had been hinting about that. "Right now, yes. But Ace knows I've been planning to spend some more time in Tessa's studio, so it's all good." As long as Payne didn't mind. No one had exactly been clear about that.

Once they'd reached the room, he turned on the light and stood in the doorway for a moment, marveling at how it seemed untouched by time.

"Someone cleans in here regularly," Fiona said when he spoke that thought out loud. "Otherwise there would be dust everywhere."

She had a point. He wondered if Payne took on that particular task himself or if he had household staff do it.

They spent the next hour going through photo albums, most of them of Tessa's children, Payne and a beautiful border collie who must have been the family pet.

After they'd gone through the tenth album, Jake pushed to his feet and stretched. "I think I've had enough photo albums for now. Maybe we should check out some of the more artistic shots she took."

"Where?" Fiona asked, sweeping a wayward strand of hair back from her face as she too stood.

"I think she filed them in those large portfolio things." Moving toward them, he eyed the assortment of cameras. One of them, a big, bulky, rectangular thing, didn't look like a camera at all.

"Look." Jake pointed. "Is that…?"

"A Sony BMC-100. One of the very first personal camcorders." Fiona moved closer. "Look how freaking huge it is!"

Jake carefully picked it up. "Heavy, too. If I remember right, these guys recorded to those old clunky video tapes." He pushed a button, and a compartment on the side slowly opened. "There's still one in here."

"I wonder if there's anything on it?" Fiona smiled. "Wouldn't it be awesome to be able to actually see your mother's face and hear her voice?"

"It would." Carefully, Jake closed the camcorder door. "Though if she were the one using it, I doubt she'll be on any of the recordings. Still, it wouldn't hurt to look. I wonder if Payne happens to have an old VCR sitting around so we could watch it. I'll ask Ace later."

A quick tap on the door had them turning in unison.

"Hey," Ainsley said, smiling tiredly. "I got Payne released and he's home. He's exhausted, so he's gone to his room to try and get some rest."

"That's understandable," Jake said, relieved. "I'm so glad you were able to get him out of there."

"It wasn't easy. I had to do some serious convincing. I mean, come on. He's elderly, no prior record, and it's not like he's a flight risk or danger to society. Luckily, the judge took all that into consideration and set a reasonable bail amount."

Jake didn't want to ask what she thought was reasonable.

"Do you happen to know if there's a working VCR in this house?" Fiona asked, explaining why.

"Seriously, a video tape?" Ainsley appeared intrigued. "That'd be cool if something really was on it. I know Payne has a DVR, but maybe he might have hung on to one of those old VCRs. Ace would probably know for sure."

By the time Ace returned home, both Ainsley and Grayson had gotten excited about the tape and wanted to find a VCR. The instant he strolled through the door, Ainsley immediately grabbed him, demanding to know if he had any idea where they might find one.

"A VCR?" he asked, incredulous. "Why on earth would anyone need one of those? Did you find an old stash of videotapes or something?"

As soon as they explained, his eyes lit up. "I'd love to see that. Honestly, though, I don't remember her ever using a video camera."

"Probably because you were so young," Ainsley shot back. "Duh."

Ace laughed. "Good point." He thought for a moment. "Did any of you look for one?"

"Not yet," Ainsley chimed in. "We wanted to wait for you."

Jake envied the easy camaraderie between brother and sister. "We actually figured if anyone would know, you would," he said.

This made Ace grin. "You guys didn't even try, did you? Because I'm pretty sure Dad still has a VCR hooked up to the big flat-screen television in the media room. Along with his DVR and Blu-ray player."

"Seriously?" Fiona looked both flabbergasted and intrigued.

"Yep," Ace replied. "He has a huge cabinet in there full of videotapes, DVDs, etc. There's a ton of old movies, along with newer ones."

Jake cleared his throat. "Does Payne know we've been in Tessa's room?"

The three siblings exchanged looks. Ainsley shrugged. "I didn't say anything. I figured he had enough on his mind already."

"I didn't, either," Ace added, his expression rueful. "To be honest, I was afraid he'd say no, and I really wanted you to learn about your mother, Jake."

Fiona crossed to his side, once again slipping her fingers through his. Grateful, Jake smiled at her before eyeing the others. "I was just thinking Payne might like to see whatever is on the video."

"Let's wait and see what it is first," Ace suggested. "For all we know, it might be a blank."

A sobering thought, but Jake knew Ace was right. No sense in stirring up Payne without good cause. The poor man had already been through enough.

"Come on, let's go see." Ace led the way. They all trooped upstairs to the media room, a large, windowless area with theater-style seating and a huge flat screen hung on the wall.

"There it is," Ace said, pointing. "Let me make sure it's still hooked up." When he pressed a button, a light came on.

"Yep." Jake handed Ace the remote so he could power up the TV. "From what I remember, I think you have to change the input."

Finally, once Ace had everything ready, Jake handed him the videotape. Once he'd inserted it, he pressed Play.

"Here we are." A woman's voice. *Tessa*, Jake thought, his heart skipping a beat. His mother. A quick glance at the others revealed similar expressions of wonder. Just then, he realized none of them had actually truly known their mother. They'd all been so young when she died.

The video showed the interior of the Triple R house, looking much newer, with totally different furniture, of course. Tessa continued to narrate, naming each room as she filmed it.

Jake struggled not to show his disappointment. He didn't want to look at the others, aware they probably felt the same. Fiona squeezed his hand, offering her silent support.

Finally, Tessa stepped outside. She filmed one of the barns, a few horses frolicking in an outside paddock, still speaking in her soft, pleasant voice.

As she rounded the corner of the house, she froze, still recording video. Two men came into view. One of them, a much younger Payne, appeared to be arguing with the other.

"Damn it," Tessa cursed, still quietly. "That's Randy Stanford. Payne fired him last week. I'm not sure what he's doing here, but it can't be anything good."

While trying to keep the camcorder focused on the

two men, Tessa took pains to stay out of their line of sight. She ducked back behind the house, which briefly sent the video feed swerving crazily, showing sky and dirt and brick before she got herself situated and finally turned the lens back on her husband and the intruder. They still appeared to be arguing. Because of the distance, no one could make out what exactly about.

When Randy pulled a gun on Payne, the entire room gasped out loud.

A second later, Payne pulled his own gun and shot the other man, so quickly he didn't have time to react and fire his own weapon. A clean shot right to the chest.

Tessa gasped, muttered something and took off running, forgetting to turn off the camcorder in her haste. Because the thing was so heavy, she lugged it along with her, recording all the way until she got back to her room.

Breathing hard, she finally pressed the button to power it off. The recording ended.

For a second longer, everyone simply sat in stunned silence. Then they all started talking at once.

"Was that…?"

"Clear case of self-defense."

"But if Tessa had this all along," Jake asked, "why wouldn't she have shown it to Payne so he could be exonerated?"

No one knew.

"Maybe they never discussed it," Ace said. "We can't ask her and clearly Payne had no idea this tape existed."

"I need to get that to the prosecutor immediately. We'll request a meeting with the district attorney's office." Ainsley marched to the front of the room and extracted the videotape from the VCR.

"What if they don't have anything to play it?" Fiona

suggested. "I'd run it again, and this time, record the relevant part with your phone."

"Good idea." Ainsley smiled. Then she did exactly that.

Once she'd finished, she handed the tape to Jake. "Keep this safe, please."

He nodded, absurdly pleased. "Will do."

"This should be enough to get them to drop the charges," she announced, smiling. "We'll deal with the media once that's done." And then, to Jake's complete and utter shock, she strode over and hugged him. When she finished, she hugged Fiona, too.

"This would never have come to light without you two," she said, her voice breaking. "Thank you, from the bottom of my heart."

Once Ainsley left, Ace came over and slung his arm over Jake's shoulder. "Good job," he said. From his seat, Grayson echoed the sentiment.

True to Ainsley's prediction, once the video evidence had been reviewed, backing up Payne's claim of self-defense, the DA refused to prosecute. And the media covered the story, the headlines stating Payne Colton had been cleared of any wrongdoing.

Payne, too relieved to mind that Jake and Fiona had been in Tessa's room, took a particular delight in phoning Selina to let her know. He reported she told him to go to hell before ending the call.

The FBI wrapped up its investigation into Micheline and the AAG. The government would seize the property, which would soon be locked down until it was auctioned off. Jake figured Fiona would have to leave Mustang Valley—and Jake—soon. Part of him wanted to ask her to get a room at the Dales Inn there in town, just to stay close.

The DNA test came back. He'd had it sent to Payne, who phoned him with the results. The match proved beyond a shadow of a doubt what everyone already knew: Jake was a Colton.

Finally, Fiona called and asked him to meet. When he pulled up, he saw her suitcase in the back of her car, along with a few other belongings that she'd accumulated since arriving in town.

"We're done," she said simply. "After all this time, all this work, what happens next is out of our hands. I'm not sure when, but multiple indictments will soon be handed down. I don't think Micheline will be getting out of prison in her lifetime."

"Good." He pulled her into his arms and held her, breathing in the scent of her hair. "Good job, Fiona."

She tightened her arms around him, though she didn't speak. "Where are you going to go now?" she asked, her voice muffled since she'd pressed her face against his chest. "Back to your ranch?"

"No. I'm staying here," Jake said, pulling back a little so he could watch Fiona's face for a hint of how that might make her feel. "At the Triple R, with my family."

She nodded, her expression neutral. "What about your ranch? Are you going to sell it?"

"No. I worked too damn hard getting that ranch up and running. I'm proud of it, especially since I did it on my own. I've got capable people taking care of it for me and keeping it going. I'll just drop in and check on things from time to time." He smiled. "Ace says once Nova and Clara are up to it, we're going to have a big shindig, even if we have to have two parties. It'll be huge, since I hear the Colton Oil branch of the family and the Colton triplets are all much closer now."

Fiona nodded. "That's a lot of people to get to know. It must be pretty awesome," she commented. "Finding out you have an entire family you never even knew about."

"It is," he replied, still unable to tear his gaze away from her. "I consider myself lucky that they're all so welcoming and generous with their love."

His comment made her blink. Was that sheen in her dark eyes from unshed tears? "They've even asked me to consider changing my last name legally from Anderson to Colton."

"Wow." She smiled then, though her gaze remained serious. "Are you going to?"

"I think so. Yes." He hadn't been certain until that very moment. "Micheline and her fake last name never should have been a part of me. I'm a Colton by blood, and I'm honored that the entire family wants me to make that official."

"How does Ace feel about that?" she asked. "It must be difficult for him, knowing he's the interloper here."

"He's not, nor will he ever be." Heart full, Jake couldn't suppress a grin. "The family is throwing a big party for both Ace Coltons, as they call it. We're both Coltons, no matter what."

"Wow." She blinked again. Now he was almost positive she was keeping back tears. His precious, wonderful Fiona. Was she wondering what place in his life would be left for her? "Will you be spending the summer holidays with them?"

"I am. How about you?" he asked. "Are you close

to your family?" Testing the waters, to see if she'd be willing to spend time with him.

"No siblings—I'm an only child." Her smile wavered a little.

"I hate that," Jake began.

"Don't." She shook her head. "Don't pity me. It's all right. I'm used to being alone." Then, clearly trying to change the subject, she told him she'd heard that some of Micheline's followers had turned against her, particularly after having learned she kept people in a basement. "They're willing to testify against her," she said. "Including Harley Watts, who sent the original email to the board about the baby switch."

"That's great," he replied, refusing to be deterred. "But I don't pity you, Fiona." He shook his head. "Never that. I was used to being alone, too. I told myself that I didn't even mind it. But being accustomed to something doesn't mean you have to like it."

Did she get the hint? Heart pounding, he waited for her response.

"Of course." Now she wouldn't look at him. "And I envy you that. But how do you think it would be for me, knowing you dragged me to your family's celebrations, just because you didn't want me to be by myself?"

He took a step closer. "That's not why I want to spend more time with you," he said. "I want to be with the person I love the most in the entire world. You."

Now she got it. She froze. "Do you really mean that?" she whispered, her gaze locking on his.

"I do." Now he went to her, pulling her into his arms. "From the moment we first met, I knew there was something special. A connection. I know you felt it, too."

Face against his chest, she nodded. "I like how you

let me be vulnerable," she said, her arms wrapped around him as she held on tight. "Being strong all the time can be tiring."

"I know. We've been through hell and back in the last few weeks. You're the strongest person I know. That's one of the many things I love about you."

She sniffed and started trembling. Stunned, he realized she actually was crying now. "Please don't cry," he said, helpless in the face of feminine tears.

"I'm trying not to." Lifting her head, she angrily swiped at her face. "It's just that's the nicest thing anyone has ever said to me."

"That you're strong? I find it hard to believe no one's ever remarked on that before."

"No." She gave him a watery smile. "That you love me. I love you, too, you know."

He debated pretending shock but settled for kissing her instead.

* * * * *